PENGUIN BOOKS

FEARLESS

Rafael Yglesias is the author of six novels, including *Only Children* and *The Murderer Next Door*. He lives in New York City with his wife and two children.

RAFAEL YGLESIAS

———

FEARLESS

PENGUIN BOOKS

PENGUIN BOOKS

Published by the Penguin Group
Penguin Books Ltd, 27 Wrights Lane, London W8 5TZ, England
Penguin Books USA Inc., 375 Hudson Street, New York, New York 10014, USA
Penguin Books Australia Ltd, Ringwood, Victoria, Australia
Penguin Books Canada Ltd, 10 Alcorn Avenue, Toronto, Ontario, Canada M4V 3B2
Penguin Books (NZ) Ltd, 182 190 Wairau Road, Auckland 10, New Zealand

Penguin Books Ltd, Registered Offices: Harmondsworth, Middlesex, England

First published in the USA by Warner Books 1993
Published in Penguin Books 1993
1 3 5 7 9 10 8 6 4 2

Penguin Film and TV Tie-in edition first published 1993

Copyright © Rafael Yglesias, 1993
All rights reserved

The moral right of the author has been asserted

Typeset by Datix International Limited, Bungay, Suffolk
Printed in England by Clays Ltd, St Ives plc

For Jules & Charlotte

The author wishes to thank Kenneth Platzer
for explaining, not impersonating, the lawyers
in this novel.

CRASH & BURN

───────── I ─────────

Max lived scared, always alert to the threat of disaster, and yet when disaster finally arrived he was relaxed. Relaxed because takeoff from Newark airport had been smooth. Of course during the ascent he had been afraid. He had concentrated on the plane's progress, clutching the armrests while it made the wrong-way climb up the slide, convinced if he let go the jet would fall. He stayed worried until a chime alerted passengers that the seat-belt sign was off and they could move about the cabin. He knew that also meant they were successfully airborne and clear of competitive traffic and he could feel pleasure again.

Until descent.

Thanks to his morbid study of air disasters he allowed himself to be panicked only during takeoff and landing. That psychological bargain was the best he could do to master his dread of flying. And it worked. During the cruising time of a trip, while the aircraft was level, Max was even capable of joy, convinced by the statistics that he was safe.

But he wasn't safe. Forty-two minutes into the air (Max glanced at his watch immediately) there was a boom. A dulled and yet definite explosion. It was a punishment, Max felt, for the brief minutes of comfort and security he had recklessly allowed himself.

The luggage compartments above rattled. A wheezing, metallic moan vibrated underneath the hollow carpet. The steady background noise of power altered ominously. Taking advantage of the view from his center seat, Max checked each wing's engine. They looked okay, but that was no solace since he could hear the loss of power came from behind. The engine mounted on the tail was quiet and Max knew it was the one to worry about, the turbine that had fallen off a DC-10 out of Chicago and killed a planeload. Long ago the original design had been exposed as defective. Supposedly the flaw had been corrected, except in third world countries that the manufacturer had failed to notify. But after all, Max thought, this flight was to LA, not Beirut.

'Oh my God,' a woman two rows up said softly. Partway out of her seat, turned to head for the lavatory, she had been nudged across the aisle into the row right in front of Max. She looked horrified.

'What the hell was that?' Max demanded of his companion.

Jeff didn't reply. Max had a view of his profile. Max expected impatient reassurance from Jeff. Something along the lines of: 'Calm down. It's turbulence.' Instead Jeff was pale and managed only a stiff, slight side-to-side motion.

'I'd better sit down,' the woman said at Max, but she was really speaking to herself. As she attempted to move, there was another, even louder, boom.

This time there were a few shrieks when it happened. He thought they were human, but they could have been cries from the craft itself.

For one strange blessed moment there was no consequence.

And then they fell. The floor seemed to drop away and they were following it down. Max arched up against his seat belt as if he could hold up the plane by himself. He saw a businessman, three aisles ahead on the left, open his mouth wide. The man was dressed coolly in a seersucker suit. Since takeoff he had held a *Wall Street Journal* before him, folded into a tall column of print, like a soldier carrying a banner into battle. He continued to fly this flag during the free-fall, although he also appeared to be screaming. Max couldn't be sure since all interior sound was muted by the straining noise of the wing engines. A flight attendant came hurtling through the first-class curtain and dropped on to the cabin floor. Immediately after her the metal food cart rolled out and whacked her in the head.

'He's lost an engine!' Max yelled at Jeff. There was blame in his tone.

Jeff's long face and lazy eyes usually gave off an impression of boredom. Not now. His cheeks were sucked in, his lips were disappearing. He squinted toward the front and nervously denied the charge, shaking his head no.

'We're going down!' Max shouted, but they weren't. They were flying sideways. Tray tables on the left-hand aisle popped open. The sky slid away through the porthole windows and Max saw the thin land, flattened by the height of their view, not below him where it should be but directly to his left. They were upended. Still they weren't going down, not yet. They were rolling, the same as in the Chicago crash. That jet had lost the rear engine and rolled and rolled until it was utterly destroyed.

Aware of the DC-10's history of death, Max had boarded this one only after losing a fight against doing so. Max, as usual, had been careful to phone ahead to find out what model plane was scheduled. He had been told their flight was on an L-1011. At the check-in counter (always making sure, always cautious) he casually asked again and was terrified the instant the agent said that the equipment for their flight had been changed from the safe L-1011 to this, the DC-10 deathtrap. Pulling at Jeff's arm and whispering shyly, like a little kid coaxing a parent, Max argued to Jeff that they should wait for a later flight.

Jeff lost his temper, shouting at him in front of the amused airline agent. 'We're grown-ups for Chrissake! We can't call Nutty Nick and say we're not going to make the meeting because we're scared to fly! Look!' he almost spat into Max's face. Max had never seen him so pissed off. 'Your life isn't so great anyway.' Jeff smiled sickeningly at this joke.

Now that they were spinning down toward the fatal earth, Max longed to say, 'I told you so,' but he couldn't talk. He was pinned against his seat by the plane's roll, unable to turn Jeff's way. My face is going to hit the ground at six hundred miles an hour, he believed, and received a vivid image of his features smashed flat into a Halloween mask. He saw his teeth covered with blood, displayed on the ground without the rest of him. He wondered about an old terror from childhood: does the guillotined man see his headless body from the basket?

I'm dying, he screamed into the onrushing river of terror in his brain, drowning all other thoughts. His muscles went into spasm. The sun flooded his vision, the plastic ceiling opened, and he was in the sky. He saw white everywhere. He had let go: he was free of life.

No he wasn't. With a nauseating jerk the plane

6

leveled. And then Max heard his own voice speaking, in a muffled tone captured within his stuffed and popping ears. 'Where the fuck are we? Where the fuck are we?' he begged Jeff.

'In the air! In the air!' Jeff answered him.

Max smelled bowel movements, urine. He opened his eyes, only then realizing they had been shut. What he saw first was the flight attendant crawling down the aisle, reaching for armrests, but having a hard time getting a hold. The right side of her face was covered with thin and runny blood that almost looked fake. The rest of her still had the dry-cleaned stiffness and perfection of her job's uniform. Jeff was seated on the aisle right next to her.

'Help her,' Max nudged him. As he made the gesture liquid seemed to spill out of his ears, and they opened up: sounds came into his head at a higher volume.

Above him a little voice squawked. 'This is the captain,' it said and then something else. His tone was calm, but the electronics were not: they squeezed and garbled his voice. '. . . a loss of power. We're going . . .'

'What did he say!' Jeff's fingers, rigid and arched into a claw shape, dropped over Max's wrist. He seemed unaware of the bleeding flight attendant at his feet.

The woman passenger who had been out of her seat when the two explosions happened appeared, rising over the headrests. She had been thrown into the row in front of them; it was empty and she seemed unhurt.

Max heard children crying. The flight was loaded with kids. 'A good sign,' Jeff had said as they boarded. After Max caved in about taking the DC-10, Jeff did his best to reassure him. 'Planes with kids on them don't crash,' he whispered. There were a lot of children,

7

but one of the flight attendants explained why and it had nothing to do with guaranteeing Max's safety. To fill its seats off-peak the airline discounted their tickets seventy-five percent for children flying on Tuesdays and Wednesdays. Some were very young – four, five, six. Max had seen at least three pairs of siblings traveling without parents and he had noticed one child, a towheaded boy, going it totally alone.

Max had flown alone as a child. His parents put him on a plane (for the first time when he was six) to visit his maternal grandparents in California at Christmas and for two weeks every summer. A shrink had told him that the fear he repressed then, pressured by his parents to pretend he enjoyed the experience, was forever resurfacing now that he was an adult. At first Max had been in love with this theory; but its uselessness (the next time he flew his terror was keener) eventually caused him to lose faith in it. Just last week Max had offered his own explanation to the doctor: 'The simple truth is: I'm a coward.'

The towheaded boy seated alone three rows up had sat through boarding in a very grown-up, dignified, slightly shy and sad manner. Max used to put on a similar behavioral disguise when he had to travel as a child to California: he was concealing fear. Max wondered whether the boy was injured by the plane's roll to the left. But the noise of crying children wasn't coming from up ahead where the boy sat, it originated from behind Max. He freed himself of the handcuff Jeff's fingers had made around his wrist and unbuckled his seat belt.

'Help her,' he ordered Jeff, pointing to the flight attendant, who was still unable to get off her knees.

Twice she had reached for the top of the seats, gotten hold, risen slightly, only to have her legs give out. She seemed to be in shock: her pupils were big and she didn't react to the blood running down the side of her face.

Jeff's face had calmed, but his arms and hands were rigid. 'I can't move,' he said.

The bad smell, at least some of it, came from Jeff's pants. Max, out of his seat by now, touched his rear to make sure that his skin had correctly informed him that he hadn't crapped. He hadn't. He was glad – and then disgusted by Jeff. 'Clean yourself up!' he shouted and breathed through his mouth. He reached over and took hold of the flight attendant's hand –

The little world of the plane in which they were trapped, wobbled and bobbed and then . . . dropped.

'God!' Jeff shouted. Max stumbled into Jeff's lap and imagined he was falling into shit. The flight attendant lost her grip again and flopped over like a Raggedy Ann doll into the narrow river of blue carpet.

Engines fought the air. Max pushed himself up from Jeff. He was facing backwards. He looked at the rows and saw mostly little faces and young parents, younger than he. On every one there was frozen the terror of imminent death.

This is it.

Max was forty-two. He announced his age to himself, paused to consider how the fact of his death would read in the paper, and felt surprised. Not at dying so young, but to have lived so long and feel that he hadn't really done anything.

The plane found a ramp in the air and swooped up it, leveling. They were much lower, perhaps no more than ten thousand feet off the ground; Max didn't know, he was guessing. He noticed that the right wing dipped and then rose abruptly, without the usual smooth sway. Instead the plane jerked like a drunkard stumbling on his way home, landing heavily on each foot, threatening to topple over, rescued only by an equally precarious tilt the opposite way. Max peered at the wings and saw the flaps were up. They had been in that position before the roll, and after it, and again before the sudden drop. They hadn't moved. Their immobility probably wasn't a choice made by the captain; more likely he had no control over them. If so, Max knew that meant they would eventually crash. He had read about the safety backups: everything was supposedly designed to prevent such a catastrophic failure. If somehow the impossible had occurred and the captain couldn't steer, then they were doomed.

You're going to die, a voice in Max's head informed him, not his conscience, maybe his God. Anyway it was someone with a lot of authority, no fear, and very little sadness. Consider it over and done with, he was told. He felt the terror leave him, discarded below as inconsequential. Relieved of his own dread, he concentrated on the others. The passengers' faces still showed fear, but there was hope, desperate and fragile, returning. Max pitied them, because they continued to fight the inevitable and therefore had no peace.

Max stepped over Jeff, careful not to hurt the floundering flight attendant. He helped her up, hooking her by the armpits. The fabric was rough and scratchy. His fingers accidentally grazed the sides of her breasts. Even through the starched material Max had an instantaneous sensation of soft and bouncy flesh, probably a hallucination, and he was sad to think of sex just then. He gently maneuvered her down into an empty seat next to a silent and pale, but calm, elderly male passenger who applied his tiny cocktail napkin to the flight attendant's cut. No one spoke.

When Max turned back to apologize to Jeff for yelling about soiling his pants (why meet the end on a quarrel?) he saw the senior flight attendant – her name tag read Mary – open the curtain from first class and grab hold of the food cart. It was stuck sideways in the aisle, wedged into the seats. She couldn't budge it. Max moved up to help her from his side.

The cart was jammed against the armrest of the seat of the boy traveling alone. The boy watched them and pitched in, pushing from his seat with both hands, frowning with a manly seriousness at the effort.

'You okay?' Max asked the boy after they freed the cart. During the roll it must have struck him in the side of the leg.

The boy's nod was casual, but there was a lonely fright in his eyes, a plea for rescue. At the thought of the loss of this child's life Max wanted to cry.

'Could you help me stow it?' Mary asked, nodding down at the cart. She was stocky and almost completely gray-haired, cropped short, as if she wished to give a military appearance of neatness.

Max and Mary pushed the cart to the galley. They passed a lot of frightened people but no one was panicky or made any demands of Mary, not even to ask what was happening to the plane. Most of the overhead baggage compartments had opened. A few passengers were out of their seats shutting them; otherwise people sat still, clutching their armrests. There was a smell in the air, not only of rectal fear but of cold sweat. The plane was hot, too, as if the air-conditioning had been shut down. Outside it was sunny. Beams of yellow light streamed in from the windows, bobbing with the plane's rough bouncing motion. Their touch was warm to the skin, and their glare intrusive and blinding. On the ground it was a hot July day.

Another flight attendant joined them in the kitchen, approaching from the other aisle. She had come up from the back of the plane. She was small and skinny and wore a lot of makeup. She must have slid against something because her lipstick was smeared down one side of her mouth, transforming that half of her face into a clown's sad paint. Her name tag read Lisa.

'Anyone hurt?' Mary asked.

Lisa shook her head no, but she answered, 'I think the man in 33A may be having a heart attack.'

Was that the businessman reading the *Journal*? Max wondered.

'Stay with 33,' Mary told Lisa.

'What about Stacy?' Lisa asked. That must be the flight attendant who had been hit by the food cart, Max assumed. Lisa was young, probably in her twenties, and had lots of freckles on her neck and arms. She had covered up the ones on her face with makeup. Why do that? Max wondered. He liked freckles.

'I'll check her out,' Mary said. 'Get back to 33.'

Lisa moved off right away, scared but obedient.

'I'll be there soon,' Mary called after her.

The captain was on again. This time the electronics were fine. After some preliminary reassurances he got to the point: 'We've experienced a loss of power in number three engine. One and two are okay and this plane is designed to fly, if necessary, with only one engine. But we may have some trouble steering because we've sustained some damage. That's why we can't give you your usual smooth ride. We're going to make an emergency landing. As a precaution, when we're cleared for landing, the flight attendants will instruct you to get into crash positions . . .'

While the captain talked the co-pilot opened the cockpit door and came out.

'What the fuck is going on?' Mary demanded of him. Her obscenity provoked no attention. It seemed natural.

The co-pilot didn't look her in the eye. 'Three blew up. Took out the hydraulics,' he said. He cut himself off from saying more as he became aware of Max's presence. The co-pilot shook his head at Mary and then mumbled, 'Visual check.' Max glanced past him into the cockpit. He saw a man dressed in civilian clothes, kneeling over a panel in the floor that had been opened; the man fussed with something hidden from view.

Before Max could study what he was doing, the co-pilot pulled the door shut and said to Max, 'Return to your seat, sir, and fasten your seat belt.'

'Thank you,' Mary added.

They wanted him out of earshot. Max moved off. He would not interfere with them. They had to ignore the fact that they were doomed. That was their employment, the part of it they hoped never to face, but really the best part, a hopeless fight against death.

Max had a sweeping view of all the passengers as he returned. There were so many kids. He saw an Indian sister and brother, about ten and twelve years old, traveling without an adult. They both had shiny black hair and rich, almost purple, skin. The girl had put her head on her older brother's shoulder and had reverted to an old habit, sucking her thumb. She stared fearfully out the plastic porthole window as if she were having a night-terror and saw monsters in her closet. To comfort her the boy caressed his sister's long hair with his small hand. But he was also scared. He kept his eyes shut and aimed at the ceiling, as if he wanted to be sure, in case he forgot and opened them, that he would see nothing dramatic.

Max touched the brother's head as he passed, rustling his hair, aware that his casual touch was a cliché and probably would do nothing to calm the boy. The boy didn't react. Max, however, felt more in command; he believed that because of the contact he knew the child better and could protect him.

Two aisles behind them sat a young black couple with a baby. The mother was calm. She concentrated on rocking the infant seat from side to side to lull her child. The young father had sweated big ovals under the arm of his blue shirt. He was partly out of his seat to get a view of the cockpit. He looked as if he felt inadequate to some internal demand of manhood. He met Max's eyes and almost seemed to plead: give me something to do.

'Baby okay?' Max shouted at them.

The young father frowned and nodded. The mother smiled her yes.

Across from them were two mothers traveling with four kids, presumably two each, although it was difficult to say who belonged to whom because of their blond sameness. Each child had the same row of yellow bangs and pair of pale blue eyes underneath apparently hairless and yet heavy brows. Three of them were boys, bouncing in their seats with nervous energy and anticipation; they could have been waiting for an amusement-park ride. The girl meanwhile shouted, not scared, but angry: 'Mommy, my ears are hurting!' Neither mother answered her; they had their eyes on the co-pilot, who moved down the other aisle at a faster pace than Max's.

'Tell me we're okay,' one of the mothers said to the co-pilot as he passed.

The co-pilot smiled and winked but he said nothing.

At the co-pilot's failure to reassure, one mother cursed. The other winced, pulled one of the blond boys to her chest, and hugged him hard.

It was heartbreaking. Max was angry that God had made this choice, when he could have picked out a planeload of rich people, smashed the Concorde into the Savoy Hotel, for example, instead of killing a bunch of kids put on planes by parents meeting a tight budget.

Max copied the co-pilot and used the headrests as crutches, alternately placing a hand on the next forward one as he moved down the aisle. The plane had definitely lost some part that lent it stability, something roughly equivalent to a car's shock absorbers. Either that or they had turned on to a poorly maintained paved road of the air with nothing but bumps and potholes. Insulation seemed to have been lost all over: the noise from the two remaining engines was fierce. Max's muscles clenched against the insecure machine, especially his legs: their springs were fully contracted, prepared to make a great leap. Don't fight it, he lectured his body, and consciously tried to relax them, allowing all his weight to settle into his feet before he took the next step.

Jeff was out of his seat. He had gotten one of the blankets (vomited out of the gaping overhead compartments by the dozens) and wrapped it around his waist. As Max reached him he understood what his partner was doing: Jeff was wriggling out of his soiled underwear and pants.

'Can you find my bag?' Jeff demanded. 'Get me the dungarees.'

Max had to open their compartment to get Jeff's overnight – theirs was one of the few that had remained shut. He dropped Jeff's bag on the seat. 'Get it yourself,' he said, still furious at him for insisting they fly this deathtrap.

'Sir!' the injured flight attendant called out from the seat where Max had put her. She still had a tiny drink napkin, completely soaked with her blood, pressed against the cut on her temple. 'Sir!' she insisted sternly to Jeff. 'The captain has put on the seat-belt sign. You should be seated.'

'Are you nuts?' Jeff answered her.

'She's hurt,' the elderly man next to her explained.

Max went past Jeff and stopped at the flight attendant's seat. He didn't want to watch Jeff change his clothes, although he wondered what he was going to do with the soiled pants.

'How are you doing?' Max asked Stacy, after checking her badge and verifying that was her name.

'You should be seated, too,' Stacy answered. She removed her hand to take a look at the napkin. Only half of the tissue came away. The rest stuck to her temple. Stacy stared at what she held of the bloody paper, too saturated to be of any further use.

'I don't have any more,' the older male passenger

commented and gestured at several soaked cocktail napkins tossed on to the floor.

'Remove all sharp objects from your clothes. Pens, combs. Also take off your shoes and eyeglasses,' Stacy said, her eyes on the bloody tissue, squinting and blinking, trying to focus. 'The flight attendants will gather them.'

'Un huh,' Max said. He picked up a fallen pillow, removing the pale blue cover, and tore it up. The muscular effort of ripping the fabric was satisfying. Activity soothed his nerves: helping with the cart and touching the boy's head had also made him feel good. He was able to fashion a crude bandanna. He tied it around her head, covering the wound.

While he tied it their eyes were only a few inches apart. He studied the tiny blond hairs of her mustache and wanted to kiss her lips, painted a brilliant red, but again he was sad to be feeling sexy.

'Why doesn't it stop bleeding?' Stacy asked him.

'I think it is,' he told her.

Out of the corner of his eye Max saw the co-pilot hurrying back to the forward cabin. Because of his haste Max understood that what the co-pilot had been able to discover from his visual check terrified him. Well, what the fuck did you expect? Max argued with him silently. You said yourself that number three blew up and the hydraulics were out. Did you think you were going to be able to Krazy Glue it back together?

Max knew enough about planes to understand that if they had lost all the hydraulics, not only was there no way to steer, there was never going to be. Unless a runway happened to be directly in their path, where could they land safely? A highway? An empty field?

Max wasn't even certain that a controlled descent would be possible.

A small, cold welling of fearful saliva blocked his throat: the coward come to life. But when he straightened and saw the packed crowd of kids and businessmen and the occasional mother, he felt sorrier for them. After all he deserved death. He had plotted to avoid it, quit cigarettes, forsaken red meat, jogged and power-walked, loaded up on vitamins so that his urine looked almost psychedelic – yet it had stalked him anyway. And into its bland merciless face what did he have to show as his proof that he deserved to live?

Nothing but that he was afraid to die.

2

Carla's little boy, two-year-old Leonardo, named for Leonardo da Vinci, but called Leo the Lion by his father, and Lenny by his aunts and uncles, and Bubble by his mother (because as a suckling infant, after a meal of Carla's milk, he manufactured them by the dozens: little shimmering bubbles that slid along his puffy lips), was asleep in the seat next to her when the explosion happened. He had collapsed only minutes after takeoff, his head sagging on to the spongy armrest, the rest of him crumpled up with the spineless compactability of babies – and Bubble was still a baby, even though two. His sleep was so deep that he drooled out of the side of his mouth, darkening a circle of the light blue fabric into navy. The initial jerk of the explosion lifted his unconscious head up – Carla's eyes went to him immediately – and then bounced it down again on the armrest.

That woke Leonardo with a meow of complaint. Carla twisted in her seat and used her hands like earmuffs to protect the sides of his head. She peered toward the front of the plane and waited for what was next.

It didn't occur to her that they might crash. She vaguely assumed they had hit unexpected turbulence, something inconvenient, not tragic. She called out in the direction of the cockpit: 'What's going on!' But there was a lot of noise from the engines and the confusion of other passengers and then . . .

A big fall. Nothing below. She was dropping and

Bubble fell also, sliding out from her grip and down through the seat belt until he was caught by the armpits. He seemed, for one horrible second, to be choking: his legs and torso hung from the seat and the belt was taut across his chest and throat, more a noose than a safety device.

Carla reached to free Bubble. But she couldn't fight the plane's roll. It was like trying to walk in water against the ocean's undertow: her body sank into the foam cushions while her arms seemed to separate from her as they flailed for forward momentum. She struggled as hard as she could to reach her son. Bubble's dark eyes gleamed with fear. She imagined he called to her, but the noise was too loud to hear him.

At last, with a jolt, she was unstuck from gravity's quicksand. She yanked Bubble away from the killer seat belt. He bawled into her neck. She clutched him to her, in a rage at the plane and distrustful of allowing any part of it to touch her son.

'What the fuck is going on!' she demanded into the noise of the engines and, almost as if answering, they were abruptly quieter. Their sudden calm, like the end of a temper tantrum, was a profound relief.

But Leo was screaming without surcease or any suggestion that there ever would be. He didn't like to get up from naps anyway, and this method of waking hardly improved his reaction. She tried to rock him from side to side, but the constraints of the seat limited her swivel. Her comforting did reduce Leo's hysteria to sobs. While he cried she clutched the back of his sweaty head, kissing the moist skin of his neck, a hot cream she loved to taste. 'Stop necking with my boy,' her husband complained from time to time. It pissed her off that he made something sexual out of what was pure and innocent love. After these two years raising Bubble, it seemed to her that was the difference between men and boys: boys understood only love and men understood only sex.

The plane fell again. Jerked backwards and then dropped. She became a cage around her baby: the long muscles of her tall skinny body felt as stiff and as hard as metal. She had a crazy belief that she could cushion him if they hit the ground, that she would die and he would live.

This drop wasn't so bad. More like what she remembered of turbulence from the time she flew to Florida and they passed through a storm.

'Is your baby hurt?' a flight attendant asked while on the move up to the front of the plane. Her name was Lisa. She had been friendly and helpful during boarding; she figured out how to fold up Bubble's new stroller, which seemed to get stuck just at the worst times, such as today when Carla was in the aisle trying to manage Bubble and his bag of things and answer his endless questions or notice what he was exclaiming about. Carla nodded no to Lisa, assuming that if Leonardo was able to scream then he was okay.

Bubble yawned some words through his bawling. She couldn't understand him. She yelled back, trying to puncture his loud grief and also get through the noise of the plane's engines, its air vents, and the overhead compartments being reclosed. 'Stop crying!' she begged and scolded. 'Please, Bubble. I can't understand you. Did you get a big boo-boo? Stop crying, for Chrissake, for one second and talk so I can understand.'

He's a baby, Carla, shut up and give him a break.

21

She often talked to herself in a scolding voice to keep her temper in control. She was famous in her family for her sudden and quickly dissipated rages. From when she was a little baby to her maturity as a wife and mother, everyone who knew her had seen her stamp her right foot, flash her black eyes, and clench her fists so that the muscles and veins in her arms popped the smooth skin. 'You look like Popeye with tits when you're pissed off,' her husband Manny teased on their honeymoon. That answered a mystery: the wonder of Manny wanting her. Then she understood that her anger – what scared the hell out of most men – actually turned her husband on.

She hugged Bubble tighter, squashing her breasts. She distracted herself from Bubble's assault on her right ear (he was crying right into it) by scanning what she could see of the passengers. That wasn't much, given her angle: her sight was narrowed both by her proximity to the window and because her periphery was blocked by Leo's bobbing red face. Nobody seemed hurt. Some-one had thrown up. A couple of people must have crapped: the smell was disgusting. Out her window she saw land, a flat checkerboard of brown and green squares. The captain had come on. She heard the phrase '... emergency landing ...' although Bubble continued to bawl, because the speaker was positioned just above and behind her free left ear. She was crowded by all the noise and glare from the window and the rows of pale blue fabric and the low cream-colored ceiling. Also, the whole body of the plane creaked and rattled, as if all the screws were loose. She wanted out.

'Just get us on the ground,' she answered the captain.

'That's right,' the man in the seat in front of her said.

22

The fields below were empty: it looked safe to land there. She thought about what a story this was going to make. Uncle Sal had the scariest airplane story in the family: landing in Las Vegas, his jet's tires blew out and it had skidded off the runway a few hundred feet. There was lots of excitement in his account: sliding down emergency chutes, fire trucks, TV crews interviewing them later, their choice of a free flight home or a free night in a hotel, compliments of the airline. But if you paid attention you realized most of the danger was in Uncle Sal's mind.

And that's what this is going to be: just a good scary story to tell.

But Carla's plane rolled down ... dropping without any hint of a brake ... and then swooped up violently.

They all gasped. Bubble's tears stopped, shut off totally, as if he were a toy. Someone shouted, 'Oh God!' That was all there was to it: a sudden ride on a roller coaster, a fast dip down and a quick climb up. It was nothing compared to what had happened before, only it seemed to mean there was something still broken, that their troubles were far from over.

A pilot passed her, heading for the back, where the problem must be. Maybe he could fix it, she hoped, although she knew better. After all, he had no tools and how could he reach whatever was broken?

But with each shiver of fear, the scolding voice in her head told her it was ridiculous to believe that they were in serious trouble: *When planes crash they go down right away*. This was the big outside world where people weren't hysterical or stupid like some of her relatives. That pilot who had just gone by looked like a hero; with his sandy blond hair and sharp chin he would figure out how to get them down okay.

23

'Mommy.' Bubble's voice was alert. He had straightened in her arms, his heels kicking down, poking her in the stomach.

She was heartened by the clarity and strength in his voice. She was impatient with his crankiness after naps; this was the Leo she adored. 'Yes, baby,' she said and squeezed the tall length of his body. Bubble stood on her lap, pressing his tiny sneakers into her, trying to peer over the seats.

'I want a drink,' he said, enunciating so clearly he could have been twenty years old.

'I got some juice. How about that?'

'No!' He disciplined her with the word, like someone instructing a disobedient dog. She recognized that tone as the way she spoke when trying to stop Leo from doing something either dangerous or very destructive.

'Hey! Don't talk to me that way.'

'Don't want juice.' He whined this a little.

'Baby, I can't get you anything else right now. I got some juice in the bag. You want it?'

Bubble didn't answer. The mess of the plane had gotten his attention. He cocked his head to study the passengers retrieving scattered bags, clothes, blankets, pillows. 'I smell poop,' he said.

It happened again. Another roller-coaster ride. Her stomach flipped and Bubble flopped back: his stumpy legs kicked out, his head crashed into the seat. Carla exclaimed and grabbed him. As the ride came up from the valley she tasted her breakfast at the back of her throat. *Get me the fuck out of here*, she begged.

'Bubble,' she called to his little face. His eyes were shut tight. 'Bubble,' she said and gathered him.

He laughed. From his belly. The way he did when she

tickled his feet, a laugh of his whole body. 'Funny!' he called out between his hissing laughter.

'Come on,' she lifted him and swung him around so that he would be secure in her lap.

'Do that again,' he said.

'No, no. We got to sit still.'

'Do that again!'

'You want your juice?'

Bubble butted his head back. Carla wasn't sure if he meant to whack her in the nose (which he did) or if it was simply his willfulness pulling against her lead. For a moment, while her sinuses tingled and her head buzzed she couldn't talk.

That pilot passed again, heading back up to the front.

'Excuse me,' the man in front of her called to the pilot. 'What's going on?'

But the pilot rushed past, in a nervous hurry.

'Play! Play!' Bubble bucked in her lap. She had to dodge his head, which threatened her with more blows.

'Cut it out!' She hugged him close, crossing her arms in front of his chest. She buried her face in Bubble's black hair. He needed a cut; it was curling up the back of his neck. He had her hair, or her hair when she was young: so black and shiny your eyes couldn't accept the color and they would see velvet or glints of amber, but it was only rich black hair, dark and straight. Made Carla think of an Indian in Bubble's case, her poppa used to say Carla was Cleopatra when she was little.

Who's Cleopatra? she asked him.

The most beautiful woman who ever lived, he said.

She forgot the plane, didn't see the humps of blue fabric, the cave-like ceiling, or the recessed lights glowing from its curves. The sun warmed her face and she smelled Bubble's hair (she had shampooed it this morning so that her mother wouldn't right away criticize) and remembered her father.

She saw Poppa's coarse face, round and pockmarked, his nose was small and curved like a thumb, his tiny teeth were yellowed from the cigars he liked, his hair was all gone. He smiled at her, welcoming . . .

Carla gasped and shunted the image away. Her father was dead.

He's calling to you.

'No,' she answered.

'I want it now!' Bubble told her, he thought she was answering one of his demands.

'Okay, baby,' she said dutifully, too scared to be amused by their misunderstanding.

Carla bent down to reach around her feet for her bag. She held Bubble in her lap while bending over, and the strain on her back made her groan. Luckily, the disposable juice carton was on top, bright yellow with slashing red letters, easy to spot and somehow exciting. All the new stuff for babies was great. Manny often complained enviously that when he was little toys were crummy compared to today. There was so much to buy, much more than they could afford, but she wanted to get all of it, not only so that Bubble wouldn't be deprived, but because she liked the looks of the stuff, all the brilliant new gadgets; and she enjoyed the feeling, the excitement of giving him a new toy.

But she wasn't thinking of consumerism then. With her head lowered she could better hear sounds from the plane's injured structure. The noises it made were scary. The thin floor rumbled, the seats creaked, and the sides seemed to roar, as if there were tigers behind the panels. Was that normal? Had to be, she told herself.

'I want it,' Bubble said, grabbing for the juice container as soon as she brought it into view.

'Let me open it,' she yanked the carton away.

Poking the straw through the designated hole, she punctured the membrane of foil too hard and a jet of juice splashed her cheek. Fear and her baby made managing everything awkward. She had a squirming Bubble on her lap, her feet were unwilling to put their full weight on the floor for fear it would give way, and her squeezed legs were reluctant to rest against the sides because those roaring tigers might tear through any second. After she gave Bubble the carton, she glanced out the porthole window. They were low, close to the ground.

Good. You see? Everything's going to be all right. No problem.

The flight attendants were suddenly on the move: wobbling in the aisles, talking and picking up . . . shoes? Lisa appeared a couple of seats ahead:

'Take off your shoes if they have hard heels or soles. Remove all sharp objects from your pockets and stow them in the seat pocket. Eyeglasses also.'

This is nuts, she thought, and kicked off her shoes, one of her best pairs. She tried to decide if her house keys were considered sharp objects.

'Ma'am, baby better go in the seat.' Lisa took Carla's dressy shoes and added them to the armful she was carrying.

'Don't want to!' Bubble stiffened his back.

'We're going to be landing soon,' Lisa said.

'At an airport?' the man in front of her asked.

As if he heard, the captain came on: 'We're cleared for landing at . . .' She couldn't hear the airport's name. 'Flight attendants, prepare for emergency landing.'

Right away Lisa began to yell at them. Carla could see two other flight attendants forward of Lisa do the same as her, shouting with their arms full of shoes – red, black, brown, white, yellow – like a bathtub full of Bubble's toy boats. Lisa shouted: 'Bend over, put your head in your lap. Stay down until the plane comes to a complete stop and then find the nearest emergency exit.'

The plane took another dive down. Recklessly down. Carla yanked the squirming Bubble against her and winced at the proximity of the earth: 'Too close!' she pleaded to the porthole.

They swooped up from the land. But that was sickening also. Her stomach levitated up from her pelvis to her throat, while the rest of her was pinned down, paralyzed.

'Cut it out!' Carla said, addressing her advice to the captain. She couldn't help feeling that he was behaving like a macho teenager, intentionally doing crazy stunts in his souped-up car to scare the girls in the back seat.

Lisa was almost flipped by the plane's action. Her knees gave out. She stayed on her feet by grabbing the headrests. The shoes spilled all over, under and around the nearby rows.

'Come on, baby,' Carla said and pulled at Bubble, trying to get him off her and into the empty seat. His hands and sneakers clung to her clothes like pasta drying on the edges of the boiling pot. There was no one available to help. Lisa and the passengers nearby were preoccupied by picking up the scattered shoes. People made their motions in a quick and jerky manner, nervous that the plane was about to take them for another dip on the roller coaster.

'Come on, Bubble!' She pried one of his gluey hands off. But when Carla reached for the other hand, he stuck it to her again. 'I don't have time for games!' she yelled into his chubby determined face.

'No,' he said calmly.

She shoved him into the seat rudely.

'Ow!' he complained and kicked at her with his tiny sneakers.

She grabbed the heavy buckle of the seat belt and pressed it into his puffy belly, pinning him down while she hunted for its mate. *What good is this!* she yelled silently to herself so as not to scare her son. *It's no infant seat. He'll get cut in half.* She found the other end and locked him in.

Bubble kicked out his legs, scrunched his shoulders, and let himself slide down, wriggling so that his legs and his stomach slithered off the edge of the seat and the belt came up to his chest and neck.

'No!' Carla cried in despair. She pushed at his dangling feet to move him up. It was as hopeless as attempting to put toothpaste back into the tube. His rubbery two-year-old body squashed together for an instant, oozing back down the instant she stopped.

Another swoop . . . down . . .

Carla twisted her neck to glance out the window. A highway – looking very hard and firm – rushed at her . . .

The plane swooped up and the gray pavement was gone. Carla flopped back and lost Bubble altogether. He slid until hooked by the armpits. There was frantic activity in the plane. The flight attendants were shouting, pointing. The shoes they had gathered were gone. Where?

Hurry! she scolded herself. She didn't have much time. God knows what disaster would happen next. Problems jumped at her out of nowhere, the way they do in nightmares, and there seemed to be a diabolic presence thwarting any progress. She was back at the beginning: the seat belts were endangering Bubble, not protecting him.

Carla decided to try another method. She pulled Bubble up by the arms.

'No!' he shouted. His cheeks were bloated with stubbornness; his tiny lips disappeared into a pout of refusal.

She slammed Bubble against the seat, pinned him with her left hand and pulled at the loose end of the seat belt to tighten it all the way, despite the horrible images of Bubble being sliced in half.

This is no good.

'Shut up!' she said.

'I don't wanna!' Bubble answered.

Her plan was fine except that the belt didn't tighten all the way. She had him immobilized, ready to pull everything taut and secure him, and it was stuck.

'Fuck!' she said and didn't even bother to feel bad that she had cursed in front of Bubble. It was a vice she had promised not to indulge before her baby. Not that she had any hope he wouldn't eventually learn to use bad words: just that he wouldn't associate them with her.

'Need help?' Lisa had leaned in. She was a kid, Carla realized, seeing her up close. Her lipstick had been smeared down one cheek and it made her seem even

30

younger, like a little girl who had gotten into her mommy's makeup. She couldn't be more than twenty-one.

'I'll hold him,' Carla said and allowed Lisa to work on the belt, glad to have both hands for restraining Bubble, who was fighting with every muscle to break free. 'Stop fussing,' she said mildly, impressed by the total commitment of his effort to escape. Bubble's fat cheeks puffed out, his brown eyes bulged, his porcelain nostrils flared, his shoulders narrowed. Carla had to use all her strength and both hands to hold him in position. 'You're crazy,' she told him, cheerful at the thought that she didn't have to worry about how he would manage in the big world against all the other tough guys. 'You're so stubborn,' she lectured him, but in a mother's wondering singsong of praise.

'Damn,' Lisa said after several tugs. She had succeeded somewhat more than Carla, but there was plenty of slack for Bubble to slide through. Lisa paused and seemed to hear something. Had there been a chime? 'That's the best we can do,' she leaned back.

'That's no good,' Carla said.

'Let me go!' Bubble kicked out with his sneakers.

To illustrate the problem Carla let go of Bubble. Immediately, without shame, he stiffened his back and shoved with his ass. That propelled him down until the belt caught him at the chest and threatened to choke him.

'It's going to choke you, Bubble! Sit up!'

He didn't care: he wanted to be free at all costs.

'Hold him in your lap,' Lisa said. 'That's the drill, anyway.' Lisa seemed to hear something, something Carla couldn't, or didn't know she was hearing. Lisa ducked her head to get a view out the windows. 'Runway,' she whispered passionately.

Carla followed her glance.

There was an airport straight ahead. A long gray path with broad painted lines and small flashing lights, blinking their welcome. They were safe.

Bubble cried out.

Even as she rescued Bubble, Carla chuckled: he had worked himself so far down that now he was being hung by the neck like the outlaw he was.

'He'll be okay in your lap,' Lisa said, moving up the aisle, obviously surer of the situation. 'Everyone keep your head down,' she called out as she moved up toward the front. The authoritative and casual tone of the routine had returned to her and the other flight attendants' voices: 'And remain seated until the plane comes to a complete stop. We'll be on the ground in a few minutes.'

Carla put Bubble in her lap, nuzzled in his black hair, wrapped her thin muscular arms around his soft squirming body, and squeezed him with pleasure, eager for the scare to be over. *We're safe.* Carla hugged him and took another look at the land below. She smiled at its promise of safety.

3

While Max took care of Stacy, he saw Lisa across the way, tending to the business traveler in the seersucker suit. He was the man in 33A, but he wasn't having a heart attack. His shortness of breath was panic; the pain in his chest was fear. Lisa helped him out of his jacket and loosened his tie. He hung on to the *Journal*, although it drooped in half. In his white short-sleeved oxford shirt he looked older. Lisa seemed young enough to be his daughter.

Max learned from Mary that the businessman was okay when she joined him in ministering to Stacy. *En route* she had paused by 33A and Max asked her right away: 'Is he having a heart attack?'

'Are you a doctor?' she asked eagerly.

'No,' Max said and he felt a profound regret.

'Oh . . . I don't think so. Just scared.' She focused on Stacy. 'How you doing, hon?' Mary greeted her colleague with an informality that touched Max; speaking to one of her own she switched off the harsh public-address voice. 'Sorry I couldn't hold on to the cart.' She lifted the bandanna and winced in sympathy: 'Ow!'

'Doesn't hurt,' Stacy said and moved to rise.

Mary touched her shoulder. 'Don't be crazy, honey. Everything's okay. We got it under control.'

'I can help,' Max said.

Mary's virtual crewcut of graying blond hair seemed to harden into a shell as she stared at Max with a lot of suspicion and a little outrage for his making this offer.

He had no sexy feelings toward her and this was a relief. 'You can help by returning to your seat and buckling up We'll be on the ground shortly.'

Max laughed a little. A sardonic, doomed chuckle.

'Go back to your seat, sir,' she insisted, turning her public-address microphone back on. She ignored him by calling out to this section of passengers: 'Please remove all sharp objects, pens, eyeglasses, and take off any hard-soled shoes. The flight attendants will collect them.'

Max crossed over to Jeff and his seat. He listened to the plane. Although they were presumably descending there was no whine of back-thrust, no letup in the engines. The machine was fighting just to stay aloft.

Jeff had the dungarees on. He was stowing a bulky blanket in their overhead compartment. 'I put the pants in there,' Jeff explained with a mixture of feverish pride and shame. His partner's narrow face often resembled a high-strung pedigree, a wary greyhound. The scare Jeff had been through sharpened his angles. His eyes bulged a bit and moved from side to side as if checking for enemies. His mouth hung open, exposing his biggish teeth and their slight overbite; he was almost panting. 'What the fuck do they want our shoes for?'

'So the heels don't puncture the emergency slide. It's inflated. They want the pens and other stuff in the seat pocket so we don't stab ourselves. Move over,' Max said, indicating he wanted Jeff's seat. He had intended to say something pleasant instead of his gloomy explanation but every time he looked at Jeff he was reminded of their argument at the airport, of Jeff's contempt for his fear, and that made him want to punish his friend.

'Why?' Jeff might be scared, but he was still contentious and paranoid. 'Is this side safer?'

'No,' Max said. 'But the middle row is. So it doesn t make any difference. Just move so I can be on this side.' Max wanted this change in order to sneak up to the boy traveling alone and check on him once Mary had finished collecting all the shoes.

Jeff shifted seats. Max glanced down to see whether the fabric had been soiled by Jeff's spasm of fear. It was clean. Max settled in and buckled up.

This is where you're going to die, Max, he told himself, merely as a matter of fact, satisfying a lifelong curiosity. There was something comforting in this execution of himself: this certain knowledge of when and how.

Maybe that's what had me so scared, he thought. Maybe it was the uncertainty of the appointment, not the fact that it had to be kept.

The captain lost control again. The plane fell. Jeff grabbed his arm. He heard a child's scream. Was it that boy traveling alone?

'Get her up,' Max said into the wheezing noise, struggling to live even if he was ready to die. He thought he felt movement under his feet from the mechanisms that should be stilled if the hydraulics were gone.

They swooped up, just as out of control as when they fell, but at least it was away from the deadly ground.

'That was bad,' Jeff hissed.

We can't land, Max thought. The captain can't land it with no way to steer. He could imagine the frantic upset in the cockpit, the fury the pilot must feel at instruments that refused to yield to his skill.

Max looked toward the windows across the aisle. Two rows ahead Mary knelt at the feet of a male teenager, trying to pull off his pink boots. His leather jacket was trimmed with chains and buckles. They trembled with each attempt at freeing his foot from the boot. Above Mary's head Max saw that the effect of the downward and upward swoops had left the DC-10 lower, perhaps no higher than a few thousand feet. He could see a chain of buildings and silos off to the right, maybe the outskirts of a city.

But the captain can't get us down smoothly, Max reasoned. What could he do? Wait until they ran out of fuel? Unable to steer, the pilot would have to chance the first cleared space. He might have to attempt a landing any second, without warning. Max glanced out the windows again. He saw a mall with a Sears pass them in the distance. The store was several floors high and they were way above it. No, they weren't low enough for a sudden landing.

'I should have let you buy us the flight insurance,' Jeff said.

'What are you talking about?' They didn't look at each other while speaking. They kept their heads facing forward, braced for the worst. The sun slanted across Max's jaw and neck, heating him.

'When you found out this was a DC-10 you wanted to buy some.'

'I wanted to take another flight!' Max sighed, exasperated not by Jeff's manipulative alteration of the facts (that was typical) but because he couldn't hold himself back from being drawn into an argument. I'm about to die and I still can't ignore him, he thought bitterly.

'Oh? Yeah ... but you also wanted to get some insurance right?'

'Are you actually worried –'

The plane flopped in the air again, dropping into the

hollow of the wave and riding up its back, an awkward surfer. They were silent until it was level. Mary had gotten one of the teenager's boots off and was at work on the other as they took the wave. She ended up with her head between his knees. When she rose from this position she had a pained expression on her face. Max assumed she had been inadvertently kicked in the stomach by the pink boot. She got to her feet and moved away without the second boot. The teenager hurried to work on removing it himself.

Jeff banged Max with his elbow: 'What were you going to ask?'

'What do you care about the insurance?'

'We have wives and children, remember? When it seemed like we were going to crash that's all I could think about. I mean, if we die, there's no business. How are they going to make it?'

Max relished this moment. He moved his head to see the effect: 'Jeff, I got news for you. I overheard the co-pilot talking to the head flight attendant. We're not going to make it.'

The greyhound was stilled. Jeff's mouth stayed open, his teeth exposed to the air, but the panting was arrested and his eyes no longer nervously scanned the periphery. 'What'd they say?'

'The rear engine blew up. There are no hydraulics. They can't steer.'

For a moment he had no reaction. Then Jeff nodded and his great eyes were dulled by a film of something, not tears, but a kind of liquid glass, a protection against pain. 'What about manually? Can't they –'

'Not in something this big.'

Jeff accepted it, nodding again. His attitude was

much braver than Max had expected. No whining, just curiosity. Max felt ashamed of himself for his desire to torment Jeff and now wanted to comfort him. 'You know, there'll be plenty of money for Nan and Debby and the kids. The average settlement on a plane crash is three-quarters of a million dollars. And we have the business partnership insurance, which goes to them if we both die while conducting business. That's another quarter of a million each –'

'Are you sure?' Jeff's interest was intense. That's why they were partners, after all. They had peculiar attitudes, more concerned with the structure and mechanisms than the feelings and philosophy. It was almost as if their debate over whether they could afford to die was as significant as the pilot's efforts to land. 'I thought the business policy was only for the surviving partner.'

'No. There's a provision –'

Max stopped because he noticed that Mary and Lisa and the other flight attendants were tossing the shoes into the lavatories. That answered a question which had worried him, namely where could they stow them so they wouldn't become missiles. With the shoes put away, the flight attendants began their final surveillance of belts, their chant of emergency procedures, first illustrating the crash position, and then arms akimbo to point out the exits. The teenager continued unsuccessfully to pull at his boot.

Jeff banged Max again. 'Go on!'

'– if we die on a business trip, the widows get the money. And also –' Max smiled at Jeff. But his partner wasn't looking. The greyhound head had fallen back against the seat, its eyes shut. '– we paid for the tickets on the gold American Express card –'

Jeff twisted his head abruptly and interrupted: 'What difference does that make?'

'Automatic flight insurance. That's another half a million for each of them. They'll end up with one point five million apiece.'

'Jesus,' Jeff mumbled, upset. 'I didn't know.'

'Didn't know what?' Max asked.

Jeff hesitated, his narrow dog's mouth hanging open. Then he barked: 'We're worth more dead than alive.'

With a shudder and an alarming whine, the landing gear was lowered. It felt and sounded as though the floor were being removed. Jeff cursed into the noise:

'Fuck! God damn it! I can't take this! Fuck! Hurry up!'

'It's the wheels,' Max tried to calm him. But they *had* made an unusually loud and terrible sound. Was that an illusion? Max wanted to know much more about the how of his death. He envied all those people who would spend tomorrow morning secure at home, sipping coffee and enjoying their superior knowledge about the cause. He pictured the spate of newspaper articles based on leaks from the investigation until months later, when the final judgement of the National Transportation Safety Board would be followed by orders for the defect that produced this fatality to be repaired in all the DC-10s, luring passengers on to more planes which would fail in some other insidious way. As an architect he had come to understand that most things were made shabbily and more so with each passing day. The deterioration was first in their look, now it was in their fundamental engineering.

Mary and her helpmates were done. She returned to get Stacy, guiding her up to the front, to the jump seats by the bulkheads. That put them beside one of the emergency exits. While they made this maneuver someone shouted:

'Look! The airport!'

All heads turned together in a uniform movement of hope that Max pitied.

Jeff stabbed Max's biceps with his elbow. 'Hey! He did it!'

Max hunkered down to get a better angle on his side view of the landing strip. Sure enough they were heading straight for a medium-sized airport. He saw spinning red lights atop a row of tiny trucks, miniaturized into toys by the perspective of their height. The presence of rescue equipment wasn't a clue to their chance of survival: fire trucks were a standard precaution for any unusual landing. Instead of being dismayed by the sight of this wary welcome, for a moment Max believed in the continuation of his life.

But then the captain lost control again. This time the plane tilted instead of dropped. The right wing disappeared below and their bodies followed. All the passengers were unwillingly linked on this wild ride and they moaned together in dismay . . .

The right wing reappeared with a sickening jolt and then continued past the horizon, rising to the heavens. The seesaw now pulled everything the opposite way, tilting down to the left, and Max was unnerved to see the ground pass vertically, as if the floor he wanted in a department store had just gone by, lost forever, and he tried to cry out, to tell everyone – *I'm sorry we aren't going to live anymore. I'm sorry we don't have time to change* – but no sound came out of his mouth into the horrible roar . . .

And they were abruptly level, everyone's stomachs arriving late, jarring into place.

The teenager threw up on the pink boot which he still hadn't gotten off.

'He's doing it, Max,' Jeff's voice said faintly. The engines were screaming at this point, howling with pain as the jet descended in jerks, as if they were bumping down a flight of stairs on their ass.

Max checked what he could through the windows. The plane did seem lined up properly with the runway and it was close to touching down, moving fast at the ground. But they were rushing to an earth that wouldn't forgive airborne clumsiness.

Max unbuckled his seat belt. 'I'm going to sit with the boy,' he said to Jeff, more sure than ever, after that awkward maneuver with the wings, that they were going to crash. He expected Jeff to plead, to beg him to stay.

'What?' Jeff called, bewildered instead. Max had no time to answer. He was frightened to be up and walking on the breakable floor. He stumbled his way forward three aisles, found the boy seated alone, waved a casual goodbye to his partner, and fell into the empty seat.

'Hi,' he said and buckled himself in. He put his hand on the boy's neck. 'Head in your lap.' The child obeyed, dutiful, concealing his loneliness and fright to the last. Max thought of how proud this child's parents would be of their son's bravery and he wanted to weep.

Max bent over as well, turning his head so he could look at the boy. 'What's your name?' he shouted.

'Byron,' he said, also placing his head sideways to see Max. There was something comforting about their huddled position, as if they were lying in a bed and chatting intimately. As recently as a year ago Max used to do

41

that with his son at bedtime, listening to stories of boyhood quarrels and contests, providing advice that only a child would think wise.

Max thought he had misheard. 'What did you say?'

'Byron,' he repeated. 'Like the poet.'

There was a sudden lull, the engines cutting as they were about to touch ground. Max had succeeded in distracting Byron for a second, unfortunately the change in sound refocused the boy on his terror.

'Everything is wonderful,' Max said into Byron's worried face. 'Are you scared?'

Byron nodded, with that admission his lips trembled.

They were floating just above the earth, gliding in their big ungainly airship. The back wheels touched pavement –

Max gently pushed Byron's head flush to his knees. 'We made it,' he said, lying.

On the right they banged into something. Max felt the error. All the passengers did, as if they had stretched their nervous systems to the machine, growing into the skin of the plane. Fear flashed in Byron's eyes and Max tried to comfort him before the roar of impact reached them:

'It'll be over –'

But he never finished that sentence. Everything was on the move: their seats, the floor, he saw something black and heavy spin into a part of a person, he thought he was sideways and he shut his eyes and he melted to nothing except for his eyes, he was alive inside his blinded eyes until the crash engulfed him and Max was alone in his brain, cornered.

Goodbye, he whispered to life.

4

Carla dodged her bobbing son's head to keep what she could see of the airport in sight. Bubble was excited, although she couldn't imagine by what, since he faced the back of the seat in front of him, a dull sight made less interesting by its empty pocket. Both the plastic card which illustrated emergency procedures and the airline magazine had long ago been taken out. Bubble had used the card as a sword until he swiped her across the cheek. Carla retaliated with confiscation. Then he tore up the magazine until there were so many bits of paper all over the place that Lisa, in passing, embarrassed Carla by asking if she could throw the magazine away for her. Both removals provoked fits, two of three quarrels that were resolved only when Bubble passed out shortly after takeoff. He had been tired, poor baby. His strong will degenerated into petulance when his body was exhausted; otherwise he was demanding, not whiny; charming and manipulative, not sulky and a complainer.

While they came down toward the airport his post-nap energy was comforting. She needed encouragement because after first seeing the runway and enjoying a moment of complete relief, Carla lost some of that hope at the additional sighting of the fire trucks and ambulances waiting for them. And her fear came back completely when the jet, which had seemed to be going smoothly as it went lower and lower, suddenly rocked back and forth. It swayed so far to the right that

43

Bubble's head went below the seat level and then jerked him back with such violence that she had to restrain him with all her might to prevent his skull from colliding with the curved window frame.

This isn't safe.

She decided the aisle seat was better because of the cleared space on both sides. 'Come on, Bubble, we're going to move.' She fumbled between his back and her lap to release the seat belt with one hand, while she clutched her baby with the other.

When she made the short hop over to the aisle seat, Bubble resisted. Only his lower half came with her. He had hooked the pouch with both hands and clung to it, stretching the elastic band to the limit.

'You're going to break it!' Carla shouted, ridiculously she knew. *You sound like Mama*, she mocked herself.

The bottom of her seat hummed, her feet rumbled.

'Jesus!' she yelled, frightened by the noise and vibration, and worse, panicked at their vulnerability. She was unbuckled and Bubble was stretched out as if he were a diver frozen in midair.

A loud mechanical whine overwhelmed her shout and even the noise of the engines. What was happening? It sounded as if her part of the plane were coming apart.

Carla yanked hard and Bubble lost his grip on the pouch. They were flung back into the aisle seat. His head struck her chin and she was stunned.

For a moment she made no move and watched the passengers. It was surprising that they all faced forward, ignoring her area. No one seemed to care about the noise she had just heard. Also it confused her that the sound was gone and the trembling had been stilled yet there hadn't been any result.

Bubble was complaining. 'Mommy hurt me,' he said. He tried to reach around to touch the back of his head, but his arms were too short.

'Sorry,' she whispered and kissed his black head of hair. She glanced out the window. They were almost down. The earth scared her: huge and clumsy and gray like a whale, the runway filled her porthole. It seemed in the way.

She hurried, fastening her seat belt. She opened her legs wide until Bubble slipped down on to the cushion and then squeezed them together, wedging her baby between her thighs. He squirmed and complained. She put her arms over his shoulders and crossed them in front, imitating the secure style of Bubble's car seat. She was proud of her invention.

The engines were quiet. They must have touched the ground, she assumed. Everything felt smooth and the sound was gentle.

Bubble bumped his head back and then forward, rocking his body to gain momentum to break her grip while making noises of protest.

Carla glanced at the middle rows of the plane and across to the far rows on the right side. Most people were bent all the way over. Very few were sitting up like her –

Beneath her there was a bump.

The wheels had touched the ground!

'Yay!' she called to all those huddled people. She wanted to lead the cheers. They were safe!

She released her fingers from their entanglement in front of Bubble's stomach just enough to free the tips. She clapped them together delicately.

A woman screamed.

A shudder went through her right side and her row of seats rose up above the others. She hung there for a weird second, twisting. The middle rows moved by her as if they were a car passing hers on a freeway, passengers' profiles zooming out of sight until a man's head and shoulders flopped like a doll and were squashed by something and she knew that what she was seeing was horrible and her brain went numb.

Her eyes shut. She heard and sensed the rest of the crash –

The tigers roared. She was spinning up and around and over, like a sock in a washer, and she prayed hard –

Please God, please God, please God, at last filling her mind with Him and longing for life and wishing herself away from this . . .

Something hit her legs. Then her back. A hand was burned.

It was over. The tigers had gone and she smelled their rage: everything stung her nostrils and only then did she remember Bubble. She clasped her arms tight. She touched nothing but herself. Her baby was gone.

Carla screamed, opened her eyes and couldn't see. She couldn't breathe. Her face fell free. She had been inside the ceiling. Only it wasn't the ceiling anymore. It was foam rubber. Also the floor wasn't beneath her – the blue carpet was to her right. Where was the aisle? The windows?

A cloud of smoke washed over her face. She reached around for Bubble and called to him.

Somebody passed her, breathing hard, and she remembered her seat belt. That's why she couldn't move. And the smoke meant fire . . . coming at her.

Panicked, she released the buckle and tumbled side-

46

ways on to a lump. It was the middle of someone's body. She felt liquid on her bare wrist that she realized was blood. 'Help me!' a voice cried. There were lots of sounds she didn't recognize. She smelled things burning; she feared to know what. Terror was alive in her bones and she screamed, rolling off the corpse. She crawled away and got up as best she could with the space so squashed. Behind her, the other way, were light and voices. People called and pleaded.

Flames appeared ahead in the dark. She turned to the sunlight behind her and ran for it. She passed a lifeless face staring upward. She ignored a man digging for something in the foam. He yelled at her for running but she couldn't stop, she had to get out from the horror, the torn-apart world, and the fire.

Max was alive. He knew that first. And so was Byron. He knew that when he opened his eyes. He did not understand much else, especially what he was seeing: Byron's hair floated in a burst of yellow light.

That was the sun.

The hair wasn't floating – the boy was upside down.

Facts gathered speed, catching up to each other in his head, and soon he could make sense again.

The plane is on fire. He smelled the acrid fumes of plastic and synthetic fabric burning. It's poisonous. We're both upside down and strapped in to our seats. He released his belt and dropped right on to his knees. He knew that the fall must have hurt them, but he felt nothing. He wasn't numb, yet he felt no pain. You're in shock, he told himself. Out of the corner of his eye he saw a woman compressed between what must have been two or three rows jumbled together. She was dead, of

47

course, but what sickened him was the irrational look of her body, squashed into a shape that he couldn't comprehend.

He reached up and unbuckled Byron, catching the boy's legs as he dropped. Lowering himself to cushion the fall he saw another incredible sight —

A newborn baby nested in an infant seat. The upper edge of its cradle had been caught and was suspended in a mass of wires and twisted metal. The baby was no more than a few weeks old. It was untouched and untroubled; its little fingers played in the air.

Byron was talking; he seemed to be hitting Max in the side. Max ignored him and reached for the infant. Smoke covered him. He inhaled some of it and felt a sharp pain in his stomach. He got dizzy . . . The death tide pulled at him, wanting him to linger . . .

Go Max, hurry!

He sprang out of the morass. He had the infant seat and a part of Byron, hand or arm or foot, he didn't know what.

There was light off to the side where it shouldn't be. But he pushed Byron that way.

They passed unforgettable nightmares: bodies smashed or impaled. He shouted at Byron – 'Don't look!' – and it was then that Max saw the worst of all:

Jeff's greyhound face, eyes filled with blood, lying on its side without a body.

Max looked no more and pushed Byron at the light. Everything, inside and out, screamed at him: Hurry! The yellow cloud filled their vision. They ran right into it and fell out of the plane . . .

As he dropped, Max let go of Byron in order to hang on to the baby. He twisted while they went down, his back to the ground. He expected to be broken by it . . .

He landed on straw. No. A sharp green leaf stuck him in the cheek. It was a cornfield. He faced where they had come from, a severed portion of the plane, gaping with torn wires, insulation and destroyed seats. A body was splattered against one edge, merged into the metal.

They were out! They were alive!

The joy of this knowledge coursed through him, electrifying his body with power.

The jet could blow up, he realized, smelling its kerosene fuel and feeling heat from the ruins.

'Come on!' he shouted at Byron, who seemed paralyzed, lying motionless, suspended above the ground by a hammock of cornstalks. On his feet, carrying the baby in the infant seat, Max was surprised that his own body worked so well. He glanced down at his jeans and white sneakers and saw no blood, no soot, nothing: he had escaped pure and untouched.

A man in a white T-shirt and jeans caught Carla as she jumped down from a part of the plane she didn't recognize. Nothing made sense. The airport was gone. Behind the man and the other people running at her was a farm field, nothing else.

'My baby,' she told him and couldn't talk, ashamed.

Sirens and people answered her. She couldn't stand up. Carla slid down on to the T-shirt, resting her head against the belly massed above the belt.

He said something about her leg. But not to her.

'My baby!' she screamed hard, because of all the noise and because she couldn't be sure of how much volume she was producing.

'Where's your baby?' This question was asked by a

different face, a young one, with shining brown eyes. He seemed to know the truth of what she had done.

'I don't know!' she begged him to believe her.

'Move it. They're going to douse her,' a different person answered.

Why? Why do that to me?

'My baby!' With this pronunciation she confessed her cowardice and also told him where to look. His brown eyes didn't seem to get her meaning, but they grew lighter and forgiving.

'I'll find him,' he said and was gone.

'From there,' said the belly carrying her, not talking to her. 'Here, put your arm around –'

She was lifted above the green trash which had swallowed her feet. Now she could see more. There was the airport and everywhere there were people and cars and fire trucks and openness. She could see the sky and the buildings and soon the ground turned hard underneath and the fact came running at her . . . Racing alongside all the people was the fact –

Bubble is dead.

'No!' she doubled over. She pushed at the T-shirt and looked back at the horror.

The plane was smashed on the ground, broken in huge pieces like a great animal felled and dismembered and feasted on by insects. They crawled everywhere, spraying water and insinuating into its wounds.

'My baby!' she showed where he must be. In her head she could see Bubble trapped, perfectly fine and happy, but scared, caught inside the smoking tube surrounded by mangled corpses. The T-shirt and a woman in white didn't pay attention. She pushed at them and ran back.

Only she couldn't. There was a sharp tug in her left calf, a clean slicing stab, and she fell.

It's broken, she knew. And she knew that her injury wouldn't be enough, wouldn't satisfy God at all. A broken leg was not enough and she sobbed at the woman in white and the T-shirt because nothing would ever make up for this.

5

Max carried the baby and urged Byron through the high rows of corn until they were past the smoking filet of plane and could see a mob of rescuers running at the wreck from their trucks and cars. The fire fighters raced at the mechanical corpse without hesitation, charging both on foot and in their vehicles.

How brave, Max thought. Passengers stumbled out of white and black snakes of smoke. A man whose pants were torn off and whose shirt was bloodied fell on to the runway as an ambulance reached him. Fire fighters scurried into the jet's various wounds. It was all so sad and hopeless: they were pygmies unable to save their toppled idol.

Max had to restore the baby to its mother. He believed she was alive although he had no fact to support his faith or any idea who she was. The infant might belong to a number of couples he had noticed while boarding: there were at least a half dozen babies on the plane. Max also felt Byron needed to be restored to normal authority and life. The boy had been dangled over a limitless chasm; he ought to be yanked back to a flat safe world as quickly as possible.

Max carried the infant seat in the crook of his left arm and held Byron's hand with his free one, guiding him out of the cornfield and on to the runway. There were dozens of tiny cracks in its gray surface that Max had never observed through an airport's tinted glass or a plane's plastic windows.

The baby made no sounds. It stared calmly at Max. Byron winced at the hot concrete. His shoes had been collected by the flight attendants. Max was protected by his sneakers. The sun inflicted its glare and heat everywhere, soaking into the pavement and flashing off windows and trucks.

'Ow,' Byron complained. He skipped on the balls of his feet.

Their progress toward the rescuers seemed to be in slow motion. Nobody noticed them. All eyes were on the three sections of the wreck. A long jet of foam peed from the top of a fire truck on to a smoking engine. Passengers continued to appear from the wounds of the DC-10. There were shouts and sirens and an ominous hiss from the plane.

'Look!' an ambulance man pointed at Max.

And then lots of people noticed him, only it couldn't just be him and he turned to glance back. Behind him, like ghosts, walking at a slow stunned pace were maybe fifteen or twenty people, emerging out of the cornfields.

Quickly they were surrounded by a variety of helpers, in uniform and out. A man lifted Byron and it was only then that Max saw one of the boy's legs had been scraped and he was bleeding.

'Who's baby is this?' Max shouted back at the other passengers. He called to one woman. 'Is this your baby?' But she didn't even seem to see him, much less hear what he said. He recognized her as one of the blond mothers he had noticed on the plane traveling with all those look-alike blond kids. None were as young as the baby he held. And none were with her.

'Help!' That was Byron's voice.

Max turned and saw that Byron was reaching for him.

'Don't worry,' the man carrying Byron said. 'Your daddy is right here.'

'I'm not his daddy.'

Byron still had his hand out, yearning for Max.

'Take care of him,' Max told the volunteer. 'Who are you?' he added lamely.

'Red Cross,' the man said. Max was surprised by the speed of their arrival until he remembered there had been about twenty minutes while the jet was in trouble in the air. Plenty of time for all the services to be prepared on the ground.

'He'll get you back to your parents,' Max told Byron and the boy actually had the presence of mind to nod his agreement. 'He was traveling alone,' he told the Red Cross man.

They reached the ambulances and trucks. Max leaned against a green station wagon. Three bags of groceries were loaded in the rear. He noticed a box of Rice Krispies. Byron was carried off toward the airport buildings. Max wanted to close his eyes but he thought he would die if he did. He pushed off the car and moved toward the other collection point of surviving passengers – a pair of ambulances parked near an open hangar.

He walked holding the infant seat outstretched, offering it to each person he approached. 'Is this your baby?' he called to a woman who was in hysterics, but he realized the moment his question was out that she was in her sixties.

A few rescuers blocked his path. 'Are you okay?' one said.

'I got this baby out,' Max answered. 'Maybe we can find the mother.'

'You weren't in the crash?' a paramedic in white

54

uniform asked. She bumped shoulders with him and looked closely into his eyes.

Max shook his head no, hoping she would ignore him. 'I found this baby,' he repeated. He just wanted them to make an announcement or something so he could relieve the mother's anxiety.

'Over here!' a fire fighter shouted at him and bounced up and down. A hatchet on his belt danced. He looked fake, someone in costume. 'This way!'

Max was urged along until he reached a woman seated on the edge of a station wagon's back panel. Her head was bowed and the hair cut in a pageboy style; the bangs obscured her face. She was small; her feet dangled without reaching the pavement. As she lifted her face to look at him he was impressed by her youth. She was hardly older than a teenager.

'Is this your baby?' he asked his forlorn question.

For a moment she stared lifelessly. Then she was on him, frantic. She grabbed the infant seat as if Max had meant to do her baby harm. She knelt on the ground, unstrapped her child, and clutched it desperately, repeating its name in between wild kisses.

Max was crying. The tears came down his cheeks. He felt them hang and drip off his jaw. One curved around his chin. When he tried to wipe it away his palm slid off into the air.

The doctor in the hangar injected Carla with something, something that made her feel she was atop a mass of large cushions, that every muscle could give up and leave the living to these giant pillows, each one devoted to relieving her of the slightest effort. In fact, she lay on a portable cot beside a number of other injured passengers.

She told the T-shirt man Bubble's age and size and general appearance. She knew he was thirty-seven inches and weighed thirty-four pounds because he had gone for his two-year-old checkup last week.

'I'll find him and bring him to you,' T-shirt said. After he left, Carla decided he must have had a reason for being sure that he could succeed. Maybe very few passengers were dead. She knew some were because . . .

There was a nausea that accompanied any recall of the sights she had passed while running out of the plane, especially of the body she had fallen on. If she forced the ghastly images away then her stomach settled. She made a great effort to raise herself up and look at her right arm to check whether that corpse's blood was still there. No. Maybe she had imagined it. Maybe things weren't so bad.

Her leg was in a cast, or a kind of cast, something that the doctor had been able to put around her calf instantly. It was inflated and held in place by straps fastened with Velcro. She felt a dull sensation, not pain really, right below her knee. The doctor told her it was broken although there hadn't been an X ray –

Why wasn't she thinking of Bubble?

She was a horrible person. Selfish and scared. She had learned that in the plane.

The hangar had a tall ceiling, vast and curved like an old-fashioned train station or a cathedral. Her head fell back on the pillows. She stared into the receding dark of the roof.

Please bring him back, she asked God meekly. *I'll do better next time.*

She waited for someone to answer. She wasn't dumb or crazy, she knew God wouldn't. But wouldn't He send someone? Or was Jesus himself scared?

She felt hot although the hangar was cool. She shut her eyes.

She was floating on waves. She opened her eyes and saw a man carrying her into an ambulance.

'What's wrong?' she asked.

'Going to the hospital.'

'Get your leg fixed up,' a voice from behind added.

'What about my boy?' It took all her energy to speak. She couldn't lift herself either. A weight had her pinned, as if someone were sitting on her.

'Everybody's going to the hospital.'

They slid her into the ambulance. She saw sky out the window, that soft perfect blue sky which makes people say, 'Oh, it's such a beautiful day,' and she thought –

He's dead.

The thought hurt. She wept. The tears rained on the cruel fact and she just didn't care, didn't care where they were taking her or whether she would ever get up from lying down.

She couldn't stop crying. One of the medics held her hand. He had a plump face, small dark eyes, and messy brown hair. She noticed all that but she kept on crying. She wanted her head to feel, not think about what happened, not judge, not hope.

'Where are you from?' he asked.

'New York,' she stammered between sobs.

The medic nodded and covered her hand with his other. 'Does the leg hurt?'

She had forgotten all about it. 'My baby,' she bawled.

That made him look away. He knew something. He knew Bubble was dead.

She stopped crying and felt cold. The perspiration

covering her was chilled; she felt as if a thin blanket of ice had been thrown over her. She shivered.

The medic's attention returned. He noticed her condition and fussed, covering her with another blanket and taking her pulse. Her head lolled toward the window. Outside the sky remained empty and pretty. She couldn't find a single cloud, not even a wisp. In the plane she remembered they flew above a puffy floor of them.

She felt Bubble in her arms again, his sweaty head bouncing underneath her chin, his stomach pushing against her hands.

Why couldn't she remember losing him? She had him and then he was gone and she couldn't remember. Why?

She was uneasy about herself and her actions. She shouldn't have allowed them to carry her off. She shouldn't have left the airport.

Carla braced her elbows against the stretcher and pushed up.

The medic said, 'Whoa,' and gently stopped her progress with a hand, coaxing her to lie down.

'I can't go to the hospital without my son. I got to go back and help them find him.'

'Everybody's out of the plane. They're taking everybody to the hospital, okay? You'll see him there.'

He was lying. He didn't know a thing about Bubble.

She was nauseated suddenly, so powerfully that she threw up all over the blankets without giving a thought to how disgusting she was being.

'I'm sick,' she told them after it was out.

'Jesus,' one of them muttered.

She fell back and watched the blue sky while they cleaned her up.

*

Max accepted a drink of orange juice from a Red Cross volunteer and watched the mother and baby enjoy their reunion. He moved away from them, however, in order not to overhear whether they had been traveling with the father. He didn't want to learn that she had been widowed.

He caught sight of the blond mother standing beside a fireman, intent on the people and bodies they brought out of the wreckage.

A man wearing a uniform and a name badge and carrying a clipboard with what Max presumed to be the DC-10's passenger manifest stopped at his elbow. 'Were you on the plane?' he asked breathlessly, pen ready to check him off.

Max disliked this fellow. Although the airline official was in his twenties, his hair had thinned, his belly had grown, and he had the nervous sweaty manner of a middle-aged bureaucrat. Max crumpled the half-sized paper cup and shook his head no.

The airline man frowned at this response and hustled over to the blond mother. She answered him, her mouth moving angrily. She gestured at the plane, pointing.

Where had she been sitting? Max tried to find which of the three sections of destroyed plane had been hers. It was the first part. A bite had been taken out of the right side of that piece. It was charred and disintegrated, scarring the cornfield. Max turned away.

I'm alive, he thought without shame. He looked at the glass walls of the terminal. A gang of people had stayed indoors to watch. He walked toward them.

His face was very hot. Nobody stopped him from entering the terminal. He didn't know what airport this was, although it was obviously somewhere between New

York and Los Angeles. He found a water fountain just inside the building's doors. A reporter and a cameraman came through jangling equipment and went out on to the runway while he splashed himself with cold water.

Jeff is dead.

That was a complicated thought and he had no desire to consider its implications.

He walked away from what had everybody else's attention, making a reverse commute into the heart of the building. The baggage carousels were bare and still. The car rental counters were deserted. The ticketing terminals flashed green at nobody.

He found a newspaper vending machine. The local paper inside told him he was in Canton, Ohio. If he remembered correctly then he was at the home of the Football Hall of Fame. That seemed funny.

'My big chance,' he said aloud.

Max went out the airport building entrance. He saw a few empty cabs. Farther along, standing at the edge of a chain-link fence, were a number of men who might be drivers. They were watching the wreck and the rescuers. A bench against the wall invited Max to sit, and he was tired enough to accept, but he wanted to keep going, to move away from the crash and its cover-up, the steady accumulation of details all designed (he knew this now, understood the process so much better) to reassure the rest of humanity that it couldn't happen to them.

He walked up to the men and asked if they were taxi drivers.

Two said yes, one a haggard young man with long unkept hair, the other a fat elderly man wearing an electric-green short-sleeved shirt.

'Is there a good hotel nearby?'

'Sheraton's the best,' said the young man.

'Give me a ride there?'

The young man looked at the scene: at the trucks, still spewing liquid; at the smoking slices of plane; and farther back, at the hangar where a semicircle of survivors limped into the arms of volunteers or peered back in shock or wept beside the ambulances and cars. 'Think I should stick around,' he said, leaning his elbows into the fence.

Max noticed that a man on the other side of the driver was recording the scene with a home video camera.

'I'll take you,' the fat man said.

Max followed the shimmering green shirt to a white station wagon.

'No bags?' the old man asked Max before getting in.

The interior had been cooked by the sun. Its upholstery smelled of manure. 'Sheraton?' the driver asked.

Max nodded. He felt guilty, as if he were fleeing a crime.

With tantalizing slowness and grace the old man drove around the circle that led them out of the airport. He had to dodge a number of cars stopped at random, presumably abandoned by rescuers in too big a rush to park properly. 'Were you in that crash?' he asked as they straightened out and exited on to a regular road.

Max denied it with a vigorous shake of his head. 'Thank God,' he added.

A young man in a blue hospital gown looked at Carla's leg and at her left hand and flashed a penlight into her eyes. 'She's okay,' he said in a clipped dismissive voice, almost a rebuke. He hurried away, followed by an attentive nurse.

Because of him Carla noticed for the first time that the back of her hand had an inflamed red stripe across it. She remembered the burning sensation she had felt during the crash. Other sensations and images came fast: Bubble wedged in her lap, his hair brushing against her chin; the spinning people and seats, the roaring tigers, and the horrible shock of her empty arms.

'Help me up!' she called. She tried to will her legs over the edge of the gurney. The broken one refused her order.

She looked around. She was in a hallway. Blue letters pasted on a glass panel told her she was outside the emergency room. Through the window she saw a middle-aged man's chest split open like a chicken on the butcher's counter, his mouth overwhelmed by tape and a white funnel. The sight was fleeting – they drew a curtain around him. Everywhere there were people and hurried activity.

The people here are really sick, Carla. So lie down and shut up. You're all right.

'Oh God,' she said sadly. A state trooper glanced over at her. He stood with his arms folded facing the entrance's double doors, as if expecting wrongdoers to make a charge. She waved to him. He frowned. And then he came over. He made noise when he walked. His belt was loaded with things. 'You seen a two-year-old boy with black hair?' she asked.

'They took the kids to Pediatric Emergency,' he said, still stern, as if she were at fault for not knowing they would. 'Looking for your son?'

His accent squeezed the sounds into a whine. She had to repeat his sentence to herself before she understood it. 'Yeah,' she drawled. Her tongue was thick and slow.

Must be the shot. 'What did they give me?' she asked. When the cop didn't understand her question Carla mimicked an injection with her thumb and fingers.

'Don't know. Could be morphine. I'll ask somebody about your boy.'

He moved off behind her. She attempted to turn herself in order to watch where he went. Her eyes were surprised by the glare of the fluorescent panels on the ceiling. She blinked, her elbows slipped, and she fell back with a thud.

Just relax. Give yourself a break.

'Hi, honey.' A voice wakened her. She wasn't aware of having fallen asleep.

The face she saw was wrinkled and big and square. Large glasses twitched. They were lightly tinted and had a twinkling jewel at each corner. Carla recognized the frames as being the same as her mother's. They were an extravagance, costing over two hundred dollars.

'My name is Bea Rosenfeld. I'm a social worker and a family therapist . . .' she smiled beneficently, tilting her head as if making a joke: '. . . and some other things. My husband says I like being a student, but you know how men like to belittle what they don't understand. I guess women do too – but what do you care? You're in pain. How's the leg? Has a doctor seen you?'

Carla nodded. 'It's broken.'

'That looks temporary,' Bea said, glancing at the cast. 'I was told you said you were traveling with a little boy. Your son?' She studied a sheet of paper. 'What's your name?' Before Carla could answer, she added. 'Or what was the name on your ticket?'

'Carla Fransisca.'

'Beautiful name. Franchesca –'

'No. Fran*sis*ca.'

'Right ... uh huh. Okay.' Bea's glistening frames rose up from the paper and shined at Carla. 'Well, I think you should know that he's missing.' The glasses reflected two bars of fluorescent light. She told Carla the fact boldly. She put a big warm hand on Carla's uninjured one. 'Was he in a seat or in your lap?'

'I couldn't get him in the seat! The belt wouldn't work!' Carla felt stupid yelling, but she was nervous that her story wasn't going to be believed. 'Ask the stewardess,' she pleaded in a hoarse voice. 'Even she couldn't make it work! It got stuck!'

'Nobody's saying anything to contradict you, honey. Okay? I'm asking questions to find out some fact that might help us find out what happened to your son.' Bea studied her sheet of paper. 'The airline hasn't made a seating plan available. You don't remember your seat number, do you?'

'Forties. It was in the forties. Forty-eight?' Carla pulled on Bea's hand to prompt her.

'I don't know. Really. I'm telling you everything I do know.'

'Is he dead?'

Bea was neither shocked nor wary of the question. 'I don't know. I know he isn't here in this hospital and they tell me that all the children are here. But that's not definite. I don't want you to assume that they've got all their facts straight. There's a lot of confusion. Can I call someone for you? Your husband? The airline is supposed to notify everyone they can reach, but you probably know how to get to him faster. If you tell me a number I'll call him now and tell him you're here and you're fine.'

'He's at work,' Carla said.

'Do you know that number?'

'It's in Manhattan. It's 555–4137. That's a 212 area code.'

Bea was writing it down. 'Okay. What's his name?'

'Manny.' Carla was exhausted by this conversation. After Bea left, she collapsed. Her head hurt. Feeling returned to her injured leg, it throbbed and there were pangs just below the knee. All her muscles also wakened to pain. Up and down her back, through her shoulders, down to the tiniest muscle in her arms, they were bruised.

She moaned.

A nurse came over and said, 'They'll be getting to you in a jiffy. We've got a lot of people who are badly hurt.'

Shut up. What have you got to complain about? You're alive, ain't you?

She cried as quietly as she could.

In his room at the Sheraton Max took a shower. He turned on the hot water so high he nearly scalded himself. When he was done he stood between the twin beds facing a wall mirror, rubbed himself dry, let the towel drop and studied the full length of his body. He had a trim and vigorous figure, thanks to both genetics and regular exercise. A fine down of black hair draped over his pectorals and swirled about his dark nipples. Max shut his eyes and touched his chest lovingly, as if it belonged to someone else. Then he skimmed down with the flats of his palms, feeling his rib cage and fatless flanks, his pulsing stomach and rubbery penis. It was a young man's body. He opened his eyes and saw a

65

middle-aged head on top. His kinky bush of hair was all gray and the curls were exhausted, squashed at their apex, unfinished circles. His face looked overused and it was. He wondered how many times he had scraped the skin with a razor, fried it in summer, blasted it with exhaust or cold. His ears were big, growing into the elephantine excess of old age. His mouth was pinched by fatigue and his pale lips showed disappointment at the corners. Worst of all, his light blue eyes, which used to twinkle with wonder and mischief when he was young, were dead. They cowered beneath a prominent forehead inhabited only by worried and angry thoughts.

He stroked his penis with one hand and held his testicles in the other. He had no sexual fantasy in his head, no tickle of desire prompting him. He wanted to be erect.

The old unhappy face changed. His eyes brightened, his skin relaxed. His cock lengthened, surged away from his shadowed pelvis, and announced him to the world.

Satisfied that everything worked, Max dressed. While putting on his clothes he remembered his fight with Jeff over his choice of jeans and a polo shirt. The purpose of this trip to LA was to win a major job from the owner of a chain of discount electronics stores. The owner was interested in hiring them to design and oversee the construction of his expansion into New York City. The immediate project was worth a lot of money – as much as their architectural firm had earned over the past two years - for what would probably be six months' work. And there was also the promise of more. Nutty Nick stores planned similar expansions into Philadelphia, Washington, Atlanta and Miami. If Mr Nutty Nick approved, it was possible that their design might become the basic model, which meant money coming in for years and years with a minimum of additional effort.

As always, under pressure, Jeff didn't contribute to the work. He chose instead to fight bitterly with his wife in the evenings and to spend his day at the office placing make-up phone calls. After a week of that he caught a cold and had to go home early to prevent it from becoming much worse. When Jeff finally did put time in, he made elementary errors which required re-drafting, no matter what one thought of the concept. In short, by the time Jeff had overcome all his difficulties and announced he was ready to 'pull an all-nighter' so they could meet Nutty Nick's deadline, Max was finished with a complete plan.

'No need,' Max said and showed him blueprints with Jeff's name listed as co-designer.

Jeff was generous in his praise of Max's work and he had a suggestion about inventory storage that, although minor, was neat, impressive, and even inexpensive. Jeff seemed unembarrassed to have contributed so little Perhaps that was because, as Jeff never tired of reminding Max, his socializing had gotten them this opportunity in the first place. A year ago, at his country club on Long Island, Jeff met Nutty Nick's accountant and got the assignment to renovate a Nutty Nick branch in Great Neck. Max's work on that minor job so impressed the boss in LA that they were given this chance.

But it was *my* work on the store in Great Neck, Max said to the Sheraton mirror. You spent that whole month arguing with your wife.

'You want us to get turned down, is that it? You want to fail? That why you're dressing this way?' Jeff had taunted him as they entered Newark airport.

'He's hiring architects, not salesmen. These nouveau riche businessmen want to think they've hired an eccentric, an artist. That makes them a patron. Suddenly he's not Nutty Nick interviewing second-rate architects, he's David Rockefeller hiring I. M. Pei.'

Jeff had blinked, rolling the lids down over his bulging eyes, as if what Max had said was too ugly to see. He said mildly: 'We're not second-rate.'

Max was alone in the room once this memory stopped its replay. More alone than he had been before. He was absent Jeff and also absent the desire to finish their business.

He sat down and considered how he felt.

He felt pursued.

So he ran. He left the room less than an hour after renting it.

The crash's activity had spilled into the Sheraton's lobby. A group of men who had helped in the rescue efforts stood around a fake stone fireplace telling a few of the hotel staff what they had done and the gruesome sights they had seen.

Max waited at the front desk behind a television crew who were loaded with equipment. A reporter, or at least the only one in a suit, told the desk clerk they were from ABC.

'National news?' the clerk said with a hush in his voice.

But the clerk got no answer since the network reporter, overhearing the rescuers' talk of the crash, had drifted in their direction.

'I need to rent a car,' Max said to the awed and distracted clerk.

The reporter gestured to his crew to start shooting

while he interviewed the rescuers. They answered eagerly. A camera appeared and was pointed at the storytellers.

'Excuse me,' Max said to the clerk.

'What?' The clerk had contorted his position behind the desk to put himself in the background of the camera-man's shot.

'My car's going to be in the shop for two days. Where can I rent a car?'

'The mall,' the clerk said and pointed behind him.

Max left without checking out. They had an impression of his credit card anyway.

The car rental was a glass room set by itself in the middle of the mall's parking lot. The agent, a skinny red-haired girl, probably a high school student doing a summer job, asked him: 'Is something going on at the airport? My boyfriend drove by and shouted that he heard a plane had crashed.'

'I don't know,' Max said, wishing to make sure his business was transacted without conversation.

Unfortunately she got a phone call while writing up Max's agreement form. 'No shit,' she said to the receiver and then apologized for her obscenity with a look. 'A jet's crashed at the airport,' she explained. 'No. A customer,' she said to the phone. 'Oh my God,' she gasped, hearing a horrific detail. Her pen was idle. The paperwork lay half-done underneath.

'I'm in a hurry,' Max said softly.

She ignored him. She had paled at another ghastly item. Her face went slack. 'Really? I'm never getting on a plane. I swear to –'

Max knocked on the counter, rapping it hard until she looked at him. 'Fill out the form and call him back. I'm in a hurry.'

She stared at him, in dumb outrage.

'Please,' he said.

'Yeah . . .' she drawled sarcastically to the phone. 'Story of my life. I'll call you back.' She put the point of her pen on the form and demanded angrily: 'You want insurance?'

The question reverberated for him. He couldn't answer right away.

'I thought you said you were in a hurry. You want insurance?'

Max smiled. 'No,' he said. There were tears in his eyes even though his mouth was spread wide in a goofy grin.

'That means you're responsible for any damage to the car.'

Everything seemed to be chock-full of ironies. 'I'm responsible,' Max said and he let out a laugh. It sounded loud and a little deranged.

'Okay,' she said and now hurried, obviously leery of him.

He took what she had available, which was a small white Ford, not glamorous or fun to drive. He was thrilled to control it, however.

He studied the map the redhead had included in the envelope containing his rental agreement. He understood it with ease. That was unlike him. Usually maps blurred into incomprehensibility, service roads melting into freeways, turnpikes becoming rivers, huge urban centers disappearing; and what he could decipher inspired little confidence: he worried that what he thought he understood would inevitably turn out to be wrong in the greater reality of the road. It was embarrassing, he thought, for an architect to have so much trouble reading a blueprint of the earth's surface design.

Not this time. He found the interstate just where the map said it would be and he got on. His heart soared at the sight of the almost empty road. He put the air-conditioning on high, was pleased to discover that the previous renter had tuned the radio to a rock station, and flattened the gas pedal, delighted by a novelty: the speedometer readout was in digital numbers. He watched the old numbers blip off, the new numbers blip on, seventy, eighty, higher and higher, until he was driving into strange territory going faster than he had ever gone before.

THE GOOD SAMARITAN

6

Max saw that death was everywhere, had been everywhere all along, only he hadn't seen it as death. On the highway he passed four cemeteries and a car being towed from an accident that was probably fatal. He noticed the stains of several recently killed animals on the pavement; and there was the corpse of one, lying gray and squashed, on the road's shoulder.

He laughed when, after driving east for a little more than two hours, he saw this sign: WELCOME TO PITTSBURGH. He had gone to college at Carnegie-Mellon and at age seventeen the same words, maybe even the same sign, had always made him laugh, especially because Carnegie-Mellon's location was the best argument against enrollment. 'Pittsburgh is the asshole of the United States,' his Uncle Sol had commented when Max announced his intention to go there.

Recently Max had read that Pittsburgh was voted the most livable city in the United States by a survey. No doubt its air had benefited from the collapse of the steel industry. The article said Pittsburgh had made a particularly successful transition to a service economy, the same transformation that had become the fate of the United States generally. Max knew what that meant. It meant lots of yuppies and renovated brownstones, maybe even the same ramshackle ones that he and his friends used to rent. Actually he remembered there were plenty of great old buildings whose dilapidated utility could be converted to the current fashion of living in work spaces and working in living spaces. He could easily imagine young lawyers turning the ruined town houses into offices and the old warehouses into living lofts. Pittsburgh had always had pretensions to civilization. Even in Max's day there had been Carnegie's guilty and self-ennobling charities to the arts, housed in great buildings that probably looked much better without the air filled by the belching of his money machines.

Truth is, Max had liked the asshole of the United States. It was a real melting pot, where you could see steel sizzle and glow: a town of genuine production. There were workers who hated him because he was young, dirty and free. There were students who wanted to become engineers and get ahead even if it cost them participation in the sexual revolution. He thought both groups admirable. He also liked his own kind, the students who wanted to act and take drugs; or play music and take drugs; or write plays and movies, and take drugs. And, above all, there was a higher purpose: the Vietnam War to march against, and a black population that had been taking shit for centuries and was amazed you were on their side. At least for a while. What he didn't know, and understood now as he toured through his old campus, was that he had been in the middle of death all the while, the end of both Americas, imperial and idealistic.

Max drove to a hill only a mile from the campus where he and three buddies had rented a four-story turn-of-the-century brownstone. He pulled into a spot in front of a hydrant and looked up into the windows. The predictable had been done: root-canal therapy on the decay. The inside had been gutted and replaced with the embalming fluid of renovation: plasterboard, polyurethaned pine flooring, Thermopane windows. In what had been his bedroom he saw a young mother carry a baby across to a dresser. From his angle he guessed she was changing the infant. Her long hair was straight and brown. Her expression was intent on her chore, neither happy nor harassed.

Max had stood on the window ledge of that room twenty-one years before, high on LSD. He remembered the red face of a student who had the thankless job of being the 'control' (namely the sober one) for that day of tripping. The control was flushed from the effort of holding on to Max's legs while Max shouted back at him, 'Let me go! I know that if I jump I'll die! I'm not going to jump!'

Max laughed.

He hadn't remembered that moment in years. That Max had died without a funeral.

He had to pee. He hadn't since takeoff, hours ago, and although this was the first request from his bladder, the need was pressing. He went up to the door of his old quarters and pushed the white button. The sound it made was different from the old harsh buzzer. Chimes played softly in the distance. The urgency of having to urinate was delicious and brought tears to his eyes.

The young mother asked, 'Who is it?' warily. She opened the door guardedly, only a crack, peering out at him.

'Excuse me. I really have to use a bathroom.' He didn't mean to be comic, but he swayed from one foot to another, unable to stand still without releasing his bladder.

'I'm sorry,' she said and shut the door.

He peed on her steps. He didn't blame her for keeping

him out, but he had no patience, and so he unzipped and splattered the granite. She saw him do it from the window and rushed away, probably to phone the police. A man across the street stopped to watch him. In the summer heat it would smell when her young husband came home. Max had been full. Minutes seemed to pass and yet it poured out of him. Max thought there was plenty of time for the cops to arrive. He imagined her report:

'There's a man peeing on our renovated brownstone.'

The whitish gray of the granite darkened from his pee. 'I'm aging you. I'm giving you a more European look,' Max said as his stream became arched, then sporadic and finally a trickle.

'That's disgusting!' the man who had been watching from across the street yelled at him.

The young mother looked out the window again. Max stared at her as he zipped up. She jerked back at his intensity. Her brown hair fell across her face like a curtain.

'Sorry,' he said to her, mouthing the words and gesturing helplessly. He moved toward his car.

Seeing Max come in his direction, the man across the street trotted away fearfully.

A world of suspicion and cowardice, Max thought. A world without enough public bathrooms. Unvandalized bathrooms, he corrected himself. He had designed a pair for a city renovation of a small park in Brooklyn. 'No nooks and crannies for muggers,' the Parks Department official advised. 'And keep ledges to a minimum. Avoid anything that would encourage people to sleep or camp out.'

Max had worked to make the structure bright and

airy – an outhouse with plumbing. He drew a skylight, aware that its protective cage would cast a medieval shadow; and he planned a row of windows just below the roofline that would also be marred by bars; but the extra light would keep the space open anyway. The stalls were generous, thanks to the new regulations for the benefit of the handicapped. Max also insisted that the urinals have barriers between them for privacy. Max hated public bathrooms that forced unnecessary intimacy. He remembered the shame of modest and insecure adolescence when obliged to go in public.

The city liked his design and built them. Unfortunately, both were kept locked to bar drug dealers and the homeless. If you wanted to use them you had to hunt down a ranger. Max had visited the park twice and not seen one. He wondered if anyone besides the work crews had ever used the facilities. By his second visit, the exteriors of his bathrooms were covered by a spider's web of graffiti written in black paint. One window had been smashed somehow, despite its inaccessible height and bars.

'Frank Lloyd Wright it ain't,' Jeff had said about the finished product. He was bitter because the city didn't contract for more. 'They think your bathrooms are too elaborate. I said: "What? You don't care for the bidets?"'

Max didn't laugh at the memory of Jeff's joke. He saw Jeff's severed head instead and felt pity for him. Jeff whined and itched and complained about everything in his life, but he had loved the world, and believed that every day held the promise of his redemption. Even if he did see redemption in the form of a long-term contract from Nutty Nick stores.

Could I say that at his funeral? Max wondered. He was lost in Pittsburgh, driving through an unfamiliar suburb past the campus. There was a youthful air to the neighborhood. He stopped at an intersection next to a pair of college-age kids. They came up to his car right away, before he had begun to lower his window, as if they knew he needed directions.

'Hey, what's up?' asked the one who was blond and thick. His muscles had the shape of a bodybuilder's. His friend was small and skinny and dark. The blond's tone was hostile and challenging.

'It's rented,' the skinny one said, nodding at Max's car.

Max asked how to get back to the city proper. He wanted to find the International House of Pancakes where he used to have marijuana-inspired orgies of pancake consumption in the pre-dawn hours, at the end of his day, the beginning of it for the resentful workers.

'You want directions?' the blond said and laughed with contempt.

Max confessed his real goal to the pair.

'You looking for pancakes!' the skinny one cracked up. He seemed to have an accent, Caribbean maybe.

Who were they? They were like a punch line he hadn't understood. 'You guys cops, or something?' Max asked. They had the police's arrogant curiosity.

'Shit,' the blond said and smiled.

'Don't joke around, man,' the skinny one said, not smiling. He turned away. 'Come on,' he called and walked off.

The blond put his elbows on the door of Max's car and leaned in. He looked at the backseat as if searching for something. Maybe he's a thief, Max thought, excited.

80

He watched the blond carefully, ready to hit the gas and spin him off. 'Just take this right and go. You'll hit the city in a mile. I don't know about your pancakes . . .'

'Thanks. I can find it.'

'You want smoke, man? That what you really want?'

So that was the punch line. Max smiled at the blond. The skinny one was across the street now. Another car pulled up beside him. Skinny leaned on its window. The driver handed him an envelope and he produced something from his own pocket. Max had come to the local pusher.

'Only thing I feel like taking is acid,' Max said in a friendly tone to this monster of modern America, the villain of almost every drama on television, the Nazi for today's screenwriters.

'I got lysergic diethylamide.' The blond said the scientific words rapidly, proud of his familiarity with them. 'Hey, I'm a fucking Sears. Cost you fifty.'

'Fifty!' Max would never become accustomed to the shock of inflation.

'You want one?' The blond looked over toward Skinny and made a gesture.

'Forget it,' Max mumbled. He had been kidding.

The blond hadn't heard. He was distracted, answering a hand signal from Skinny with his own cryptic gesture. He talked to Max sideways, casually: 'I'll sell you one for thirty-five. Okay? A sample. A fucking loss leader.'

Max handed over the money and was given a tiny white pill, certainly too small to be potent, maybe too small to have any effect. He assumed he had been taken, but he drove off without a complaint in the direction the blond had suggested.

That advice proved to be correct, anyway. He found

the International House of Pancakes where it used to be. It had been redone, although probably only in lieu of a repainting, since the design had the same dull reds and browns and standard shapes. He liked that, however. Max believed serviceable places should look serviceable.

'Do you have strawberry pancakes?' he asked the young waitress as she handed him a menu.

'Sure,' she said.

He ordered them and a side order of bacon. He hadn't had strawberries since he was eight years old. For that matter he hadn't had bacon in five years. He looked at the LSD pill resting in the palm of his right hand. It was hardly wider than his fate line. Max had been taught how to read palms in college, not from a local Pittsburgh Gypsy, but from a moody drama school student. The line ran deep and unbroken from the base of his palm to between his middle and index fingers. It finished with a very distinct and tiny star.

'That means you'll be famous,' she had said. Later they made love and he had the most passionate and unselfconscious sex of his young life, inspired by her reading: 'You're very directed and independent. You'll do one thing your whole life, you'll do it very well, and you'll be a success.' They were strange words in 1967. You weren't supposed to care about such things. In fact, to be called a directed person might have been taken as a put-down. But Max wasn't insulted, although he asked her to help him 'unfocus', whatever the hell that meant. In his heart, control was his ambition; losing it, his terror.

That was why acid had been such a horrible experience. Grass and speed enriched or heightened sensations, but they never took control. Acid was different. For most of the trip he wasn't even aware of having a consciousness. Feelings were pure and unmitigated. All fear was as acute as the fear he had felt while falling in the plane: sheer electric terror. And physical sensation was overwhelming. It took an hour to absorb all the details from one sip of orange juice.

He swore off all drugs after that. Why repeat the experience? He had spent most of the trip in a fetal position shouting: 'I am Max Klein! My father is dead! My mother is Rachel!' The chant became legend among his druggy friends from whom Max was soon to be alienated. They decided he was 'weird and uptight'. But the chant was necessary. He knew if he stopped he would forget that he existed and disappear. The most enjoyable part of taking LSD was at the beginning when he stood on the window ledge and yelled at the 'control' that he wasn't going to jump. Yelling temporarily gave Max the illusion of knowing what he was about.

He hadn't thought back to those days in years. Why remember now? Because since then he had tried so hard to keep life battened down. He had been rigorously cautious. And what had happened? The plane had fallen out of the sky and so many had died.

He took the LSD. After all, it was fake. Why fear an illusion when he had survived the reality?

The pancakes arrived. Max was disappointed. The strawberries were pale slivers impressed into the pancake dough.

'Don't you have whole strawberries?' he asked.

'I could bring you a dish of strawberries. I thought you wanted strawberry pancakes.' She had a mop of

83

black hair, a flat brow, a short nose, and small eyes. Everything she said, like her looks, was toneless. She had a perfect deadpan. 'If your thing is strawberries, I can make it happen for you.'

'I want lots of strawberries,' he said and worried about it all for a moment. But why worry? What more could happen now? He started to eat the pancakes. She brought a dish of whole strawberries and he ate one slowly. It wasn't very good. The other time he had eaten them, when he was eight years old, they were sweet and succulent. He remembered that his fingers were still red from their juice while his father drove wildly to the hospital to get Max treated for his severe allergic reaction. Max had lain in the back seat, his mother's frightened face looming, his father cursing and honking the horn, and he noticed the strawberry stains on his fingertips. He could still picture the long needle they used to inject Adrenalin into him as he gasped for air, dying. In his panic he had thought the needle was meant to stab him in the heart, to kill him faster because the agony of his suffocation was too painful for his parents to witness.

The waitress came by to refill his cup of coffee. 'Are these good strawberries?' Max asked.

'They're fresh,' she said.

'Really?' Max was surprised.

She thought for a moment, her pot of coffee suspended above his cup. 'You know, I don't know for sure,' she said, pouring. 'I guess nothing's fresh.'

He ate them all and the pancakes too. He waited for something to happen, either due to the LSD or the strawberries. After half an hour and two more cups of coffee, nothing had.

'Everything okay?' the waitress asked, slapping his check on the table. 'Want another?' she gestured at his cup.

'Everything's great,' Max said. 'I seem to be invulnerable.'

'Yeah?' she frowned and shrugged. 'Good for you. Maybe you can fix my car.'

Something in her tone reminded Max of his first girlfriend at college, Alison. He knew Alison had married and had three kids with a drama professor who taught at Carnegie. Her husband was a long-faced pale man named Ramsey. She had sent Max a Christmas card and called once, both a long time ago.

He got up and looked for the phone outside the men's room, where it used to be. It had been moved, he discovered, to an alcove just inside the entrance doors. Unlike a New York booth its phone book was intact. He found five Ramseys listed. He called each one, but they weren't right. He knew why after finishing. His memory had been faulty, actually, he remembered, her husband's name was Paulson.

Maybe the acid *is* having an effect, he thought, wondering how he could have come up with Ramsey for Paulson. He also had trouble dialing, twice missing and hitting the wrong button. Maybe he was tired, although it was still early in the day: three-thirty in the afternoon he noticed while listening to the phone ring. Her husband should be teaching. Sure enough Alison answered. She knew him as soon as he spoke.

'Hi, it's Max. Max –'

She shouted out, 'Max Klein!' before he got to it. He was flattered by the happiness in her recognition.

He said he was in town for the day and asked right

away if she could meet him for a drink. She suggested he come to the house but he declined. He wasn't in the mood for a house of marriage and children.

'Anyway,' he said and his voice trembled a little, 'I just want to see you. No one else.'

'Oh . . .' He could hear fear in her tone. Was it fear? 'It's been a long time,' she said. 'I have four kids.'

'Four? I thought it was three.'

'I know. We're insane. We had another monster. No, no, I don't mean that –'

'Sure you do. Can you get away? For an hour? I don't know when I'll be back.'

She suggested, hilariously he thought, that they meet at a restaurant in the lobby of a Sheraton near her house.

'Oh, if it's in a Sheraton I definitely want to meet there,' Max said.

She laughed nervously, misunderstanding his meaning. 'We're meeting in the restaurant in the Sheraton, wise guy.'

'Just as good,' Max said. 'I checked out of a Sheraton about three hours ago. I guess I'm fated to be near a Sheraton every few hours.'

She wanted to meet in an hour. He insisted on a half hour. She arrived fifteen minutes late. Seeing her he understood why she had brought up the fact that she had four children as soon as he asked to meet her alone. She was fat. Not all over. In fact, her face was almost the same as years ago: a high shiny brow, long skinny nose, lively green eyes, and smooth white skin, still unwrinkled. But her waist and ass and thighs were inflated, and her once defined and high-flying breasts had been diminished by the girth of her middle and the thickening of her neck and shoulders. The worst atrocity to his memory of Alison, however, was her hair. As a college girl it had been long, straight and auburn – a gleaming fur as silky as a deer's. Now it had been cut short and dulled to a muddy color.

'Jesus!' she exclaimed and almost blushed as she entered his arms for a hug. She kissed him fast on the lips and pushed away, saying, 'You bastard. You look the same.'

'I do not!' Max said and gestured at his diminished curlicues of gray hair and his regretful lined face.

'That makes you look even handsomer,' she said, meaning his hair he supposed. She got out of his arms and backed into a chair, studying Max. Her beautiful skin still registered pleasure and surprise. 'I can't believe it, Max. Makes me want to cry.' And her eyes filled.

'Why?'

'I don't know . . .' She shook her head, the way she used to, but now there was no curtain of shimmering hair to sway with the grace and self-possession of an animal. Instead, with a helmet the color of worn leather, her movement was insecure and sad. 'I'm glad you look so good, Max. You must be happy.'

'Are you crazy? I'm not happy. Do you know anybody who's happy?'

'Well, you look happy, you bastard.' She surveyed him again and shook her head. 'Can't believe it. You're the same!'

'I'm the same because nothing's happened to me. I've been hermetically sealed.'

They were the only customers of the restaurant. They ordered coffee and cheesecake. Max's tasted grainy and his coffee was weak. The place wanted to be more than a coffee shop, covering its tables with white linen and putting its customers in ugly captain's chairs whose hard seats and high circular armrests had plenty of room for large waists. In fact, slight Max was swimming in his. He felt as if he had fallen into a toilet bowl. He kept lifting up his behind to seek a higher perch. He listened patiently to her jumpy narrative of the past twenty-odd years.

'My kids are great,' she said. Except for the third, she added, a girl named Halley, who had a slight learning problem that for two years the doctors thought was behavioral. There were two years of psychotherapy. Then Halley was diagnosed as suffering from a chemical imbalance and there were two years of pharmacology. Finally they went to a nutritionist and there were two years of expensive vitamins. Now there was nothing except diminished expectations.

Halley's dumb, Max decided. They couldn't accept a daughter who was dumb so they decided she was ill.

'But my kids are great,' she said and added that the eldest, another daughter, was no longer a ballet prodigy, after breaking her ankle in a freakish accident stepping out of a car. 'She's adjusted really great,' Alison said. 'She's got a lot more time for boys so she's happy.' She lowered her head mournfully and Max knew that again Alison had been disappointed.

Her husband was great, she said, but she added that he was a little bitter because he hadn't been made head of the drama school, although it had been understood for years he would be and yet when the time came someone from outside had been brought in.

Her pain was tangible. She pushed it at him in a bumpy aggressive way, like a subway passenger elbowing to get past. 'What about you?' he asked. 'Are you still writing plays?'

'No!' She scorned the idea and then said, 'I'm a mess. I *am* thinking of going back to school. Get my Ph.D. and teach.' She reached out and slapped Max's knee. 'Tell me about you! You have a boy, right?'

'A ten-year-old.'

'Bet he's smart like you.'

'Smart . . .' Max thought about his son, who was certainly a good student, articulate and precocious. Does that mean he's smart? 'He's like all the kids I know. He's smart, but it's copycat intelligence.'

'What do you mean?'

'He imitates grown-up attitudes and says what his teachers want to hear. He's a mirror of them and so they say he's smart.'

Behind her there was a fierce glow from the windows facing the street. The summer sun flashed on the cars parked outside and a beam pierced into the restaurant, striking Alison on the head. It seemed to come out of her mouth as speech: 'That *is* being smart, Max,' she said. 'What do you want him to imitate? A baboon?'

'I just can't shake the feeling that a really smart, an authentically brilliant child, wouldn't seem brilliant to us. He's smart in the same way we all are: he knows what we know, he believes what we believe. He's being educated to be as dumb as the rest of us.'

'Come off it, Max.' She was irritated. A truck drove into the restaurant's windows without shattering them. But it covered the glowing light behind her, and her eclipsed face went dark with anger. 'That's crap. Believe me, I've seen plenty of dumb students. Students so dumb they couldn't imitate what you know if you put a gun to their heads.' The sun bleached her face again and she was shooting him.

Max reached out and caught her hand, frozen in an imitation of a gun, index finger threatening his brain. He could see how angry he had made her: the pain glowed about her eyes. 'Don't hate me,' he pleaded.

'I don't hate you. Don't be ridiculous.'

Max pulled her hand to him and kissed the fingers. They were plump and soft. He had remembered them as long and elegant, their touch cool. These were the hot whitened hands of a baker. She ignored him and said, 'Just don't tell me your son is a genius and it doesn't make you proud.'

He let go of her hand. 'He's not a genius. I didn't say he was a genius.' He thought back and couldn't remember what he had said, except that it was contemptuous of his son. 'Did I? I mean if I did –'

'Max, I'm exaggerating. Remember me? I exaggerate.' She covered the space between them, her head bobbing like a doll with a spring for a neck. 'You just said he was bright. But you know what I mean.'

'Let's make love.' His belly was full and warm. He wanted to hibernate in a cave with her – dark and close and fucking slowly. She disappeared in the darkness again and he couldn't see what she was feeling. She said something softly, but he didn't hear and anyway he kept talking, right out of the center of his being, without censorship: 'We'll probably never see each other again and I've forgotten everything about myself. Haven't you? I don't remember who I was or what I am and that's too sad. Makes me too sad to eat or sleep or argue. So let's get a room now and make love.'

He couldn't see her face clearly. The restaurant's window had altered the sun and now it had no light of its own. He tried to focus and see her eyes but they were hollow. He got up and she did too so he supposed she was willing. He put a twenty down on the table and she said, 'That's a twenty.' He assumed it was her way of saying yes.

They walked. He put his arm around her shoulders and they felt comfortable, the right height, fitting easily within the shape of his reach. 'Do you have a room?' she asked and laughed at what he answered, shaking her head as if he had been foolish. He didn't know if she was right because he hadn't heard his own voice. 'I'll wait here while you get it, okay?' She slipped away and sat down in a chair he hadn't noticed. It seemed to appear under her just as she lowered herself. He looked down at her and had no idea who she was.

The clerk seemed overjoyed about Max checking in. 'Certainly, sir! We have a room.' He was a boy. Max was fascinated by his partial beard, a skinny line trailing erratically under cheeks that looked permanently flushed.

Max didn't talk while the clerk did the paperwork. His lips got stuck together and then he wasn't sure he could talk. He nodded when the clerk asked if he was staying for one night and shook his head no when asked if he needed help with his bags.

The carpeted floor undulated beneath his feet. He was able to walk on it without any trouble, like a graceful surfer. Alison was in the chair waiting. Many other chairs had been bred in his absence. A whole row of them flanked her, their empty arms gleaming sullenly.

'I can't believe I'm doing this,' she said as they rode on the sea together to the elevator.

'Yeah, it's amazing,' Max thought or answered, he wasn't sure which, and he also didn't know what he was referring to: the surfing, the crash, the acid, or checking into a hotel with Alison.

Maybe I'm her husband, he thought, and giggled. Maybe I'm the father of her four children, of the dimwit and the cripple. I have tenure but insufficient power and money. My wife is fat.

'Stop it,' she whispered and giggled.

He was kissing her neck. He had found the familiar beauty mark that appeared at the start of the slope toward her shoulder. He tasted the dot with his tongue, a drop of chocolate that had no sweetness.

They were in the room without Max knowing how. He searched for her face and found an eye, a nose, and at last her lips. He kissed her dry lips and snuggled deeper to find another pair that were moist and kinder; he wedged himself in and nestled. A sound thundered from a canyon and vibrated him.

Sky appeared in his vision. A gray sky, but bright anyway. He glided warily, a hawk searching for his home.

She laughed in the clouds. Her head was a painting, and yet it breathed, expanding out from the canvas. 'Max! Let's get into the bed . . . I'm too old to stand up,' she joked, her smooth skin wrinkling with laughter.

'I'm sorry,' he tried to say, but he droned like an old turntable; the record moved too slowly under the stylus.

'I love it. Don't be sorry.' She moved away, a boat separating from the dock and he hung on, desperate, afraid he would fall in the water. She kept laughing. He fell on the bed. It was cool like water, but of course it bounced.

I'm tripping, he thought.

'I have stretch marks,' he said in his own ear.

'I do?' he asked himself.

More laughter. The sun set when she drew the curtains. Dark passed over the room as if a giant's hand were blessing them. If God existed He could pass His palm over the earth and blacken it like that.

'Don't you believe in God?' she asked.

Max opened his eyes. The ceiling was low, pressing down. A smoke alarm's red light warned him: You are tripping and you have your eyes closed and you don't know the fucking difference.

'Where are you?'

Her answer came from behind. He turned and saw her, mountainous beneath an unreal yellow bedspread. The color was unlike anything in nature. Her young face was scared.

'Max. I didn't bring my . . . you know . . . I didn't think this was going to happen.'

'You think too much,' he said and stared at the curtains. They were drawn but light glowed from all the edges. He listened to the whooshing noise of the air-conditioning and felt the low ceiling of prefabricated panels close in. It was similar to being in the DC-10. Everything modern was a coffin. He had struggled so hard to use the new materials, cheaper and faster to manufacture and install, and yet you could make nothing but death containers out of them. There was no wood on earth wide enough to make the floors of even the meanest barn of a hundred years ago. Nothing could achieve the simplest beauty of a Shaker table without their purer wood, their purer paint, maybe without even the pure air of a world gone forever. He had only colors that never lived, fabrics fused in laboratories, and walls created out of the letters and numbers of the periodic table. He had turned his back on the past and its impossible abundance and impractical patience; he had embraced the technology of his world, determined to be a man of his time, and it had tried to assassinate him.

'Max, we don't have to . . . Max!' Her head was a gargoyle snarling: 'You bastard, I just wanted to talk!'

She was lying under the bedspread, covered up to the neck, embarrassed and angry. I'm not being dutiful, Max realized. He moved from the floor (how he got there he didn't know) to beside her on the bed. His body sloshed as if it were a half-full pail of water. He heard the cheapness of the room: everything creaked and groaned. He pried her hand away from the bedspread. Her fingers seemed to break under his pressure, but she didn't cry out in pain.

'Oh . . .' she sighed and shut her eyes as he lifted the covering off and exposed her.

The white slab of flesh shivered and talked to him. He touched the palpitating hollow of her throat with the tip of his tongue and she was animate, rumbling. He trailed down the soft body, tasting salt and flour, and all over him happiness tingled. There was nothing skimpy or flimsy here: this was pure.

He found a nipple and fed. He found folds and more nipples. He fed and fed. There were teats everywhere and heat, terrific heat, a sauna of love. 'Take off your clothes,' he told himself, but there was no body to remove them from. He was only a mouth of liquids. He

94

counted the breasts. There were five. He counted arms and there were eight. He counted the lips and there were six.

'Oh my God,' she said.

He was a mouth but no voice. He tried to ask why she wanted to discuss God but forgot the previous word as each new one was formed. Anyway, it wasn't important. A sea poured up his body: hot, unwinding his muscles, and melting his bones.

Where's my cock? he wondered and opened his eyes. He didn't have one. He had grown an abundant woman from his stomach. She swam out of him, her face relaxed.

'You're not angry anymore,' he said, the words sounding through his nose.

'Oh God,' she answered.

He laughed and told her. 'There is no God.'

The FBI man's head was wide to begin with; and yet his ears stretched his face even more, comically projecting flesh farther from the center of his face, which was a small nose and tiny red lips. 'Are you Max Klein?' he asked.

Everything in Max's mouth was stuck together; there didn't seem to be any free space inside. 'Hmmm,' he mumbled his yes. He realized he had no clothes on and hid his body behind the hotel door, clutching the edge of its frame. He had a headache too, he noticed, two lines of pain running from his cheeks and crossing his forehead, burning to the back of his skull.

The wide-faced man opened a leather wallet. Inside there was a picture of that face with FBI in big letters beside it. 'I'm Agent Parsons. This is my partner, Agent

Smith.' Smith was black and skinny. The cool white collar of his shirt shimmered against his ebony neck. He seemed to be staring at a point above Max's head. 'You're registered as a Mr Max Klein of 505 West End Avenue? Is that correct?'

Max felt shame. He knew he had been naughty, but he wasn't sure what to select from his buffet of guilt: taking LSD, committing adultery, eating strawberries, the death of his partner, the abandonment of the children he had saved, peeing on private property . . .

Meanwhile he mumbled, 'Wait,' hurrying into his pants – he couldn't find his underwear or his shirt. He let the G-men in, prepared to surrender. It wasn't the sixties anymore: his behavior deserved punishment.

'Do you have any identification?' Agent Parsons asked.

Max gave Parsons his wallet and watched Smith wander around the room searching for something. 'No bags?' Smith asked when he opened the closet and saw it was empty except for Max's underpants and polo shirt.

'It's him,' Parsons said and showed his partner Max's photo on his New York State driver's license.

I didn't call my wife and son, Max remembered. That was the crime he had committed.

'Were you on a flight to –?'

'Yes,' Max interrupted. 'I was there.'

'You took a hike straight from the scene?' Smith asked. 'Just upped and left?'

'Yeah . . .' Max's head throbbed and he held it in his hands. A vivid neon flash of his first and ultimately rejected drawing for the Zuckerman house on Long Island pulsed against his eyelids.

'Your head hurting?' Smith asked and knelt in front of him, staring into his eyes. 'Did you get checked by anybody?'

'What time is it?' Max asked, wondering how many hours delinquent he was in telling his wife that she was not a widow.

'One o'clock,' Smith said and then added: 'P.M.'

'One o'clock . . .?' Max was confused. The crash had happened at about twelve.

Smith understood. 'One o'clock, Wednesday afternoon.'

He was a day delinquent. Max shut his eyes and the redesign of the Zuckerman patio flowed away from the boxy Cape, easing your eye toward a fantasized and improbable garden. In fact, everything Linda Zuckerman touched seemed to wither and die. He wished the things he drew were never built and never seen by his customers. What both his clients and his pencil imagined was always more satisfying than the compromise of their finished constructions.

'Mr Klein,' Agent Smith tapped him on the knee. 'Can I ask you something?' Max opened his eyes. Smith's right eye was bloodshot and he sounded as if he had a head cold. Max nodded. 'What the hell are you doing here, man? You walked away from that crash, rented a car and drove here? Why?'

Max's eyes filled. He tried to hold the tears back, ashamed to cry in front of these very grown-up men. The image of the end had returned: twisted metal and lifeless bodies carried across the runway. Under the bright sun, the colorless concrete had pained his eyes. 'They were starting to line them up,' Max mumbled. 'They line up the corpses and tag them –' And they gather the scattered body parts, such as Jeff's head, until all the broken pieces are put together again. He knew from watching CNN, he knew from the harsh magazine photos, he knew from years of accident voyeurism. 'They didn't need me anymore,' Max said.

'Mr Klein,' Smith said softly. 'Why don't you come with us? We'll get ahold of your people and get you home.'

'You're not going to arrest me?'

'You haven't done anything,' Agent Parsons said.

That's what they think, Max answered silently.

7

He was taken to a hospital first. 'I'm all here,' he told them, but they made sure anyway, X-raying and poking, evidently amazed by his wholeness.

'No concussion.' A woman doctor who looked as if she were only slightly older than his ten-year-old son. 'But he's definitely suffering from some sort of post-trauma reaction.'

'He's in shock?' Agent Smith.

Max listened. While they discussed him his legs dangled on the examining table. His behind crinkled the light blue sanitary paper that covered it.

'No,' the child doctor said low, trying to whisper. 'He's having a stress reaction.'

I'm still high, you dummy, Max thought and giggled. The doctor raised her eyebrows to Agent Smith about the giggle with the air of a lawyer who had established the proof of his case.

The government men phoned the airline. Why the airline? Max wondered. It made the company seem very important, as if Transcontinental Corporation were the highest authority in the United States. Agent Smith asked him whether he wanted to call home.

'You do it,' he said. 'Tell my wife I'm free.'

'What?' Agent Smith asked.

'I mean, fine. I'm fine and fancy-free.'

They put him in a darkened area, with a curtain drawn all around, something in between an examining room and a hospital bed. There was classical music playing through a speaker in the wall. He lay down and slept.

'Hello,' a freckled face said and smiled brightly, mouth wide, teeth showing white for a few seconds and then going out, like a camera's flash. 'Sorry to wake you. It's about three-thirty now. You're still at the hospital in Pittsburgh. I'm Cindy Dickens from Transcontinental Air. I'm here to help get you home. How do you want to go? We'll arrange any flight or transportation you like. I'm sorry. You look tired. Can I get you some coffee?'

He felt much better for the nap. She got him coffee. Cindy watched him drink. When he was done he felt he had his brain back in residence. He asked Cindy if his family had been informed.

'Oh yes. We had someone from the New York office go personally to your home and give them the good news. We offered to fly them here but they said –'

'That it's time for Max to come home,' he completed the statement for her.

For a moment Cindy's performance of a human being was paused; she peered out into the audience like a puzzled actress wondering who had heckled her. She seemed about to ask a conversational question and then switched back to her efficient checklist: 'Should I get you on the next flight to New York?'

Max waited for his terror of flying to appear in his head – but it didn't come. His thoughts were merely practical. For the first time in his life he considered only how to get somewhere quickly, not safely. 'Sure. Do I get to go first class?'

Cindy cocked her head to one side and a smile appeared briefly, but she answered in her role's neutral tone: 'All complimentary, sir, of course. May I book you on Transcontinental Air?'

'Definitely,' Max said. 'And can I have some more coffee?' Caffeine increases the anxiety response of people who are fearful, a phobia specialist had once told Max. Before yesterday's flight, Max had avoided any beverage with caffeine. He had drunk herbal tea instead of coffee at breakfast, ginger ale rather than Coke in the airport lounge.

That had helped a whole lot, hadn't it?

Max laughed; Cindy skipped back a hop, startled. She had a very slight, almost nonexistent, figure. She wore a gray suit, a pink shirt, and a partially tied yellow cravat. Max fantasized she would be wildly passionate if only you could unbutton her jacket and vest before she had a chance to call the police. Max was draped on a cot. Cindy had turned on the light. Max saw that he was in some sort of resting area, maybe for the residents, judging by the lockers and stuff right outside his curtained area. He was bare-chested, his jeans rumpled, his legs spread, vulnerable and emotionally disheveled. Cindy not only wore her suit for armor, she carried a fake leather folder stuffed with formal papers that she could take out and consult to avoid looking at Max's sensual posture and emotional nudity. Max took the time to study Cindy's legs, or what he could tell about them from the knee-length skirt and black stockings. They were thin and finely formed, her ankles as delicate as a bird's. He didn't think that sexy, although he admired its abstract beauty.

'They sent you here alone?' Max asked.

'Excuse me?' Cindy was writing on one of her papers.

'TransCon Air. They sent you alone?'

'Actually, someone else is supposed to be here,' Cindy finished writing. 'I don't know what's happened to Mike,' she mumbled and then spoke up: 'I'm going to make the arrangements. I'll be right back.'

Cindy accompanied Max to the airport in a limousine. He found it all interesting and comfortable: the interior of the limo and the new sights *en route*. At the terminal Cindy told Max another airline employee would be seated next to him on the plane. 'His name is William Perlman. He's had a lot of experience with people who've been through what you've been through. You'll like him, he's a great guy.'

Max was impressed. He thought: They found a Jew in the baggage pile to keep me company.

Cindy asked Max once again if he wanted to phone his wife before boarding.

'Do you know my wife?' Max asked, trying to figure out why she was so insistent. They were heading toward the gate. The telltale, usually unsettling smell of burning kerosene fuel penetrated the glass windows. In the distance a big-bellied 747 stumbled upward into a curved blue sky.

'Me . . .?' Cindy was astonished.

'I almost get the feeling she's asked you to get me to call her.'

Cindy looked as if she'd been caught doing something underhanded. 'I talked to her briefly,' she mumbled. They had reached Gate 5, which evidently was the departure point for his flight. 'Want to board early?' she asked.

'First class boards early anyway,' Max answered.

'Of course,' Cindy said, 'that's right. Anyway, I told

Mr Perlman we would be right at the gate,' Cindy added. She guided Max toward the ramp. Max noticed the plane attached to it was a 727, which, like the DC-10, was another old jet.

'You folks at TransCon ought to upgrade your fleet.'

'Pardon me?' Cindy said, in exactly the tone Max thought she might use if he reached over to unbutton the top button of her navy vest.

'All your planes are twenty years old,' Max nodded at the 727. The burning kerosene was stronger here. He smelled the acrid death of the DC-10's smoldering seats. He could see the infant seat suspended among the plane's dissected electronic veins. He felt Byron pulling at him to hurry. 'How come you don't buy new planes? Too much junk-bond debt?'

'Sir,' Cindy rebuked him, showing her profile as she gestured toward the 727 with a righteousness that suggested Max had slandered it, 'the design is twenty years old, but that plane has been completely rebuilt several times. I don't know the exact figures on this particular 727, but the average TransCon 727 has no part older than eight years.'

'That's not strictly true, Cindy,' Max answered, imitating her travel-brochure style of polite argument. 'I'm sorry they told you a lie and I understand that you've repeated it to me innocently, but it's not really accurate.'

'Mr Klein, it *is* true,' Cindy was upset. She opened her folder and peered inside as she spoke: 'I wish I had it here. In my office I could show you the repair records for the entire fleet and you'd see that no part is older than eight years.'

Max admired her pride and felt sorry for her

commitment to TransCon's integrity. She had that most vulnerable of human possessions: a faithful heart. Sadly, she had given her love to a corporation. He put his hand on hers, on the hand that had spread her folder open. Her fingers were cold. 'Not everything. Just the engine parts. The skin of that plane, some of the bolts, some of the welding, little things here and there are original and more than twenty years old. Trust me. I know. And as for your maintenance crews and the records in your office, I guess you've never had construction done in your home or spent any time on a job site. What's in everyone's repair files and what's out there is the difference between high school civics and Washington politics.'

'You must be Max Klein,' a male voice said behind him. The sound terrified Max. The voice was his dead father's. As if a murderous hand had grabbed his throat, he shivered and couldn't swallow or breathe. Max shut his eyes. He certainly couldn't turn and face the ghost's greeting. He reminded himself that his father had been dead for thirty years. He argued to himself, I don't really remember what Dad sounded like. 'Mr Klein?' the specter insisted.

'This is William Perlman,' Cindy said softly in Max's ear.

Max opened his eyes and saw a big frizzy red-haired man. He stood well over six feet and had the weight and thickness of a football player. His eyes were pale blue, his forehead as flat as if someone had meticulously starched and ironed it. 'Did I startle you?' Perlman asked.

Perlman was a big cheerful man, a clown without makeup. Max relaxed. 'I guess I'm still a little on edge,' Max apologized.

'Who wouldn't be?' Perlman said.

Cindy said, 'I'll be going now, Mr Klein.'

'Thanks for everything,' Max said and offered his hand. He imagined she had very small breasts, that her freckles trailed down from her long neck until just below the bra line, where her skin was probably pure white. He had a conviction her nipples would be pink. 'You were really nice,' he lied.

'My pleasure,' Cindy said. 'And I hope someday you have a little more faith in people.'

'Me too,' Max said. He smiled but there were tears in his eyes.

Perlman watched Max the whole time they sat strapped into their first-class seats, sipping complimentary drinks and listening to the captain's dutiful accounting of their position in the line for takeoff. Perlman also talked, cheerfully, about where he had grown up and so on, but his eyes were not in harmony with the light conversation. Instead they observed Max coolly, flickering only when Max seemed interested in the plane's movements.

Such interest prompted Perlman into self-interruptions of his banter with curt bulletins of obvious information. 'I used to love to travel. When TransCon hired me as a consultant – we're taxiing now – they of course offered unlimited free travel for me, but they got me flying back and forth so much – that's just the captain keeping the engines up to speed – that now my idea of a vacation is to stay put. Besides, TransCon doesn't – we're turning to be in position for takeoff – fly to Venice, which I'm romantic enough to want to go to again and again.'

'I'm not scared,' Max said. 'But I'd like another

drink when we're airborne.' He smiled and elbowed Perlman. 'Or should I say, *if* we're airborne.'

'We're beginning takeoff,' Perlman said as the large hands of the jet's engines started to push from behind, giving them the bum's rush out of Pittsburgh.

Max smiled at the window. 'Look at us go!'

Perlman frowned, puzzled. 'Your wife said you're terrified of air travel.'

'Everybody seems to know my wife,' Max said. He leaned forward and across Perlman's lap to watch the speeding runway. 'Go, baby, go!' The front wheels released the earth with a slight thud of regret and the land tilted.

'I called her before meeting you –'

The pilot banked away from the areas of noise abatement, up through what he, the tower, and the passengers hoped was a cleared corridor to his flight path. 'This is the most dangerous time,' Max interrupted Perlman with a bulletin of his own. 'Right now every bolt on this plane is stressed, and the air is full of deadly obstacles, each one moving as blindly and as quickly as we are.'

'We're safe.' Perlman's voice was soft and smooth as a loving parent singing a lullaby.

'Why did you call my wife?'

'To gain some insight into who you were before we met.' Perlman had his head back, looking straight ahead. His hands were holding the armrests. Not desperately, but with a firm and worried grip. 'I didn't know, tell you the truth, whether you were going to be communicative or what. They told me *you* were the one who was stressed, not the bolts.'

Max chuckled. He tapped Perlman on the shoulder. 'You're a funny man, Dr Perlman.' The jet's engines were humming, cycling to their maximum, revving so fast there was a brief illusory moment of silence at the climax of their power. Max saw Stacy clutch the napkin to her forehead and remembered the thin line of blood trailing down. He saw Jeff's eyes, sideways on the carpet, red and outraged by his fate.

What about Nutty Nick, god damn it, Max! You're blowing off a million-dollar meeting!

Oh fuck off, Jeff. Money isn't everything.

Perlman had his own concerns. 'Who told you I was a doctor?' he asked.

'Nobody.' For once Max didn't fight the captain's maneuvers. The jet banked, turning to head to New York. Max relaxed his body into the seat, swaying in the air, a cradled baby lying in loose-limbed comfort. Perlman was a statue, neck twisted to see Max, but rigid in that position, his arms stuck to the rests. 'And you're not a doctor,' Max said, shutting his eyes to flow better with the graceful arc of the turn. 'You're a psychologist.'

'You're right. How did you figure that out?'

This time, hearing only Perlman's voice, unaccompanied by the clown's bright red face, Max detected anxiety, not his dead father. 'You talk like a shrink.' The pilot had completed the turn. The chime sounded. Max had survived again. He was going to survive everything. He felt he could outlive even the exhausted and defiled earth. Max opened his eyes and noticed Perlman's shoes were expensive. In fact, his outfit was quite fashionable and costly, although casual. 'What kind of shrink works for an airline? You said you consulted?'

'I specialize in posttraumatic stress reactions. I've written a book about it. I worked with a TransCon crew that survived a pretty rocky flight –'

'The Hawaii one? The pop-top jet?'

'Pop top?' Perlman's voice got deep and quiet. His red eyebrows came together above his nose.

'Isn't that the 727' – Max indicated the cabin of their plane – 'this very model plane – whose top came off on a commuter flight?'

'Pop top . . .?' Perlman repeated Max's joke to himself in a mumble. 'That's a cruel way of talking about it.' He was almost inaudible, practically speaking to himself.

'What would be a kind way of talking about it?' Max asked. 'Excuse me . . .?' he called forward to the senior flight attendant, a formidable middle-aged woman with a stiff hair-sprayed arc of blond hair and a shiny wide brow. 'Could I have another?' he indicated his empty drink cup.

'Would you like a Valium?' Perlman asked, nodding at Max's drink cup.

'No, a Scotch,' Max said and laughed hard, delighted by his irreverence. He was usually solemn and respectful of authority. But was Perlman authority? The flight attendant acknowledged his request from a distance with a nod. Max lowered his cup and said to Perlman, 'Sorry. Dumb joke.'

'You're doing fine. Don't apologize. Your wife was amazed that you were willing to fly home.'

Max could imagine her anxious whisper of a voice responding to Perlman, rising to a louder incredulity: 'Max is flying back to New York? That's crazy!' Max thought he had better show some concern for her, lest Perlman think him a barbarian: 'How is she?'

'Well, we spoke on the phone for a little while. She sounded all right. Upset that you hadn't called. Worried about you, of course '

'My wife is very beautiful,' Max said and remembered her ten years ago, not very different from today, the same weight, skinnier if anything, her hair still a luxuriant brown, her pale skin still smooth, her light brown eyes wide and worried. What had changed was the animation of her features. Her mouth used to be open and laughing, teeth generously exposed, her throat vulnerable. That was how she showed her age: she didn't laugh; she smiled with sealed lips, polite and without enjoyment. She was tall and desirable, a dancer's figure holding up at forty as if she were exercising daily and injecting collagen monthly. Although she wasn't taking collagen, she taught ballet to children and kept herself in shape. She wore little makeup and usually dressed in jeans and plain tops. Even her few and rarely used formal dresses were basic colors and unadorned by complicated fashion. But Max thought her vain, anyway, vainer for her indifference to cosmetics, believing her intention was to emphasize her beauty by showing that it required so little help. 'Could you tell from her voice that she's beautiful?'

Perlman paused before answering. He frowned and stared ahead. After a moment, he swallowed, as if he had at last ingested Max's meaning. 'No. Why do you ask?'

'She has a friendly voice,' Max explained. 'But it doesn't sound like the voice of a beautiful woman. She sounds short and sympathetic and smart and nervous. But she's actually tall and a little cold, and I've come to the conclusion she's not as smart as she seems. She's selfish and that holds her back. She can't see beyond her own point of view. She is nervous, though. Terribly nervous that something will come out of her. Something ugly and irreversible.'

'What do you think it is?'

'I don't know. And I think maybe I should stop caring.'

'Does she love you?' Perlman was grave. He rattled the ice in his plastic cup, concerned.

'Yes. Very much.' Perlman beamed at this answer. Max smiled back, delighted to have pleased the furry red giant. 'That's the worst part. She thinks I'm great.'

'And why is that bad?'

'Because I'm not who she thinks I am. You know, I already have a therapist.'

'Yes, your wife mentioned. I tried to reach him, in fact.'

'We spent quite a lot of time these past weeks discussing my fear of flying.' The flight attendant arrived with Max's second Scotch. 'He told me I had nothing to worry about.' Max held up the plastic cup, toasting Perlman. 'Cheers.'

'Cheers. Are you angry at him for being wrong?'

'No!' Max smiled into Perlman's serious, evaluating eyes. 'That would be neurotic. And I wouldn't want my shrink to think I'm neurotic.'

'Do you want to talk about the crash?' Perlman tipped his cup all the way to get at an ice cube. It bounced off his upper lip and rolled back to the bottom.

Max saw the DC-10 in sections, in flames on the bleached runway, but the action was stilled, as if photographed for a picture postcard. What had happened to him was inside the pieces, deeper in his memory. He didn't want to give up the safety of being outside the wreck for the sake of Perlman's curiosity.

'No,' he told Perlman and turned away. Across the

aisle, outside this jet's windows, the sun had lowered and yet was fierce, unveiled in the cloudless blue sky, its dominance threatened only by the horizon's rim. Max stared at it until the brilliance forced his lids to shut. The impression danced on the red world of his closed eyes. He thought the innerscape was like his childhood visions of the red planet, Mars. He remembered his thrill at hearing JFK vow that Max's countrymen would reach the moon before the Russians. Max had immediately wanted more – a mission to Mars – an advance that would take them to other worlds, other peoples. During his college years, in spite of the druggy cynicism about national policy, Max had rejoiced at *Apollo*'s success and assumed the United States would conquer the solar system within his lifetime. Landing on the moon was still, to his mind, the only achievement of his country worthy of its stature as an Empire. The space shuttle blowing up and the cowardly aftermath were further proof of how second-rate the United States and its leaders had become. The hostility of conservatives and liberals to further space exploration was all that he had to point to – surely anything both sides agreed was a waste had to be worthwhile and noble. Sitting next to the airline's hired therapist, Max understood something that had bothered him for a decade, that he had known only in a sleepy, evasive way. He was living in a reductive age, a time where any diminishment of person or goal was popular. The astronauts were now considered to be frauds and no one believed racism could be conquered. The two longings of his youth, to live in peace with all the races and ethnics of his city, to see men walk on other worlds, were laughable, even stupid desires in the eyes of the smart and sophisticated and powerful people of his time. It wasn't the disappointment of designing discount electronics stores that had embittered Max; it was living in a nation without dreams that made reality so hard.

'It was stupid,' Max said at last and his cheeks felt heavy. His eyes watered.

'What was stupid?'

Max rubbed the tears back into his eyes. He drained the plastic cup. The Scotch made him feel empty.

'What was stupid, Max? The crash?'

'Yeah,' Max said, returning his attention to the furry red therapist. 'It was pointless.'

'That makes it very hard,' Perlman agreed. 'That seems to be the hardest thing for everyone who's hurt by an accident to deal with. They feel it's senseless.'

Max's heart hardened, his tears evaporated. He looked over at the big man. Perlman filled up even the relatively spacious first-class seat. 'Have any of your patients succeeded in making sense of it?' he asked the plane-crash therapist.

'Well . . . after a while – it takes a while – they find a kind of peace about it. I think it's appropriate for survivors and relatives to feel that it's senseless, because it *is* senseless.'

Unless I give it sense, Doctor, Max thought. Unless I give it a point. Max nodded agreeably at Perlman, pretending to agree with his philosophical bumper car, bouncing merrily off all the hard jolts of life. Max had his mission now and saw no reason to share it with a civilian. He was glad the FBI had found him and turned him around. He had been going the wrong way, into the failed past. Now things were set right. He put his head back and listened to the engines, thrilled by their power.

Mr President, he thought, I'm ready. Max was launched, roaring out of Perlman's orbit, able and willing to land on the strange terrain of his home.

8

Max was aroused by his wife. Debby greeted him with a firm wholehearted embrace, pressing herself against him from toe to head. They were almost the same height, had always seemed to fit nicely, although it had been years since Max had felt so thoroughly hugged. He squashed himself against her, ran his hand down her strong straight back until he reached the top slopes of her ass. He was erect.

'Isn't almost dying a wonderful thing?' Max whispered in Debby's ear.

She bit his earlobe hard. He jerked his head away and saw her face was animated, eyes brilliant, face flushed. 'Why didn't you call?' she said, angry and excited. Her voice was loud, loud enough for everyone to hear.

Everyone was Debby's parents, Max's mother and sister, his son, his wife's closest friend, and someone he didn't recognize, a mild fellow wearing a light gray business suit. The man in the suit had a youthful, fleshy face, no chin, bashed-in shoulders, and appeared both shy and obtrusive, that is, his body hung back while his head jutted forward, apparently straining to overhear what Max had to say.

Entering his home Max had ignored them, even his son Jonah, who was half-hidden anyway, slouched by the hallway to his bedroom, willing to observe, but keeping distant from his father's arrival. Max moved past them all into Debby's open arms.

Getting to her arms from the airport had been difficult

and dramatic. On landing at La Guardia two Transcontinental employees entered the plane before anyone had a chance to depart. They led Max out into a car that was waiting on the runway. The other passengers from Pittsburgh watched him go, impressed by how Max was ushered ahead in this special way, hustled off as if he were an important official. Max had said goodbye to Dr Perlman at their seats. The therapist handed him a business card and said, 'Call me anytime. I'm either at that number or my service will know how to reach me.' Perlman then shook Max's hand and stepped back to wave goodbye. He did this with the insecure reassurance of a parent sending his child off to the first day of school.

Max went down the ramp and into a waiting car, an ordinary dark sedan. One of the airline employees got in with him. He was a short blond man with wire-rimmed glasses. He introduced himself as a media liaison for the Transcontinental New York office.

'Does that mean you're in public relations?' Max asked.

The blond admitted it did. He got right to his job, even before they had cleared the airport, while their sedan still swayed through the exit loops on to the Grand Central Parkway. 'There's probably gonna be press at your apartment building. I saw two TV crews at the terminal, but we've got you past them. They have your name. Not from us. Our policy is not to release names – but you were wandering out there for a day – and we didn't . . .' he waved his hand, 'Anyway, do you want to avoid them at your building?'

Max wondered why reporters wanted to talk to him. What did they know? Did they know he had seen Jeff dead? Did they know he had left the scene? Did they know about his dropping acid? No, of course not. What was especially interesting to them about his experience?

'That is,' the airline man said, '*if* we can avoid them. Is there a back entrance, a service entrance?'

Max told him there was, although it was only halfway down the block, within view and a quick jog from the front doors. This information caused a long silence from the PR man that lasted until they had crossed into Manhattan. 'You know what?' he came to life as they bucked on the city's streets. 'We don't know if they know what you look like. They may have paid the doorman to tip them off, but they'll be expecting you to come by car. If you approach on foot – no,' he interrupted himself guiltily, as if he had committed a taboo. 'That's a nutty idea –'

'What?' Max was game. 'You mean, let me out and I'll walk in? I'll do it.'

'No, no,' the PR man said, vehemently shaking his head. 'I can't.'

He's not supposed to let me out of his sight, Max guessed. They're worried I'll run again. Why do they care? Was there some sort of general faith in Max's life, in his marriage and his work, in his friendships and family relations? What was it to Transcontinental Airlines whether he returned home? 'I don't mind going in alone,' Max said.

'No, no.' The blond took off his wire-rimmed glasses and rubbed his eyes. 'Terrible idea,' he mumbled.

'I'd prefer it,' Max insisted.

'If anything went wrong,' The blond replaced his glasses and stared earnestly at Max to emphasize his point: 'They'd fire me.'

'Come on,' Max protested.

'Oh yes indeed,' the blond nodded solemnly. He turned to the driver. 'Can we take a pass by the entrance and see how bad it is?' The PR man bit thoughtfully on his index finger. They were about twenty blocks away from Max's building on 84th and West End Avenue when the PR man abruptly turned all the way in his seat to face Max, removed his finger from between his lips and demanded, 'Why did you leave the crash site?'

Max said, 'I'm not sure,' which was the truth.

'Shock?' the blond offered.

'Probably,' Max agreed.

There was only one television crew and one print reporter camped in front of his building. They loafed under the awning. The video and news reporters were chatting near the doors; the TV crew was idle by the curb, their video camera drooped to the pavement, unprepared for a sudden appearance by Max.

'Let's do it now,' the blond decided on the first go-by. 'Stop it here.' He spoke rapidly and with great excitement. 'Come on, Mr Klein, get ready. We're gonna run past them. My suggestion is just say, "No comment." Better still, say nothing.'

The driver stopped. The blond hopped out, rushed around to Max's side, opened his door, and practically dragged Max from the sedan. They had to squeeze between two parked cars on their way to the curb. That allowed the television crew time to start shooting and for the reporters to get between Max and his building. The television reporter stood to one side, angling a mike at Max's face; the newspaperman bounced ahead of him, hopping back as Max advanced.

'How do you feel?'

'Why did you run away?'

'Are you hurt?'

'Where did you go?'

They were at the door by then. The blond pulled Max relentlessly, interposing his body with quick adjustments to the constantly shifting positions of the crew and reporters. The PR man shouted at the doorman as they got inside: 'Keep them out!'

The television reporter was an Asian woman, her smooth puffy cheeks so young and vulnerable she appeared to Max to be a lost waif. The doorman blocked her off. Max felt sorry about abandoning her to her bosses without a quote, so he called back: 'I'm just happy to be alive.'

'That was great!' the blond praised Max in the elevator. 'That was the perfect thing to say.'

And also upstairs, at home, everybody was so pleased with Max. As he made his beeline for Debby he heard a sigh of relief from someone and applause from others. Even Debby, who should have been angry, hugged him with a conviction and desire that was usually absent from their life together. Although she bit his earlobe and complained to the room about his not calling in a formal almost mockingly stern tone, she then hugged him again with welcome and passion. She felt him harden against her; her eyes were tearful and amused. 'You seem to be in good shape,' she half whispered.

'Give your father a kiss!' Debby's mother instructed Max's son in a harsh and high-pitched tone. Max tried to separate from Debby to greet Jonah, but he succeeded only partly. His wife hung on to half of him, gathering his left arm and hugging it between her breasts.

Jonah had his head down, eyes averted, as he

approached Max. This was the shy approach he took with his grandparents, or any adult he was strange to. Jonah was shy anyway; but especially with adults he radiated discomfort and distrust. Not with his father, however, not until now.

'My son,' Max called to him encouragingly, sounding for all the world like a biblical character. Jonah ducked his head under his father's free hand and snuggled into Max's stomach, a furtive embrace. Max bent over and whispered in Jonah's ear: 'Were you scared?'

Jonah shook his head no. Max felt Jonah's nose rub against his belly. His son stayed silent and kept his face obscured.

'No?' Max prompted.

'No,' Jonah was muffled, talking from another dimension. 'I was worried.'

'Aw . . .' said several relatives in the room. Someone laughed softly. Debby's eyes flooded, big drops overflowing, but she smiled also, her head tilted sympathetically in the direction of her child.

'Who are you?' Max asked the half-shy, half-nosy man in the suit.

'Excuse me,' the man answered and came forward with a spurt of energy, extending a small hand. 'I'm Steven Brillstein.'

Max had to untangle from the clinging growths of his wife and child to free a hand. 'Nan asked me if he could be here when you arrived,' Debby said in a quick, confidential way to Max while he shook hands with Brillstein. The small hand was strong and energetic and quick to escape the contact.

'I'm an attorney,' Brillstein announced gravely. His voice was wringing its hands. 'I'm sorry to intrude. Mrs

Gordon is frustrated. She's gotten some conflicting information from the airline –'

'Jeff's dead,' Max interrupted. Brillstein's tone, agonized by seriousness and gravity, had irritated him. Max wanted to shut him up. What Max hadn't wanted or anticipated was the reaction of the rest of the room. His bald statement had shocked them. His mother, whom Max realized with a pang he had so far completely ignored, gasped and staggered, until she was steadied by Max's sister.

'Max!' his sister complained, not about the weight of their mother, but his cruel statement.

'He is,' Max insisted, although sheepishly. Jeff was long gone for him: he had forgotten that it was news to them. 'I saw his –' Max gestured toward the floor, at his red Oriental rug, which he used to think was blood red, but he realized was nothing like the color on the man whom he saw stumble out of the plane, or the smears on the fractured metal, or Jeff's blood-filled eyes. He never finished the sentence. They all waited for him to. Instead he said, 'He's dead. I'm sorry.'

'You know that for a fact?' Brillstein asked. 'I don't want to give Mrs Gordon any false hope, but I also –'

'Who are you?' Max demanded. 'Jeff doesn't have a lawyer.'

'I'm a family friend –'

'Whose family? Not Jeff's?'

'Max!' his sister repeated. She guided their mother to the couch, helped now by Debby's father. Evidently his sister thought he should be helping.

'What?' Max asked his sister.

'Your mother!' his sister gestured to her. Max's

mother sat stunned on the couch, staring forward, as if beaten into idiocy by the blow of Max's news.

'What's the matter, Ma?' Max asked.

'It's horrible,' his mother muttered.

'What's the matter!' his sister repeated Max's question sarcastically.

'I didn't realize you felt so close to Jeff,' Max said.

His mother looked up at him. Her eyes were red, her cheeks sagging. She shook her head slowly, in an incredulous way. 'Oh you didn't?' she said rhetorically, with heavy disapproval.

'Well, he was *my* partner,' Max found himself explaining to them all, although he didn't know what he was explaining or why he felt he had to.

Debby, no longer titillated or amused, walked back into Max's arms. This time she was frightened. She leaned her head against his chest and tried to pull Jonah along with her. He resisted and then yanked free. Jonah was suddenly bold, his shy light brown eyes peering at his father. 'How do you know?' Jonah demanded, not skeptically, but urgently.

Max separated from Debby and faced his son. 'I just know,' Max said. He was suspicious of them all suddenly. He was no longer like them. Max knew that they felt what he said about Jeff's death and how he said it were as significant as the fact. They were almost mystics, virtually believing Max could breathe life or death into Jeff with his choice of language.

'You saw him?' Jonah's voice rang out, again demanding and hurried. But Jonah had reason to consider himself an exception and want an answer. Jonah was close friends with Sam, Jeff's elder son. They had played together in the park as toddlers, had been given video games with synchronized forethought; together the sons of the partners had fought side by side, little fingers flashing on the game controls, conquering the villains of the Japanese computer. 'Oh, damn it,' you could hear them cry out from rooms away, 'I died again!'

So Max waved to his son to come close, and bent over to whisper, 'I saw him die. He didn't know it. He didn't feel any pain.'

'How do you know *that?*' Jonah's incredulity was so strong, he almost laughed.

Brillstein leaned over as well. His head appeared next to Jonah's. They had formed a football huddle.

'Excuse me,' Max said to him.

'Can we speak privately?' the lawyer asked.

'No,' Max said to Brillstein. He returned his attention to Jonah. 'He was killed instantly. I was right there. I know.'

'Okay,' Jonah agreed to the death. His bright eyes shone inward, worried.

'We'll spend a lot of time with Sammy,' Max said.

'Okay,' Jonah said, very low, eyes going down, down to the floor, down to someplace in his heart unknown to Max. Was he afraid of his friend's loss? Or embarrassed by his comparative good fortune?

'Excuse me,' Brillstein insisted. 'In fairness to Mrs Gordon, I would like to hear the details of what you saw in order to make sure before I tell her.'

'*I'll* tell her,' Max said. He straightened, a hand still resting on Jonah's head.

Brillstein straightened with Max, unfazed by his responses. 'I understand,' the lawyer said. 'But I have a problem. Mrs Gordon asked me to call as soon as I spoke with you, so when do you think you'll tell her?'

There was nothing for it: Max had to dance to their choreography for at least a little longer. 'All right, we'll go together to see Nan,' he told Brillstein.

'What!' Debby's body was rigid. There had been only a hint of anger from her until then. And even with this release she seemed to be trying exceptionally hard to hold back more. Max was surprised: he wasn't used to her being shy about that emotion.

'I'm going to see Nan and tell her. I don't think she should hear from a stranger.'

'You just got home.' Debby let this furious remark escape and then returned to a self-imposed silence: lips together, arms folded.

'I'm going to be home for a long time. Jeff isn't.'

'You could call her,' Debby said in a furious mumble, still a miser with her annoyance.

'I should tell her in person,' Max said.

'You should be here with us,' Debby insisted, forcing herself to speak in an unnaturally slow and reasonable tone. 'You nearly died. After something like that you should be with your family.'

'Don't scold me.' Under the terms of their marriage he was supposed to give way when she invoked his duty to the family. Not anymore. 'Don't make me apologize for being a good person just because this time it isn't being good to you,' he said and he could have sworn someone, probably his in-laws, had gasped.

'Good to me!' Debby could keep it in no more. 'Good to me!' She clenched her fists together and appealed to the others: 'You didn't tell me you were alive for twenty-four hours!' She looked at Max and released him with contempt: 'You want to go to Nan, then go.' Debby turned and walked out into the hallway leading to the bedrooms. They all waited together for the inevitable noise of a door slamming. It didn't come.

Instead Brillstein spoke. 'I'm willing to tell Mrs Gordon myself provided I know what I'm talking about.'

'Could you give these people a break?' Debby's father protested. His interruption surprised Max in two respects. Harold was usually a mild man, almost timid with strangers, and as a prominent professor of American literature, he rarely spoke a colloquialism such as 'give these people a break'. The change of character lasted for only one sentence. 'My son-in-law has just been restored to us,' Harry continued. 'It's a shock for all concerned. We need time to ourselves.'

'Thanks for trying, Dad,' Max told him. Harry wanted to smooth over the quarrel with Debby. He had no son and Max had no father. Years ago they had decided – it was a willful act – to fill in each other's family gaps. As a consequence Harry seemed to have more invested in his daughter's marriage than the typical father-in-law. The rare – indeed, Max could think of only two – occasions when Max and Debby fought in his presence, Harry had become agitated and tried to distract them by comparing their argument with marital disagreements in nineteenth-century novels.

'Debby is frightened,' Harry murmured to Max. 'She needs reassurance.'

'But I owe it to Jeff to tell Nan myself,' Max explained to Harry, sorry that he wasn't sufficiently well read to find an appropriate literary allusion. 'The sooner I do it, the better.' Max turned to Brillstein. The lawyer had his chin lowered, his arms folded across his chest, waiting without any overt sign of impatience and yet radiating a desire for speed. 'Let's go,' Max said to Brillstein.

'No!' Jonah blurted out. He had retreated to the far end of the living room, by the hallway where his mother had stormed out. When everyone's eyes went to him, he lowered his head shyly.

'You want to come with me?' Max offered.

'No,' Jonah mumbled and looked horrified.

So his friend's loss was scary, something Jonah didn't want to witness. Max was disappointed in his son. He has his mother's stingy heart, he judged harshly. Yes, there was a lot wrong with these people – things that would have to be corrected.

'Goodbye,' Max said coolly to the roomful of his family, no longer applauding his survival, instead they either glowered resentfully or looked away in embarrassment. Only the neutral and impatient Brillstein wanted Max. He had immediately moved into the small foyer to unlock the front door and now held it open for Max's exit.

'Let's do our duty,' Max mumbled and followed the lawyer's lead.

9

The lawyer had come in his own car, a blue Volvo station wagon, complete with an empty infant car seat, the trash of frequent trips to McDonald's, and wrappers that indicated a boy's interest in baseball cards. Brillstein hadn't expected to chauffeur Max. He apologized for the condition of the interior with a hasty curse. 'Shit,' he said, pushing stuff off the front seat. 'I'm sorry. I'll arrange for a car to take you home.'

'This is fine,' Max said, pleased to see someone else's kingdom ravaged by familial occupation. 'You have two kids?'

'Doesn't everybody?' Brillstein mumbled and pulled out of his parking spot with a cabdriver's sudden, angry acceleration and violent steering. 'Sure you want to tell Mrs Gordon yourself?'

'I'm sure.'

Brillstein made a face: scrunching his chin and raising his eyebrows; at once impressed and doubtful. He nodded as they sped past Max's block. 'There were a lot of TV people when you got here?'

'Just one,' Max said. There had been none on their way out. 'Got bored with me fast,' Max said. Brillstein drove madly, faster approaching yellow lights, running through the red if he didn't make it in time, weaving around paused cars or tentative drivers. Max was relaxed; he even enjoyed the pace. The lawyer merged on to the West Side Highway at top speed. Brillstein was either unconcerned by whether there was conflicting traffic or gifted with extraordinary peripheral vision. Max asked, 'You drive a cab to put yourself through college?'

Brillstein whistled. 'Good guess. Yes. For two years. Don't have any kidneys left. I think Mrs Gordon is going to take it hard.' He added the *non sequitur* without any indication that it wasn't a logical continuation.

'She must suspect.'

'I don't think so. That's why her father called my father to get me to find out. I'm not an aviation lawyer.'

'There are aviation lawyers?' Max asked, surprised.

'Oh sure,' Brillstein frowned, appalled at the prospect of there being such a lack. He rocketed over the West Side Highway's bumps with pleasure, a happy cowboy riding his bronco. 'In the New York area there are two law firms that specialize in crashes. Most of my practice is automobile accidents,' he explained as they took a pothole so hard that Max's head grazed the car roof. 'Or medical malpractice – wrongful death – but as I explained to Mrs Gordon, I'm not, uh, I just don't deal with this kind of thing. I would be happy to ...' he added in a singsong, and even smiled at Max, 'but as I say, there are two firms that pretty much have it covered in New York. Nevertheless, they wanted me to step in until we've at least confirmed Mr Gordon's death.'

'Well, you've done your job.'

'You actually saw him die?' Brillstein simply couldn't resist. He fired the question across at Max.

'No.' Max sat pat, enjoying this role as witness.

'Did you see his body after the crash?'

'Yes,' Max answered. And offered nothing more.

Brillstein sighed, beset by the world and yet willing,

after all, to lend a helping hand. 'Let me give you one bit of advice for when you speak with your lawyer. I'm sure he'll ask, but just in case he doesn't, you should emphasize that you saw your partner's dead body with your own eyes. And, if by any chance you remember later that actually you *did* see him being killed, I would suggest you, uh, not, well not to be crude about it, but make that very clear. Also, if Mr Gordon did not die instantly, if there was any conversation, any indication that he was in pain, or suffered, details like that, you'd be surprised how significant they might be for both Mrs Gordon and yourself.' Brillstein skimmed the Volvo across two lanes of bumps, heading for what was supposed to be Westway. Instead, because of environmental disputes, the city's lack of money and coherent vision, there was a simple open roadway, curiously more functional and beautiful than any of the grand designs that had been proposed. Although he cut in front of a car, Brillstein removed a hand from the wheel to warn Max, 'Don't say anything now. Just think about what happened. Sometimes, in terrible accidents, people don't immediately remember everything that happened.'

Brillstein's maneuver off the highway on to the extension had put the Volvo on an apparent collision course with the concrete divider that separated the road from the river. Max in particular, given his position in the death seat, felt he was being rushed right at the wall. Even when the lawyer returned his free hand to the wheel, he still did not drive straight. His car continued toward the wall. Max waited for the impact with mild curiosity. His body was relaxed. Brillstein had a plan, however, jerking the car away at the last moment and steering on to a crosshatched section of pavement, clearly marked not to be used, so that he could pass a line of cars stuck behind a white van that was attempting an illegal left turn. New York was a riot of lawlessness, Max thought, and laughed.

'Something funny?' Brillstein said with a pounce in his tone, a hunter's alacrity.

'You want me to make things up about the crash so that I can get more money.'

Brillstein wasn't offended. He didn't even seem to react. He was behind a taxi that he must have felt wasn't going fast enough. He glanced to his left, hopped to that lane only barely ahead of another car (its driver honked a complaint), sped past the cab, and hopped back in front of it. Max noticed the driver as they superseded him. The cabbie was a dark hairy man with bloodshot eyes; he stared at them with loathing. 'To be honest with you, Mr Klein, I wasn't thinking about you at all. I was thinking about Mrs Gordon, who, although I don't know her well, I know doesn't come from a rich family, and is now a widow with two young children in an expensive city, full of single women her age and with very few men who want to marry them.'

'You're telling me that if I testify –'

Brillstein shook his head vigorously. He was well suited to be a parent: his expressions were as exaggerated as a puppet's. He denied Max's comment with the rapidity and strength a dog uses to shake himself dry. 'I doubt that it'll ever get to court. It's very rare for airline cases to go to court. This'll be settled.' The lawyer nodded up and down, again in a dumb-show manner, going farther up and farther down than people normally do. He continued to make this marionette's movement as he elaborated: 'But yes,' nodding down and then nodding up, 'if you say in a deposition that Mr Gordon suffered,' nodding down. 'that he knew he was dying,' nodding up fast and then down slow, 'that he was anxious as to the fate of his wife and children, of course that could influence the settlement.' The puppet was done. He cocked his head and waited cheerfully for an answer.

Max pressed the button for the electric window. It squealed in agony at first, but then hummed down quietly the rest of the way.

'I've got the air-conditioning on,' Brillstein complained.

The summer-baked smells of urine and food covered Max's face as if he had put on a mask, along with a vague pungent odor of the ocean, and also a hint of fire, of something always burning in the city, acrid and angry. He didn't mind the rotting sea or spoiled food or human wastes – he minded the fire. Its smell had been in the DC-10; this new burning mixed with some left over in his nostrils. He wanted to scream. So he did.

Brillstein was shocked. He twisted the wheel and shouted, 'Hey!' The Volvo bounced across the road, on to a graveled area marked off by cones, presumably for work being done along the riverside. Their wheels crunched on the pebbles and the car went into a skid. As they twisted and slid sideways, Max enjoyed his view. The summer night had finished its gradual progress to darkness. The river came closer, veiled by a chain-link fence. The city's lights glowed on the water, painting long tails on the black river. Max had grown up next to a magnificent body of water that he had never touched and could never know. He waited willingly for Brillstein's car to crash through the barrier and submerge him into the Hudson's dark and restless flow.

They were out of control only briefly. The tires squealed as Brillstein remastered his car. The Volvo slid easily into the fence, like a baseball player pursing a foul ball with gentle recklessness. When they came to a stop, Brillstein shouted: 'What's wrong!'

'I don't want to tell any lies,' Max said.

Brillstein released air. 'Okay. Next time just say no. I'm a *nudge*, but I'm not deaf.'

Max and Brillstein stared at each other for a moment and then Max laughed. Brillstein grinned back, a toothless and tight look. His eyes were still nervous, but he tried to appear friendly 'What's your problem?' Max asked. 'Why are you in a total rage?'

'A what?'

'You're in a total rage. You drive like you want everybody on this road dead.'

'Are you okay?' the lawyer countered. 'I mean, you were in a horrible crash. No settlement hype. For real – you've been through hell. Are you all right? I've got Valium in the glove compartment.' Brillstein leaned over and released the door. Maps slid out, a flashlight rolled on to the floor. Left in the compartment was a hypodermic filled with liquid and several bottles of pills.

Max laughed again. 'It's a pharmacy!' he announced and laughed harder.

'Are you kidding? My wife has us fully stocked. Carsick? Dramamine. Nervous? Valium. Allergic to beestings? Here's a shot of epinephrine. Got a kidney stone? Here's Percodan for you.'

'The way you drive I'm surprised she's still functioning.'

'I like to go fast.'

'Why?' Max demanded, surveying Brillstein as he replaced the fallen flashlight and maps in the glove compartment. The lawyer was a medium man, average height, his hair dark but not black, his eyes small but not beady, his hair thinning but not gone, his skin pale but not white. He looked dull and typical. Certainly no thrill seeker.

'Why?' Brillstein repeated the question, surprised. He stared past Max at the river until he had an answer. 'Because waiting is for suckers.' He laughed at himself.

'That's not the reason,' Max dismissed him. 'Let's go.' He waved at the highway extension. He could still smell the city burning faintly; somewhere, it was being destroyed.

'What's the reason? What do you mean?' Brillstein guided the car back into the flow, now driving calmly. 'Oh, I'm insecure, that's what you're saying. Of course I'm insecure. Who isn't? I'd like to meet somebody who isn't.'

'Sure you're insecure,' Max agreed. 'But that's not why.' The fire seemed to die out – a warm breeze reached him from the water and it wasn't polluted or stale. Its touch was gentle. 'You're angry. You want to impose yourself on everyone. You want them out of your fucking way. Why? Where are you going? What train are you late for?'

Brillstein turned off the extension at 23rd Street. That was an error, since Jeff's apartment was on 8th and Broadway and they could have continued down to 14th before exiting the highway. Surely, with an ex-cab-driver's knowledge, the lawyer knew that. Had Max messed him up with self-examination? Max wondered if that was why Brillstein had to be on edge: perhaps unless the lawyer was nervously alert, his skills deteriorated. 'I dunno, I dunno, I dunno,' Brillstein said rapidly three times, with the haste and emotional conviction of an adorable children's character. 'This is sounding like a sixties conversation. Let's drop it.'

'What's wrong with a sixties conversation?' Max asked.

'I hated the sixties.'

They lurched on the streets. The city had left a repaving half-accomplished, which meant that they had to ride on a rough striated undersurface, vibrating their feet and teeth. They also had to swerve around manhole covers placed at the higher level of the now demolished paving. Driving over one would have involved a hammering drop into the surrounding moat of underroad. Such a fall would probably destroy even Brillstein's Volvo. 'If you hated the sixties that means you supported the Vietnam War and never got laid,' Max said. The words were hummed out of him by the rumbling tires.

Brillstein smirked, not looking Max's way, and swung them on to Seventh Avenue heading downtown. 'That's right,' he said in a singsong. 'And I didn't help destroy our educational system with open admissions and I didn't give kids the idea that taking drugs is okay and I didn't get AIDS and I –'

'– didn't die trying to kill gooks either. College deferment and then what? High lottery number?'

'Fuck you,' Brillstein said in a sweet tone. He was back in the flow again, shoving his fenders in the way of other cars, daring them to choose: have an accident or let me go first.

'National Guard probably. You didn't give up your

career to stop people from dying and you didn't risk your life fighting.'

'No one should have had to fight. We could have won the war in weeks –'

'Yeah!' Max's heart was thumping. Why do you care? his head complained to him – it's the dead past. 'We lost the war,' he said sarcastically, 'and now communism is overrunning the world!'

'Okay. Take it easy.' Brillstein chose 12th to go crosstown, a wise decision since 8th or 10th would be slower. 'It's been a tough day. All I wanted to say to you, all I wanted to emphasize is that Mrs Gordon and her children's future is at stake. You get the partnership insurance. You're sitting pretty. I think you owe her anything that would improve her settlement discussions with the airlines.'

Max opened the glove compartment and again the flashlight rolled out. He tossed bottle after bottle of pills on to the seat.

'What the fuck are you doing!' Brillstein yelled.

'I'm admiring how well you discourage the use of drugs.' Max rattled the bottle of Valium in the lawyer's ear. 'Your children will be impressed!'

'Those are my wife's! They're her pills.'

'Oh, I see. So it's okay to marry drug addicts!'

'This is ridiculous! This is a ridiculous fucking conversation.'

'And the Percodan?' Max demanded, shaking the appropriate bottle. 'Your wife is the one who's passing kidney stones?'

'Jesus!' Brillstein steered the car curbside and stopped. He grabbed the bottle. 'Don't talk about kidney stones! You'll jinx me.' He was sweating. 'I feel like I've got one coming . . . all night and day since Nan Gordon called. I'm telling myself it's psychosomatic.' Brillstein pointed out the window. 'We're here.'

Max was disheartened by the news. The lobby to Jeff's building imposed itself on his vision and he realized how frightened he was to face Nan.

I'm alive and he's dead. He felt cold in the hot smelly air.

Then, as clearly as though he were leaning forward from the backseat, Jeff talked in his ear. '*You've fucked us with Nutty Nick for good. A professional would have made that meeting.*'

'She's going to get money from American Express,' Max told his ghost.

'Well,' it was Brillstein who answered. He carefully replaced the bottles, studying each label. 'This is expired,' he commented about one and put it aside. 'Does Dramamine spoil?' He flashed a smile and then lowered his head to read another label. He mumbled, 'The American Express insurance was something I wanted to bring up later with you.'

'You know about it?'

'Even though I'm not an aviation lawyer, the family asked me to look into things and I had all night and day . . .' He seemed to apologize with a shrug. Max didn't know for what. 'I'd better put the car in the garage and come up with you.' Brillstein steered them past the entrance to Jeff's high rise. Through friends of his parents, Jeff had gotten a deal on a three-bedroom rental in one of Greenwich Village's few tall modern residences. The cheap rent was Jeff's excuse for living in a structure that was ugly and out of character with its surroundings. The orange brick tower rose forty-four stories above the area's Federal houses and nine-story loft buildings. The tall monster's synthetic façade was pockmarked with cantilevered slabs that were supposed to be terraces. Each slab shadowed and boxed in the terrace below, lending them the inviting gloom of a cave. The building's parking garage was in the sub-basement. Brillstein turned into it. 'You made the original plane reservations with your company's American Express card?'

'Right.'

'And then Mr Gordon changed the reservations?'

'When our meeting in LA was changed.'

'You gave him permission to act as your agent in changing the travel arrangements?'

Max remembered Jeff's anger at the check-in counter when Max wanted to delay and go on a different flight. He also remembered Jeff's surprise when Max included the credit card insurance in his running total of the benefits Nan and Debby would receive. No, Max whispered to himself. He couldn't believe his partner was that much of a loser. 'What is it? What did Jeff do?'

'Well, evidently Mr Gordon got a different deal on the second reservations. He took a credit from American Express and paid in cash.'

'Jeff made a cheaper deal on the tickets and pocketed the difference?'

'Well, we don't know that. He probably restored the money to the firm's petty cash account or business checking account. Or intended to. It's unfair to assume a petty theft. And it would have been petty. The refunded money was a couple hundred bucks.'

'Not to Nan. To Nan it's a half a million dollars. Our wives are beneficiaries on the credit cards. That idiot!'

Jeff haunted him all right. He was still a burden to be carried.

'I know,' Brillstein said, presumably referring to the information about who benefited. 'That's why I wanted to stress that what you say about the crash may be important.'

Max felt something he hadn't since the explosion: irritation at the mosquito bite of the morally confused world. He had been free of it since the crash. Max hadn't measured the relief of its absence until now as he felt the itch of its return. Why was this choice imposed on him? He was so near to freedom.

Brillstein had stopped his car under a huge sign that read: STOP HERE. A sleepy man approached filling out a claim ticket. Max looked around at the family mess of the Volvo and the lawyer's nervous curious eyes, darting from him to the parking attendant, as if they were both potential threats. 'Can you represent me and Nan in this?' Max asked. 'Or do we have to get an airline lawyer?'

'Look – if Nan Gordon weren't a family friend – I mean, I'd love to – but it's not my expertise – I'm sure I could do it, truth is, compared to malpractice it's taking candy from *niños*,' Brillstein accepted the ticket from the attendant. 'Probably about an hour,' he mumbled to him. 'But Stoppard and Gray have got aviation liability down to a clean quick formula. They'll package you all together, get reasonable settlements – I mean, they may not pay enough attention to each individual case –'

'Shut up for a second,' Max said. Brillstein immediately made a great show of stilling himself. He put his hands together, pressed his lips tight, inclined his head a notch forward, disappearing what little there was of his chin into his neck – an attentive bird waiting to see if food would be offered him. They were in front of the elevator in the parking garage, only a minute away from the widow of Max's best friend. Yes, Max had to admit, after all, Jeff was his closest friend; a man he had spent at least forty hours a week with for over a decade; a true intimate, a man who trusted Max not to mind when he stole from him. 'If I'm going to lie my head off, I don't care for how noble a reason, I want my lawyer to know I'm lying –'

Brillstein was again a dog shaking off his swim in the pond. 'No, no, no, no,' he waved a hand at Max. 'This is very bad talk. I haven't heard this. A Range Rover roared past us just now and I didn't hear what you said. You want me to handle your case? Great. I can do the job. We understand each other. We're grown-ups. We know this is a game. We don't have to sit side by side and read the instruction manual aloud together. Right?'

'No.' The elevator arrived. Max blocked the inner rubber safety door to hold it open. 'I don't need you for that bullshit. I can get the fancy guys for that kind of advice. I don't trust my abilities here. Okay? I'm not saying I'm too moral to lie, I'm saying I may not be good enough at it. If I hire you it'll be because you *will* read the instruction manual out loud.' The elevator doors tried to close. They bumped Max's hand and withdrew in horror.

Brillstein let out a lot of air. He inflated first, cheeks puffing out like a blowfish, before releasing it all in a huge sigh of resignation. 'You don't work for "60 Minutes" or the DA, do you?' Brillstein entered the elevator laughing at himself. 'Just kidding. Just kidding.

Come on,' he urged Max in. Max followed. The familiar interior – fake paneled wood, mirrored ceiling – brought Nan vividly to life as a dreaded obstacle. Brillstein spoke into an intercom to the lobby to announce where they were going. The doorman verified they were expected and then allowed the elevator up. They waited in silence until they were moving. 'We'll have to have all our conversations after rowing out into the middle of the Atlantic,' Brillstein said, 'but that's okay. Just kidding.' He put his hand out to Max, an offer. 'It's a deal.'

Max shook the little hand. It fled quickly from his grasp. The lawyer had manipulated him, of course Max knew that, but he was a willing dupe. A man he could see through was always more reliable than a man he couldn't.

Max didn't care for Nan's looks. Her yellow hair, pleading blue eyes and tender pink skin, her puffy cheeks and rounded face resembled an old-fashioned doll's, a vision of helplessness, stupidity and easy sexual prey. Actually, from what he knew about her through their limited social contact and from Jeff's complicated explanations of their marital dissensions Max believed Nan to be sexually inaccessible, nervously smart, and helpless only in the sense of wanting help. Up until the birth of their second child Nan had worked as a writer for *Newstime* magazine. In the last two years she occasionally did freelance pieces for women's magazines but had basically become a talker: she talked about writing a book, she talked about organizing workshops, called Stopping Short, for non-working mothers who used to have high-powered careers; and she talked about returning to full-time journalism.

Her lack of income combined with the costs of raising their two boys in New York City had made Jeff hungrier and more frantic about money than ever. During the elevator ride, trying to make sense of Jeff's petty theft, Max harkened back to his dead partner's complaints. Jeff said, 'We're so in debt,' at least twice in any conversation on any subject. He worked it into any topic. Subject: The Berlin Wall is torn down. Jeff's response: Remember how cheap things were in 1961?

'You were eleven,' Max protested.

'That's why things were so cheap. All I needed to be happy was twenty-five cents for a new Pinky if Fat Joey hit a home run.'

Nan didn't look helpless that day. She was distraught. She stood waiting at the elevator doors for them. Her straw hair was pulled back into a ponytail and her skin didn't look pink. It was pale, almost translucent. She had pimples on her forehead, nose and cheeks that she hadn't bothered to cover with makeup. She wasn't made-up at all. That was also unusual. Her lips weren't painted red. They looked thin. Her eyes were less prominent and she had a more authentic American look than ever, a rural woman abandoned to poverty and back-breaking labor. Only Nan was from New Jersey, had gone to Yale, didn't know how to plant a flower and was lazy. Even though she claimed to be anxious all the time and insisted daily life was too much for her, she had a frantic competence and strength.

Both were gone. Instead, she was eager and brave. Her pupils looked odd, big and uncertain. Max decided she was tranquilized. She stood right at the elevator doors when they opened, eagerly waiting, and yet she backed away as Max appeared and moved toward her.

He realized Nan – the actual physical presence of Nan – was strange to him and that in the past he had often been cool to her, not because he truly believed Jeff's version of their marriage, but because he couldn't help but feel that as his wife she ought to make him more diligent, rather than provide excuses for his lassitude about work. Max avoided chatting with her on the phone or any friendly overtures she made at their rare social encounters. But this was not the time to withhold himself from her.

Max opened his arms and said, 'Nan, I'm sorry.'

Beside him, Brillstein shrank away, hiding near the apartment door. The lawyer spoke in a whisper to someone inside and then Max heard Jeff's mother's voice say, 'Oh my God!' followed by weeping.

Max reached Nan and embraced her. She was tall. About an inch taller than Max. She didn't cry. He peeked at her profile and her eye was still clear. She wasn't breathing. At least he couldn't feel any inhalations. She was motionless in his arms. She had gained weight after the second child and her back felt soft and loose.

'Breathe,' he whispered.

She did and exhaled words: 'I knew it,' she said quietly but in a steady tone. 'I just knew it right away. Isn't that crazy?'

'He loved you,' Max said.

'God, we're stupid.'

Max leaned away to look at her full in the face. Her big pupils swallowed Max's reflection. 'What do you mean?'

'We lived like jerks, always nagging. We wasted it,' she said. That judgement broke her down. She sobbed and covered up. She bent over quickly, so fast that by the time Max hugged her he was hugging a human bundle, a falling human bundle. They sagged against the hallway and slid down together.

Max said, 'No, he loved you. You made him happy.' He kept on saying those sentences into her sobs. 'You made him happy. He loved you.' Max remembered all the times his partner's greyhound face had snarled. 'Nan's sucking the life out of me. I've got to leave her. I love the kids, but she's killing me.' Yet Max believed what he told Nan wasn't a lie. 'He loved you,' he said again to Nan. 'You made him happy.' That was the truth because Jeff couldn't know any greater pleasure than to have someone to blame for all his dissatisfactions.

Nan answered him through the tears. The sobbing made it hard to understand her words. Relatives had appeared in the hall, including Sam, her elder boy and Jonah's friend. He was holding a portable video game in one hand. It drooped forgotten, still a part of him, the way a toddler might drag along a security blanket. His pink face, usually expressionless, was scrunched up in a frown that was the result of mixing fear with tears. Max nodded encouragingly at him. Sam mumbled a 'Hi' and Max knew that Sam was another legacy from his dead partner he couldn't refuse. Sam came over and leaned against his mother's back.

'He loved you,' Max repeated. 'You made him happy,' he droned and then paused to hear what Nan was mumbling.

He heard her this time. She said, 'Shut up.'

Max refused Brillstein's offer of a ride and took a taxi

home. It was after ten-thirty. As he entered his apartment Max heard the eighth inning of a Mets game playing on a radio in Jonah's room. Max glanced down the hall but saw no light coming from his son's door. He was probably still awake anyway. The living room was also dark. Max moved into it, heading for the kitchen, 'Max . . .' Debby called in a whisper from their bedroom. She came rushing out. She had on a long nightgown and reminded him of the romantic ghosts in old black-and-white movies: she glided to him in a blur of flowing white. She rushed into his arms and whispered, 'I'm scared.'

He plied her off gently, but with conviction. 'I don't have patience for that anymore.'

Debby seemed genuinely puzzled. 'Patience?'

'I can't make it all okay.'

Again Debby seemed to make an unusual effort to restrain herself. She moved up on her toes as if he were too tall to see. 'Max, what's wrong? I don't know what you mean.'

'I want you to know. Things are different. I can't fix everything for you.'

She opened her mouth to speak, shut it, and looked away toward the bright windows. They glowed from the streetlamps and the shimmer of the river. When she looked back her face had relaxed. There was anger in her voice, but it was real, not posturing. It was the thrilling truth. 'You don't fix everything for me,' she said.

'I know,' Max agreed. 'And I can't try anymore. I'm hungry,' he added. He moved off to the kitchen, flipping on all its lights. He had removed the fluorescent fixtures and replaced them with halogen spots. It was elegant, but not a kitchen, he had to admit to himself. Kitchens should have the merciless glare of pragmatism. Food. He was so hungry he wanted to eat everything in the cabinets.

'You want something?' he called to his wife, the beautiful ghost, standing in the doorway with confusion on her face. She watched him without answering. He started his feast alone.

BURYING THE DEAD

10

Carla noticed a shadow waiting at the door of her small private room. She turned her head on the pillow, crinkling the stiff hospital linen, and there her husband stood, pale and silent and ominous, like a ghost come to accuse.

Carla wanted to call to him, but she had no energy in her body. For hours she had watched the medical personnel come and go, tending to her numbed limbs. If they said anything about Bubble it was to say there was no news. Some spoke to her gently, some were annoyed. She had no voice to answer, anyway, no desire to be aware and talking.

'Carla . . .?' Manny called in uncertainly.

At the sound of his voice she cried. The tears first stung, then soothed her irritated eyes. A doctor had explained that the smoke from the plane was poisonous, and her eyes might burn for a few days.

Manny entered. She was ashamed and afraid. She lowered her head, diminishing herself, prepared for whatever he might do, ready for a blow or an embrace.

Manny adored his son. His passion for Bubble had surprised her. After all, he had agreed to have children with a shrug, and while she was pregnant he talked incessantly about how much it would cost to raise a child. He never seemed to look forward to becoming a father. Yet from the moment Manny held Bubble in his arms he was nuts about him. He bragged about Bubble's size, his looks, his smartness, his boldness and his strength. When Bubble stripped off his clothes and paraded naked (pulling on his little cock, belly thrust forward, a cartoon of masculine pride) Manny beamed. He was unashamed and unafraid of his son's self-love. The pleasure he showed at Bubble's ability to wrest a toy from another tot embarrassed her. But the clearest proof of Manny's great love was that anything Bubble asked for, his daddy bought. Immediately. Without giving consideration to the cost or whining about the expense. And if, after a few minutes, Bubble lost interest in the toy, Manny might frown, but that was all. 'Anything for my boy,' he'd say.

She had let his son die. How could he feel anything but hate for her?

He approached her bed warily. He looked all around it, suspiciously, as if there might be someone hiding in ambush. 'You okay?' His voice was husky and quiet. 'A doctor told me you're okay.'

She nodded. She was okay, although her leg was broken in two places and the top of her hand had been badly burned. 'You were lucky,' a nurse had said without irony. 'Some of those people . . .' she added and didn't finish. Carla knew. The longer she lay in that room the clearer the images from the crash. Gradually, things she had seen, things that her brain had refused to understand, were reseen in vivid horror. The body she had fallen on top of was only half a body. The man who yelled at her as she ran out was missing an arm.

Was that what he yelled at her for? Did he want help looking for it? Horrible. It was horrible.

Did he get out? She didn't want to know. She wanted to forget.

Manny kissed her on the cheek, the way you would a

grandparent, and backed away a few feet from the bed. 'I'm here,' he said grimly. 'You hurting?' he nodded at her leg.

She shook her head no. When was he going to ask about Bubble? Or tell? Did he know more than she?

'The airline got me here as fast as they could.'

She shut her eyes at the idea of that, of anyone she knew in an airplane. 'Don't!' she croaked in a panic at the thought.

'Sorry,' Manny mumbled. 'Anyway, they did it.' He bent down to be at her level, carefully raised his hand to her forehead and touched her delicately, like a priest's blessing. 'I love you, babe,' he mumbled.

There was a scream inside her. The drugs had buried it underneath her numb skin. She shut her eyes at her husband's touch. She was back in the burning plane. The man missing an arm yelled at her for running. Inside, she screamed to chase it away.

'Bubble . . .' she managed to get out, but she kept her eyes shut.

'Okay,' Manny pressed his face against hers. She felt his arm over her chest, his voice at her ear. 'I'm here.'

She cried for a long time and was grateful Manny said nothing and did nothing. He waited. He was patient. That wasn't like him. He was an active man who hated to sit still. When she stopped weeping, he moved to a yellow chair by the window and just sat, staring.

They were quiet. It was night outside. She could only see the silhouettes of a few trees. There wasn't much light, a little cast by other windows, but no city lights, no distant lit-up buildings. They were nowhere.

After a while Manny said, 'They gave you a private room.'

She knew what he meant. Why? She wasn't badly hurt. Maybe that was why.

'Things are crowded out there,' he nodded toward the corridor.

Why put me here alone? He was right. It meant something. She wished he would stop thinking so clearly.

'I ought to call home and say you're okay.'

Everything he was thinking made good sense. Even the fact that he didn't use the phone. It was over by a beige night table with some discarded extras from her bandage. How could he talk to anyone without knowing about Bubble?

But really they did know about Bubble. That's why Manny sat in the chair and did nothing.

Eventually a nurse gave her another shot. She felt she didn't need it for pain or any medical reason, but she allowed it. The drug didn't raise her on a bed of pillows this time. Her ears got hot, her legs first felt thick and then were numb. The painful sight of Manny in the chair softened to a blur. Her eyes wanted to shut. She let them.

She felt something in her arms, something warm and wonderful that squirmed and snuggled her.

She was holding Bubble. She cried in her sleep, knowing it wasn't him, just the memory of him, a thrilling bundle that vanished as soon as she tried to carry it back into the wide-awake world. She was asleep and yet she was weeping. She thought: That's strange, I didn't know you could sleep and cry at the same time.

She forced herself to open her eyes. Manny wasn't in the chair anymore. Good, she thought, glad he was gone, even though she missed him.

She slept. A dark sleep without feeling.

She woke to harsh morning light. She was sober. Everything hurt. Any movement was painful. The tiniest muscle in her body had been bruised. Her neck was so stiff it might as well have been locked in a steel brace. She would have gone back to sleep, only the pain kept her awake.

Manny was asleep on a cot by the wall. His mouth sagged open. The presence of the cot was new to her. He was fully dressed and looked uncomfortable.

She realized she had made a bargain last night. She had agreed to go to sleep in the hope that she would be wakened by her rescued baby, by a miracle.

There are no miracles, Carla.

For the first time she knew without any doubt that Bubble was gone. In a cold hopeless way she understood he was dead.

She wanted to get out of the hospital.

'Manny . . .?' The sound of herself was shocking. Not only was she hoarse, but the tones were old and hard. I'm an old woman now, she understood. I'm only twenty-nine but I'm an old woman.

Manny startled awake. His legs slipped off the cot and he fell half out. The right side of his thick straight black hair, the side that had been on the cot, was ironed the wrong way. It stuck up in the air. 'What is it!' he said.

'Let's –' She wanted to say, 'Let's get out of here,' but her battered muscles overwhelmed her with pain. She moaned.

'You need another shot?' Manny was already up, heading for the closed door.

'No!' she cried out as loudly as she could.

'Yeah, babe. You need it.' He opened the door and stuck his head out. He called out for a nurse and told someone that his 'wife is in pain and needs another shot'. He mumbled more; she couldn't hear what.

She wanted to get out of bed. She pulled off the sheet. She was shocked by the fact of her cast. She had forgotten about her broken leg. How the hell was she going to walk?

The tears started again. This time in anger and frustration.

'How can I walk!' she yelled at Manny. 'I can't walk,' she blubbered, wanting to be angry, but falling into sadness, into a bottomless loneliness.

'It's okay, babe, it's okay,' Manny rushed at her, nervous and scared. 'They're coming. They're coming.' He said everything twice, his repetitions a plea for her to be quiet.

'I'm sorry,' she admitted her shame. She covered herself in his arms and begged: 'I'm sorry, honey, I'm sorry . . .'

'Shh, don't talk. I'm here . . .'

You're so weak. Calm down. Stop making a fuss.

'I want to get out of here! I don't want to be here anymore, Manny! Get me out of here.' She pulled and pushed his shoulders, rocking him back and forth as if his weight were what kept her stuck in grief.

'I can't.'

'Why not!' She hit him on the chest. The blow made a hollow sound. She shied away, afraid she had hurt him.

'There's nowhere for us to go. We've got to stay until they –' he interrupted himself. He looked away from her and shut up guiltily.

He did know something. 'What? Until they what?'

'Where's the nurse?' he avoided her ineptly, moving off the bed and returning to the door. He poked his head out and called for a nurse.

'Stop it, Manny,' she reached after him. The gesture shocked the left side of her body. From the ribs to the neck, her muscles jumped as if they wanted to escape her body. She moaned and fell back. She was in agony and it scared her: the bones and muscles were hot and brittle. Maybe she was in very bad shape, not okay, but seriously, maybe permanently injured. She lay still, tears rolling out of her eyes. She was trapped and helpless: she was never going to get out of that plane.

Manny charmed the nurse while she took Carla's temperature and blood pressure. This time the nurse said that instead of an injection, Carla would get two pills. One was Tylenol, the other a muscle relaxant. Manny talked cheerfully. Carla recognized the tone as his I'm-going-for-my-Christmas-tip voice. She heard him use it when she called him at work and one of the residents at his building interrupted with a repair problem. According to Manny it was the old people, the nontippers, who complained the most. *Los ricos*, the yuppies, who paid incredible rents and handed out Christmas cards with as much as one hundred dollars inside were grateful no matter what you charged, so long as what you did worked. But the old people were irrational, ungrateful and miserly. A few years ago an old woman for whom Manny had slaved all year gave him an envelope with eighty-five cents, fifteen of them in pennies. She complained the next morning that he hadn't been sufficiently appreciative. Manny talked in the same tone to the nurse that he used with the stingy old people: a singsong that sounded a little dumb and cheerful and very friendly, but also, if you knew Manny, had an echo of mockery.

'How am I going to walk?' Carla groaned.

'There you go,' the nurse said, handing Carla the muscle relaxant.

'I can't walk with this,' she tapped the cast.

'We'll give you crutches,' the nurse said and nudged her with the pill.

'I hurt all over,' Carla could hear herself whine like a tired toddler, the way Bubble whined . . . And again her sore puffy eyes were wet with tears.

'All charley-horsed, right?' the nurse nodded sympathetically. 'Same thing happened to me after my brother totaled a car with me in the death seat.'

'My God!' Manny put a hand on his cheek. His mouth dropped open and his eyes were comically wide. 'Were you badly hurt?'

'Nothing. Not even a scratch.' The nurse turned to Manny, pleased by his responsiveness. 'But I couldn't move the next day. Comes from the adrenaline rush. It's the same thing you'd feel if you'd lifted weights for hours.'

'Poor baby,' he said, looking at Carla, but his tone was so general he might mean the nurse's old accident.

What is their problem? Why don't they shut up and leave me alone?

The drug untied her muscles. Soon they were warm and caressed. Her head, she realized, must have been squeezed by a headache before, because now she felt there was blue sky up there, plenty of space without pain.

Manny hustled to put away the cot the minute the

nurse left. He was afraid of her. Manny would sooner chase a crack dealer from the corner than argue with a nurse or a city bureaucrat. She watched her husband strip the cot, fold it and the sheets, and stack them neatly with anxious speed. He could be a marine hurrying to get ready for inspection.

'They were very nice to get me this,' he said about the cot when he was all done. He sat on the chair admiring his neat pile of bedding. 'Against hospital rules,' he nodded at her.

She was about to mock his gratitude when she was stopped by a good look at his eyes. His smoky skin, alloyed from his olive Italian father and coffee Filipino mother, was especially dark under his brown eyes. The shadowing lent them a romantic aura. But that morning the skin was blackened by fatigue and grief; it looked almost charred. His eyes were wasted in their burnt setting.

'I got something to tell you,' Manny said. His legs were spread, elbows on his knees, his head braced by his hands. He looked at the floor. 'A guy from the airline came by while you were sleeping.'

'They found him?' she was able to ask without any trouble. It surprised her. Hearing herself, she thought she sounded bored.

'They can't indenti –' Manny lowered his head and took a deep breath. He started again, breathing fast: 'They can't be sure it's his body –' He had to stop. His chest heaved with anxiety. He looked away and mumbled, 'Oh God ...' He pressed his lips and swallowed. Then he spoke fast: 'They're sending for his hospital records. They're going to use his footprint.' Again he stopped.

She remembered. When Bubble was born they took a footprint. So part of him had survived. Her baby's foot.

'They don't think there's any reason for us to look at–' Manny covered his mouth with his hand and breathed noisily through his nose.

Not enough left for her to recognize. The image of her beautiful boy being torn apart came into her head without mercy. Manny rushed to hug her, but she looked past him at the ghastly visions of Bubble killed. 'I – want – to – go home!' she gasped between her sobs. 'Get – me – out of here!'

'We have to wait, honey,' he whispered. 'We'll go soon.'

The nurse poked her head in. 'She want a sedative?' she asked Manny, as if Carla weren't competent to answer for herself.

'No!' Carla shouted. She shook her head vehemently to prove she meant it. 'No more drugs!'

'Relax you,' the nurse said.

Carla grabbed Manny's short-sleeved shirt by its cuffs and yanked. 'Leave – me – alone!' she choked the words out.

'Shhh!' Manny pressed her head against his chest. He wasn't only comforting her, he was worried about her rudeness to the nurse.

The nurse didn't care. 'You sure?' she asked Carla. 'I'll get somebody . . .' she said and rushed away.

Carla concentrated on the look of Manny's arm. It appeared smooth and soft, but to the touch the muscles were defined and hard. You might think he spent all day weight-lifting rather than fixing leaky pipes, replacing hallway lights, and rewiring intercoms. She stroked the bulge of his forearm, brushing its few hairs. He had lots of thick hair on top of his head and little elsewhere. He was a bastard, the product of his father's weekend leaves while stationed in the Philippines. Carla assumed Manny's mother must have been a whore, but he never said so, and he punched a friend who once suggested it. As soon as his mother died Manny made the trip to the States. He was still a teenager when he came to Little Italy to find his long-lost biological father, retired from the service and then the superintendent of a row of tenements on Broome Street. The meeting was a disappointment for both men. At least Manny did get a job out of it. Through a friend of his unacknowledged pop Manny was made assistant porter in a Greenwich Village apartment building, which meant he got all the shit work, running the service elevator, collecting the garbage from each floor and mopping the halls. Once a month he polished all the brass doorknobs. Manny didn't like the hours or the work, but he liked New York, its ethnic and racial stew, and its promise of doing better. He took the abuse of the doormen and befriended the handyman, who gave him books so he could teach himself about carpentry, plumbing, electricity and compressors and all the gadgets that people use but don't know how to fix. Eventually, the super was fired, the handyman was promoted and he elevated Manny as well. Manny was the handyman now, and the heir apparent to the superintendent. 'You know what that means,' Manny liked to crow to Carla about his vision of their future. 'That means someday you get a fancy Manhattan address.' She admired his ambition and willingness to work hard, his belief in the American dream; but she wished he wasn't so willing to accept insults and pretend thankfulness.

After she had stopped crying, after her breathing had slowed down, and after she had been quiet for a while, Manny said softly, 'I called your mother while you were sleeping. She says it's all her fault.'

She nodded, not to agree, just to show she had expected that. Her mother was being literal: Carla and Bubble had gotten on the plane to visit her and her husband in their new home. Carla sighed for an answer. She thought, my mother is crazy.

'She wanted to come here. I told her that was crazy.'

'Good,' Carla mumbled. She missed her mother and didn't want to see her.

'She said she's going to New York. She'll be there when we get back.'

The whole family would gather. They would fill the house with black clothes and food and tears.

She shivered. Manny rubbed her arms. Her mouth was dry and tasted bad. 'I need a toothbrush.'

'Okay,' Manny said. But he didn't move, didn't get out of her arms.

The door opened and Bea Rosenfeld looked in. Carla noticed the glasses first, the big square frames sailing on her nose and two glistening jewels at the corners. She remembered that she had spoken to this woman, but not where or when or about what. For a moment Carla thought that Bea was also a passenger and that they had talked on the runway.

'Hi, I'm Bea Rosenfeld,' She said to Manny. 'How are you doing?' she asked Carla.

Carla nodded.

'I heard the news about your son. I'm very sorry.'

Manny's arms got tight, the hard muscles bulging out from the smooth skin. And he held his breath, as if waiting for something terrible to happen. *What was his problem?*

'I also heard from the nurse that you didn't want any tranquilizers. I told her I thought you were right. Throwing blankets on a fire may put it out, but covering feelings only makes them burn inside.'

Carla thought Bea was interesting. She remembered they had met in the emergency room. But she felt no need to answer.

Manny took a breath and shifted. Carla slid off him and reached for the pillow. She had to hang on to something. Manny said: 'We don't know for sure. They're sending for his records to check the footprints.'

'Oh . . .' Bea's tone was hesitant for the first time. 'I see. Did they tell you how long that would take?'

'They said it wouldn't take long. They send it through a fax machine. You know?'

They could be talking about anything.

'Who are you?' Carla asked Bea.

Bea smiled at her, as if she were an intelligent child. 'You mean what's my job?'

Carla nodded.

'I'm a thanatologist. That's a very long word which means that I try to help people who have lost someone – isn't that a funny way to talk?' Bea shook her head. 'The words we use for death. "Lost someone," I said. What I meant was, when someone close to them has died.' She looked at Manny to include him. 'I also work with people who are dying.'

'That's very nice of you,' Manny said in an awkward mumble.

'No. I do it for myself.' Bea, still calm, her jeweled glasses bobbling slightly, focused on Carla. 'My daughter was killed in a car accident when she was sixteen. She went out to the movies and she never came back. Every time I cried they gave me a sedative. Every time I asked a question they told me to forget. And I never saw her body. They said it was nothing I would want to look at. I'm sure they were right. She must have looked horrible. But now I wish I had seen it. As for the drugs – it took three years for me to stop taking pills and they didn't get rid of my grief. When I stopped taking them, the grief was still there as if she had died the day before. It's better to cry and scream bloody murder. You can't cry for three years.'

'We're not looking at the body,' Manny said very definitely. He was so positive that Carla thought he must have already seen it.

'Why . . .?' Carla asked. Her mouth was dry. Her top lip peeled off from the bottom. The skin tingled afterwards. She touched it to check if she was bleeding. No.

Manny meanwhile answered her question with a stare. 'They just said there's – I mean – if it's him – there's not much to . . .'

'I don't know,' Bea's hand went up. 'If there's nothing to recognize, then . . .' She came over to the bed and asked with a gesture if she could sit. Carla didn't have the energy to answer. Bea took that as a yes. She settled next to Carla's head and put a hand on her hair, stroking. The gooseneck reading lamp hung over the bed, brightening only a circle. Bea's head looked big. The jewels in Bea's eyeglasses darkened in the shadows just outside the lamp's spot. 'What happened in the crash? Were you holding him?'

'Oh!' Manny cried out. Carla shifted to see him. Manny was sweating, although the room was cool from the air-conditioning. He shook his head at Bea.

'What?' Bea asked him.

Manny glanced at Carla and went back to Bea. 'Can we talk outside?' he pointed to the hall.

Carla understood. He knew Manny couldn't bear to hear about her cowardice: he would hate her forever.

'We should talk,' Bea said to Manny. 'But I think Carla needs to talk right now.'

Manny and Bea went back and forth arguing in a whisper about whether she needed to talk. Carla watched them with interest, but she was hardly with them. She hugged the pillow, enjoying its bulk. She remembered that while she slept Bubble had come back into her arms. She had felt him warm and squirming, so real her heart ached with joy. She shut her eyes and longed for sleep.

'Are you sleepy?' Bea gently shook Carla's pillow to bring her into the conversation.

She nodded. *Leave me alone.*

'Are you really sleepy? The nurse told me you were out all night and most of the morning. Are you sleepy or very blue?'

What do you think!

Bea studied Carla, searching out from her boat-like glasses into the fog of pain between them. 'Tell me what happened,' she spoke almost in a whisper. 'They say the plane was in trouble for a long time. It must have been very scary.'

Carla remembered Lisa the flight attendant. She remembered her face next to hers as they tried to get Bubble's seat belt to work. Her chin was smeared with lipstick. Lisa tried to fasten his belt, which would have saved his life. Carla peered at Bea through the sharpening focus these thoughts gave her. She noticed parentheses of wrinkles on each side of Bea's mouth and that her lipstick was redder than Lisa's. Was Lisa alive? Lisa could tell them she had tried her best.

But what if Lisa didn't say that? What if she told them that Carla was hysterical and all thumbs and that it was her fault, that everybody else could make the belts work.

But Lisa had tried and failed also!

'It's okay, honey,' Bea said and stroked her cheek. She touched a tear that Carla didn't know had slipped from her eyes. 'Tell me. Were you very scared the whole time?'

She had clapped. She remembered her stupid, stupid clap. Jesus, I opened my fingers to clap! Her whole body shivered with the memory: she had loosened her hands just as they crashed. That's why Bubble had been ripped from her. She had opened her hands. Because she was so eager to think everything was okay. Just like this stupid old Jewish woman who wanted to feel everything was okay. Well, nothing was okay.

I opened my hands and killed my son.

'Okay, babe, okay, babe,' Manny pushed Bea away and smothered her face.

Someone in the room was sobbing.

'Talk about it, honey,' Bea's silly glasses were tossing above the waves in Manny's hair.

'She don't have to talk about any fucking thing! She don't want to! Leave us alone!' Manny yelled at Bea even though she was a *yanqui*, as Manny called them, yelling without any worry about his Christmas tip.

'I don't remember,' Carla said to the glasses as they were tossed back by the storm. 'I can't remember anything!'

That's right. Don't tell them anything.

Carla was carried places. Picked up and put down, regarded doubtfully, and sometimes ignored. She was silent or as silent as they would let her be. Manny nagged her at first. Especially about using the crutches.

'Your muscles'll get weak,' he said.

She didn't bother to point out the obvious: that no matter how much she used her crutches the broken leg's strength would be diminished. She said, 'Leave me alone.'

All their conversations were arguments, only she didn't fight for her side, except to be silent and refuse. The first was about how they would go home. It surprised her that Manny tried to convince her they should fly back to New York. She expected understanding.

'I understand,' Manny said. 'But, babe, you know what they say. It's like falling off a horse. You got to get right back on.'

What does he know about horses?

'It don't have to be on Transcontinental. They'll pay for any airline we want.'

'I don't care about the money, Manny. I want to go home by train.'

'It ain't the money! You think it's the money? They'll pay for any way we want. They'll pay for a car. I'm just saying, you can't give in. We won't go anyplace ever again.'

'Good.' Carla nodded at him. 'Good!' she repeated with as much strength as she could muster.

Talking hurt her. She complained to the doctor that her chest and sides ached every time she moved; a deep breath could be painful. He said her ribs were bruised. She had thought it was from all the crying, but the doctor told her that probably something had whacked into her during the crash. She couldn't cry without feeling sore; she couldn't yell either. Or laugh. Being unable to laugh was not a problem, however.

She decided that the bruise was the loss of Bubble, the wound from where he had been torn away. They identified what was left of her son from the hospital records and what she had known in her heart became fact to the world: her two-year-old son was dead. Evidently he had been found in a horrible condition. Even Bea Rosenfeld agreed that Carla shouldn't look at his body.

They went home by train. That was scary, too. At one point the brakes screeched and the car lurched. Carla screamed and buried her head in Manny's chest. He said, 'It's okay, babe, we're coming into a station.' She hit him as hard as she could in the arm. He didn't even flinch. She decided that once she was back in Little Italy she would never travel again.

And yet all of her hadn't returned home to Mulberry Street. On the plane was where she really lived. Over and over she considered the choices she had made. She wondered if moving from the window seat to the aisle had been an error. She decided no. The ceiling had completely collapsed on the outer seats. The man missing an arm had been on the aisle, the window seat beside him had disappeared and that was also how his arm had been severed. And she knew that the man seated directly in front of her by the window had been killed. She had overheard him introduce himself to his neighbor and his name was listed among the dead in the newspaper.

No. If she had stayed put she would be dead. That was how close she had come, a last-minute decision made for a reason she could no longer remember. She could see herself squashed and sliced by the metal. She had to squeeze her eyes shut and curse in a whisper to shoo away the picture from her brain. Even in this misery she didn't want to have died.

Carla read in the papers that Lisa the flight attendant had lived. All of the crew survived. Sure they did – they had safe seats and belts that worked. The reporters wrote that the flight was a miracle, the landing a great accomplishment, that by rights everyone should be dead. They were full of stories of bravery, especially one man whom the papers called the Good Samaritan. He had saved – an especially bitter fact for Carla – a couple of kids from burning alive in the wreck. From all the coverage, Carla got the impression she was supposed to think the crash was almost a blessing in disguise.

The worst thing was Bubble's coffin. It was heart-breakingly small: a little mahogany box with tiny handles, its wood and brass highly polished, the length so short there could be only two pallbearers. She had come to the funeral with her grief exhausted, determined to be dignified. But the sight smashed her.

The best thing about the funeral was that no one was bothered by her weeping. Her grief was no longer solitary; she had plenty of sorrowful company. For most of the service her mother's red face and bloodshot eyes blocked her sight of the priest and the small coffin. Her aunts wailed behind her. At the graveside her two closest friends linked arms as Bubble's miniature casket descended into the earth. Their heads bowed toward each other until they touched and made an umbrella. Carla turned her back on this last sight of her son and moved under their covering, not to be shielded, but to be comforted.

Her relatives and friends visited every day after the funeral. Her mother sent her new husband home to California and slept on the living-room couch. They made meals, they pushed Carla in a wheelchair when she got tired of her crutches. Her mother even held a tissue under her nose and said, 'Blow,' as if she were a baby.

Each night the apartment was full of her relatives' talk and it came around again and again to the lawsuit. Manny was the first to bring it up with Carla. 'Tony's got us the name of a lawyer to call,' Manny said. Tony was his illegitimate father. 'He's a big shot. His sister lives in one of Tony's buildings. She's an artist or something.'

'No,' Carla said.

'I'm calling him,' Manny said.

About a week after the funeral she overheard Manny tell her mother and aunts and uncles at the kitchen table that two other lawyers had phoned asking for the job. She lay still in her dark bedroom straining to hear them as they ate lasagne and argued in mumbles. She could distinguish her mother's voice. Her mother was upset and she kept contradicting Manny about something. At one point Carla thought she could make out what her mother said: Don't talk about money for a dead baby.

That's right, Carla cheered her mother on. She worried Bubble's soul might be punished for their greed. She had never seriously considered the consequences of people having souls until then, but it seemed to her there was no point in taking chances. Bubble was being judged now, if anything the Church said was right, and she thought: There's nothing to judge about him except us. God will judge him by the kind of people we are.

At the funeral Father Conti had said babies were innocent and have a special place in Heaven, that Leonardo was smiling in Jesus' lap. Carla remembered the boys in junior high used to say Father Conti liked to give them long hugs and asked to hear details of masturbation in confession. What he had to say didn't seem to her hypocritical; it sounded foolish and that hurt her feelings.

The voices in the kitchen became frantic and angry. Her mother's got loud enough for Carla to hear her say, 'Listen to me, Manny. You're going to be sorry!'

That convinced Carla to attempt to use her crutches and get closer, to be able to hear all of what they were saying. Her bedroom was at the end of a narrow hall opposite Bubble's room. His door was kept closed. The sight of its glass knob (scavenged from the luxury building where Manny worked) was a rebuke. When he was alive, Bubble's door was never shut and the knob was out of sight. Now it was the first thing she saw if she left her room. She was stopped by its facets; like a hypnotist's watch they held her vision and mesmerized her. She forgot the crutches and the airless hallway smelling of tomato sauce. She felt Bubble in her arms, she smelled his hair, she heard him make demands.

'No!' she whispered intensely to scare the memories away.

There was shushing and quiet from the kitchen.

'Carla?' Manny called.

She didn't answer. Her left crutch began to skid on the bare floor of the hall. She wedged it against the wall and waited silently.

'Nothing,' Manny said. 'She's sleeping.' He resumed their discussion about the lawsuit in a whisper.

Carla fit herself into the narrow hall, so narrow there was hardly room for the spread of her crutches. She wedged the rubber tips into the crevices and hung like a puppet, limp from her shoulders down. She didn't like to use the crutches because she couldn't get the hang of swinging her weight forward without the handles digging into her armpits. Her body was a misery, aching the full length, from broken leg to bruised middle to sore underarms. She loathed her body anyway: bony and weak, her skin dusky and loose. She wished she could shed herself. That's why she cherished sleep: her energy and freedom of movement returned and so did her baby boy. From her position in the hall some words became audible, but not enough. She moved closer, the tips squeaking against the wall and floor.

'He told me we can sue the government here in New York,' Manny said.

Aunt Mary, whose voice was always loud and complaining, said, 'The government! What did the government do, for Chrissake?'

'They don't make the airlines use infant seats,' Manny said.

Carla wished her mother would interrupt again and stop them. Tell them: You don't take money for a dead baby. If not, then she would have to, even though the prospect of facing her aunts and uncles made her sick with exhaustion. She couldn't eavesdrop indefinitely, though. The crutches were wearing through her skin. Her shoulders felt as if they were about to pop out of their sockets.

'What difference would an infant seat have made?' Uncle Bob asked. He had a degree in engineering, the only college graduate of the older generation, and he enjoyed thoughtful discussions. His question was posed with a mild curious tone, the inquiring student.

'Who knows!' Aunt Mary complained as if the issue were mystical and irritating.

'Carla was holding him on her lap,' Manny said. 'You can't hold on to a baby – that's why you have to have a car seat when you drive.'

'We used to put Pete on the floor in a little bed,' Mary said. 'Remember? Nothing ever happened.'

'You were never in an accident!' her sister Florence said.

'It was safer that way!'

'Mary, how can you be so stupid? There's nothing holding them down.'

'Excuse me. I don't understand.' That was Uncle Carmine talking; he was all business, a practical man. 'You don't sue the airline?'

'No,' Manny said. 'We do. We sue the airline, the government, the manufacturer –'

'Sure! They made the plane badly! *That* makes sense!' Aunt Mary banged something, gaveling her verdict.

'Will you shut up, please,' her sister Florence said calmly. 'Let him finish.'

'I don't remember what I was saying,' Manny said.

'Listen to me, Manny!'

That was Carla's mother. Exasperated, ready to take

charge. Carla was thrilled to hear her mother take command. She would shut them up.

'Listen to me!' her mother repeated.

'He's listening,' Aunt Mary whined. 'You're shouting. We're all listening. What is it?'

'I'm telling you, Manny, don't use the Irish lawyer.'

'He was born here,' Manny complained.

'He's an Irishman,' Carla's mother insisted. 'The Irish like doing two things: drinking and stealing from Italians.'

Under the best of circumstances Carla didn't enjoy listening to their collective wisdom. She had thought at least her mother was defending the dignity of her loss. A surge of rage came up through her crutches. She bolted down the hall clumsily, whacking the tips into the wall and the floor, jarring her shoulders and head. 'Get out of here,' she yelled as she reached the kitchen entryway. 'I can't take listening to your stupid opinions!' She lost control of the right crutch attempting the turn. She reached for the wall, missed, and stopped a fall by taking hold of the nearest support, the refrigerator handle just inside the entrance. The working part of the kitchen was narrow and painted yellow. At the far end, open to the living room, was a small dining ell, almost entirely filled by a yellow Formica table with a metal band around its edge. Right now the table was especially dominant; Manny had put in the extra leaf to accommodate her aunts and uncles. 'It's none of your business! You don't know anything about it!'

They ignored her scolding. Aunt Mary smiled idiotically at her, as if Carla were a toddler having an amusing tantrum.

Aunt Florence called out blandly, 'Hello, honey.'

Her mother turned to Manny and accused him: 'I thought you said she was sleeping.' Manny was out of his chair in a rush to prop up Carla. Both uncles peered at her as if she were a total stranger. Uncle Carmine added a frown to his perplexity, the way he might if caught in a subway car with a rude and deranged panhandler.

'Get off me!' Carla yelled at Manny.

He ignored her and wedged his shoulder under hers, becoming a crutch. 'Let go of the other one and I can get you over to my chair. You want to sit?'

Carla looked at the crammed box of the dining ell. The yellow paint seemed to have aged since she last noticed it, the color changing from what had been a bright mustard to the dried-out and dingy look of something left out overnight. Five very old, wrinkled and foolish faces watched her. They were packed into the space like eggs in a carton. 'I'm not a child,' Carla yelled at them.

'Of course not,' Uncle Bill said.

'I want you to leave. This is my home. I want to be alone with Manny.'

'That's not very nice,' her mother said, using a familiar phrase of criticism.

'I don't give a shit about being nice!' Carla yelled back. She was crying, although she felt angry, not sad. 'There's nothing to be nice about,' she mumbled in a blubbery voice.

Manny picked her up. He wasn't much bigger than her, yet lifting her appeared to be effortless for him. She was furious at his presumption. She yanked on his thick black hair. 'Put me down!'

He cursed at the pain and shouted: 'Let go! That hurts!'

'Put me down!' She pulled again, outraged and glad to hurt him.

Manny cursed and pleaded, 'Let go! I'll take you to your room and get them out.'

'We're going, we're going –' Aunt Mary called.

Carla released Manny's hair. 'My mother too!' She didn't care if they all hated her or if she never saw them again. She was more than indifferent to their opinion of her; she wanted them to dislike her. She wanted the connection to them severed from both ends. 'I want you out of here, Mama. Go home, Mama,' she called back almost in tears. Manny bumped the foot of her broken leg into the wall and that sent a pang up to the tender spot where it was mending. She moaned.

'Sorry,' he mumbled and hurried her into the bedroom, dumping her on the bed. He immediately touched his hair – tenderly, as if expecting to discover raw scalp.

'Get them out!' Carla shouted.

Aunt Florence appeared in the doorway. 'Honey, we're just crazy old people. Don't pay any attention to us. We love you.'

Carla pressed her face into the bed and held her breath. Her leg ached. She concentrated on the pain. Vaguely she heard her mother complaining, probably about where she could go. Go to California, Carla pleaded in her head. She was thirsty. She couldn't get herself a drink since the crutches were still in the kitchen. She mused: It's a good thing Bubble is dead, I couldn't take care of him. Aware of the callousness of that thought, Carla was disgusted. She pressed her lips together, squeezed her eyes tight, and voicelessly shouted into the mattress: *You're horrible. You're horrible. You're horrible.*

Eventually Manny came in with her crutches and offered her espresso or tea or beer. She said no and sat up to watch him. Manny straightened the room, gathering the clumps of tissues and disheveled magazines and half-empty glasses of juice and cans of soda. She followed his every move.

'What?' he asked after he was done and she was still staring.

'Where did my mother go?'

'Florence's. Just for tonight.'

'I don't want her to come back here.'

'She's not.' Manny looked exhausted. But he seemed to have unlimited energy and no tears. She hadn't seen him cry, really weep, over his son's death. He had teared up a little at the priest's sentimental talk about Bubble bouncing in Jesus' lap – 'Leonardo knows only His goodness, blissfully ignorant of His awesome power.' Manny had lingered at the graveside. Her mother commented on it while Carla pressed her face against the limousine's glass and looked up, above the level of the headstones, wishing to see unlimited sky. A helicopter buzzed past and her mother said, 'Poor Manny. Look at him.' Carla turned and saw her husband at the foot of the opened ground, a solitary and unmoving figure. There was something unusual about the sight, apart from the fact that he was in a suit and standing sentinel by a grave. She didn't know what – until he moved. It was seeing him at rest, stilled and sorrowful. That was the last time for such calm. Since then he had fussed around the house, serving drinks, rushing out to buy forgotten groceries, making mysterious phone calls in a hushed mumble. Whenever her eyes met his, Carla talked to him with them, in the silent and expressive language of their marriage. He answered in the clumsy words of their grief: 'Can I get you something? Does the leg hurt? Are you hungry?'

Manny was tired. She noticed his shoulders were slumped, his eyes were burned out, the skin surrounding them charred. 'Hold me,' she said.

He did, moving to the bed and sliding behind her so she could nestle in his arms and lay her head on his thick and lulling chest. But he did so in the same hurried and dutiful manner he rushed out to buy more groceries for her mother to cook. She wondered how patient he would be about making love. They hadn't since the crash. That must be two weeks, she figured, a long time for them, even since the baby. Carla didn't trust a marriage without lovemaking. She knew men and she especially knew Manny, and Manny was the kind of man who, if he didn't desire his wife, couldn't be trusted to keep his heart faithful. There were men who had no connection between their two beloved organs, but for Manny loss of desire would be the death of love. She had no sexual feelings. None. Her body, if it wasn't in pain, was numb and foreign to her. And she couldn't imagine ever having them again. But she had no illusions about Manny. Maybe his need for sex was why he couldn't talk to her in words or looks. She urged herself to touch him.

Instead he talked. 'Tomorrow I'm calling a lawyer and making an appointment. He'll come here if you want. But you got to talk to him. This is a lot of money we're talking about. And we can do good with it.'

Carla held her breath. She thought she was going to be angry, but she was tired of feeling apart from her husband and she let the crude words flush out of her head, catching hold of the last phrase. 'What good?' she asked dreamily and was happy to feel sleepy again. She could make another journey away from misery.

'For later,' Manny said in a low harsh tone. 'It can do a lot of good later.' He said 'later' as if planning a revenge.

She was frightened by his ominous voice. 'What – later?' She raised her head from his soothing chest. 'What are you talking about?'

Manny pressed his chin against his chest to see her. That doubled his chin and puckered an old scar. 'For Leonardo's brother or sister. We could use the money for their education.'

Manny's words made a weird hole in her memory. She fell in and searched for a brother or sister of Bubble's. She was happy and anxious all of a sudden. Who were they?

'I always worried about Leo's schooling . . .' Manny sighed heavily. His chest rose up and caught her head. 'Something good has to come out of this,' he mumbled.

And the obvious shivered through her, a wave of nausea as she understood Manny meant children she didn't have yet, children they would create all over again; with her body changing shape again; feeling the pain of birth again; fighting the grinding war of infancy again; again watching it grow day by day until – centuries from now – they would have another two-year-old who could be killed at any moment. It was an insult. An ugly joke. That was why Manny didn't cry over Bubble. He planned on getting a new son; like changing a bulb in his building's hallway, indifferently replacing his dead son with a new baby.

'Get off,' she said glumly. She lifted her head and pushed at his billowing chest. 'I want the bed to myself.'

'I didn't mean right now!' Manny squealed.

'I need more room. Lying like this hurts my leg.'

'It shouldn't hurt you anymore.'

How do you know what hurts?

'I asked Dr Galletin,' Manny insisted. 'He said it shouldn't hurt anymore.'

'Well, guess what?' she answered with lugubrious scorn. 'I got news for you and Dr Galletin. It does hurt.'

12

Carla's family ignored her fit of anger, just as they had ignored her during childhood, adolescence and young adulthood. The next morning her mother and aunts were back, cooking, cleaning, gossiping.

Carla said nothing. She was so hopelessly angry at them there was nothing she wanted to say. All morning they came in and asked questions.

'Would you like breakfast? How about some cereal?'

'Manny called from work. He said you should go for a walk. How about it? Uncle Bill'll come over. He was always your favorite. Remember, he'd carry you on his shoulders through the San Gennaro fair?'

She didn't answer. Anyway, she didn't remember. Her aunts had all these pretty memories that, it seemed to Carla, had never occurred. She could recall only family quarrels and cooking and roomfuls of men slouched in easy chairs with their bellies distended, suppressing belches.

She couldn't fight them anymore. All her life she had fought. Fought to dress the way she liked, fought to be friends with the kids she liked, fought to go out on dates, fought to move out of her mother's house, fought to get married to a half-breed. Yes, in the beginning her relatives hadn't wanted her to be in love with Manny, a bastard and almost a nigger, as one of the uncles that Carla supposedly doted on had said. Now Manny was simmering in their pot, mixed in with their spicy glop.

She said nothing. Her mouth was heavy. Even to sigh

would require that she part her lips, and they were thick and stuck together.

'She's not talking to us,' her mother commented to Aunt Mary by lunchtime. 'Let's put some food in front of her. She'll eat it.'

Carla's great-grandmother had killed herself by staying in bed and refusing to eat. Carla didn't remember the passive suicide herself, except for a dim and fading snapshot of a memory: a dark room, dusty light streaming through wide blinds, and a tiny ancient woman lying still in a big bed. Carla knew the story as family legend. Mama Sofia had decided to die when she broke her hip. She refused to get up and use her walker. She refused to eat anything. She only sipped water from time to time. She wasted away for three weeks, caught pneumonia and died.

The story used to terrify Carla. Now she thought it was beautiful and comforting.

She lay in bed and said nothing. They put food in front of her and she watched it gel. She turned off the television and the air-conditioner and returned to bed. She felt sweat grow out of her skin and drip down into the sheets. She hoped the heat would make germs breed faster in her lungs.

She looked at the mahogany dresser inherited from her grandmother, dark and sulking in the corner. Her eyes skied down the curling sweep of her green drapes, noticing dirt and stains she hadn't before but that now seemed glaring. These were going to be the last things she would see in life. The television, the screen gray and hostile, stood at the foot of the bed like an overheated, sleepy dog. There was a scratch on its wood paneling, a gash caused by the yuppie who had thrown it out believing the set was broken. In fact, it required only an eighty-nine-cent fuse that Manny promptly bought and installed. He gloated about the ignorance of the rich college graduate. For months Manny dragged friends home to show them the set and tell the story. 'He throws it into the garbage room. I tell him, "Don't you want to have a repairman look at it? Maybe it can be fixed?" He says, "No, I know about these things. Once they're broken, costs as much to fix them as it does to buy a new one. And they're never right again."' Manny would then turn it on and gesture, laughing with his dark mouth, at the television's perfect image.

Beyond the television, on the wall, there was a painting she had bought as a young unmarried working girl during a walk through the Washington Square Art Show years ago, before she had met Manny. A funny old man had a stall on the corner of Tenth and University Place jammed with pictures he had made of the neighborhood. The one Carla bought was a painting of the outside of the Grand Tichino restaurant on a lively summer evening, the street busy with tourists going by. What she liked about it was the old lady leaning on the windowsill in the tenement above the restaurant. The old woman didn't look anything like her grandmother but it reminded Carla of her anyway. Since her grandma had died only a few months before, she bought the painting, although it cost fifty dollars, a huge sum to her then. She hadn't looked closely at the painting for years. Since the crash, with the television always on, she had given it no more than a glance. She was interested in it now because of the association with her grandmother. Her mind wanted to go back to people who had died, people she was used to forgetting.

In the dark hot room she studied the painting. It was the only thing in the apartment that she had really bought and picked out all by herself. Everything else was handed down or salvaged by Manny.

She decided she didn't like it anymore. The colors looked too bright; and the old woman was leaning out too far forward from the window. She seemed eager to see what was happening below. Carla's grandma used to lean on the window ledge as if she never planned to move from that spot. She wasn't curious about what was below, although she looked down. She had stopped there to rest, to be away from the complaints and duties inside, to be – Carla understood suddenly – alone. The ledge was as alone as she could be.

She cried for her grandmother. Only a few tears. No sobs. Slow-moving sad drops of regret. She had ignored that old woman. She had waved her grandmother away morning and night on her way out of the apartment, annoyed by the old lady's nagging warnings about her revealing clothes, the boys she was seeing, drugs, sex, whatever was the latest horror that television told the old lady to guard against.

Carla fell asleep.

Her baby returned to her arms. Hot, sweating, feeding from her.

Manny's stern voice yanked her out of her shallow grave of dreams: 'Carla! Is the air-conditioner broken?'

She could have been swimming: her T-shirt was stuck to her belly; a translucent oval revealed her deep navel. She remembered the sight of Bubble's thick trunk bursting out of his stomach, wiring him to her insides.

'You want an innie or an outie?' the doctor had asked.

'It's working!' Manny complained, standing by the air-conditioner. He switched it on. The overhead light dimmed for a moment.

'Leave me alone,' she said. Her mouth was dry and her lips thick, numbed. The words sounded like a trumpet player clearing his mouthpiece.

'Somebody's here.' Manny opened the glowering dresser. He tossed out a yellow-and-black-striped polo shirt. 'You'd better change.'

'I don't want to see anybody,' she tooted. She was on her back. Twisting to get on her side, away from Manny, her head throbbed. The first wave of cooled air skimmed over her soaked shirt and its temperature clung, a freezing sheet tossed on to her skin.

Manny's feet thumped, walking around to her side of the bed. His round face and charred eyes popped in front of her. 'The lawyer's here. I had a lot of trouble convincing him to come to see you. I know you ain't up to leaving the apartment. I been patient, but it's over a month now and we have to do something. They call me every day and I have to make a decision. You got to help me, understand?' Manny lifted her, one hand on her elbow, the other on her shoulder. He had no trouble doing it. She couldn't lift herself; Manny got her up with no effort at all. She was a helpless child.

'Let me die,' she said into her husband's mouth as he pulled at her drenched T-shirt. She no longer tooted: she growled.

'Don't be crazy. You're in mourning. You're not dying.'

What did he say before? It's been a month? You've been feeling sorry for yourself for a month?

He pulled the T-shirt off her. Sweat collected in the

hollows, dripping down her breastbone, her armpits, the back of her neck. Manny took his callused hand and smoothed the perspiration all over her exposed ribs and breasts, small and empty of milk. He hummed with appreciation and looked at her nipples.

She was appalled: *He wants to have sex with the lawyer waiting in the hall?*

'You look good to me,' he mumbled. 'I miss you,' he said and kissed between her breasts with a loud smacking noise. He spread the sweat on her hollow stomach. A pool filled her big belly button. 'This is no good. You'd better take a shower. I'll get your mother to help you.'

He left her halfway up out of bed. She could still feel his sandy palms sweeping across her chest and belly, squashing and squeezing her. She was warm and small while he handled her: a baby being bathed.

'Come back, Manny,' she whimpered and sagged back on to the bed. The air-conditioner vibrated and struggled.

'You're a mess,' her mother said casually and lovingly, the way mothers say it, the way Carla used to say it to a food-smeared Bubble or a dirt-encrusted Bubble or a red-eyed, temper-tantrum Bubble. 'You don't want to take a shower. We'll go in the bathroom and sponge off.'

Carla allowed her mother to wipe her with the washcloth, although she was capable.

'You're too skinny,' her mother commented, running the cool towel over her ribs.

'I'm always too skinny for you,' Carla said.

'That's right. Something sick about those models. It's not real men who want that. They're selling you a bill of goods.'

'Nobody's selling me anything,' Carla said sadly.

Her mother was done. Carla sat on the toilet, staring at the blackening edges of her cast. Her mother brought in a clean white long-sleeved blouse – too formal and too hot to wear with her shorts. Carla didn't argue about it although she wanted the yellow-and-black polo shirt that Manny had picked out. If it pleased her husband then she should wear it. What did she have left to do but to please him? But she had no energy to fight her mother's choice.

When the blouse was on and she was ready to go out to meet the lawyer, her mother said, 'If you really want me to go back to California before you're back on your feet, able to do for yourself, I'll go. I didn't want to while you were yelling because you yell things you don't mean and then the next day you're sorry but you're too proud to take them back. You're my baby,' and her mother was crying suddenly. Although she had sounded annoyed right up until she said 'baby,' she was quickly a wreck. Tears rolled down her cheeks, her wide mouth trembled, and her old hands came together in a prayerful gesture. 'I'm trying to help you,' she said.

'Okay, Mama,' Carla said and they hugged awkwardly, Carla still on the toilet, her mother arching past the rigid leg to embrace her. 'I love you,' Carla said. *You mean, if you still could love anybody.* Later, as they hobbled together out of the bathroom, she added, 'Stay until the cast is off.'

'Now I'm a mess,' her mother said, brushing away a tear. She smeared mascara across her cheek toward her temple.

'Fix yourself up. I can make it.' Carla took her crutches and faced the hallway. She made sure not to

183

look at the jeweled doorknob to Bubble's room. From the sound of it Manny had taken the lawyer into the living room. The hall smelled dusty and was only half-cooled. She listened to their conversation as she maneuvered in the narrow passage.

The lawyer was a fast talker: '– these new seats, they're called sixteen-Cs, were ordered on all new planes by the FAA. They've been proven to be much safer in the kind of crash your wife was in.'

'No kidding.' Manny was grim.

'They don't break loose. Passengers aren't turned into human missiles –'

'And they knew about them?'

'Knew about them? They're using them. All new planes have them. About fifteen percent of the old planes have had them installed. The FAA is going –'

Carla had reached the living-room entryway. It had no doors and she faced the two windows at the far end. The sun was bright, irradiating the red drapes Manny had been given by the son of one of the old women in his building when she died. The glow rouged Manny's and the lawyer's faces as they turned toward her.

The lawyer was a little man, very nervous, or at least jumpy. When he moved at Carla, he seemed to leap out of his body, his motion was so sudden and quick. 'Hi, I'm Steven Brillstein,' he said. His small hand was flat, he kept the fingers together and the thumb close. He noticed she was occupied by the crutches and removed his offered hand abruptly. 'Stupid of me. Last thing you need now is to shake hands. Here,' he stepped aside and offered her the couch. 'Sit.'

'They didn't have these seats in the jet my wife was in?' Manny asked, preoccupied. He made no move to help Carla as she tried to get herself around the glass coffee table on to the couch. The living room looked weird. She hadn't ventured there since coming home. She checked all the furniture, trying to understand what was odd about it.

No bottle lying on its side.

No abandoned toys.

No sleeping baby nestled in the yellow-and-white-print couch. She dropped on to it heavily. One crutch kicked up and banged the coffee table. It vibrated. The lawyer put a soothing hand on the glass and said, 'No harm done.'

Across from her, on the credenza, in a silver frame, was the portrait of Bubble taken by the same man who had photographed her wedding. It was one of a series of photos that Manny had mailed off to modeling agencies. Carla hadn't objected to the cost and the fuss because she agreed with Manny: Bubble was such a beautiful boy, probably companies would want him to sell their products.

'Did you hear that?' Manny demanded of her. 'They had seats that would have made a difference. Do you believe that? They can't get away with this. It's wrong. You know?' Manny was serious. He paced in front of the glowing red drapes. 'I don't care about the money. You understand?' Manny was talking to the lawyer. He had a grim expression on his face. His eyes were intense. Carla assumed Manny was saying that he didn't care about money to improve his chances of getting the lawyer to ask for a lot. She knew that he cared about the money, that he had been poor his entire life, that he blamed everything on his lack of money, probably even the crash. It was ridiculous hearing him say he didn't care. Manny persisted in his theme. 'If they aren't made to pay for this, then they won't do anything about fixing it so other babies won't die.'

'That's the way the world is.' The lawyer cocked his head at Carla and twisted his small lips back and forth. 'Corporations don't volunteer to do the right thing. They have to be persuaded by the economics. Look at what the car companies tried to do to Ralph Nader.'

'What?' Manny asked eagerly.

The lawyer was taken aback momentarily. 'Ralph Nader, the consumer advocate?'

'I don't know about him,' Manny said freely. 'What about him?'

'The car companies – he wrote a book about unsafe cars – and they sent girls, you know, ladies of the night, to his apartment, hoping to get him into trouble. They sent a couple of goons to threaten him –'

'They did that?' Manny shook his head. He seemed truly surprised and disappointed that American corporations would behave so badly. 'What happened?'

'Didn't work. That's why we have seat belts and air bags and all –' the lawyer seemed to wind down. He came to a stop, small flat hand poised in midair, his nervous head still. 'What am I talking about?' he asked the floor.

Brillstein was like a precocious little boy, Carla thought. His hair had thinned; his pale skin was tough and there were wrinkles around his eyes and mouth; but he had the nervous energy of a smart child, an intent, asexual creature pretending to be grown up.

'How are you?' Brillstein suddenly asked Carla, pivoting on his feet, pointing his small hands at her, a teacher calling on her to answer.

She didn't. She looked back at him in a friendly way, she hoped, although she wasn't going to smile. He didn't care how she was, not really, so why answer?

'Carla . . .?' Manny said gently.

Brillstein held up a hand to stop her from answering. 'I'm here to introduce myself. This is a horrible time for you. No money, nothing the law can do will change what's happened. But you're entitled, you *deserve* to be compensated for what's happened. It could have been prevented. They could have been better prepared. If they had been more careful your son would still be alive.'

He seemed sincere. His small eyes were intent and dark with passion. She believed him. She nodded, to be encouraging, but she still said nothing, mostly because she wanted to be out of the room and back in bed. She didn't want to look at her living room with it so clean and neat.

Brillstein sat on the love seat at an angle to the couch. He perched on its edge, head slightly bowed, hands together, an aging choirboy, although of course he was Jewish. 'The airline, the plane manufacturer, all of them, they know they're in the wrong and they already want to make things right. But they need to deal with a lawyer and you need to have someone who knows –'

'We need an expert, Carla,' Manny interrupted, exasperated by the gradual logic of the lawyer's speech.

She gave Manny a dark, angry look He obviously thought she had turned into an idiot. He talked to her as if she were retarded. 'I know it's cruel to have to talk about it, to tell' – Brillstein gestured to himself – 'strangers about what happened to you and your boy. Why is it our business?' Brillstein stared down at the coffee table and shook his head. 'It's cruel.'

This is crap.

'I'm tired,' Carla said. She reached for her crutches.

'We have to have a lawyer!' Manny said and flopped his arms up and down, a frustrated bird trying to take off.

'I know,' she mumbled, annoyed.

'This is crazy,' the lawyer said and they both stared at him. 'I know this is a crazy process. But I have to know, any lawyer would have to know, what happened to you during the crash. If you don't want to tell me directly, that's okay. I have a tape recorder' – he gestured toward the hall – 'in my bag and I can leave it and you can tell it to the machine or you can tell your husband and he can tell it to the machine.'

'She doesn't have to go to court?' Manny asked with wonder and hope.

'Oh, I don't think we'll go to court. I don't think anybody's going to want to go to court about this. They want to settle. They want to negotiate. But I have to have the facts – and that's all that your telling me would be for – so I can know what the facts are before talking with them. If I don't know what happened to you I can't even start to have that conversation with them. I'm not promising you won't have to give a deposition – do you know what that is?'

Carla nodded. She knew. 'People in the neighborhood,' she said quietly, 'have given depositions.'

Brillstein laughed suddenly and quite hard at that. 'I bet they have,' he said. 'You're a funny person,' he said and then looked solemn. 'I admire you for your strength.'

'I don't remember what happened,' Carla said. 'You can leave your tape recorder but there's nothing I got to say.'

'You blanked out? You have no memory?' Brillstein came right to the edge of the love seat, his knees thrust forward. The glass table seemed about to cut them in half. 'Have you told her doctors?' he asked Manny.

'Well . . .' he stammered.

'Why?' Carla asked. 'Why do they have to know?'

'You know, I handle quite a few medical malpractice and accident cases. I know a little bit about medicine. Memory loss can be caused physiologically. Probably it's not. But that should be checked.'

'Oh, they checked her brain!' Manny said with an enthusiasm that irritated Carla. 'They gave her a scan, all that. She's fine.'

He's always saying you're fine.

'You should check again,' Brillstein addressed Carla. He seemed to really care. 'You know, those scans are accurate and yet there's always the ability of the technician reading it and sometimes the scans can miss something. You may have developed a problem since then. I don't mean to scare you,' the lawyer put a hand on Carla's arms. He had to leave the love seat altogether to reach her, but he didn't stand up, he remained squatting in the air on an invisible seat. 'But you should have another CAT scan of the brain.'

Carla was scared. What did he think was happening to her? A brain tumor? Her heart pounded and she was afraid.

Of what? Not of death. She wanted to die.

But not because of a silent killer in her brain. Not of some cancer eating away at her, dissolving her into bone and dead skin, like her poor papa.

189

'What could it be?' she asked Brillstein.

'I don't know,' Brillstein stood up and turned partly toward Manny. 'But if you can't remember anything –'

'I can remember!' Carla said, desperate to be released from the lawyer's death sentence.

'What!' Manny said.

'Of course you can,' the lawyer nodded without surprise. 'I'll be right back.' He walked out to the hall.

He tricked you.

'Are you playing games, Carla?' Manny asked, so angry he was squinting, his eyes wanting to squeeze the truth out of her.

'I remember it happening,' she said nervously.

The lawyer was back. 'Here's the tape recorder. If you want me to be your lawyer –'

'You're our lawyer,' Manny said, his voice deep and furious.

'Great,' Brillstein said without excitement. He put a red tape recorder on the glass table. 'Tape's loaded. Just press Play and that hole right there is a microphone. You don't have to get that close to it, just talk in a normal tone, and say what you can remember. That's all I need. And if it turns out you don't feel like giving a deposition, we can talk about that. What you remember for me and what you remember for the world, who knows? Maybe they're not the same thing. It's not their right to know everything. You haven't committed a crime. You didn't crash that plane. You're a victim. I'm your lawyer, whatever you say to me is in confidence. You know what that means. No one else has to know.'

'I don't remember very much,' Carla sulked. 'That's all I meant.'

'And anything you remember and say on that tape is

for me and me alone.' The lawyer pointed at Manny. 'Even your husband shouldn't hear it.' He smiled widely at Manny, but only for a second.

'Why not?' Manny asked, frowning. 'You said before she could tell me and I could tell the tape.'

'I did?' Brillstein was astonished. He stared at the glass table as if it were a mirror and he could check if the image reflected was his own. 'Well, forget that. I was totally in error.' The lawyer looked up and said sternly at Carla, 'For legal reasons you have to promise me that just you and I will know what you say on the tape. At least for now.' He stood waiting for an answer, folding his small hands at his groin, an attentive pupil.

This time she knew he was lying. There were no legal reasons. He wanted to fool her into feeling safe about talking. Carla nodded.

Brillstein turned to Manny. 'I mean it. It's important that you not hear it.'

Manny shrugged. 'You're the boss.'

'So –' the lawyer almost sang the word, releasing a puff of air and clapping his hands softly. 'We're settled?'

Manny nodded gravely. 'Yes, sir,' he said.

The two men walked together into the hall. Manny whispered something. Brillstein answered in a normal tone. Carla didn't bother to eavesdrop. She stared at the tape recorder. Its plastic cover looked cheap. The red paint was laid on so thinly you could almost see through to the transistors inside. But Brillstein was nice and respectable, dressed in a beige suit and a tie. She knew he couldn't be trusted but she didn't feel he was dangerous to her.

'I'll help you get back to the bedroom,' Manny said

when he returned alone. He nodded at the tape recorder. 'Or you can talk to it here.'

'Not now,' Carla moaned. A reflex. She should have said nothing; pretended to agree.

'Honey,' Manny whined. He twisted his body, wriggling with irritation. 'It's just so Mr Brillstein can get started. He's the only one's gonna hear it. It's like talking to a priest.'

Talking to Father Conti after the funeral: he had bowed his head and covered her hand with his soft doughy palms, mumbled something about pain, and said, 'You know, He also lost a son.'

'But I'm not God,' Carla had answered and then cried so hard she couldn't hear what else the priest said.

She hadn't answered Manny and he stamped his foot, not very hard, but hard enough to make the glass coffee table vibrate. 'Listen to me, Carla! If you don't tell him what he needs to know then he can't do his job!'

'Manny . . .' She meant to shout back at him, but her voice was weak and trembling. 'Just –' she lost her breath she was so upset. 'Just –' she sighed to let out the nervous air and take in something calmer to keep her going. 'Just let me rest a little. You go out. I need you to go out.'

'I gotta go back to work anyway. It's the middle of the day. I'm gonna get fired the way I'm fucking up.' He moved to go and then hesitated. 'You need anything? I'll tell your mother on my way out.'

'Tell her to leave me alone for a while.'

Manny nodded solemnly. He kissed her on the forehead. His lips were wet.

Their moist impression dried slowly and coldly in the air-conditioned room. She kept a close watch on the orderliness around her, as if it might spontaneously change.

Her mother came in to ask if Carla wanted something to eat or drink. Manny must have told her about the meeting with the lawyer on his way out because she glanced at the tape recorder immediately and yet didn't ask about it. Carla told her she didn't want anything and sent her away. Again, she studied the dead room.

She remembered a newborn Bubble by the window, being shown off to all the relatives, wrapped in a blanket and half-buried in a big clumsy carriage.

She remembered carrying him in for middle-of-night feedings so he wouldn't disturb Manny. Not often. Only when Bubble was restless. In the bedroom his crying could pierce through the door, cross the hall, and wail in their room. Besides there was nothing as comfortable as the couch.

She had held her baby so close: hot and wriggling against her in the quiet apartment. His hunger pulled at her breast. The drapes were tinted amber by the streetlights and only an occasional drunken song or mysterious explosion would startle Bubble. They were so alone and so safe.

She didn't cry at the vivid memory.

She couldn't tell the truth but she could tell them what they needed. She pressed the Play button and talked.

AN UNEXAMINED LIFE

13

Max answered the television reporter's question, asked
by Ellen Kaku, the same Japanese-American woman
who had blocked his way home the day before, while
something that had bothered him all night, percolating
underneath his duties as a survivor, continued to worry
him. He talked into the microphone without energy: 'I
didn't have time to think. I just got Byron here,' he
gestured down to the eager dirty blond head of hair
leaning against his arm, 'out of his seat –'

'I was upside down!' Byron interrupted with enthusiasm.

'Were you stuck?' Kaku moved the mike from Max's
mouth down to the little boy's level.

'I had the seat belt on! It was stuck!'

'So you *did* save his life?' Kaku demanded of Max
with a stern look and sharp tone. She had obviously
decided he could not be trusted to tell all.

It was at that moment, standing on the corner of 84th
and West End, surrounded by two interrogating television crews and a crowd of eavesdropping neighbors,
that Max realized what had bothered him all through
the sleepless night, his first night home after the crash.

'Is that right, Mr Klein?' another reporter called out.
'You saved both this little boy's life and also the
baby's?'

Max heard the question. He did not answer because
the implication of Jeff's scam with the tickets had
finished brewing in his head. When their presentation to

Nutty Nick was postponed a week Jeff had switched the plans so they would arrive on the day of the appointment. He said he was being considerate of Nan, that it shortened how long she would be stuck with their two kids. The truth was: Jeff had picked that flight because he had gotten a deal on it. They were traveling to a meeting that over the course of a few years could be worth a million dollars in fees and Jeff had arranged that they would arrive with only two hours to spare for the sake of a couple hundred bucks.

That's why Jeff had been killed. God had severed his head for his small-mindedness and he deserved it too and there was nothing to feel bad about.

'I didn't save anybody,' Max said to the reporter, pissed off that they were presenting him to the public as a hero.

It had begun the night before, without his knowledge, after he got back from delivering his bad news to Nan. He had been home five minutes when Byron's parents phoned to say the boy needed to see him. Byron's father had gotten his number through somebody who knew somebody at TransCon. He introduced himself as Peter Hummel and apologized for the intrusion but explained that his son was still in a state of terror, unable to sleep or eat. What Byron demanded over and over was to be with the man who saved his life. Naturally Max agreed to their request that they bring him by.

Again Debby was annoyed, now at the late hour (it was past eleven at night) as well as by Max's willingness to give up time with her for others. She wouldn't admit that was the reason; she claimed she was thinking of Max, that he needed to rest. He had just gotten home from Nan's, she pointed out; he had not had a minute to himself.

'Dr Perlman said you need peace and quiet,' she said. Max laughed. Debby flushed, embarrassed. 'You're laughing at me.'

'I'm sorry, but that sounds ridiculous.'

'Don't you want to be left alone?' Debby demanded.

'When did you talk to Dr Perlman?'

'He called while you were at Nan's. He's nice. He's trying to help.'

Max shook his head, dismayed by her eagerness to accept help without studying the giver's motive. That was her vulnerable point. The back injury that threatened and eventually ended her fledgling ballet career was his prime example: she was too willing and too grateful to Max for nursing her through her attempted comebacks and finally comforting her over the death of her ambition. You're so kind, she used to say. Actually he had been full of lust and selfishness. 'Perlman is around to make the airline seem compassionate,' Max told her. 'He's paid to be nice.'

There was only half an hour to argue about it, or rather to sulk (Debby disappeared to take a bath), since Byron and his parents lived in Greenwich Village and were leaving immediately. Max went into Jonah's room. He was still awake, lying under the covers fully dressed, a recent fetish that used to worry Max but now seemed unimportant, even benign. Max suggested they move into the living room and watch the end of the game on television. Jonah was surprised by this violation of normal bedtime regulations and happily agreed. Debby appeared in a huge terry-cloth bathrobe just as the doorman buzzed that Byron and his parents were coming up. She stayed in it, with her hair wet, an obvious statement that she didn't want guests.

Max introduced Byron to Jonah, who had to be coaxed even to mumble a hello, and they shook hands with his parents, Peter and Diane Hummel. Both families sat down together and listened to Byron's excited account of the crash. Some of it wasn't accurate, Max thought; Byron was exaggerating Max's actions. He said Max had wrested him out of a stuck seat belt and pulled him through flames and billowing smoke and 'gross dead bodies' and found a way out when there didn't seem to be one. He also claimed that Max had called to others in the plane and they had followed him to safety. 'He saved at least twenty people!' Byron insisted. The child's story dissipated Debby's lingering anger at Max. She teared up, came by the couch where Max, Byron and Jonah were seated, and kissed Max on the top of his head, a hand squeezing his shoulder. Jonah reacted less sentimentally, at least on the surface. Although his face did flush, his shy brown eyes were clear; he watched Byron from under lowered and suspicious brows. Of course at that hour and given the tension of the past day and a half, maybe Jonah was just tired. As for Byron, he interrupted his narrative to hug Max several times with a kind of showy affection. He leaned his head against Max's chest, bright face smiling back at his parents, posed for their benefit as if Max and he were a postcard he wanted to send home.

Byron's parents, who Max decided without any evidence other than their sloppy preppie clothes and their diffident manners were rich, weren't embarrassed by their son's emotional behavior. Nor were they emotional. What they said expressed thanks, but it was pronounced with a cool sophisticated manner.

'I guess there's no way to express how grateful we

are,' Peter Hummel commented after his son's account was finished.

'I really didn't do all that,' Max answered gently, ashamed to contradict Byron.

'Yes, you did,' Byron insisted 'I would have been fried if you hadn't gotten me out. I watched. It got all burned up. A fireman said there were people still alive in there they couldn't get out.'

'Oh, *that* could be true,' Max said.

'God,' Debby mumbled. She covered her face with her hands and sighed loudly. She quickly uncovered and looked at Max with shining wet eyes.

'I don't know if talking about the danger helps make anyone feel better,' Peter said to his son.

'I think he needs to talk it out,' Diane said to her husband. She turned to Debby. 'I'm sorry.'

'You don't seem scared,' Jonah said to Byron. He mumbled this comment to his knees. They undulated as he restlessly kicked his legs out and back.

'What?' Byron asked. His parents also glanced at Jonah inquisitively. Evidently only Max had heard his son's statement. Max understood its origin. He had explained to Jonah that Byron was coming over because he was still frightened from the crash and his parents believed seeing Max would help. Max thought it was a good question. He wondered also – Byron seemed happy to him.

'Nothing,' Jonah mumbled, embarrassed to have everyone's attention. He lowered his head more, hair coming down over his light brown eyes, covering their curiosity.

'What did you say?' Byron asked. He had an energetic body. He was beside Jonah on the couch. He twisted all the way around to ask, one hand touching Jonah's thigh to prompt him.

'It was a good question, Jonah,' Max urged him. 'Ask it.'

'I –' Jonah waved his hand and stammered, 'I – don't want to. Forget it.'

'He said, "You don't seem scared,"' Max revealed his son's remark. He wouldn't have before the change. He was always supportive of his little boy, even of his weaknesses.

'Max . . .' Debby warned softly.

Byron blinked at Max for a moment and then said in a plain simple tone, the excitement gone, 'I'm not scared when I'm with you.'

Diane appeared moved. Until then Max had thought her self-possession beyond upset. Her deep tan and shiny black hair, gathered into a demure bun, seemed to make her inscrutable and coldhearted. But he noticed her sharp chin pucker inward. She ducked her head slightly and shaded her eyes with one hand. Was she crying?

Byron's father continued to be cool, although polite. 'He's been very upset,' he commented to Max. 'You seem to make him feel safe.'

'I'm sure that's temporary,' Debby said.

Byron and his parents looked at her. Max didn't know whether she meant she hoped it would go away soon, or if she was consoling Byron's father for losing his natural role toward his son.

'He also saved a baby,' Byron said to Debby, obviously concluding that she didn't realize what a paragon she had married. 'I told the mommy who you were,' he added to Max.

'Yes, that's right,' Peter said. 'Just before we called you, a woman called us, evidently the mother?' he asked Byron.

'Yeah! She's the one you gave the baby to,' he said to Max, excited.

'You saw that? I thought you were with the Red Cross by then,' Max argued. He was worried by this child's determination to reshape what they had experienced into something that couldn't fit into his own memory.

'I was watching you from the ambulance!' Byron explained. He turned to Jonah to tell him this amazing fact: 'Your dad just walked out of the airport.'

'Um,' Peter signaled he had something important to say, 'the mother, her name is Paula Pavod – I think that's how you pronounce it – said she knew that you had also rescued Byron and so she was calling us in case we knew who you were. We gave her your name, or rather Byron did – I hope you don't mind.'

And so, because of Paula Pavod and other survivors, by the next morning Max was considered to be a hero – and not merely the savior of Byron and the Pavod baby. He was also supposed to have played pied piper to another twenty or so passengers lost in the burning plane. Max found out that he was a public figure at seven-thirty in the morning on his way out to put Jonah on his bus to day camp. The doorman showed Max a *New York Post* that credited him with saving four children, an elderly woman, and a flight attendant. Max was surprised that the *Post* had assembled all these accounts of his rescue efforts without speaking to him. But the *Daily News* explained the lack of contact with its headline, GOOD SAMARITAN SAVES TOTS AND

DISAPPEARS, again shown to him by the doorman. Max stopped inside the outer doors, reading the *News* to find out where the press thought he was. Jonah poked him in the side.

'Dad! Look who's here.'

From their position they could see the 84th Street corner. There a mob had gathered, at the center of which were two television crews interviewing, of all people, Byron.

Byron and his diffident father had been waylaid as they got out of a cab intending to visit Max again. The boy's insomnia had continued even after last night's get-together; he had refused to attend his day camp (a different one from Jonah's, thank goodness) unless he saw Max first. Byron's father had tried to call ahead but Debby had taken the phone off the hook before going to bed and he couldn't get through.

Max was immediately sucked into being interviewed with an eager Byron by his side. And so he had his revelation that Jeff deserved to die while denying his own heroics. Besides, his revelation wasn't irrelevant to Kaku's questions, in fact, she provoked his silent verdict. She asked Max his reason for switching his seat to be with Byron, and that emphasized to him why his decision on Jeff's fate was so important. Max had deserted his dead partner. He knew he was ashamed of his desertion because he had concealed it from Nan. That hadn't been difficult; she didn't ask about how Jeff died, presumably too upset to hear details. And now Nan would learn it from the tabloids, find out in big black type that her husband's best friend had left him to die alone. This false life Max had returned to, this ghostly existence that he inhabited only in form and not in substance, was overcrowded with people, errands and moral ambiguities. While he said to the reporters, 'No, I didn't pull an old woman out from between seats. No, I didn't rescue a brother and sister who were buried underneath dead bodies. No, I didn't pull the baby out of a burning seat. No, I didn't show the way out for dozens of people. No, I didn't leap into flames to save Byron,' while he fended off their accusations of heroism he sagged at the dreary list of chores ahead: he had to go to the office; he had to call Nutty Nick; he had to get Jonah on the camp bus.

In fact, the bus had come and, atypically, was waiting patiently. Jonah's campers peered in awe at the mob of cameras and celebrity television reporters. A friend called and waved to Jonah.

'Dad!' Jonah interrupted another of Kaku's hostile questions. She was still convinced that Max wasn't giving her everything. 'Dad, can I get on my bus?'

Max bent over to give his boy a hug goodbye; he was immediately pushed back by his son's hand. He escorted Jonah to the bus. The mob of reporters (led by Kaku) and gawkers inched along with them. He waved goodbye and felt he was alone, more alone than ever, more alone even than when he had showered in the Sheraton and understood that Jeff was gone and his life was forever changed. Once the bus drove off, the reporters crowded him again. He backed away a few feet. They moved after him in a carnivorous movement, a hungry herd. Max felt hot and he couldn't breathe. His legs wanted to go. He abruptly turned the other way on West End and broke into a full run, ignoring the shouts from abandoned reporters and forgetting as well that he had promised Debby he would have a leisurely breakfast with her.

He remembered five blocks later. He saw a phone booth on Riverside and ran to it.

'Hello.' Debby was angry, prepared to hang up.

'Hi, it's me.'

Her tone changed: anger to relief. 'Where are you?'

'There's a mob – I'm not kidding you – a mob of reporters downstairs –'

'Oh, the phone has been ringing nonstop. I tried to call my mother and it started. Really. I can't even begin to dial. They say you saved all these people. Is that true? Why aren't you telling me these things? You just say you got this boy out –'

'It's not true. I did carry a baby out. But he was right next to me. Not – I don't know – buried in the flames or whatever the hell they're saying –' he sighed. The gray plastic receiver smelled of sauerkraut, a peculiar odor for eight in the morning.

'Max.' Debby had the irritation back in her tone. 'Where are you?'

'Uh, I'm on Riverside Drive.'

'Max.' She said his name as if making a statement about his character, with a note of finality. 'Come home.'

Last night they had lain together after Jonah went to sleep. They made love in slow motion. Her orgasm was as gentle and suppressed as a child sobbing into a pillow. Max, although he was fully erect and felt each detail of the pleasure of being inside her, couldn't climax. He was embarrassed and annoyed. Debby pulled at him to continue but when he did it was she who was again moved into passion and release, this time bucking and moaning with joy. They stayed joined for a time in the dark, lying still while Max waited – for what he didn't know.

'What's wrong?' she asked.

He pulled out: stiff, alive, and unsatisfied.

'I'm frigid,' he said.

She held his penis and kissed him. 'What can I do?' she said.

He laughed.

'What do you want?' she asked.

'I want you to save me,' he said.

But she didn't know from what or how and he didn't either. She got sadder and sadder as she asked questions that sounded straight out of a self-help book or from a therapist's mouth. It seemed to Max as if his being alive made his wife sad. He tried to convince himself she was unhappy at the thought he had almost died, but he didn't succeed. She was disappointed in him. She had been disappointed in him for years. He didn't know why. Probably because he *was* her life, or a great part of it, and that life, the life of a thwarted artist, was a letdown. But what did these distinctions matter? The end was the same: she would be better off with him dead; then his absence, not his presence, would be what made her sad.

Think of Nan. She had never shown anything but annoyance or disdain for Jeff and yet last night, as his widow, she had been magnificent in her love.

'He was my big boy, my crazy boy,' she mumbled in Max's ear. 'We were just kids when I married him and we fucked it up,' she choked, her warm breasts palpitating against Max, her strong hands digging into his back. Nan cried on Max's shoulder but the passion of her grief reminded him more of lovemaking than of sorrow.

These were dangerous ideas and he didn't want to have them.

'No, I can't face those reporters,' Max told the phone. 'They're asking me crazy stuff. I stand there saying I didn't do it, I didn't do it, like I'm a criminal.'

'It's disgusting. I'll call the police and they'll get rid of them.'

Max laughed. Well, she was trying to help him, anyway, even if she wanted to turn the job over to others. That tilted his head back and he caught sight of the West Side Highway and beyond it, the edge of park on the river. He could get near to the water there. He thought he remembered there was a wall or a low fence or something that would bar him from actually touching it, but he could get very close. 'I'll call you later,' he said.

'Max!' her voice caught him from escaping.

'What?'

'I want you to come home.'

'Not now.' This wasn't a conversation with his wife; he was arguing with his widowed mom, expecting him to leave the stickball game early to relieve her loneliness.

'Fine. You don't want to see me, that's –' she made some sort of noise and then resumed with studied calm: 'I want you to call Dr Mayer.'

She referred to his shrink in so formal a way because she didn't know him and they rarely discussed him. Bill Mayer was quite old now, semi-retired. Max was thirteen when his mother first made an appointment with the psychiatrist, concerned about the effect on Max of his father's sudden death. Throughout his adolescence, whenever Max failed to be the A-student, the compassionate son, the loving brother, his mother would call Dr Mayer. In fact, for several years Max's therapy was largely consumed by discussions with Dr Mayer about his mother's use of it as a kind of punishment. Eventually Mayer went so far as to talk directly to his mother, suggesting that she leave it up to Max whether he continued therapy. Didn't do a bit of good; one sulking look from Max and Mom would ask if she should schedule an extra session.

Debby had never invoked the good doctor, however. Threatening Max with mental health was a first for his wife.

'Fuck you,' Max said mildly and hung up. That was the end of that relationship. Who needs marriage anyway? Max decided. What was it but a way to personify life's inadequacies?

He crossed Riverside Drive. Something honked at him. A jogger brushed past and cursed. The West Side Highway hummed with traffic. Burning meat blew down the avenue from some restaurant or vendor. He was going to the river no matter what.

'Hey – you got change, man?'

That was a teenager. A dark-skinned, sluggish, threatening teenager, with a slight Spanish accent. His hand was slung at his side, the palm up, but close to his hip and easily made into a fist.

'No,' Max said and kept on, going for the wall that separated Riverside Park from the highway.

'Where the fuck you going?' the teenager called after him.

Max hopped the wall, a car buzzed past, and he landed in the warm air of its wake. A white van in the middle lane honked and swung to the other lane nervously.

A blue Chevy was heading at Max now, slowing, but still on the move and honking at him.

The van passed in the center. Max stepped there. A yellow truck was next. It didn't honk or slow. The driver kept coming.

Max let a black BMW go by and got out of the truck's way, running to the divider just ahead of another black car. He got up on the low wall and perched, three lanes of northbound traffic behind, three lanes of southbound ahead. Some cars swerved into the other lane at the sight of him. There was confusion and worry in the movements of some drivers; others ignored him and sped inches from his position. He was nearly blown back on to the other road by the passing blast of air. One driver threw a cigarette at him and yelled: 'Get the fuck off there, asshole!'

There was power in his legs, although they trembled on the divider. He could see details with magnified clarity. There were dried drops of black tar on the near lane, in a long dribble on the bleached concrete. There was a safety pin two lanes over, the top half smashed flat into the pavement. There was a fanned and blackened copy of *TV Guide* squashed at the far curb, inches from the small strip of grass between the highway and the Hudson, the mighty Hudson, a flowing gray mass slinking beside the bucking cars with a snake's menace.

The traffic was dense southbound. He had to wait for a break; when it came he had only a few seconds to clear the road. A trio of cars was coming fast: a brown van in the slow lane, a taxi with its hood loose in the middle, and a baby-blue Mercedes in the far lane. Max jumped on to the road and ran across their bows. He knew if he stumbled he was dead. He knew the Mercedes in the far lane might be going too fast for him. He would soon reach the water or be killed.

He dived and rolled on to the patch of grass. He heard another curse from a passing car. He felt a breeze of gritty exhaust. A beer can crumpled under his right knee. He smelled the river. Max got up. The grass grew unevenly down to the low cement breaker. Masses of cigarette butts were lined against it as if they had died trying to make the ascent.

He looked across the water and was happy again. He had forgotten this freedom in his breathing, this strength in his legs, the openness in his head, welcoming the world without any unhappy thoughts to bar the way. He had forgotten this freedom since coming home last night; once again his sinuses were clear of the fear of death. He would dive in the Hudson and swim away from the city. Why not?

'Okay, man,' said the teenager from behind him. 'How about now? You got change now?'

Max turned back toward the city. The skinny teenager had followed him across the highway. They were together on the narrow strip of grass, segregated by the road from Riverside Park. The hand was out, away from his body this time, again open to receive money, not begging, but demanding.

Max was disgusted. 'Aren't you going to tell me what you need it for?'

The hand retreated, moving to the pocket of his sagging dungarees. The teenager looked hot and unhealthy, dressed in long pants on a summer day, skinny ribs showing below a tight tank top. 'What?' he said, squinting past Max.

Was there an accomplice behind him? Max wondered. Teenagers did their evil in groups: rape or mugging, they needed support from like spirits. Grown-ups killed alone. Max looked back. There was nothing but a lane of patchy grass curving with the river. Max turned to the kid. Sweat streaked down the teenager's sideburns, flattening the kinky hairs. 'I don't have any,' Max said honestly. 'I just came downstairs to –'

The hand came out of the pocket holding a long brown-handled knife, with no blade showing. There was a short silver metal cross at the end facing Max. The teenager angled his body so that the handle was hidden from the passing traffic. There was a sliding noise and a blade appeared, flashing into view. 'Give me your fucking money or I'll cut you bad,' he talked fast and flicked the blade at Max's stomach, only a foot away. 'Hurry up, man. I don't want to fuck around. Just give me the fucking money.'

Max had left the apartment without his wallet or change. To call home he had had to use his phone credit card number. He wasn't going to plead that, however. 'Go ahead. Cut me. I don't have any money to give you.'

'Come on,' the kid stepped closer and flicked the blade at Max. 'Don't fuck around.'

It was hopeless. The world was a hopeless and stupid place. Max felt the heat of its selfishness and looked away toward the Hudson. He would die in sight of it. That at least had dignity.

Max shook his head no at the mugger, his mouth in a regretful pout.

The teenager lunged at Max's chest with the blade. Instinctively, Max moved one step to his right. He didn't shift far enough. The knife sank into him. Max lowered his head and watched as the metal disappeared into his arm and chest. He felt nothing. With the blade all the way in, the teenager's face was only inches from Max's; he stared at the point of entry, stunned, his mouth sagging open. The mugger's eyes were small and frightened. Max didn't like him. He put his hand on the kid's chest and pushed him away. He didn't want to die looking into scared eyes.

The mugger stumbled back, tripped over his feet and fell on his ass. Max felt the point of the blade in his armpit. He realized he wasn't cut. The stupid kid had stuck the knife in the space below Max's armpit, the gap between his arm and chest. He had torn Max's polo shirt, but missed everything else. For a moment the knife hung there, caught by the fabric. Max raised his arm and the switchblade fell to the ground.

The teenager jumped to his feet and ran away, heading uptown. Bewildered, Max peered into the jagged hole in his shirt. No cut, no scrape, no wound of any kind.

'They can't kill me,' he said aloud, the traffic drowning his mild tone. 'They want to kill me,' he admitted and he smiled affectionately at the West Side skyline, at the architecture of the city of his birth, 'but they can't.'

14

Max walked the fifty blocks to his office. The city was exposed to a bright sun, heating up the closely packed corridors between the tall buildings. New Yorkers walking in the oven were smoked by fumes of car exhaust and street cooking. Max watched their faces, fascinated. The midtown blocks were jammed with people of color and clothing of color and there were lots of glistening skins and bold hairdos. Max enjoyed their company, striding hard through the unbreathable air. He couldn't hear their conversation. It was too hot to hear: the city's noise was dampened into a continuous background roar. The only sound Max could distinguish was his own panting. He arrived soaked through from perspiration. His hair was dripping wet, his polo shirt stuck to his body. At the chilling touch of the office's airconditioning his skin crawled. He walked in pulling at his shirt.

They surrounded him in seconds: Gladys the bookkeeper, Scott and Warren, the two draftsmen, and Betty the secretary. Their eyes all looked puffy; Max was pleased they had cried for Jeff; pleased and a little amused. Betty was prepared to hug him but she held back at his obvious discomfort. Gladys, however, was too upset or didn't care. She rushed into Max's arms. Max didn't feel her plump squat elderly body; he got the clammy embrace of his own clothing.

'My God, Max,' Gladys said. 'What a nightmare.'

'Yes,' Max said and moved her away. He picked at

his polo shirt, peeling it off him. The shirt reclaimed him as soon as he let go. He decided decorum was preposterous. Bending over, Max pulled at what felt like his own skin. He shed it.

'Max,' Warren said with a hint of surprise at the nudity. The office wasn't formal, but it wasn't a dormitory either. In fact, Max usually wore a dress shirt, if not a jacket.

Gladys picked up the shirt and commented, 'It's torn,' in a wondering singsong, studying the hole.

'Could you get me a towel?' he asked Betty. Betty was a pretty woman in her twenties. She stared at Max's bare chest. Her look wasn't lustful. She seemed curious about her boss's chest, though. What was she thinking – Gee, his chest hairs aren't gray? Max wished she wanted him, but he was too old, and probably too something else, even if he were young. Betty was a cheerful person: she went to concerts, she danced, she laughed a lot, she cared about her long nails and her thick auburn hair, she enjoyed shopping. She was happy, that's the name for it, Max decided. I'm not. Even if I were young she'd think I was old.

Meanwhile she brought him a towel from the bathroom.

'Come into my office,' Max said. His employees followed him into his and Jeff's room. The offices were the front half of a loft, rented from a comic book distributer who used the windowless back half for storage. The draftsmen had space with a window on an alley; Gladys and Betty were opposite with a view of a parking lot. The partners had the large front room to themselves, their desks side by side, facing two floor-to-ceiling windows overlooking Seventh Avenue and the concrete bunkers of the Fashion Institute of Technology, an ugly view that Max liked to believe was an encouragement. No design of his, no matter how practical or commercial, was as defeated as what he looked at.

Max was unmoved by the sight of Jeff's desk. The empty chair and spread of unfinished designs weren't poignant or even unusual. It was normal for Jeff to be away, busy with lots of errands and family emergencies and long lunches and of course his daily hour in the gym from eleven to twelve. The deserted workstation, ready for his return, was more embittering than heart-tugging.

'Everyone's called,' Gladys said.

'Yeah, practically every client,' Scott said and sighed, as if he were exhausted by all the conversations.

'We're so proud of what you did,' Betty said. She flashed an embarrassed smile, a girlish smile.

'What I did?' Max looked at his cleared desk, at the row of perfectly sharpened pencils that he always made sure to leave ready to greet him the next morning, tips clean and sleek, ready to be his dutiful tools. He turned away from them.

'The children,' Gladys said. Scott and Warren nodded respectfully.

'You were so brave,' Betty said. Max understood why Betty was peering at his bare chest: she was looking for signs of the crash.

'Thank you. I know this is as much a shock to you as it is to me or Jeff's family. He spent as much time here –' Max stopped, thinking, No, he didn't. 'Anyway, I know you're all feeling upset but I want to give you as much notice as possible. We have – what do you think, Warren? – about three months' work?'

'I guess,' Warren said reluctantly.

'I don't want to keep the firm going after that. Even if we complete the work sooner than three months – in fact, I'd like us to get it done as fast as possible – but even if we finish it this week, you'll all be on salary through October. You can start looking for jobs right away and I'll help out, think up people to call, give recommendations –'

'Max,' Gladys lowered her usually high pitch, as if the deeper sound couldn't be heard by the others. 'Not now. Don't make decisions right now.'

'I know what you're thinking. And it makes sense. But it isn't like that. I intend to go on working. But I drew these houses,' he gestured at the Zuckerman Long Island drawings, 'and Nutty Nick stores for money. I liked doing it, partly because I liked supporting my family and being part of the world. Who was I to think I could do better than anyone else? I eat at McDonald's. I even kind of look forward to their french fries. So why should I disdain their architecture? I've never met a king, how can I expect to build cathedrals? I don't even know the CEO of a corporation, so who am I to think I should be designing Citicorp?'

The four people he employed looked back at him with the attentive and uncomprehending stares of kindergartners politely waiting for snack time.

'Don't you see the mistake I made? It has nothing to do with whether I'm good enough to design what I want to design. I don't have to be entitled to it. I don't have to have talent. I don't need permission. All I need is my own desire. If that's strong enough then I'm strong enough.'

'Money,' Scott objected. He was always the practical

one, suggesting that elements of the sketches handed to him couldn't be engineered easily or cheaply. He was usually correct. 'You need money.'

'Yes, that's true,' Max said. 'If I want to see my drawings built I need money. If I want to eat I need money. That's true. But Jeff has given me that.' Max gestured at the vacant swivel chair, its owner not exercising or fighting with his wife or schmoozing with clients. Its owner was beheaded in a body bag. 'He's given me the one thing he couldn't give me while alive. He's set me free.'

Young Betty blinked and looked at her elders, as if suddenly Max had broken into a foreign language and they could translate. Scott smirked. Warren lowered his head. Gladys stared, mouth open, her hands going to her hips. 'Max, have you lost your mind?' she demanded.

'I know I sound heartless. I'm not. It's the truth. You have time and effort invested here and you deserve the truth. Gladys, you've worked here for ten years. I want you to know the truth. I hated working with Jeff. I loved it and I hated it. He was the weak part of me and it's been killed and I won't bring it back to life.'

'I can't listen to this,' Gladys said. She turned to go, groaned, and looked back. Her cheeks wobbled, her eyes teared up. 'You're upset,' she told Max and left.

Betty followed Gladys out, although her eyes didn't want to go; she turned her head to look back as she exited, squinting at her boss curiously.

Warren stepped back against the bulletin board. He was in his fifties and his talents and personality didn't quite make up for his lack of skill. He cringed at the touch of the board's thumbtacks, but they seemed to prod him into speech: 'It's a bad time to look –' he began and then thought better of it.

'Bad time for what?' Max asked.

'To look for work,' Scott explained. He had both talent and aggression, except for what he claimed was his true ambition, painting. 'You know that. Real estate's soft, there's tons of commercial space. Architects aren't hiring. They're laying off.' Scott shrugged. He had long blond hair that he kept in a ponytail. He liked to stroke it thoughtfully and a predictable look of happy abstraction would come over him. He mumbled, 'I don't care. I can collect unemployment and do some real painting.'

'Max! Line one.' Gladys poked her head in the door-way. She sounded furious. 'It's your psychiatrist!' She disappeared.

Max laughed. So did Scott. He even let go of his ponytail. Warren straightened up and seemed alarmed.

'That's funny,' Max called after her.

Warren pointed to Max's phone. 'She wasn't kid-ding.'

A light was flashing. Max picked up warily.

'Hello, Max, how are you?' Dr Mayer's squeaky lisping voice came over the phone. Disembodied, it resembled a Mel Blanc voice – Daffy Doctor or Sammy Shrink. 'Your wife phoned me. She's very concerned about your state of mind. I wasn't paying attention to the news broadcasts and I didn't know you were in that plane. Otherwise I would have called on my own.'

This was one of the longest speeches Bill Mayer had ever made to Max. 'Debby really called you?' Max said.

'Yes. She's worried about you. But, as I say, that isn't why I called. Would you like to come in? Anytime's all right. I can move things around, if necessary.' 'Necessary' was squeaked and lisped loudly, making it sound as if Dr Mayer were using a walkie-talkie.

'Maybe later or tomorrow. There's a lot I have to take care of.'

'I told you the flight would be safe,' Mayer said.

'Yes, you did.'

'I'm sorry. I understand that Jeff died in the crash?'

'Are we having a session?'

'I'm here for you to talk to, Max. That's all. I don't want you to feel emotionally isolated. I know that's your pattern when something bad happens.'

'This wasn't bad, Bill.'

'I know. It must have been horrifying.'

'Actually, it was kind of great.' Max rolled the row of pencils back and forth. He noticed Warren leave the room. Scott, however, stayed, stroking his ponytail. Max rolled the pencils faster. One of them spun away and landed on the floor.

'In what way was it great?'

'I'm not scared anymore. The worst has happened and I'm not scared anymore.' Max's heart pounded. He rolled all the pencils off the table.

'Un huh.' This was one of the few things Bill Mayer could say without squeaking or lisping. It was also the doctor's most frequently used sound. Max often wondered if that's why Bill had become a psychiatrist.

Max's heart thumped in his ears. His throat swelled. He was strangling in his own blood. 'I'm going to be myself from now on, Doctor. No more hiding.' The pressure was gone. Max inhaled easily. His chest felt sore, but his heart was quiet.

'I'm glad you've found something good in it.'

'I got mugged this morning.'

'No shit,' Scott mumbled.

'Were you hurt?' Mayer asked.

'No. Nothing seems to hurt me these days.'

'I'm surprised you're at the office. I would have thought you'd want to stay home.'

'I was going to stay home. Anyway, I have to go.'

'I understand. Would you like to set up a time for an appointment?'

Max thought about what he had just claimed for himself, that he would not hide anymore. He smiled. 'I don't have to go, Bill. What I meant was, I don't want to talk to you anymore. If I do, I'll call.'

'Fine, Max. That's fine,' Mayer lisped gently.

Max hung up and dried himself with paper towels. He spread his torn polo shirt on the air-conditioner vents. Then he picked up his scattered pencils. Gladys called in: 'Your mother's on the phone.'

'Can't talk to her. Tell her I'll call her back.'

This brought Gladys into his office, hands on hips, and scolding: '*You* tell her. She's upset. She's worried about you. She asked me how I thought you were and I don't want to tell her I think you're acting cuckoo.'

'Tell her I'm cuckoo. Tell her I'll call her back. I don't want to talk to her.'

His tone was commanding. Gladys blinked, surprised by it. 'That's really what you want me to say?'

'Yes.'

Scott hadn't left the room. He was slumped against the wall, stroking his ponytail. His eyes were glazed.

'Get out of here, Scott. I want privacy and you should be stroking yourself in the bathroom.'

'What?' Scott asked, startled.

'Go. Out.'

'What did you say?' Scott moved back. He had let go of his tail. He bumped into the door frame. Young Betty appeared next to him.

'Oh, I forgot to tell you,' she said, her eyes lowered, her tone soft, head bowed fearfully. 'Mr Lobell called yesterday. He said he needed to talk to you as soon as possible.'

Mr Lobell was the real-world incarnation of Nutty Nick, the man Jeff had literally died trying to impress. Jeff had met him once; Max had only spoken to him on the phone. 'Okay,' Max said. 'What's his number?'

'I'll get him for you,' Betty said, her head up, her tone bright. She left. Scott smirked at Max as if he'd caught him at something. From the hallway they both heard Warren ask Betty in an excited, hopeful whisper: 'He's calling him?'

'I'm leaving,' Scott said and did, with the smirk still in place.

Max put his damaged shirt back on. It made him shiver. His nipples hardened. He reflected that he had gotten laid twice in the past twenty-four hours. Not since he and Debby were creating Jonah had he enjoyed such frequency. Then it had been with the same woman, of course. He wasn't a Catholic and yet the unprotected sex of deliberate procreation had felt more deep and intimate than when the act was only self-indulgent. He longed to repeat those weeks of determined love – to make a second child. They could leave Jonah with Debby's parents for a week and fly to Europe (now that the air was terrorless) and he could witness the uncompromised architecture of the Old World (now that his artistic failure was painless) and they could fuck in hotel beds and on hotel rugs and in hotel baths . . . The daydream was interrupted by Max remembering that he had ended his marriage that morning. Well, so what? he thought and allowed the images to resume. Married or not, it was still a fantasy.

'It's Mr Lobell,' young Betty said in an intense low tone. She had entered all the way into Max's office to deliver this news. 'He's on one.'

Max turned away from Jeff's desk as he lifted the receiver, hiding his face from his dead partner's post, so that Jeff wouldn't see him turn down Nutty Nick. Max didn't believe in ghosts, but why take a chance? 'Mr Lobell?'

'Just a moment,' a male voice said. Silence, then a booming voice: 'Hello!'

'Mr Lobell? This is Max Klein.'

'Hi. How are you? You look all right. I just saw you on CNN in front of your apartment building. With your son. Where's he going on the bus? To camp? Isn't it late for camp to be starting?'

'It's a day camp.'

'Isn't he old for day camp?'

'No one's too old for day camp.'

Lobell's big voice chuckled. 'Hee – hee – hee,' he laughed in a deep tone, like a storybook giant. 'Well, he has a very brave father. I'm glad you weren't hurt. But I'm sorry, very sorry about Mr Gordon. I liked him.'

'He was a good –' Max stopped himself. Lying was so easy, almost impossible to avoid. 'He was a close friend,' he amended.

'I also wanted to tell you not to worry about the presentation. I've made other arrangements.'

'You've hired other architects?' Max was startled, not

upset. That had been quick. It meant there had been competition all along, racing beside them at the same pace.

'Yes. Other things being equal, if the designs you came up with were as good as what you did with the Long Island store, I probably would have hired you, but – well, to be honest, I'm a superstitious man. I'm sorry. You don't need to hear any more bad news, but I felt I owed it to you to tell you directly.'

'What do you mean,' Max wondered, partly to himself, although he spoke aloud, 'that you're a superstitious man?'

'You know. Anyway, I expect a bill for the preliminary drawings. Please extend my sympathies to Mrs Gordon –'

'Excuse me.' Max couldn't let this mystery go. 'What do you mean, I know? I don't know what you mean when you say you're superstitious.'

'Well, you were on your way to see me and you couldn't get here. So I feel there's a jinx . . .' The giant's voice hesitated, flustered by embarrassment.

'You mean I've got bad luck and you don't want to catch it?'

'No, no, no,' the giant said, almost chuckling. He had the false good cheer of a man in a Santa Claus suit. 'This project requires a lot of immediate attention. Obviously you're going to need time to adjust to this tragedy. We'll work together in the future. Thank you for –'

'Yeah, goodbye,' Max hung up rudely. He hadn't felt angry until Nutty Nick lied. In fact, he had been grateful to hear his previous, truthful statement of worry that Max was jinxed. Max had survived all these attempted killings, he thought he was lucky to be alive, that he was overflowing with good fortune. That was wrong-headed. Nutty Nick was right. All these events were bad luck. He was dogged by bad luck, by the malicious actions of an evil god.

Was it punishment? The therapists would line up from New York to China to tell him it wasn't. But they wouldn't make much of a living informing their patients that they deserved their fates.

Okay, it is punishment, Max decided. What for? What did he do? Abandon his ambitious plans? No, not for that. Everyone had jumped off the ship of ideals. A huge asteroid would be on its way to pulverize the earth if that were a serious crime.

Gladys interrupted. 'Max, a Mr Brillstein is on the phone. He says he's your lawyer.' She had her hands on her hips again, a scolding posture

'I'm sorry you don't approve,' Max said.

'It's not up to me to approve,' Gladys flung her hands out, tossing the subject away. 'Maybe you *should* close the business. I just think you shouldn't be making decisions right now. You shouldn't turn down a job like Nutty Nick, the kind of success you've worked so hard for. You've wanted a job like that for years. You've killed yourself to get it –' She was revved up, pacing in a tight circle, full of passionate feeling and mistaken history.

'Gladys –' Max stopped her, hand up, a smile on his face. 'Mr. Lobell called to tell me that, because of the crash, he isn't hiring us.'

'What?' Gladys asked this of the rug, as if something hideous and unknown had erupted at her feet.

'And, believe me, I wasn't working hard all these

years to figure out the best way to display programmable VCRs next to microwave ovens.'

Gladys ignored his sarcasm, because that's all it was to her, Max realized. All these years she had thought his most profound statements were the talk of a wise guy. 'He's not giving you the job because of the crash?'

'Well, we're jinxed. We're on our way to see him with the prototype drawings and the plane crashes. Who wants to invest millions in a design scheme made up by people with such bad luck?'

'That's disgusting.' Gladys mumbled this as she shuffled out. She slumped, aging as she walked away. She was beaten. She had encountered a human act that was beyond her comprehension. 'What a disgusting man,' she said almost to herself.

Max was amused. He smiled at her exit. 'He's perfectly normal, Gladys,' he called out.

Gladys stopped just beyond the doorway. Her evenly divided black and gray hair, pulled back into a bun, seemed to have turned mostly gray. He was sorry to have teased her. She used to mother Jeff. He would hug her affectionately, complain in a teenager's whine if she nagged him, and ask her advice (which he never followed) about his children. For a moment, Max thought she was going to cry. 'Don't forget,' she said softly, discouraged, 'Mr Brillstein is on the phone.'

Max picked up. 'Mr Klein,' Brillstein seemed to be in the middle of a long monologue. 'I'm glad I got you. There's paperwork we should take care of right away. I didn't want you to be bothered last night, but I've got – you know, it's annoying but there are some papers you have to sign. Could you come by – I'm near you – or maybe I could come over?'

'Max –' This time it was young Betty. Even with his polo shirt back on she seemed fascinated by his chest. What was she searching for? His heart? 'I've got four calls for you. Everything's lit up.'

Meanwhile Brillstein hadn't paused in his ear. 'Nothing important. By the way, has an FAA investigator gotten to you yet? Mrs Gordon had one at her place first thing in the morning. A little tacky, I thought, a little early for that stuff. By the way, we have to give up any idea of Mr Gordon's death taking time – they know he was killed instantly.'

'Sorry about that,' Max said and told Brillstein to hang on. 'Who are all the calls?' he asked Betty.

She had her head tilted to the side and was staring at his chest wistfully. 'What?' she came out of a reverie, startled. 'Oh. Two of them I think are lawyers.' She shrugged her shoulders. 'I can't get them to really say who they are or what they're calling about.'

'Get rid of any lawyers. They want to sign me up.' Betty's young face was at last wrinkled – by a crease of puzzlement across her forehead. Max pointed toward the sky. 'To sue.'

'Oh . . .!' Betty sighed with relief. She was quickly appalled. 'God, what pigs.'

'Wait for a second.' Max returned to Brillstein. 'I've got lawyers coming out of my phone lines. What do I tell my secretary to say to get rid of them?'

'No kidding,' Brillstein was grim. 'Ugh. What a business. Well, I guess I can't be too holier than thou. What should she say? Have her tell them you have a lawyer. That *might*, I emphasize *might*, get rid of them.'

Max relayed the advice to Betty. She seemed glad to have it. Her mouth set and she clenched her fists.

'Okay. Great. Oh. Also there's somebody from the Federal Aviation Administration who needs to interview you. He said –'

'Get rid of him. Tell the lawyers I've got a lawyer. Tell everybody else you don't know where I am and take messages.'

Betty nodded seriously. 'Right.' Her lips and cheeks were as plump and fresh as a child's.

'Thank you,' Max said. 'I'm sorry about all this.'

'Hey – no problem. It's exciting,' she said and smiled. Her happiness was revealed only for a moment. She realized that it wasn't polite and was embarrassed. 'I'm sorry,' she mumbled.

'Don't be, don't apologize. You've got it,' Max said and encouraged her with applause. 'Thank you. You understand. It's terrible and it's exciting.'

Betty backed out, flushed. 'Okay,' she said. As she turned and left, Max indulged himself by admiring her beautifully thick and richly colored hair. He used to wonder if Jeff had hit on her, Jeff chatted and flirted with her every day. Max had disapproved. She's almost young enough to be his daughter, he would think, and suggest Jeff get to work. What a prude I was, he decided. What a fool. I could have enjoyed that fresh cream instead of cleverly pitching Nutty Nick's roof to create more storage. Maybe Jeff wasn't irresponsible, lazy, cheap, and a petty thief. Maybe he was a man who knew that the sensual world was the only real one.

'Betty,' he called as she was about to disappear.

She returned eagerly. She had long black shorts on. They reached almost to her knees. Her legs were white, bleached when compared to her tanned face. She wore an oversized men's T-shirt, tucked into the shorts, also black, but a lighter shade. Shoulder pads gave her a cocky attitude. Her bushy hair trailed behind, an abundant mass, a rope that could rescue him. Max gestured for her to come closer. 'Hang on,' he said to Brillstein on the phone, who shot right back: 'No problem.' Max got up from his chair as Betty came close. He stayed low at her level and kissed her on those young lips. It was a quick peck but long enough for a dozen sensations. Her lips were soft, of course, and a little wet. He also smelled cigarettes on her although he had thought she had given them up. 'I'm sorry,' Max mumbled, inches from her surprised mouth. 'But you're pretty and sweet.'

Betty's eyes lowered, her lids fluttering. Her eyes glistened. 'I like you,' she said softly and then shook her head. 'What am I saying?' she asked and stepped back.

'Thank you,' Max said. 'I appreciate that you didn't scold me.' He sank back into his chair. It rolled from the force and bumped him into the desk. He felt sore around his ribs. Was that from dodging the knife or jumping out of the plane? He picked up the receiver. Betty backed out, but she moved reluctantly. Max smiled at her. 'You want me to sign stuff and see you,' he said to Brillstein on the phone. 'Your office is clear, right? The press doesn't know about you and me?'

'You mean that I'm representing the Good Samaritan?' Brillstein grunted. 'You didn't tell me everything,' he said in a lilting voice. Then he altered his tone to church-like solemnity. 'What you did was impressive. Very brave. But that means we have a lot to discuss.'

'Don't believe what you read – why?' Max interrupted himself, tired of denying his heroism. 'Why does that mean we have a lot to discuss?'

'Well, I assume from the newspapers that you weren't next to Mr Gordon when he died.'

'That makes a difference?'

'It will to Mrs Gordon. How Mr Gordon felt at the end, and whether he knew what was happening to him, are compensable as pain and suffering.'

'Well, as you know now, he died instantly –'

'No, no. I mean, even before the crash. Each minute that you and Mr Gordon believed you were going to die is worth dollars.' Brillstein lowered his voice and mumbled it again to himself, a prayer: 'Big dollars. Of course you're alive and can testify to what you knew and felt. To Mrs Gordon and her children, the question is whether you can –'

Max impatiently cut off his roundabout approach: 'I was with Jeff until only seconds before the crash. I switched seats at the very end.'

'You were? So you *do* know how he felt while the plane was in trouble?'

'For Chrissake even if I *weren't* sitting next to him I would know! He thought he was going to die. We all thought we were going to die. For twenty minutes we were –' Max laughed. 'What was it Einstein said God didn't do? He did it with us.'

Brillstein was stern. 'I don't know what you're referring to, Mr Klein.'

'He played dice with our universe. For twenty minutes we were all looking at the odds of whether we would live or die.'

'I'm not sure we're communicating here. Do you know for a fact that Mr Gordon believed he was going to die?'

'Of course. We discussed it. We discussed how Nan and the kids would make do.'

'You're serious? Why didn't you tell me yesterday!' Brillstein was thrilled. 'Don't say anything – wait. Let me turn on my recorder. We can do this now. Go ahead. Tell me everything from the moment you realized the plane was in trouble.'

Max heard the engines roar and felt the floor tremble against the insecure air. A beam of heated light traveled up his neck and bobbled from the shaky hydraulics. Jeff's greyhound profile turned his way . . .

Max hung up. He couldn't breathe. He heard his heart thumping, expanding in his chest, aching from inflation and effort. He was sweating, but not sweating hot, sweating in the cold air-conditioning, sweating fear. He was scared he was going to die, smashed flat on the ground, his head rolling on the burning carpet.

He ran out, ran out through the outer offices, trying to catch up to the fearless Max. He saw his employees' faces startle as he passed. He banged out of the heavy metal door to the hallway.

He was cushioned by a block of hot air.

A cornstalk poked his face. He looked down at a little baby's face, wondering blindly at the sky.

You're alive.

Max ran down the wide fire stairs and his sweat was hot again, his pounding heart no longer too loud. He was growing bigger and stronger with each landing, getting free of his past, of their need to know everything was safe.

'Max!' His wife was waving a yellow umbrella as he jumped the final four steps to the lobby's landing. She stood at the elevator surrounded by the tiny dirty white tiles of the marble floor, dressed in white, her long arms raised. The bright yellow circle wasn't an umbrella.

Debby was waving a plastic shopping bag to get his attention before he raced out the front doors.

'What!' he panted.

'I brought you clothes. What happened to your shirt? Where are you running? What's wrong?'

'I'm closing the business!' he shouted, exasperated. 'I hate this place!'

Debby allowed the yellow bag to drop by her side. As she moved toward him he was struck by her grace and beauty. Her long neck and straight back, acquired in adolescence as a ballet dancer and kept up by her teaching, floated at him in the stilled air. She had pulled her hair back, flush and sleek as a bathing cap. Her sympathetic light brown eyes were awash in tears. She seemed huge. Although she was an inch shorter and skinny as any starved middle-class New York woman, he shrank in her embrace.

'Please be okay. Please be with me.' Her lips kissed him on the cheek, on the eye, on the mouth, and she mumbled, 'Come home with me, Max. I can't make it without you. I need you.'

She was so powerful and in total control. She had the strength to hold the chaos of the universe together. Why did she pretend to need him?

'Sure, honey,' he sighed and leaned his head on her shoulder. 'Take me home.'

POSTTRAUMATIC
STRESS SYNDROME

15

In early November Carla agreed to attend a group
meeting of survivors organized by Dr Perlman to be
held the week before Thanksgiving. Although Dr Perlman was paid by TransCon to deal with the effects of
crashes on their employees, Manny was assured by
Brillstein it was safe for Carla to go. The lawyer explained that all parties had agreed to consider the group
sessions confidential and exclude them from the suits.
Manny was doubtful. He found excuses to call Brillstein
back and ask for this reassurance again and again.
Manny was suspicious of everything about the airline
since he had learned that the typical insurance payment
for a dead child was roughly fifty to one hundred
thousand dollars.

'That's why they don't give a shit whether they got
infant seats,' Manny mumbled to Carla in their bedroom
the night Brillstein had broken that particular bad news
to him. 'No fucking reason to. Only gonna cost them
fifty grand for a dead baby.' He spoke softly and yet
the words 'dead baby' were like punches to Carla's stomach.

'Don't say that,' she groaned. Her husband didn't
hear her protest. He had already gone on into the
bathroom, slamming the door. The old pipes squealed
as he started a bath. Usually he took showers. He took
baths when he had a fight with his boss or pulled a
muscle.

Carla refused to go to the group meeting at first. To

her surprise Manny didn't argue or coax. A few days later Dr Perlman phoned. Manny insisted she talk to him. Or listen anyway. Manny unraveled the tangled wire from the base of a large white desk phone. He had rescued it from the garbage where he worked. An impatient tenant had discarded the phone because the speed-dialing buttons seemed dead when really all the phone needed was new batteries. Manny stretched the wire until he reached Carla's position on the bed. Manny held the receiver to her ear and said loudly, 'Just listen to what he has to say.'

She was embarrassed that the doctor might hear Manny so she said, 'Hello,' to cover up.

Perlman had a cheerful voice. 'How are you doing?' he said casually.

She took the receiver from Manny. He let go reluctantly. Suspicious and vigilant, he stayed at her side and nodded grimly for her to respond.

'Okay,' she mumbled back to the cheerful voice.

'Not great, huh? They told me your cast is off. Your leg was fractured, right? I broke my right leg a couple years ago. It ached in a funny spot for months whenever it got real humid – it hurt right inside the bone. Yours bother you?'

'Yeah. Sometimes.' She answered Dr Perlman's questions with a word or two at most; she didn't hold back, and yet she didn't add anything more than the minimum necessary to be polite.

'Been having trouble sleeping?' he asked.

'No. I sleep plenty.'

'Too much, maybe? More than you need?'

'Maybe.'

Dr Perlman explained that he was collecting all the

236

survivors he could to meet in a group and talk. 'You don't have to talk,' he said. 'You can just listen.'

'Group therapy,' she said. She knew about it from television, although she had never heard of a group being more than six or seven people. This would have to be dozens at least; if the doctor got them all to come they would be ninety-eight. That's how many survived the crash. The number blinked in her head a lot – 98–98–98. She thought about the number as if the symbol itself were significant, noticing details: two short of 100; the first digit just one higher than the last; full of curves, almost an 88 if you closed up the 9 a little. Ninety-eight. She said the words to herself sometimes: their music was special. If Bubble had lived they would have been 99, a pretty visual repetition. And a happier sound: ninety-nine. She knew these thoughts were goofy. But they were among the easiest she had had during the four months since the crash. Four months didn't seem like a long time to her. Manny would say, 'It's been four months,' as if that were forever. He was impatient with her. He complained about her sleeping until noon, staying indoors all day only to go back to bed at ten. Of course she didn't sleep straight through. She'd wake up in the middle of the night, usually about two A.M. She'd sneak into the kitchen to eat odd combinations of food: ice cream, then a peanut-butter sandwich, then some yogurt, and finally a plate of sticky pasta with cold sauce. She gained weight for the first time in her life, except of course for the months she carried Bubble. Her usually nonexistent belly, just an inwardly curved valley between her jutting hipbones, filled in and became a level surface. Manny said he liked her a little fatter. 'You ain't fat,' he said. 'You were skinny. Now you're normal.' She had sex with him once a week or so to keep him pacified, but their lovemaking had no taste and no heat, like the cold pasta and gelled sauce, only it didn't even fill her up.

She did go out. She went to church regularly and prayed for Bubble's soul. Not to the church of her girlhood, Saint Anthony's, but to Saint Patrick's Old Cathedral, just across the street from her apartment on Mulberry. She told Manny she preferred the shorter walk, but what she really preferred was the older stone building and the glimpse of its ancient graveyard, a patch of elegant grass and smoothed headstones protected from the dirty city. And she became fond of the small, gray-faced priest who led the daily masses. Monsignor O'Boyle moved with extreme slowness, not bending his knees or elbows, like a robot. But his wide face trembled all the time, the lines and loose skin as floppy and wrinkled as a bulldog's. His watery light blue eyes were sad and trusting. She liked him so much she even went to confession.

Monsignor O'Boyle pitied her. After he heard the story of the crash, no sin she admitted increased her penance from more than a token Hail Mary. Not since she was a little girl had she gone that often. She went almost every day, sitting at the back of the old church, watching Monsignor O'Boyle conduct the mass in his slow motions, his pale face then as still as stone, his gestures a copy of the day before. What was once boring soothed her. Carla believed she had found a routine she could follow for the rest of her life: going to church, telling her sins to Monsignor O'Boyle, and taking care of the soul of her beloved son.

As soon as she agreed to attend the group therapy

session this safe world became dangerous. For more than a month she had been doing the household shopping, challenging herself to get over her fear of the outside. It wasn't far to go, just down the block to the stores on her street. But the day after saying yes to Perlman, a kid on a motorcycle came roaring around the corner. He drove his huge bike right up on to the sidewalk and whizzed at Carla. She had to fling herself against a car to avoid being hit. She was so shaken she needed a neighbor to help her home. After that she refused to go out without an escort. Even to church. And yet going to church also turned out not to be safe anymore.

On the Sunday before the group meeting, Monsignor O'Boyle's right foot skidded as he turned from the altar. He had to lean on the altar boy to prevent a fall. Carla gasped. Her best girlfriend, Ginny, was with her. Manny had to cover for one of the doormen that day and he arranged for Ginny to come in and visit. Ginny now lived in Staten Island with her three kids and a fat husband who everybody suspected was in the Mafia because he never worked and yet he got richer every year.

'What is it?' Ginny grabbed Carla's hand. Monsignor O'Boyle had regained his balance, let go of the boy, and resumed the ritual. He lifted the blood of Christ in the air. Didn't matter. Carla was terrified that the priest would fall again. She couldn't watch him. She was convinced he was about to topple and crack his head on the stone floor. She imagined the watery blue eyes staring lifelessly into the dark of the ceiling, his skinny old body crumpled and twisted on the strip of red carpet.

'I'm sorry,' she apologized to Ginny. A pair of old widows shot them dirty looks for talking. 'I got to go,' she said and despite the rude noise and the sacrilege, she left in the middle of Monsignor O'Boyle's ghostly ceremony. She was trembling when they got outside.

'You cold, hon?' Ginny asked. It was November and very cold that day. There were white streaks in the gutter where the freezing wind had drained its black blood. 'It was cold in there. I forgot how cold that fucking Old Saint Pat's is.' Ginny was pious and went to church even during her druggy teenage years, but she always cursed when she talked about Old St Pat's.

'He missed a step,' Carla tried to explain. 'He almost fell.'

'Yeah, he drank too much of the blood of Christ,' Ginny said.

Carla didn't explain to her friend why the priest's misstep terrified her. Ginny would be disgusted by her nutty cowardice. She was sure that Monsignor O'Boyle would have died if he had fallen. She couldn't get rid of the picture of him killed: eyes swollen and unmoving; the look of the dead on the plane. She shivered all the way home. Ginny brewed a burning-hot cup of espresso. Carla gulped it down and yet still trembled.

They sat in the kitchen and talked. That was awkward. Carla felt Ginny wanted to tell stories about her kids. She would start to, then become self-conscious and change subjects.

'Talk about your kids,' Carla finally said.

'I don't want to talk about them. What for? I'm so glad to have a day off. They make me crazy.'

But she was lying and that made it worse. 'The kids with John today?' Carla prompted her.

'John? You crazy? Take care of his beloved children? Nah – they're with John's mother.'

'They get along with her?'

'You kidding? They love her. Not like my mother. She worries about her furniture. I say to her, "They're your grandchildren. Enjoy them. You're going to be dead soon. What do you want to be surrounded by in your last years? Your beautiful grandchildren or clean upholstery?" You know what she said?'

'Clean upholstery,' Carla answered.

Ginny threw her head back and laughed. 'You're right.'

'Your mama loves her furniture,' Carla said. 'Sometimes she'd look at your pop eating – you know how sloppy he was? Sometimes she'd look at him like she wanted to put a Hefty bag under him, tie it up and put him out with the night's garbage.'

Ginny roared. She laughed easily and often. She was happy. She had always been a plump, short girl with chubby arms and legs, strong but not fat. Childbirth hadn't enlarged her and yet Ginny looked stronger. Her biceps bulged like a workman's. Maybe she carried both kids all day. Outside the cathedral Carla had put her arm through Ginny's. The muscles were strong ropes, like Manny's, the arms of people who worked hard.

'Your kids must keep you running around.'

Ginny made a whooshing noise. 'All day. No stopping. Noise all the time. I'm exhausted.' But she wasn't. She sat on the edge of the metal chair, ready to answer any request, happy to be needed.

Carla felt glad for a moment. She hadn't wanted to think about Ginny's children before, but her girlfriend's

241

obvious pleasure in life made Carla feel a little easier about her own loss – simply because it meant there was happiness somewhere. Carla decided to ask the question about Ginny's life that she had always been too scared to ask. She had to know urgently – it was the danger to Ginny's lightheartedness: 'Is John in the Mafia?'

'I hope so,' Ginny answered without hesitation. 'I don't want to be married to a freelancer.'

'You're funny,' Carla said, unable to laugh, but knowing that if she weren't so numb she would.

'I'm funny? You're the funny one, Carly. Remember when you used to do imitations? Remember at my big brother's wedding you made me laugh so hard I had to go to the bathroom?'

Carla used to do imitations of the nuns at school and the tough boys strutting their stuff at San Gennaro. From Ginny's memory she received an image of herself the way she used to be before the crash: mischievous and fun and . . . not scared. 'I didn't have a care in the world,' she said wonderingly and stared into her friend's eyes.

Tears filled them. Ginny said, 'Oh hon,' with a sob. She lurched out of the kitchen chair awkwardly to hug Carla. 'I'm sorry,' she squeezed Carla with her strong arms. 'I'm so sorry, hon.'

Carla didn't feel bad. She patted her friend's back comfortingly. 'I didn't have a care,' she mumbled, thinking about the words, the trick in the switch of meaning: 'I was careless,' she said and held her breath waiting for Ginny's reaction to her confession. But Ginny didn't hear Carla. Her strong friend was crying too hard.

Manny drove her to the group meeting of survivors. He

242

parked his illegitimate father's car in the Sheraton's lot. It was full. He shut off the engine. Carla glanced at the people gathered by the double glass doors to the lobby. She didn't recognize anyone. There were many people and they appeared comfortable with each other. She saw a man and a woman coming from opposite sides of the parking lot embrace without even bothering to say hello.

'I can't go,' she mumbled. Her head drooped and she stared into her lap. She had dressed up for Dr Perlman's group session. She wore the blue-and-white-print dress she had bought for her mother's wedding. Ginny had taken her to the beauty parlor and insisted Carla let them shape her wild black hair. With it restrained, and wearing a dress, Carla felt young and little. She was as timid with the group as a new kid on the first day of school.

Come on, Carla, she told herself. *It'll help you.* She couldn't answer the encouragement.

'Babe, I'll go in with you.' Manny rubbed her arm. 'We drove all the way here. Just go in for a little bit. See what it's like.'

Actually it hadn't been a long drive. The hotel – Manny said they were supposed to go to a meeting room – was on the other side of the Holland Tunnel in Jersey City. Carla wished it had taken longer. 'I can't,' she said. Her fingers slid on her palms – they were wet with fear.

'I ain't going back home, Carly.' Manny's tone was hard. 'We'll sit in this fucking car forever. I don't give a shit. You can't go on like this. It's been four months! You don't do anything. We don't fuck anymore –'

'We do too,' Carla complained.

243

'That's not the real thing. You lay there staring at me like a fish.' Manny leaned his head on the steering wheel. 'I'm sorry,' he groaned. 'Go!' He shouted into the gap of the wheel. 'I can't help you. Your mother can't help you. The priests can't help you. You gotta fucking go.' He shut his eyes against tears and closed his mouth to stop the flow of anger.

She was alone. She had never, ever, been so alone. That was the truth. She pulled at the door handle and it sagged heavily out and away, swaying low until it scraped the pavement. She heard the traffic of slow-moving cars edging toward the tunnel. *Put your feet out*, she told herself. She slung one, heavy and lifeless, on to the concrete.

Manny's hand landed on her shoulder, weighing her down. 'I'm sorry,' he whispered.

'No you're not,' she answered fast and that propelled her the rest of the way out of the car. The world seemed to rock under her feet. The black pavement, the one-story hotel, the metal awning that covered the other survivors who had come, was flying, spinning under her high heels.

Manny's voice sounded behind her. He had gotten out of the car and come around to her side. 'I'll take you in, babe,' he said gently.

She ran toward the awning. Not to escape her husband's escort. She had to get off the orbiting surface; find walls that would keep her in, safe from nothingness.

She ran past a woman holding a clipboard and brushed against a young black man dressed in a suit and wearing sunglasses.

'Excuse me,' the young black man said in a loud voice.

'Excuse me,' the woman with the checklist also said, leaning toward Carla. 'Are you in Dr Perlman's group?'

Carla stumbled on a step as she tried to answer and stop and turn all at once. The young black man steadied her and answered: 'Yes she is.'

Carla looked at him. His face was a mask, the coffee-colored skin, like his dark sunglasses, an impenetrable opaque surface, giving no hint of whether he was nervously pale or blushing from agitation or haggard from lack of sleep. His hair was a thin helmet. In his elegant charcoal suit he looked as tall and sheer as a skyscraper. He kept Carla balanced with only a light grasp of her elbow, 'I remember you from the hangar,' he explained. 'I think about you a lot. Did they find your baby?'

'Honey!' a light-skinned black woman appeared from behind him. She pulled at his sleeve, 'Don't blurt it out.' She added to Carla, 'He's sorry. He has nightmares about you – not *about* you – but about whether your child is safe.'

She had no idea who they were or how they knew about her. What had they seen? Did they know she couldn't get the seat belt to work? Did they see her run away from the smoke?

The black man bent his tall stiff body toward her. His voice was soft, but deep. It vibrated in her chest. 'It was your baby that didn't make it?' he asked Carla.

'Honey,' his wife said and pulled at his arm. 'He's having trouble . . . you know, sleeping and such. Making the trip was hard. Very hard,' she mumbled.

The black man stiffened. 'We didn't bring our baby girl this time,' he said, loud, announcing the fact over the heads of the gathering.

Manny scurried in between Carla and the black

245

couple. He looked short and nervous beside the taller, still man. 'Here you are,' he said and took her hand possessively, the way a parent takes a child's to keep it from getting lost.

'Hello, everybody,' a voice said from behind Carla. The crowd turned to look at its source. A broad-shouldered redheaded man was on the top step, holding open one of the glass doors. 'I'm Bill Perlman. I'm glad you all came, but standing right here we're blocking things. So let's proceed to the conference room. Just go through the lobby to the back. There's a sign showing the way.'

'Do I check them off here?' the woman with the clipboard asked.

'Wait until later,' Perlman said.

Carla wanted to leave. She was at the head of the crowd and couldn't retreat, but she didn't want to walk forward into the lobby either. She had been upset by just one encounter with another survivor. What did the black man mean they didn't bring their baby girl this time? Was she killed on the plane? No – no babies died. Bubble was the youngest victim. Was he joking? Or angry? Or crazy? Maybe the only survivors who had come were the crazy ones, the ones who couldn't get over it, like her. She couldn't stand a roomful of herself.

'Come on, babe, let's go in,' Manny urged, pulling her.

Even if she kept her mouth shut – and she sure planned on keeping her mouth shut – others might say things about her, the way the black couple had. They might ask her questions or tell stories about her. 'I'll go in,' she said to Manny. The crowd pushed at her back. 'But alone,' she added.

'Hi,' Bill Perlman leaned down to her. 'You're Carla?'

246

'Hello, Doctor,' Manny said. They knew each other?

Although Perlman smiled at Manny, he addressed the whole group. 'I'd prefer it if only survivors came in today. Your spouse is welcome if you feel you need them, but if you can come in alone, that's even better.' He lowered his voice to say to Carla, 'So why don't you come in with me?' Perlman offered his hand.

'I'll wait out here,' Manny said.

She took Perlman's hand. His fair skin was covered with freckles: light brown spots on a pink background. She thought him ugly. In an oversized, clownish friendly way – but he was still ugly. Perlman kept hold of her hand as they walked into the lobby and down the hallway to the conference room. He swung it back and forth gently, as if they were skipping into a playground. 'Come by car?' was his only question. He nodded at her answer.

The room wasn't as big as she expected and it appeared unfurnished despite the presence of more than fifty folding chairs, the majority still unopened and propped against the rear wall. There were no tables, no lamps, only the chairs, arranged not in neat rows facing in one direction, but haphazardly, at odd angles, sometimes in opposition, sometimes side by side. Apparently thoughtless hotel employees had simply set up a few chairs without rhyme or reason and dumped the rest. Other than the same blue carpet that was in the lobby there was nothing to distinguish it from a storeroom. Carla looked at Perlman, expecting him to be angry.

'Let's arrange these in a circle if we can,' Perlman said mildly to the woman with the clipboard. 'If you want you can sit next to me,' he said to Carla. He tapped the black man who had spoken to Carla on the

247

shoulder. 'Can I deputize you to help me with the chairs?' He gestured at two more men. 'And you gentlemen? Let's get them in a circle, even if we have to make them two rows deep.'

Soon almost everybody was busy clanking the chairs as they tried to manage the unfolding and placement. Someone had the idea to space them so that the second row was centered on the gaps of the first, allowing better sight lines. While people moved about there were hellos and hugs of recognition. Many of them seemed to know each other. Carla didn't. She was disturbed by this until she remembered that the others had been together in the hospital, treated in the emergency rooms and released to be housed in motels, or kept in semi-private rooms, wandering in and out, talking in the hall, smoking cigarettes in the lounge, sipping coffee in the cafeteria. She was the only one who had been given a private room; she couldn't have walked out even if she had felt like seeing anyone, and no survivors visited her. Why should they? They had all become friends that first horrible night while she was drugged and alone.

She didn't accept Perlman's offer to sit beside him. She took a chair in the second row at the back toward the corner and watched the friendly survivors. To her they were happy. Not hurt by the accident; they had been softened. On the plane they had moved with the stiff protected motions of strangers; in this room they brushed shoulders easily and smiled at each other with their eyes, like tipsy cousins at a wedding. For what seemed to be a long time the room buzzed from dozens of conflicting conversations. Carla stayed silent and looked through the turned heads at Perlman. After delegating the work of setting up, he had taken a seat, folded his hands in his lap and watched. He noticed that Carla had her eyes on him and gestured for her to come beside him. Carla shook her head. She tensed up, ready to run for the door if he came her way. Instead he smiled. He didn't interrupt all the conversations. He waited. Gradually people fell silent, suppressing others, until finally only one person was still talking.

'Ooops, I'd better shut up,' that voice concluded and the room chuckled.

'Not really,' Perlman said to the group. 'I want you all to talk. But me first.' He smiled and leaned forward eagerly. 'You all had a very special experience. I know that sounds funny. It wasn't good, but that doesn't make it any less special. You can talk to lots of people about it, you *should* talk to lots of people about it, but only the people in this room will really hear and understand all of what you have to say. I know it can be tough to stand up and talk to a large group of people. And, of course, you don't have to say anything at all. You can just listen. There are no rules except that nothing anybody says is going to be repeated outside this place unless they want it to be. You don't have to be interesting, you don't have to be funny, you don't have to be nice, you don't have to make sense. I know some of you have become friends and shared your feelings with each other but that's not what this is. That's the way we handle most bad things that happen in life. We talk with family and friends and maybe ministers or priests or rabbis or shrinks. But that's not what this is. What we're doing here today is something as old as humankind itself.' Perlman leaned back and looked up at the ceiling. 'Before we made all these machines and people spread out into what we call the nuclear family, human beings lived in tribes. White, black, yellow. We lived in tribes. And when a tribe suffered a calamity, a great flood, an exploding mountain, a terrible shaking of the earth, they sat around their fires, under the skies or huddled in caves, and retold the event, the stories of deaths and destruction, of escape and rescue. I'm not sure why that helps us. We're still just people, I guess. We haven't invented a new human being to go with all the new machines. I have a lot of theories about why this group talking helps, but they could be wrong. What's important is that it helps.' Perlman sighed and lowered his eyes, briefly scanning the circle of faces. 'If there's anyone who wants to stand up and say what happened to them we'd like to hear it.'

Carla did want to hear. She was afraid she would have to talk, but she wanted to listen. She searched for a familiar face. The man who had lost his arm. No. Lisa the flight attendant. No. There was no one she remembered. Maybe these were the wrong survivors.

'I lost my sister,' a woman said. 'I lost my sister and my niece and my nephew.'

'Could you stand up?' Perlman asked mildly.

She had blond hair and a deep tan. She wore jeans and a T-shirt. She looked athletic and pretty. To Carla she was the sort of midwestern American woman who had been a cheerleader in high school. While continuing to speak in a strong clear voice, she stood up: 'I was sitting right next to them. Their seats were ripped away. Right in front of my eyes. I'll never forget it. My sister just –' she gestured into the air, miming something moving off, hovering away, out of reach. 'My kids –' she resumed, 'my two boys, were on the other side of me. They're okay – I wish I'd brought them. My mother said no.'

Somebody laughed for a moment and then swallowed it, embarrassed.

The blonde answered the laugh: 'Well, she thought it would make it worse for them to relive it. I don't know how to explain to her you can't stop – you can't stop reliving –' without warning she was weeping. She choked on the tears and doubled up, covering her face with her hands. The people seated on either side of her reached out to support her. A man got up to guide her back to her seat.

Perlman spoke sharply at the blonde: 'What's your name?'

The man trying to help her back to her seat said, 'What!' to Perlman as if he were mad.

By now the blonde had forced her tears down. She straightened and looked at Perlman, puzzled.

'Could you say your name, just your first name, and then finish telling your story?' He added quickly to the man supporting her. 'You can sit. She's all right.'

The woman collected herself. She rubbed her forehead. 'Uh,' she seemed to be concentrating. 'I'm, uh, I'm – everybody calls me Jackie,' she flashed a shy smile.

'Why don't you tell us about the crash, Jackie, or even about things that happened before anything went wrong? We don't just want to know who lived and died. We want to know everything. Tell us from the beginning. Tell it all the way through.'

'Jesus,' a man in Carla's row mumbled. He stood up and addressed Perlman. 'This is going to take forever. I can't stay. I've got to get back to work.'

'What's your name?' Perlman asked.

'I'm John Wilkenson.'

'Why were you flying that day, John?'

'Pardon me?' Wilkenson had on a gray double-breasted suit. He buttoned the inner flap of the jacket as if preparing to leave.

'What were you flying to Los Angeles for?' Perlman asked.

'I was going on business.' Wilkenson spoke matter-of-factly.

At this answer Perlman tilted his big head. He resembled a quizzical dog wondering if what had been put in his dish was food. He said softly: 'You must be very committed to your work.'

John Wilkenson sat down as abruptly as he had stood up. 'I'll wait,' he said from his chair.

It was comical, but no one laughed. 'Go ahead, Jackie,' Perlman said.

Jackie told her story. She, her sister and their kids were flying together to visit with their brother in Los Angeles. They planned to see Disneyland. It was the first time all the siblings would have been together since they were teenagers. 'Now we'll never be together again,' she pointed out. Perlman got her attention again with a sharp question and she went on calmly. Carla understood that his behavior was a technique, although she thought it was tricky and unfair.

If listening to other people's tragedies was supposed to make Carla feel better, then Perlman's group wasn't working. Jackie had none of Carla's problems. From what she said, going outside didn't scare her, her husband was great to her, and she and her kids had never been closer. Perlman didn't seem to appreciate Jackie's easy adjustment either. He interrupted her and said, 'Let's just talk about things that happened the day of the crash. You said you saw your sister and her kids go flying off. What happened to you?'

'I don't know. I guess I closed my eyes and then there was incredible noise and I couldn't see anything. I was choking on the smoke and I heard that man – is he here? Are you here?' Jackie asked the crowd.

'Who?' Perlman asked.

'Max Klein. *Newstime* called him the Good Samaritan. I heard him shouting, "This way! Follow me!" And he was standing –' She stopped talking. Carla knew why. Jackie was remembering the bodies she had passed on the way out: a fast look at the crazy-looking dead, at smashed and mutilated bodies. Jackie came to: 'Is he here?' she asked Perlman.

'No, he couldn't come,' Perlman said quickly.

'I couldn't see anything but him. I only knew my sons were with me 'cause I was holding on to them. That man saved our lives. I came hoping to thank him.'

'How did he save your life?' Perlman asked.

'I was so scared. I couldn't see. And he sounded so normal. "Follow me."' Jackie imitated the call and the way the Good Samaritan had raised his hand and waved. 'So I went that way even though I couldn't tell what was the right direction. Then there was this light behind him. I didn't know if it was the flames. He disappeared into it. I could still hear him. "We're alive!" he kept saying and so I wasn't scared. I took my kids in my arms and jumped into the yellow light. It was the sun shining through the smoke. We landed on the corn and we were okay. I was so scared, my kids were screaming, the smoke was everywhere. We might've

253

gone the wrong way and choked on the smoke. I came here today mostly because I wanted to thank him.'

'Same thing happened to me,' someone said.

'Stand up,' Perlman said. One after another six people got up to tell stories of following the Good Samaritan out. Carla didn't pay attention to them. She leaned forward to see past the heads at Jackie. She wanted to ask her something. Had Jackie searched for her sister and her niece and nephew? Jackie had returned to her seat. Carla moved back and forth to keep watch, in order to see past the shifting heads of the people seated between them. Jackie looked flushed, listening with interest to the other stories of escape. Why didn't it bother Jackie that she had run away from the plane? She had left her sister and those two children to burn alive. If they were alive. Carla still didn't know whether Bubble had died from the crash or the fire. She had asked Manny to find out; he came back with the answer that they didn't know exactly how Bubble had died but they were sure he didn't suffer. Carla knew that made no sense: how could they know whether he suffered if they didn't know how he had been killed?

The woman sitting on Carla's right stood up. 'I'm not one of you,' she said.

'What?' said a voice.

'I don't belong here,' she said. Carla stared up at her. She was a broad-shouldered woman with completely silver-gray hair, although she didn't look any older than fifty. Her left hand dangled inches from Carla's face, the fingers clenching and unclenching. 'I'm sorry. I wasn't on the plane. My son died in the crash.' She raised her hands toward Perlman, almost a pleading gesture. 'I sneaked in – I don't belong here.'

'Why did you come?' Perlman asked.

The silver-haired woman moved between the folding chairs to get out of the circle. 'I'm sorry,' she mumbled.

'Wait,' Perlman stood up and pleaded. 'I wish you had asked me but it's okay that you're here. What did you want from them?' He gestured to the curious faces of the survivors.

The gray-haired woman noticed the stares of the group. She was pushed back as if the looks were a strong wind. 'I don't know. I'm sorry. I just wanted to know if anyone had talked to him or knew how it was . . .' She wound down like a toy with a dying battery and mumbled, 'I'm sorry,' and moved back, bumping into the wall.

'Who was your son?' a man called out.

'Where was he sitting?' a woman asked.

The silver-headed woman paused in her retreat along the wall toward the exit. 'They said he was in 21C.'

'That was right behind me.' An elderly man stood up. 'Did he have red hair?'

'No,' the dead man's mother answered. 'Brown.'

'Kind of a reddish brown?' the old man asked.

'I don't know,' she stammered. 'It might have looked that way. But it was brown.'

'Tall?' the man asked.

'He was six feet tall,' she said with a hint of pride.

'And he was wearing glasses?'

A young man fitting that description stood up. 'You mean me,' he said. For a moment the trio stood at different corners of the room and looked from one to another in a triangle of disappointment. The gray-haired woman sagged. The old man blinked. The young man shrugged apologetically. 'We were on the other side of the plane,' he said to the mother. 'I think you're talking about me,' he said to the old man. 'Remember? We met at the hospital.'

The old man's head bowed. 'I'm sorry,' he mumbled and sat down.

Perlman moved toward the gray-headed mother. She continued to leave slowly; she took small despairing steps.

'Anyone else remember that row?' Perlman asked. 'What was it? 21?' He had reached the woman and stopped her progress.

In front and four seats to the left of Carla a young woman turned to her companion and whispered: '21C was three rows ahead of me. They were smashed flat.'

Carla's heart raced. With it pounding so fast, she couldn't sit and breathe comfortably.

'Does anyone else have any information?' Perlman said.

Carla leaned forward to better eavesdrop on the young woman who knew what had happened to the silver-haired lady's son. Her neighbor, the man she had spoken to, bumped her shoulder: 'Go ahead. Speak up.'

'Stop it!' Carla was on her feet shouting at Perlman. 'Let her go!'

The silver-haired mother was frightened by Carla. She slunk away from Perlman, heading for the exit.

'Why?' Perlman asked Carla.

'This isn't gonna do any good,' Carla said.

Perlman stepped toward Carla, arguing. 'What harm can it do? She just wants to know what happened to her son.'

'My son died,' Carla said in a clear voice.

'But you know how he died,' Perlman said. 'You

were with him.' He turned back to the embarrassed woman leaning against the wall. Her hand searched its surface as if hoping to find a secret exit. 'When was the last time you saw your son?' Perlman asked the grieving mother.

'His birthday. About a month before. I don't remember kissing him goodbye.' She lowered her head and mumbled. 'I know I did. Just can't remember.' She raised her eyes and seemed to notice Carla. 'You're very young,' she said.

Carla knew what that meant. Her aunts said it often enough: You're young – you can have another. As if Bubble were something on sale that had been thrown out by accident and Carla still had time to rush to the store for another just as good. 'I'm not young,' Carla said.

'How old was your son?' the silver-haired woman asked gently.

'He was gonna be two,' Carla said. She felt ashamed. She wanted to cry, of course, but that was nothing new. The shame was. She had to look away from the older grieving mother. She stared at the blue carpet.

'I'm sorry,' the silver-haired woman said. 'He wasn't with you for very long.'

'Jesus Christ!' a man shouted. 'This is sadistic! We're not accomplishing anything.'

'Who says we're here to accomplish something?' Perlman answered. 'We're here to talk.'

The silver-haired woman talked; Perlman answered; there was shouting between some men. Carla couldn't follow their conversations anymore. She didn't know, for a moment, where she was or who these people were. They seemed to be memories or nightmares. She knew the facts: she was in a room of survivors and she was one of them; but that was nothing compared to the shriveling feeling that the faces of these people came from a dream or a television show, that none of it was real. I'm going crazy, she thought, and felt the room spin.

'Manny,' she said in a weak voice, hoping to summon him. He was real and if he appeared, then she was too.

'Hello,' a woman in front of her said. 'Remember me?'

It was Lisa the flight attendant. She stood right in front of Carla. The rest of the group was silent. What had happened to their conversations? Why was everyone looking at her and Lisa?

'Sure,' Carla said. She stared at Lisa, registering the changes in her. Without makeup and with her long hair cut as short as a schoolboy's she looked different. No, not just her face; it was the weight. Lisa had gained a lot, maybe as much as thirty pounds. But she still had her friendly smile, her happy smile of helpfulness.

'I really wanted to see you. I came mostly to see you.' Lisa put her hands together and seemed to pray for an answer.

Carla remembered the streak of her smeared lipstick and her gaunt cheekbone as she bent over Bubble. He had kicked out his chubby legs and slid down. The belt tightened on his neck. *'Hold him in your lap,' Lisa had said. 'He'll be okay.'*

'I think about you and your baby a lot,' Lisa said. She was smiling. Why was she so cruel? Her smile was mean and got bigger as she came even closer, only inches from Carla. 'Remember I tried to help you with the seat belt?'

'Help me?' Carla said. The strange faces popped, expanding into Carla's world. They *were* real, not memories or dreams or television actors. 'You told me everything was going to be okay!' She was angry. Her voice filled the room. The friendly survivors shrank away like scolded children. Lisa's smile was gone. Tears came, pushing Carla's chin up and clogging her nostrils, but she didn't lose her voice or her righteousness. 'Help me? You think you helped me? You didn't help me. You told me to hold him. I couldn't hold him.'

Lisa's smile wasn't coming back anytime soon. Perlman had moved to Lisa's side. The big clown had her by the shoulders, trying to back her away from Carla.

'No – don't say that –' Lisa begged Carla.

'Yes!' Carla shot at her, refusing to stop. 'You said everything was going to be okay. It wasn't okay! My baby died!'

'Okay, okay,' Perlman said. Lisa hid in his chest, sobbing. She wouldn't smile ever again. 'That's enough,' the doctor said sternly. 'You've said it. That's enough.'

He was full of shit, too. He wanted Carla to talk, but only if she was a pretty blonde who was happy that the people she loved had died, who was going to cry a little and say nice forgiving things.

'Fuck you,' Carla said. 'Don't tell me when I've said enough. I'll never say enough! She told me it was okay! And it wasn't!'

Perlman let go of Lisa and moved at Carla. His spotted and beefy arms reached for her.

'Don't touch me!' Carla shouted. Perlman was so startled by her ferocity he came to a halt.

'If you don't have anything to say but to blame people then I want you to go.' Perlman was firm. He was a bastard, Carla realized. He pretended to be gentle and easygoing, but really you had to play by his rules or he would get rough.

'I'll be happy to get out of here,' Carla told him. She walked out, passing the silver-haired mother. Now she was the one who hung her head, ashamed. 'Take my advice,' Carla said to her. 'Go home. He can't help you. He's a witch doctor.'

In the corridor outside the conference room she could hear the slow traffic grumbling toward the tunnel. Her heart pounded with rage. But she felt good. She felt better than she had for a long time, maybe the best she'd felt since it happened. As she walked to the front of the lobby, her legs – even the damaged one – had spring and energy. She was eager to find Manny and go.

She saw her husband's back leaning against the half partition of a public phone. He was always on the phone since the crash, either talking to Brillstein or telling his friends about the lawsuit.

She hurried to him, dancing across the blue carpet. The prospect of being alone with her husband was thrilling. She imagined them returning to New York in the car with the whole day ahead of them. They could go to a movie. She hadn't been to a movie since the crash. Was the Rockefeller rink open? She had taught Manny how to ice-skate – a passion of hers – and she imagined skimming on the big-city ice with her husband, just having fun for no reason at all.

She was stopped by a strange ugly sound. She looked around to find its source. It frightened her when she realized the noise came from the phone booth.

'Manny,' she called faintly. She hung back, afraid to touch him.

He had on a tan windbreaker. Huddled forward in the booth, his head was bowed. He hadn't heard Carla. His muscular shoulders flexed and stretched the material to the limit. It quaked from his sobs.

'Oh baby,' he moaned into the receiver. 'I can't take it anymore. You can't leave me. I can't handle this by myself. I need your help, baby.' The words were yawned out of his weeping.

He's crying, Carla comprehended, amazed. He had never cried in front of Carla, not for his dead mother, not for his dead son.

'Don't leave me, baby,' he blubbered.

The lobby was cold. Chilled air leaked in from the glass doors. Her throat closed. She knew in her bones that he was talking to another woman, crying for her. Crying for a woman! All those whispered phone calls; Manny acting so strong, rushing around doing things for the lawsuit, concerned only about the money, all of it, bullshit and lies – he was chasing after another woman.

'I can't do that to her,' he spoke abruptly, supposedly in answer to something the bitch on the other end of the line had said. His voice had cleared.

Think of what kind of person she must be. To sleep with the husband of a woman who had just lost her baby. But that's exactly what makes the world so disgusting: they tell you they feel sorry for you, that they care about you, but everybody is only out for themselves, relieved that it didn't happen to them, that you're the one with the bad luck.

Carla walked right up behind her husband and grabbed his straight shiny black hair, his bastard mulatto hair. She pulled as hard as she could. He yelped like a dog.

Manny twisted out of her grip, cursing. His hand was up, ready to punch his attacker. At the sight of Carla he looked terrified.

'You fucking bastard,' Carla said. 'You're going to burn in hell.'

Manny must have agreed with her. He let go of the phone and fell to his knees. He pleaded silently with Carla, begging with his black eyes. Only for a moment, though, before, scared by what he saw in Carla, he shut them to whisper, 'Oh Jesus.'

She wanted to kick him in the face. She was going to but she couldn't breathe and her legs buckled. She tried to call out to Manny to help her. Instead she fainted on to the Sheraton's blue carpet.

16

Max closed the business Thanksgiving week. Gladys continued to believe he would change his mind up through the last day. She didn't seem to be convinced even then.

'Max, I won't look for a job until the summer. But if *you* need me, just call.'

Max found Warren a job at Turner Construction, where Max had worked when he was fresh out of graduate school. Young Betty was going West with her boyfriend and didn't plan on looking for work until the spring. Scott stuck to his plan to use his unemployment insurance and his savings to fund another go at painting. Warren's new situation meant he was secure (as was Gladys, who didn't need to work; she needed to be out of the house to escape from her retired husband) and yet Warren was the most upset and nervous.

'I'll probably get fired in six months,' he mumbled whenever someone congratulated him or encouraged him to be cheerful.

The funniest part of the shutdown was the reaction of clients, old and new.

'Why?' prospective clients asked. They sounded appalled and nervous.

'I've decided to retire early.'

'How old are you?' one astonished woman asked. When Max said forty-two, she said, 'Well! Lucky you.'

Another man who wanted Max to design a house for him – 'Just like the house you built for my brother-in-law, only better' – was more persistent. 'How the hell can you afford to retire at forty-two?'

'I was in a plane crash,' Max answered.

'They pay you for that?' the man asked.

'Yep,' Max said. 'Big dollars.'

'Were you hurt?'

'No,' Max said and smiled at the thought. He didn't want to bother to explain the insurance money was for the death of his partner.

'They pay you even if you don't get hurt? Gee, I would think it would be kind of exhilarating. Living through something that horrific without a scratch. Maybe even a positive experience.'

'It was,' Max said, 'and one of the things that makes it so positive is that they're paying me.'

'Well, I'm glad it's so nice for you,' the man said, anger joining his surprise. 'But frankly this is the kind of cockamamie arrangement that's destroying this country.'

Old clients were hurt or concerned. 'Are you okay?' one asked and then added, with a nervous laugh, 'Guess you'll be glad to be rid of your pain-in-the-ass customers.'

'Yes,' Max agreed, calm and unimpressed by their reactions. He moved through conversations and day-to-day errands as if he were a passenger on an express train watching small towns go by; they blocked his vision for a moment, only to be quickly forgotten by his steady, armored progress.

He took a final walk through the empty offices on Thanksgiving morning to make sure everything had been taken. Shutting the door behind him, he decided to leave it unlocked since there was nothing to steal. He had a moment of fear, the bitter taste of cowardice rising from a hollow stomach, and then bursting through it came happiness: he was walking away from the scene of so much compromise and frustration.

Thanksgiving dinner was held, as usual and as required, at his mother-in-law's. Required because her self-satisfaction and family fame came as a cook. Flora shared Debby's height, excellent posture, and slow, graceful movements; but decades of dinner parties for her husband's academic colleagues and family celebrations had thickened her body and given her face the warm, well-fed appearance of mothers in children's book illustrations. And she played the role as well, treating her forty-year-old daughter as if she were six and maintaining a quiet but ominous presence about her grandson's health, like that of a Secret Service agent guarding the President.

Shortly after two in the afternoon Max, Debby and Jonah walked to his in-laws' apartment on 103rd and Riverside. It was a dangerous neighborhood when Max and Debby first married. Harry and Flora bore the danger because their ten-room apartment with a high unblocked view of the river and a working fireplace was cheap and kept cheap by rent-control laws. Besides, his father-in-law Harry could walk to work at Columbia University – even though he was mugged once a year. He once went to the hospital to be stitched but otherwise was not badly hurt.

The indiscriminate renovations and conversions of the 1980s had changed the area. It was now an expensive dangerous neighborhood. Since their building had gone co-op, they paid a large monthly mortgage and an ever rising monthly maintenance. Of course on paper, at the height of the real estate boom, they could have claimed to be millionaires. Boom or bust, however, Harry continued to be mugged yearly.

Max was not happy about this year's gathering. In line with tradition, Max's mother and sister were both coming, but this year Nan and her two fatherless boys would also be there because Nan had quarreled with her own parents. She insisted on living in New York City rather than moving in with them in New Jersey and saving money. This combination of people didn't seem promising, but that wasn't the worst of it. As they walked up Riverside Drive, Debby told Max that her mother had also invited Byron and his parents at the last minute. That was odd. Even odder was the fact that they had accepted.

Presumably they had said yes because Byron was still fixed on Max as a living security blanket, even though four months had passed. The boy didn't make any demands on Max; Byron simply wanted to be in his company. His parents had arranged for Byron to be dropped off at Max's office after school on Tuesdays and Thursdays – Mondays he had after-school French lessons; Wednesdays he took a course for kid chess whizzes taught by a Russian émigré; Fridays his parents left early for their country house in Connecticut. He liked to sit at Jeff's desk, near to Max, do his homework and then play chess against a portable computer outfitted with a tiny board and miniature pieces. He promised to be quiet. He was. But he was still there, occasionally exclaiming with dismay or triumph, his machine beeping whenever it made a move and playing songs of victory or dirges of defeat.

Max got tired of the sounds of intellectual combat

and had recently set up Byron with art materials. The idea really came from Byron's father, Peter Hummel. Peter had taken Max aside to say that Byron was obsessed with painting and drawing before the crash but had given them up since. He expressed surprise that Byron hadn't asked to borrow Max's colored pencils. He told Max he hoped Byron would go back to his artwork soon. Next visit Max put out all the drawing materials on Jeff's desk. Byron didn't want to draw, however, at least not people or things. He wanted to design buildings like Max. He pored through architectural manuals and Max's finished designs. That impressed Max, but Byron's haste didn't. He scanned the manuals, absorbing images impatiently, eager to make his own. Lately, he had sketched a prodigious number of elaborate complexes that Byron said, 'People will live in someday, when there's no more room on earth for homes.' In fact, they reminded Max of medieval fortresses, with cramped quarters and a central court ringed by grim defenses.

Peter was pleased and undisturbed by his son's renderings. 'What a complicated and intricate mind,' he commented to Max while Byron gathered his school things, out of earshot.

'I think it shows a desire for security,' Max said.

Peter spread his hand possessively over the onionskin paper Max had laid over Byron's design. 'Oh, I don't think so. I think he wants people to live communally. This stuff is really neat,' he said and added casually, 'I guess your son must have been drawing plans like this since he was a baby.'

'No,' Max said. 'My son has no interest in architecture.'

Peter made no comment. He raised his eyebrows in surprise and looked slightly pleased. Max suspected him of thinking something was superior about Byron for showing such interest. Suspecting Byron's parents of having a feeling was as close as Max could get to hearing them express one. They had an odd, detached manner. They continued to be grateful to Max, but diffidently. Sometimes their thanks even took the form of a teasing rebuke that Max was easily duped.

'Thank you again,' Peter said one afternoon as he and Byron left. 'You don't mind if tomorrow I bring my senile grandmother? The adult diapers have great capacity. She only needs to be changed twice a day.'

The Hummels had attempted polite material compensations, inviting Jonah to share their box seats to Mets games, inviting Max and Debby to use their spare *Phantom of the Opera* tickets. Since tickets to the show were sold out for months into the future and were known to cost hundreds of dollars if bought through scalpers, the adjective 'spare' caused Debby to laugh, then flush, and finally mumble to Max, 'They must be richer than God.' And the Hummels had attempted a more integrated family friendship, inviting Max, Debby and Jonah out to Connecticut for the weekend. Debby wanted to go, but Max declined. He resisted any attempt at forcing a friendship between his son and Byron; and he had no interest in knowing the parents. Besides, he believed Jonah didn't like Byron. He didn't know what he felt about Byron for that matter. He only knew that he couldn't ignore the child's need for him, that he was responsible somehow. Nevertheless, Max didn't think he had to take on the parents as well, and especially not on national holidays.

'I don't want to go,' he said, coming to a stop on the corner of 103rd Street.

'Come on,' Debby said and ambled on. She reached for Jonah; her long dancer's arm, even in a down coat, made an elegant hook in the air.

'It's absurd,' Max said, resuming his steps. 'We don't know these people.'

'You know Byron,' she said, capturing Jonah's head with the crook of her right arm. Since the crash they were closer than ever. Jonah seemed to snuggle with her more than he used to as a toddler. 'You see more of him than you see of us.'

That wasn't true, although it was the truth as Debby knew it, only camouflaged so Max couldn't answer bluntly. He tried anyway. 'You see? I'm already being blamed for other people's weaknesses. That's exactly why I don't want to go.'

'Then don't go.' Debby and Jonah staggered up the hill together, pretending indifference, unbalanced in each other's arms like drunken lovers.

How long has it been? Max asked himself. Two weeks? Three? He felt sluggish. Must be three, he decided. Maybe he shouldn't go to his in-laws. If he waited much longer before another joyride, perhaps he would lose his nerve. Watching his wife and son enter his in-laws' courtyard, he thought: That would be worse than anything: to live scared like them.

'Come on, Dad!' Jonah called cheerfully. He made a dumb show of urging Max, waving his right arm with sweeping movements as if his father were an ungainly truck he had to maneuver into a narrow loading dock.

Crossing his in-laws' pretentious inner central court to the recessed lobby Max was reminded of Byron's medieval renderings. Since high school, when Max first learned all he could about the building of the city of his birth, he had known that the then-disreputable upper Riverside Drive apartment buildings were originally built for the prosperous new middle class of the turn of the century. Perhaps the cracked cement courtyard, painted a dark dull red by the co-op board, had once been colorfully tiled, probably with the bright yellows and blues of Mediterranean Europe. Max had seen photographs of one building from the period with such romantic flourishes. And there had almost certainly been a water fountain in the center where now there was only a discreet drainage grate. At the four corners of the courtyard that had once been overseen by cherubim statuary, there were security mirrors to help tenants spot potential muggers. For Max, these were banal observations about the frightened utility of the modern world, but that didn't prevent his eye from making note each time, and to feel disappointed each time. He couldn't shake the thrilling and eerie sensation just as he entered the courtyard that this time he would find 370 Riverside Drive restored to its petit bourgeois elegances.

Harry opened the door to them. Flora's cooking accompanied him.

'Smells great,' Max said over Harry's hellos. 'Let's eat right away. No drinks in the living room. Show me the bowl of stuffing and I'll put my face in it.' One of the many marvelous aftereffects of the crash was that Max could eat without restraint and without gaining weight, whether he exercised or not. It's my crash diet, he told Debby. She was appalled by the pun.

'That would be appetizing for the rest of us,' his wife

commented. She embraced and kissed her father with the abandon of a little girl, even though she was his height, taller in the heels she had on and broader in the shoulder. 'Hi, Daddy,' she said, her consonants as soft as a two-year-old's.

The sound of a child running came at them from the long hall that led to the living room. It was Byron. A color printout of a design fluttered behind him. 'Look what I did.' He waved what appeared to be another elaborate fortress. 'My dad got me a MAC and a color printer and Architron.'

They *were* rich. The computer, printer and architectural design software must have cost them at least six thousand dollars. Max had wanted to get one for the office but Jeff – never a fan of speediness – had said, 'For what? We should buy an expensive machine and get our work done faster so we can bill them for fewer hours?'

Byron pushed his way between Jonah and Max. 'Isn't it cool? You can design anything with Architron.'

'Rad, man,' Jonah said in a soft, mocking voice. 'Real rad.'

'I taped the *Civil War*,' Harry said. He waved the back of his hand dismissively at the floor, scrunching his thick gray-and-black eyebrows together. 'Despite its flaws. I've set it up in the bedroom with the video recorder. I thought the boys might be interested.'

Jonah lowered his head, a child turtle, hiding in his protective shell, staying dry from the downpour of his grandfather's love of imparting learning.

'I'll be happy to watch the *Civil War*,' Max said. 'But I'm sure the boys would rather have molten lava poured down their throats.'

Startled by the joke, Jonah laughed hard. His head

popped out and his teeth showed. The unrestrained pleasure lasted only a second. Embarrassed, he covered his mouth and moved beside his mother, glancing nervously at Harry. Harry was upset. His face had widened at Max's comment, dense eyebrows untangling, eyes shocked open. And he flinched at Jonah's laughter.

'I want to!' Byron said, bouncing in front of Harry. 'I'm interested.' He turned to Max. 'If you watch and explain stuff.'

'You see,' Harry said, pointing at Byron with desperate satisfaction. A flush of embarrassment was still on his cheeks although he now had Byron for a willing student. He rewarded Byron for his eagerness by tousling his hair. 'It's pretty good history. A hell of a lot more interesting than your teachers can make it,' he commented to Jonah. He added to Max, 'Of course they make short shrift of the causes and Shelby Foote's sentimental anecdotes are both pointless and misleading but I think its treatment of the battles is first-rate. And boys like battles, don't they? Are you sure you aren't interested, Jonah?' Harry said, saying his grandson's name with a hint of displeasure. It was implied anyway since he said Jonah instead of Nonah. Nonah was the affectionate nickname Harry routinely used.

'Okay,' Jonah said, drawling the word. But he took another step back from his grandfather and closer to his mother. 'I'll watch it for a while.'

'If you don't want to, say no,' Max said.

'I do!' Jonah insisted.

'No you don't,' Max said.

'Max, for God's sake give him a break,' Debby said, but mildly, and called toward the kitchen entrance as she walked in that direction: 'Ma? You need help?'

'Come on, boys,' Harry said, gratified by his grandson's agreement, even if it was bullied. He draped an arm around Jonah's shoulders and pulled him down the hall. 'Do you know about the second battle of the Wilderness? They fought two battles in the same woods only a year apart. There were soaking rains in the weeks before the second battle and the dead from the first – they had been buried in shallow graves – rose to the surface.'

'You mean, they came up out of the ground?' Jonah asked.

'Exactly,' his grandfather patted his head as though giving him an A.

'Gross,' Jonah said.

'I know what dead bodies look like!' Byron shrieked proudly.

They had reached the open double-door entrance to the living room. Once there had been sliding oak doors or perhaps they were glass-paneled. When these buildings were designed apartment dwellers still had the romantic desire to imitate the gracious compartments of large homes, each room dedicated to one aspect of living. Modernism had taught New Yorkers to accept that they were creatures of a concrete and metal arbor – apes with elevators living in one-room tree houses. Byron's parents stood just inside the open doorway, drinks in their hands. They had been listening to Nan with polite expressions. Peter and Diane Hummel were dressed formally, he in a suit, she in a sedate dress that could easily be a suit. Nan was wearing jeans and a white T-shirt. Underneath the T-shirt she had on a black bra that showed through the white. Her breasts were large, and the effect was more obscene than if she had put on nothing. She waved her arms in the air, talking garrulously as Max, Harry and the boys approached. She looked wild, her usually straight blond hair teased out from her head, her widespread arms showing off her breasts, targeted by the shiny black bra – but even she was stopped by Byron's remark.

'I do!' Byron repeated in a scream. 'I've seen lots of dead bodies!'

Peter's mouth puckered sourly as if he were tasting his son's words. He said, 'Hello,' to Max, trying to smile.

'They look really dead!' Byron screamed at Harry.

Harry's thick eyebrows lowered as if trying to shade his eyes.

Not so eager for knowledge, are you? Max thought. Nan still held her arms up. Max looked at her black-cupped breasts. Had they always been so big? Why hadn't he noticed? Some sort of polite blindness for Jeff's sake?

'But they must have been mostly skeletons,' Jonah said.

'No they weren't!' Byron continued to shriek.

'Byron,' Peter said softly, although he pronounced the *n* firmly. 'Speak in a lower voice, please.'

'They had their skin!' Byron lowered his tone to the volume of mere shouting. 'They were smashed –'

'Byron!' his mother shouted in a panic.

'I don't mean them!' Jonah also shouted, arms out, frustrated. 'I mean in the battle Grandpa was talking about!'

'We're all going to go deaf,' Peter mumbled.

'I don't know any black people,' Max announced to all of them. 'When I was in school I knew lots of black kids.'

'What are you talking about, Max?' Nan said. She lowered her arms. With them down, although her highlighted breasts were less provocative, they looked even bigger.

'Civil War,' Max said. He passed between the Hummels and entered into the living room proper; he saw that Harry had the liquor out on top of the stereo cabinet. Should I get drunk? he wondered. That would make tonight more dangerous – but also less real. 'All those dead,' he continued, considering whether to have Scotch or vodka. 'Fought to free the slaves and I live in a supposedly integrated city – our mayor's black – and I went to public schools and I marched on Washington and I don't know a single black.'

'I do,' Diane Hummel said. 'I have two good friends who are black, I work with –'

'Are there any living in your apartment building?' Nan asked. 'Any in your son's school?' Nan laughed at herself, an apologetic guffaw.

'There are blacks in our . . .' Diane trailed off, uncertain.

'Only one and she's there by marriage,' Peter said.

'By marriage?' his wife asked, sloshing her drink a little as she turned toward him abruptly. 'What do you mean by that?'

'Anyway,' Peter said, making no response to his wife. 'They didn't fight to free the slaves. They fought for economic dominance.'

'It's the same thing,' Max said.

'Well,' said Harry. He brushed his eyebrows with the thumb and ring finger of his right hand. 'Well,' he said again and thrust out his chest, fingers still scratching the gray and black hairs. 'I suppose in the ultimate

275

sense a fight for what kind of economy a nation is going to have was necessarily a fight over slavery in the case of the United States, but Mr Hummel is referring to whether the motivation was moral or pragmatic – and on that score –'

'I know what he was referring to, Harry,' Max said. 'Don't recapitulate the obvious.'

His father-in-law dropped his fingers from his eyebrows, they parted from his eyes, suddenly nude with surprise. Max decided to have a drink. He took the vodka in one hand, a glass in the other, and moved toward the ice. 'The only reason historians make the economic point about the Civil War is so that we don't feel morally inferior to the people who lived a hundred and thirty years ago. Plenty of them – even if they weren't the majority – gave their lives for at least the stated goal of ending slavery. I don't know anyone who would do that today. Anything else people say about the subject is just bullshit. The rest of its lessons are dead and uninteresting except to history nerds. They should be forgotten, not rehashed.' He had his drink made and he took a long swallow.

'That's the new you, Max,' Nan said. She saluted him with her glass mockingly.

· 'What's the new me, Nan?' Max asked.

'Expert on bravery and charity. They should have replaced Father Ritter with you.'

'They wouldn't do that,' Max said. 'I don't believe in God and that means I can't molest little boys, accept payoffs, or suck up to corrupt politicians.'

'Oh yes . . .?' Nan smiled; lasciviously, it seemed to Max. She approached him with her arm out like a grappling hook, only it was her drink at the end that threatened to stab and gather him to her. Instead, it went around his shoulder and moistened his shirt. He noticed she had covered her pink cheeks and forehead with lots of makeup. From a foot away he could smell its musty powder. She kissed him on the cheek, wetly, and whispered, 'And why can't you do those bad things?'

'Because there's no one to forgive me,' Max said and pushed her a little, on her soft right hip, to move her enticing warmth away.

Nan skipped back a step gracefully. With a sweeping gesture, she brought her drink to her lips. 'You've become a self-righteous asshole,' she said softly in a neutral tone.

A voice, reedy and full of hope, called into the living room from the hall. 'Jonah?' it said. 'Is Jonah here?' the voice pleaded.

'Yeah, I'm here,' Max heard Jonah answer. 'I'm right in front of you.'

The grown-ups parted enough for Max to see the tableau: Jeff's sons were in the hall. Sam, the older, had spoken. He was trailed by Jake, his four-year-old brother. Jonah left his grandfather's side to stand almost nose-to-nose with his friend Sam. Jonah's wide mouth displayed the unevenly sized teeth of a ten-year-old, front teeth as big as an adult's, incisors small and still coming in; Sam beamed back with a mouth of oddly proportioned teeth. Instead of saying hellos, they laughed with delight at each other. Sam had his portable video game with him; a dirty white blanket with a frayed satin edge trailed behind little Jake.

'I was looking the wrong way into the living room!' Sam said in a nasal whine, his typical tone of voice. 'I didn't see you.'

'Well, I'm here, dummy,' Jonah said and touched the back of his friend's head gently. 'And you have *Gameboy* with you. Big surprise.'

'*Boxxil* is really tough!' Sam said. He had switched on the game. His head was down; his thumb flickered speedily from button to button. A tinny electronic song could be heard.

'Did you die yet, Sam?' his little brother Jake asked and sniffled. A dark streak under his nose, a mix of dirt and smeared snot, gave him a fake Hitlerian mustache.

'My beautiful sons,' Nan said and cleared her throat.

Peter Hummel laughed, but briefly. It wasn't clear if Nan was kidding.

Jonah knew instinctively they had become a spectacle for the grown-ups. He pulled on Sam's elbow, but gently, respectful of the game in progress. 'Let's get out of here,' he said.

'On pause,' Sam said, pressing a button on the portable video game. The tinny music was stopped in mid-melody. 'Change screens,' Sam said and ran out of sight. Jonah followed, laughing.

'Wait for me, guys!' little Jake yelled and lumbered after them, his blanket swishing on the floor.

'I thought we were going to watch the *Civil War*,' Harry called to his grandson.

'Don't want to!' Jonah shouted back.

Harry slumped, exaggerating his disappointment comically, but it wasn't funny. There was too much real disenchantment in his eyes. 'Well,' he gestured to Byron. 'How about you? Do you care to learn anything about the most significant period of your country's history?'

For an answer Byron turned to Max. 'You said you were going to watch with me.'

278

'Byron,' his father said in a soft voice. 'That's not polite.'

'Oh, you can't expect Max to keep his promises,' Nan said. She had finished her drink, she put the glass down on Harry's bookshelves with a bang. The shelves lined one entire wall of the living room and were filled with old hardcovers missing their jackets. Max thought they had a pompous and depressing look, dusty sentinels of useless knowledge. 'Max has been reborn so he doesn't have to keep his promises.'

'Why don't you play with the other boys?' Diane Hummel said to her son.

'I don't like video games,' Byron said.

'Then ask them if they want to do something else.' She ran a hand over her smooth black hair, pulled flush to the scalp, fingers combing all the way back to the bump of her demure bun. Finding it in place, she patted it.

'A boy who doesn't like video games!' Nan said in disbelief.

'I have a weird son,' Peter Hummel answered in the same tone of pride he used when telling Max that it was odd of Byron to enjoy drawing.

'I'm not good at them so I don't like playing them,' Byron said blandly. 'I don't think that's weird, Dad. What I think is weird is a dad who says his son is weird for not wanting to play video games. That's what's weird.'

'Your father's weird, there's no doubt about that,' Diane said.

Peter listened to his wife's and son's comments thoughtfully and then nodded in agreement.

'What promise haven't I kept?' Max asked Nan.

279

'You said you'd help Brillstein and you're not,' she said, her onstage tone turned down, the sexiness gone. She was serious. Serious, she looked older.

'I'm helping him as much as I can,' Max said, sighing.

'Bullshit,' Nan said. She turned away and announced, 'I'd better see if the womenfolk need any help.' She marched out, the heels of her loafers clattering on the bare hallway floors.

They watched her go. Harry raised his bushy eyebrows and opened his arms. 'What is she talking about?'

'I don't know,' Max said. He was tired. Nan always made him feel tired. He backed into the wing chair that Harry liked to read in. Flora complained it was too big for the room. Max agreed but then most comfortable things didn't fit anymore. Max let himself drop into it. 'Every week she finds some new thing to add to the lawsuit. This week it's negligence on the kind of seats they had in the plane, even though Jeff's seat didn't come loose, that's not what killed him. And she wants me to exaggerate how hysterical and terrified Jeff was at the end.' He remembered Jeff crapping in his pants. He had never mentioned this to Brillstein or Nan or anyone. What an excellent proof of his partner's fright. It was so faint in his memory that he wondered if it had really happened or if he had just invented it for the sake of the lawsuit.

'Well,' Diane said, running her hand over her head and touching the bun in back again. Her sharp chin bobbed forward, like a bird pecking. 'I hate to say it, but it's good strategy. At this stage the lawsuit is largely a game of bluff. You're pushing for a settlement really and you want the other side to know that you've got so many shots on goal to make with a jury that you're sure to score at least one. And one is all it takes.'

'I thought you were a public service lawyer,' Max said, annoyed by her tone of absolute knowledge.

'She used to work for the pigs,' her husband Peter explained, flashing a polite smile that Max imagined he might have used on a fellow member of the Century Club. Who were these people? So rich they could give their son a computer system Max wouldn't indulge in himself, so uptight he had never seen them hug their damaged son, and yet agreeing to come to 103rd Street to have Thanksgiving with a gaggle of crazy Jews. Who were any of them? Why was Nan dressed up like Madonna? Why was Byron standing there listening to the adults rather than going after the other boys? Was Byron special, like Max, a creature of the unafraid living, a true son of his spirit, while Jonah, obsessed by the fakery of computer life and death, was forever lost to him?

Nan wants me to sleep with her, it occurred to Max abruptly. He was stunned by the clarity of this revelation. That's why she's angry. She's lost a mate and she wants me to replace him. But it isn't me, she doesn't want me, she wants any replacement – I'm just the nearest to her dead husband. For a moment he felt he understood her but then he wasn't sure. If she didn't want to sleep with him, the real Max, and it was merely a desire for a generic male, then why did she persist no matter how often he was cool to her? None of her actions, her wildness and sensuality, fit the person Jeff had lived with. Jeff had talked to Max about Nan daily, had told countless stories, whined and analyzed her at length, and yet not one of Jeff's judgements was helpful. They didn't seem to have anything to do with the widow Max had to deal with every day.

'Max,' Byron said. He had come to the wing chair and leaned against Max's knees. 'Come and watch with me.'

'Leave Max alone,' Diane said. 'Go and play with the other boys.'

'We'll be eating soon,' Harry said to no one in particular.

'Max,' Byron said, his elbows digging into Max's legs.

'I can't help you, Byron,' Max said in a low voice. He felt near to tears and yet he was angry.

'I just want you to watch TV with me,' Byron said in a shy voice.

'Go on, Byron,' his mother said. 'Go play with the other boys.'

'All right!' Byron shrugged his shoulders and walked out miserably.

'Should I put on the –?' Harry began and then despaired. 'I guess they're not really interested. I loved the Civil War at that age,' he wondered aloud with unembarrassed self-admiration.

'That's why you became an historian,' Peter said.

The doorbell rang.

'My mother,' Max said in a voice of doom.

'I'm not a historian,' Harry said. 'In fact, I can appreciate your old-fashioned and quite correct usage of "an" historian. I teach American literature,' Harry said in a modest mumble, as though mentioning something so secret and precious that he had to be careful not to be overheard by the wrong party.

The doorbell rang again.

'Harry, can you get that!' Flora's voice called from the kitchen.

'Don't my daughter's legs work?' Harry asked rhetorically; he had already begun a shuffle down the hall.

Max looked up at Peter and Diane Hummel. Both stood in formal poses holding empty drink glasses. He was alone with two strangers.

'You know I decided to ask around about your lawyer,' Diane said. Peter shifted from one foot to another. For him that was almost feverish behavior.

'And you found out he's a shyster,' Max said.

Diane's dark eyebrows lifted. 'No. Do you think he's a shyster?'

'I don't think he's honest.'

'In other words, he's a lawyer,' Peter said and laughed gutturally in his wife's direction.

She winced and her nostrils tightened, as if she had smelled something foul. 'No, but ... he's, well, he's second-rate. And he has no experience in aviation liability.'

'I know that. I gave him the job because he's second-rate.'

'Do you always do self-destructive things or are you planning to sue him for legal malpractice?' Peter Hummel grinned at Max, pleased by his own wit.

'My old firm is handling Byron's case,' Diane said. Her small mouth spread, revealing small yellow teeth. She was attempting a friendly smile. 'They're very good. If you want I can arrange for them to take over.'

Max's mother and sister, looking more and more as if they were sisters, gradually moved down the hall toward them. Their chubby faces and deep amused voices were strange to him. He had a flash of memory – a still photo of his mother as she knelt on the sidewalk beside his dead father. She was skinny. Her black hair, rich and curly, bounced with each of her sobs and cries for help. Recalled to his consciousness years ago by his therapy, Max knew what he had thought about his mother at that instant, at that sad and by now legendary moment of their family history, as she tried to cradle his dying father's head, lifting it from the concrete of New York. *She's so beautiful*, thirteen-year-old Max had thought. How old was she, with her lover dead, her children fatherless? Thirty-seven. Five years younger than Max now. Poor woman. She had remained alone for all those years.

Diane Hummel said softly, 'Are you okay?'

Max looked at her. She seemed surprised by something on his face. He reached for his cheeks and discovered they were wet with tears. Max dabbed at them with the palm of his hand. Peter no longer appeared self-satisfied. He stared at Max with dispassionate curiosity.

'I'm sorry,' Max said. 'Thank you for your offer. But I picked Brillstein because he's second-rate, because it's a big score for him. He's been second-rate his whole life – just like me – and he thinks he needs just one break. I know he's sleazy – I understand that he's gotten several of the other survivors as clients by introducing himself as the Good Samaritan's lawyer.'

'So you know about that?' Diane said in a musing tone.

'Max,' his mother said, arms and hands out. She and his sister Kate had arrived at the living room. 'No kiss?'

'Sure, Mom,' Max said and rose dutifully. He talked to Diane while crossing the room to his mother. He touched his mother's cheek with his lips briefly. The skin was soft and flabby and cold from the outdoors. Thirty years before, the widowed woman on the sidewalk had tight skin and gaunt cheeks.' I don't really believe it's going to take any skill to make a killing off this and I wanted that schlepper to have his big break.'

'What schlepper?' his sister said. 'Are we talking about one of my old boyfriends?'

Max kissed Kate as well. Her skin wasn't soft or loose. He finished his explanation to Diane: 'Brillstein may blow the case but he'll never be able to say he didn't have a chance at the big time.'

'Is this man a friend of yours?' Peter said. He frowned resentfully as though he suspected Max of being a tease.

'No,' Max said gently. He continued softly, apologetically to Diane: 'I guess it sounds crazy to you. But you've been at the top always, right? I mean I don't know, but I get the feeling you were top in your class and that you've had your pick of jobs –'

'Diane's a killer lawyer,' Peter said with a confusing mix of pride and acerbity.

'I haven't had my pick,' Max said. 'And yet I think I'm as smart as you. And I know in his heart of hearts Brillstein thinks he's as good as any lawyer. Maybe we're both kidding ourselves. But we deserve a shot, don't we?'

'Max,' his mother said, a note of alarm and urgency in her tone.

'Yes, Mom?' he waited for her predictable reassurance, her usual tepid spoonful of soupy praise. What would it be? You're not second-rate; in fifth grade Mrs Horowitz said you were a visual genius. Or one of her negative palliatives: You do your best, Max, that's all

285

anyone can ask and your best is very good, better than most. Or perhaps the gift of her physical compensation: a kiss on the forehead, a mumbled 'You're a good man, Max,' her eyes shining into his, hands lingering on his waist a few Oedipal seconds too many.

'Max,' she said, again insistent.

'What?'

'No lawsuit talk on Thanksgiving. No crash talk. We're supposed to give thanks today, aren't we?'

'We're Jewish, Ma,' Kate said. 'We don't give thanks, we just stop complaining.' Kate enjoyed her own joke, laughing hard. So did Harry. Their mother also; she laughed hard and reached for her daughter's hand to give it an appreciative squeeze. Even Peter smiled – cautiously.

'That's ridiculous,' Diane Hummel said angrily. The amusement was embarrassed into silence. She stood rigidly, her sleek black hair as tight and shiny on her scalp as if it were black enamel. Her lips had thinned to a pale red line. Her hands were clenched at her waist, lowered but ready for a fight. She raised her bony chin and declaimed in a voice fit for argument before the Supreme Court: 'Thanksgiving belongs to all Americans.'

Later, when Max passed Diane the plate of stuffing, she said in a low voice, 'They're all ghouls anyway. Even the best.'

'Who?' Max asked.

'The aviation liability lawyers,' she mumbled. 'Ghouls in Paul Stuart suits.'

Max didn't have an appetite for the meal. He had lost it somewhere in the living-room conversation. He knew that he would have to test himself soon.

Jonah and Sam didn't want to linger at the table. Each time they tried to escape, Flora or Harry or Debby or Peter held them with either a bribe of dessert, a threat of failing some standard of maturity, or an unfavorable comparison to Byron. Byron was a paragon because, encouraged by his father's interviewer's manner, he ate all of Flora's dishes and entertained the adults with statements of his architectural ideas and explanations of what Architron could do.

'Why don't we have educational games like that for Jonah?' Debby asked Max.

'It's not a game,' Max said. Jonah rolled his eyes and whispered something to Sam. Max continued, 'It's a thousand-dollar piece of software that Jeff and I didn't think we could afford.'

'A thousand dollars?' Diane Hummel exclaimed to her husband. 'Have you gone out of your mind? I thought it was twenty-five bucks.'

'A thousand dollars?' Sam said in a drawling whine. 'For a thousand dollars you could buy every Nintendo game in the world!'

'In the universe!' Jonah said.

'Yeah!' said little Jake, rubbing his mucous mustache. 'In both universes!'

'I'll get you a tissue,' Debby said to Jake. 'Or you could use your napkin.' Debby leaned over and offered Jake his pristine napkin.

Jake crossed his little arms, ducked his chin to his chest, and shook his head from side to side, saying, 'No.'

Debby appealed to Nan to support her position. Jake's mucus was running again, new cloudy fluid oozing over the dried black-and-yellow mustache.

'Leave him,' Nan said. She had been sullen throughout the meal. Except for a comment, as she took a second helping of turkey, that she would have to go to an extra aerobic class.

The two grandmothers, although Jake was no relation to them, exchanged sad looks. Flora mumbled, 'It's not very sanitary.' Max's mother nodded at him to intervene. Debby meanwhile was still poised, halfway out of her chair, Jake's napkin in her hand, hovering about a foot away from his smeared upper lip. Nan dropped her eyes to her plate and resumed eating. Debby looked at Max for help.

As always she assumed it was his job to make up for the failures of others. 'You want to do something, do it,' Max said to her.

'Peter,' Diane Hummel was saying to her husband, speaking in an intense whisper, although of course everyone could hear her. 'Are you out of your mind? Spending that kind of money on a child?'

'I'm not a child,' Byron said and Debby, still focused on Jake's nose, laughed. 'I'm not,' he said to her. 'Not after what I've lived through.' Byron inhaled dramatically and exhaled with emphasis, a magnified sigh. 'I've told my dad. He's just got to get used to it. I'm never going to be normal again.'

'You know,' Nan said while chewing food. The words were muffled by her stuffed mouth. 'You ought to take him to a shrink. He's got problems.'

Peter Hummel was offended. He showed it by leaning back in his chair, stiffening to attention, eyes wide, showing a lot of white.

'I see a shrink,' Byron said, confusing Max, who didn't know it and didn't understand. If Byron was

288

seeing a therapist why was Peter so scandalized by the suggestion? 'He agrees with me. He doesn't think I'm a normal kid.'

'So you're not normal. So that's why your parents should buy you thousand-dollar toys,' Nan said and resumed eating. Jonah and Sam both smiled at each other, flashing their big and little teeth.

'I don't think that's fair –' Peter Hummel began sternly to Nan.

'We're going to have to talk about this,' his wife was saying at him.

'I need it!' Byron protested to his mother.

Debby, perhaps thinking all this confusion would distract Jake, finally got her courage up, dipped the napkin in a water glass and stabbed at his snotty mustache.

Jake screamed. A piercing howl of innocence violated.

Shocked, Debby backed away. But without the napkin. It stayed behind stuck to Jake's upper lip, adhered by his natural glue. Jake batted at it wildly with the backs of his hands, but the napkin didn't come off. His brother Sam laughed so hard he fell sideways on to Jonah. Jonah also convulsed, bits of food appearing at his lips, coughed up by laughter.

'Enough!' Max roared. He stood and reached across the table, pulling the napkin off Jake. A line of snot floated in the air for a moment and then fell gracefully into the serving bowl of cranberry sauce. Sam and Jonah both stared, mouths open, and then fell again into each other's arms laughing with open mouths, showing their odd teeth. 'Go play video games!' Max shouted at them as if he were Moses ordering his people across the Red Sea. Their laughter stopped and they hopped out of their chairs, scrambling on all fours in their hurry to escape.

'Max!' Debby protested.

'That's what they want to do. For God's sake, at least somebody is made happy by something. Let them do it in peace and without shame! Without all this goddamn shame!' Max shut his eyes and took a long breath.

He heard but could not see Nan as she said in a bored throaty voice: 'We're not talking about jerking off, Max. I don't think they'll become traumatized adults if we embarrass them about playing *Gameboy.*'

That opened Max's eyes. What he saw was clouded. His vision was blurred by something floating on his eyes. It muddied the faces of all but Byron. The boy's head was up, his eyes were shining, and he showed off a grin of awareness.

'Nan, please!' Debby said. 'What a mouth you've got tonight.'

Max blinked hard and that cleared his sight. Peter and Harry seemed to have retreated into their chests. They had the false self-absorbed looks of passengers on a subway car pretending not to notice the approach of an armed gang.

'Listen, honey,' Nan said. She dropped her fork on to her plate and it clattered loudly – a harsh cue warning of an attack.

'Take it easy, Nan,' Max's sister Kate mumbled across the table.

'I am so sick and tired of you and Max taking over with my kids! Who the fuck do you think you are! If you spent less time wiping my baby's nose and more time kicking your nutty husband in the ass to testify to the truth! To the truth, for God's sake! So that we can get what we deserve for what –' Nan stopped. Her eyes narrowed. She swallowed hard. In a minute she would be crying. That was her pattern – when making demands Nan traveled from rage to tears.

It was time, Max decided. 'Excuse me,' he said. He moved away from the table, turned and left the dining room.

Byron called, 'Wait for me.'

Max went down the hallway toward the bedrooms, seeking Jonah. In case he lost the gamble this time, he wanted to say goodbye. He was only halfway there when Byron bumped at his side.

'Hi.'

Max didn't answer. He would have to get rid of him. They passed the living-room entrance and turned down another hall leading to Debby's old room where the boys would be playing.

'I know what jerking off means,' Byron said.

'Un huh.' Another turn past a bathroom and they were there. The door was shut.

'It means playing with yourself,' Byron said.

'That's right,' Max said. He knocked.

'Come in,' Jonah said.

Max opened the door and pushed Byron in. 'I want the three of you to play together. I have to go out for a little while.'

'Okay,' Jonah said unenthusiastically.

Byron fought against Max's hands to leave with him. 'I don't want to. I don't like video games.'

'That *is* sick,' Sam said. He was playing his portable game: head down, fingers dancing, feet shifting weight in time with imagined combat.

'Shut up,' Jonah said in a friendly tone and touched

his friend gently on the back of his head as if mocking a punishment.

'Go and play,' Max shoved Byron in and then pointed his finger like a scold.

'Okay,' Byron said. He was suddenly dignified. He stepped back from Max and entered the room, his high bright cheeks shining, his small eyes unblinking and bold. He stopped and faced Max. 'But I want to know one thing. Dad says now that you've closed your office I can't visit you after school. Why can't I come to your apartment? I could even walk from school to your apartment. It's only eleven blocks. My friend Timmy walks home and that's nine blocks –'

Byron was willing and more than able to argue this point at length. Max cut him off. 'We'll figure something out. I have to go,' Max entered the room and hurried up to Jonah. His son shied away at his approach, with a touch of fear that hurt Max's feelings. He caught Jonah by the shoulder and pulled him close for a hug. He bent down – he didn't have to go very far down anymore – and whispered, 'I love you. Take care of yourself.'

Jonah was already pulling away, squirming low and out of Max's embrace. 'Okay –' he grumbled.

'Bye,' he said to Sam. His dead partner's son was still curved into the small video screen, his body jerking in alliance with his arcade alter ego.

Max left, going past Byron quickly, waving.

'Promise?' Byron said to him.

'We'll figure it out,' he said and left, shutting the door fast behind him. He didn't continue down the hall. Leaning his back against the door, Max consciously breathed steadily, to recover from the worry of his good-bye.

'What game are you playing?' he heard Byron ask.

It took a while before there was a response. Jonah finally said in a sullen grudging way: 'It's *Boxxil*. And you're not very good at it,' he continued, presumably to Sam.

'Well, how can I concentrate with all these interruptions?' Sam whined, a childish pronunciation of his dead father's favorite rationalization.

'I'm not good at any video games,' Byron said.

Max pushed off from the door, ready to leave for good, satisfied the boys had made some sort of truce.

'Nobody's good at them at first,' Jonah said. 'You have to play them a lot before you get good.'

'Ah!' Sam groaned. The game played a dirge. 'Except for me. The more I play, the more terrible I am.'

'You want a turn?' Jonah asked Byron.

Max was about to go. He waited, however, gratified by his son's civility and curious about Byron's response. 'No,' Byron answered. 'They're boring. It's not like Architron. You have to use your brain and your imagination to do Architron.'

'Well,' Sam drawled. 'What's so great about it? You can draw buildings in colors. Wow! That's really great!'

'Yeah, yeah,' Jonah said, laughing. 'Haven't you ever heard of crayons!'

'You're both stupid,' Byron said in a low confident voice.

'Well, stupid me is going to play,' Jonah said.

There was silence. Max said to himself: Go. It's time. You already know everything there is to know about their lives. You know the sad broken adults they'll become; you know how they will fail.

He heard the game's tinny music.

'Your dad thinks playing computer games is stupid,' Byron said. 'He didn't even like me playing computer chess. What he likes is architecture, that's why he's so interested in my designs.'

Byron got no response. Only the game's music could be heard for an answer.

Byron resumed after a few moments of silence. 'Your dad wanted to own Architron. You know? But he couldn't afford it. He would be good at it. He only draws small things but they work. I don't know if my buildings would work.'

'Oh, that's really great,' Sam whined slowly, a turntable spinning at an incorrect setting. 'Buildings that fall down the minute you step into them!'

'Crash!' Jonah said.

'You're dead!' Sam laughed. He laughed coarsely, almost coughing.

There was another silence. Go, Max, he told himself. There's nothing but loss and defeat in their youth. You can't rescue them.

'Your dad is interested in what I do,' Byron said. 'He likes me better than he likes you. He'd rather spend time with me. I think your dad loves me more than he loves you.'

Max waited for Jonah to answer. But there was only the game's melody.

'He does,' Byron said after a while. 'Your dad is really more interested in the things I'm good at.'

The computer beeped wildly. Sam exclaimed, 'You did it!'

'That's the highest score of any of my friends!' Jonah said, exhausted triumph in his voice.

'Big deal,' Byron said. 'Somebody in the world has a better score.'

Max walked away. He watched his scuffed leather loafers step on the narrow oak boards, bordered by the darker strips that framed each side. His feet had walked on these ubiquitous New York floors for all of his forty-two years. He had crawled on them in Washington Heights as a baby. They had split his chin on the Upper West Side as a toddler. He had raced Matchbox cars that fitted perfectly on their narrow width. He had wet them with grief for his dead father. He had fallen asleep on them in the dark while sneaking to overhear the adults talk of sex in the living room. He had stripped and sanded and polyurethaned and stained and bleached them as an architect. He had carpeted them, he had made love on them, he had tiled them, he had cursed them. How many times had they supported the tedious walk away from defeat?

Debby confronted him as he turned past the living room into the hall leading to the front door. 'Max, are you okay?' she said.

He moved into her tall body, leaning the side of his face against hers. It was strange and infuriating that he lived with this elegant and intelligent woman who said she loved him and yet couldn't salvage the wreck of his life. 'I'm going out for a walk.'

'Now?' she whispered in his ear. Her hot breath made him shiver.

'If I don't I'm going to stab them all to death with Flora's carving knife.'

'Max,' she sighed and squeezed him. 'Don't leave me alone with them.'

'You can handle them better than I can.'

Debby hugged him, pleading into his eyes. 'Before I met you I was lost in the world. I know everybody's bugging you, everybody wants your comfort. But I really need it. I need you to really *be* with me.'

He remembered the man she missed, the patient cheerful husband who always understood her nerves, her shyness, her fragility. He could almost see that husband in her eyes. But it had been a performance. How could he tell her that? How could he say: you've been married to an imitation?

'You weren't happy with me.'

'That's not true. I love you,' Debby said.

'You love me, but you aren't happy. I couldn't really comfort you.'

'You don't have to comfort me. You're confusing me with Nan. I'm not a widow.'

Max tried to pull away – there was no explaining it, not talk that she could hear.

Debby clung to him. 'You should tell Nan to get off your back. She's making you miserable. She's making us all miserable.'

'None of this is Nan's fault,' Max said and he stepped out of his wife's unenthusiastic arms. 'I have to go for a walk.'

'Fine. But we have to talk tonight.'

Harry appeared, moving with his head down, his thick eyebrows lifting and falling as if in time to some inner conversation. 'Oh,' he said as he nearly bumped into Max. He looked from Debby to Max and back from Max to Debby. 'Am I interrupting?'

'No,' Max said to him. 'What are we going to talk about?' he asked his wife.

'Later,' Debby said.

'I'm interrupting,' Harry said and resumed his shuffle down the hall. 'I'm just going for another bottle of wine,' he mumbled.

'About what?' Max asked. If it was something truly urgent he had better know right away before answering became impossible.

'Well, for one thing, what are you going to be doing now that you shut down the office? You keep saying you don't know, that you'll decide later. It's time to make a decision. I think having no plan is upsetting you.'

'No,' Max said. 'It's upsetting you. I'm going now. Maybe I'll think up something while I'm out.'

'I hope so,' she said and turned her back on him, walking away in her ex-ballerina's posture, dignified and disapproving.

Max left the apartment without any more goodbyes. The farewells were worse than staying.

The halls smelled of all the Thanksgiving feasts. Max ignored the elevator, attracted by the interior fire stairs. The games of his childhood took place on a similar set of stairs: hiding behind the banisters and shooting at his friend Gary, from whom he drifted apart when they had to move to the Upper West Side after his father's death. He couldn't remember Gary's face. But he could still hear the sound of Gary's feet rushing up behind him on the tiled hallway floor firing his water pistol and screeching, 'You're dead, you're dead, you're dead!' And his own, as he wheeled and fired back, spraying Gary's chest. 'You missed, you missed, you missed!' What a banal memory. I wasn't a very smart kid, Max thought, comparing himself to Byron with his ambitions and his awareness of the grown-up world. When did I ever get the idea I was more than an ordinary person? Max wondered. From Ma? Because my father died and that made me unusual?

He sat down on the steps while thinking all those dead-end questions. They weren't really his own questions; they were asked or provoked by his psychiatrist. His shrink's medicine used to work so well. You're entitled, Max. You have a right to be happy. You're a good son and a good husband and a good father. Good, good, good. I am Max Klein: I am empowered and glowing with self-esteem. I am worthy and deserve to be middle-class in a society where being middle-class is the nearest thing to godliness.

He wondered about his in-laws' roof. He had always wondered about their roof. It must have a great view, he thought. Not only of the river (the view he knew from his in-laws' living-room window) but also back toward the city itself. The sun, on this cool November day, was already going down, and Max climbed up the two flights, hoping to get on the roof and see the colors spread across New York.

He reached the top and found the roof door's lock broken. The metal door squealed and tottered at his touch. The city was right there as it opened, glowing pink and red, just as Max had imagined. He stepped out. New York shimmered at him: glistening glass and dignified stone. Here was the criminal who had perverted Max. Not his father's death, not his mother's Oedipal transfer of sex into ambition for him, not his own rampaging id. No, Doctor, I didn't get the idea I should be more than a second-rate, gray-haired balding Jew from your villains. I got it from this beautiful and evil city I love, this floating strip of greedy and defiant buildings.

His feet didn't want him to be on the spongy tar surface. He had lived afraid of height, skin crawling in retreat if he advanced toward the edge of any precipice. He had almost fainted when taking a cousin of Debby's up to the observation floor of the World Trade Center even though he had stayed inside, a good ten feet from the barricaded glass windows. He was sixteen stories up now, out in the open.

He felt the terror in his knees, sparking into his thighs, trying to shock him back away from the edge. But he stepped through the alarms, away from the raised safety of the door, until he was a solitary target atop the building. The wind fired at him, whipping his kinky hair flat against his skull and a few ticklishly forward at the temples. He didn't mind the cold: it was refreshing. His legs were in a panic and what he had eaten of the meal seemed to dissolve. His stomach felt empty and afraid. The building's roof wall was obviously new. The simple concrete barrier, about a foot wide and flat on top, had probably replaced something more ornate that had threatened to fall, and this was the cheapest substitute that would satisfy city ordinances and the co-op's insurance. It was four feet high, gray everywhere, except for splotches of pigeon droppings on top and streaks of tar to patch fissures on the side.

Max ignored his terrified thighs and went up to the wall, pressing his belly against it. The cold wind blew into one ear unless he turned his face north. He leaned over the wall and looked down into the frightening drop.

The window ledges were lined up symmetrically. A trick of vision separated them by shorter and shorter distances as his eyes looked down. Below, the deadly sidewalk was a bleached strip bordered by the humped charcoal street. What would have been a smooth line of ledges was broken by the occasional dirty air-conditioner. His head was woozy from the sight. Max imagined himself fall, spin, and smack on impact, embedded in the roof of a parked car.

He had always been afraid of heights, of falling. His fears were clichés. Everyone had them. Everyone knew what they meant. Did that help? No.

What am I truly afraid of? Dying? Not loving my wife and son? Loving them? Who cares what the real fear is?

It was the cowardice itself that appalled him.

He stretched his arms out flat along the top of the wall and swung his right leg up, maneuvering so he was lying on the wall along its length, the right side of his body exposed to the great fall, the left side facing the safety of the roof. He still wasn't completely on the wall. He kept the toes of his left foot touching its reassuring tar. He pressed his cheek against concrete, looking out at the sad red-stained water towers, the sullen blank faces of stone, the walls of hostile glass and, curved above them all, the dark sky, a slice of deep blue bleeding at the edge, struggling to be as vast and interesting as the New York it covered. He was inches from a free-fall to the street.

He lifted his toes from the roof and hung for a moment balanced on the wall with his belly. He raised his feet in the air. A gust of wind pushed at him. His hairs blasted off his skull. He saw one gray curl straighten over the deadly ground. His legs crawled with fear. His right eye shut against the vision of the unimpeded drop, but he fought and kept his left one open.

Get to your feet, Max.

He grabbed the sides of the wall with his hands and brought his knees up. He was clinging to the wall. A roll to the right and he would be gone.

He shut his left eye and was blind. The wind deafened one ear. He arched his back up, still holding the sides, and put both feet flat. He felt stupid, his ass high in the air like a submissive monkey. He got angry at himself and suddenly he was standing up straight, hands away, a thrill in his heart, an equal to the sky, standing beside it with nothing to hold him there.

He opened his eyes and screamed. He saw only the city flowing away from him. He was alone. He couldn't feel his feet or his legs. He screamed again. It was gobbled into silence by the raw wind.

Something hot oozed from his forehead. Blood?

A warm flow spread at his groin and down his right leg. He was peeing. He took a step forward. The mean wind blew at him, trying to knock him off.

He bent with it, swaying out over the street with his right hip. When the wind gave up for the moment, he righted himself and then he was not scared.

He scanned the slain city, standing over it, master at last of his vision. He walked on the wall, one foot after the other, walking the perimeter of the building. When the cold wind tried again to shove him off, he swayed with it, a small skyscraper that gave but did not break.

He took the corners with a smile, knowing that for a second most of him was out in the air, suspended over the fatal earth. He was glad. He moved faster on the wall, pushing back sometimes at the wind, daring it to try harder to defeat him.

I am Max Klein, he thought, death's survivor.

The terror was gone and in its place there were calm

resolutions. He would talk to Jonah about his silence. He would stop playing substitute daddy to Byron. He would tell Debby that he would never again be the beacon for her darkened life. He would attend no more dead celebrations. He would tell Nan that her unhappiness belonged only to her and he wanted no portion.

He turned the last corner. He was ten feet from where he had begun his walk. As he stepped toward the finish the wind came at him from a new direction. For a moment he was interested in the change.

And then he realized he had stepped into the air.

He didn't scream. There was no terror left in him to be expelled. He saw the walls of hostile glass jerk and the water towers tumble. He grabbed at them with his arms as he fell straight down.

He felt the pain in his knee first. His left shoulder was yanked hard, so hard he thought it might break off. Then he was hit in the jaw as it whacked into brick.

He had caught himself on the wall, hooking it with his left arm. The rest of him dangled in the air. He reached with his right hand for the wall and got only the tips of his fingers on it. The skin scraped off as his weight pulled him toward the street.

For a split second he saw it all so clearly: I'm suicidal and I've goofed and I'm about to die.

No! His body talked back. From his stomach he pushed up at the dead weight of his body with all of his energy. His left arm contracted, his feet kicked at the rough bricks. He was reminded of pulling himself out of a swimming pool in Florida when he was a child, his mouth filled with chemical water, afraid of the deep end he had wandered into. Max put everything he had into one single jerk of power in his left arm. Something punched him in the stomach.

He groaned. It hurt and made him wish to give up. He was lying on top of the wall again, spinning it felt like, and he had only a little energy left, a last bit of himself with which to decide his fate. The wind was furious and powerful.

He had to get off the wall. He couldn't see from the pain. He pushed himself off the wall without considering that he didn't know if he was headed for a short drop to the tar or the long battering fall to the street.

The suspense lasted only a second.

Immortal Max landed on the roof and laughed.

CRASH LANDING

17

Max hadn't been in Little Italy, that he could remember, since he was a young man romancing Debby. They used to have cappuccino and cannoli in the sidewalk cafes after delicious, cheap meals in Chinatown and walk north arm-in-arm, talking all the way to her apartment on Washington Square. Hadn't lasted long. Only a few months later she was injured and eventually moved in with him uptown. They were no longer sixties lovers but that ungainly thing of the seventies – a relationship.

He met Perlman on the corner of Mulberry and Canal. It was late morning on a December Monday, the last week of the year before Christmas. It was cold. The therapist's breath flowed out of him in a long arched white column of smoke, curling up past the tenements to the sky, as if he were a little chimney that had bolted from the buildings. The streets were dirty from last night's tourists. Attached to every lamppost was a gaudy and, especially in the morning sun, tawdry white-and-red Christmas bell decoration. Lights were strung between the bells; sometimes they became overgrown and smothered an awning or a tenement's banisters. On one staircase leading down to a basement, where the garbage cans would normally be, a Nativity scene of miniature figures was displayed; the steps made a steep descent for the Wise Men to Baby Jesus at the bottom. Max stepped on a green Michelin guidebook that was soggy and broken. Only one shopkeeper was out sweeping. In this cold, the quick way with a hose wouldn't work. The other store owners must be sleeping late. Or maybe hoping the bright sun would eventually warm things up.

'She knows you're the Good Samaritan,' redheaded Perlman said as they walked to Carla's apartment. He had grown a beard since their last meeting. It wasn't as red as the hair on his head, but it was full. Max thought that with his bulk Perlman would make a good Santa Claus. He sounded like one; and in the nearly empty streets the therapist's deep bass had even more resonance and volume. 'It doesn't impress her, that's not why she agreed to meet with you. She agreed to meet you because she wants to ask if you saw her child while inside the wreck. I've told her no. But she wants to hear it from you. She's completely obsessed and very – I don't know – primitive about the whole thing. She's very Old World, very Catholic, you know?'

'No, I don't.' Max no longer bothered to guess at the meanings hidden in everyone's talk. He insisted they be explicit or he would be deaf to their half-speeches.

'I don't know. She's filled with guilt and shame. You know?'

'No, I don't. I'm filled with guilt and shame. How is that Old World?'

'We're here.' They were in front of two unlocked glass doors, leading to a small tiled vestibule with an intercom and a locked door. 'You judge for yourself. I wanted to warn you. She could do anything. They tell me she's been almost catatonic for weeks. But that could change. She could scream at you. Hit you. Her mother is there and she'll keep an eye out. Carla doesn't want me to go up. I'll be across the street visiting with her priest. He's actually the one who first called me about her. But we've never met, only talked on the

phone. Would you ring the bell at that door' – Perlman
pointed to a small wooden door in a building next to
Saint Patrick's Old Cathedral – 'after you're done and
let me know how it –?'

'Isn't that where the first black American saint is
buried?' Max asked. He gestured at the long wall around
an adjoining cemetery. 'I was reading about it in yesterday's *Times*.'

For a moment Perlman was ready to laugh. He
checked that, however, and looked at the top of the
wall as though he might be able to vault it with his
vision. 'I don't know. I didn't see the piece. I'll ask the
Monsignor. Give us something to talk about.' He
opened the outer glass doors and pointed to the fake
gold buttons of the intercom. 'It's 3A.'

After he was buzzed in, Max paused in the small area at
the foot of the stairs, too cramped a space to be called a
lobby. He smelled a kind of cooking and mustiness that
reminded him of something. What was it? He waited there
until he remembered it was the smell in the halls of his
childhood building in Washington Heights. After his
father's heart attack, thanks to the insurance money and
his uncle's help, they had moved to the Upper West Side,
which, although it was decayed in those days, was still
more definitely middle-class than his old neighborhood.
Certainly the buildings smelled different and sounded
different. You didn't know who lived behind most of
those doors or what they felt about each other; in
Washington Heights he knew what everyone was eating
and whether they loved each other. Not that he missed it as
a thirteen-year-old. He had preferred the relative bourgeois dignity of the Upper West Side, despite its heroin-
addicted muggers and demented rent-control elderly.

Max winced at the fact: his father's death had improved his life. He was indulged; they lived in a better neighborhood; he was sent to a private school. Max breathed deep of the unventilated odors of ancient garlic and detergents that had worn away the tiles to a smooth rubbed finish and he had to admit it to himself – Dad's death was boom times for me. He had confessed this to his shrink years ago, but its clarity had been muddied when the good doctor forgave the observation as a generic feeling all sons are liable to. In the vestibule Max looked at the truth, admitting to himself that it belonged to him as an individual characteristic. His shoulder still hurt from his latest struggle with death the month before and he sometimes shuddered at the memory of what he had dared, but the truth stayed with him, that death was his friend, had always been his friend, and now was the source of his strength.

A little old woman, her skin dark and wrinkled, her teeth as white and fake as kitchen Formica, opened the metal door of 3A. She immediately took Max's enormous goose-down coat – removing it he felt small, as though he had shed a big man's skin and emerged as a child – and explained that she was Carla's mother. She said she would take him to the living room and then get Carla.

Max hardly answered; he was surprised by the condition of the apartment. He had expected the dented front door to squeal with age and open into a decrepit interior. But the door opened silently. Judging from the small foyer and the living room, the tenement apartment was maintained in extraordinary condition. The plaster and paint job was immaculate; Max couldn't see a single bump or crack. The walls were as smooth and pure as if it were eighty years ago and New York was mobbed with meticulous immigrant craftsmen – a Babel of geniuses who worked for what New York's WASPs considered nothing and the workers considered a fortune. The living-room windows, framed by tacky red drapes, were brand-new single Thermopane; but they weren't sloppily fitted with a slapped-together frame; they had been replastered and set with old-fashioned round-edged sills, each carefully painted so that only the absence of multiple panes made it obvious the windows weren't original. Also, the wiring seemed to have been redone throughout the apartment, judging from the three-pronged plugs and the recessed lights in the replastered living-room ceiling. Either these working-class Italians were secretly rich Mafiosi or the husband had many friends in the trades. Only love or guns could buy this quality of work.

Max was delighted to be in its presence.

'Here we go,' the old woman said, returning to the living room with Carla. The mother seemed half the size of her daughter, although that was partly because she had the beginnings of osteoporosis. The mother may have been small and bowed by age, but she was both guide and engine for her daughter.

'My God,' Max said on seeing Carla as she was steered on to the yellow-and-white sofa. He was in a matching love seat at its side. 'What a tragic face.'

Carla's mother looked at him, neither upset nor pleased by his comment, but certainly impressed. Carla had no reaction, she stared at him blankly. That surprised him. She had asked to see him and yet she behaved as if his presence were of no concern. She had an El Greco face, elegant and sad. Carla's black hair twisted away from her in places and fell off in others. The mess was richly colored even though so black – hair with the tints and shine of youth. She reminded him, although her face was different in shape and texture, of his mother when young and widowed.

Here's your chance to sleep with Mom, Max said to himself without irony.

Max didn't bother to say hello. 'My father died in front of my eyes when I was thirteen years old,' he said into her exquisite and heartbreaking face. Carla's eyes flickered to life, as if Max had only just appeared in front of her. 'I was walking with Mom and Dad and my little sister down a long hill on 174th Street in Washington Heights. I had a brand-new baseball glove, a special first baseman's mitt that they had spent a fortune to buy me, and I was tossing the ball up and down in the air. I had just thrown it up and was watching it fall toward me when I heard my mother gasp and kind of scream and I didn't see where the ball fell – somewhere, I guess, it's still rolling down the street – and I turned and Dad was dead on the sidewalk. There was a little blood coming out of his nose, and his legs were sort of twisted beneath him. My father looked as if somebody, somebody with a big hand, had just reached down, given him one good squeeze and broken the life out of him.'

'That was God,' Carla said. She smiled a crooked smile.

Max nodded. 'That's what I thought. I thought, God killed my daddy.' Tears came up in his eyes. Carla's black despairing eyes focused on him with an intensity that might be hatred. Her crooked smile smoothed to calm resignation. She nodded agreement. Max was fascinated by her long mouth and full lower lip, quite red even without lipstick. Her jaw was long and perfectly drawn by its creator. Her chin has great dignity, he decided, the dignity of a judge. 'Scared the shit out of me,' Max admitted to her. He hadn't explained it to anyone that simply. There had been such fancy talk about the effect of his father's sudden death and what did it amount to? Was it as precise and truthful as that it scared the shit out of him?

'What did your father do to make God want to kill him?' Carla asked. It was clear from her erect posture and alert black eyes that she meant her question literally.

Her mother proved that by her reaction. 'Carla!' she chided her.

'I couldn't figure that out,' Max said. 'He was a religious man. He was hardworking. He was kind to my mother and to me and to my little sister –' Max's tears had returned, blurring his vision. He paused because they had also welled in his throat.

Carla leaned forward. She thrust her beautiful and sad face at him, studying his eyes, apparently checking on his tears. She nodded. 'You loved him,' she said and leaned back, again with a judge's dignity.

'Yes,' Max said. 'I didn't know why God had killed him. There was no reason to kill him and so I decided that meant there was no God.'

Carla's mother made a noise, something in between a gasp and a groan of disapproval. 'Mama!' Carla said. She almost whispered, but there was rage in the breathy wind: 'Leave us alone!'

The little woman shut her eyes and sighed, standing still for a second. She scurried out a moment later.

calling back, 'I'm in the kitchen. Ask him if he wants coffee.'

'Do you want coffee?' Carla said, again with a crooked smile.

Max was amused. She was in blue jeans and a white T-shirt, her eyes were exhausted, her hair was chaotic, and there was no heat coming from her, no sexuality, but he wanted to take her out of the apartment and change all that. He looked at her left arm, pointing languidly at him as part of her question. The underside was smooth, its color a creamy white. One blue vein showed through, cutting across her arm until it ran into bone and disappeared. He declined her offer of coffee and she returned the arm to her side. He was impressed by the knob of her elbow, sharp, its tip pink from friction with the sofa. He wanted to kiss it. He couldn't remember if he had ever kissed a woman's elbow.

'I know it's stupid to believe in God,' Carla said. 'I can't help myself. But you're smart. You've been to college, right?'

Max chuckled. She was funny and not depressed at all, it seemed to him, in spite of what Perlman had said, and in spite of her enervated appearance and despairing voice. He didn't think it was really sorrow; she was angry. He couldn't express those thoughts so he merely chuckled. 'Yes, I went to college.'

'And you're Jewish, right?' She hardly waited for his nod before continuing, 'Do Jewish people actually believe in God? I know Jews don't believe in Jesus, but tell you the truth – and I'm sorry, I know I'm being rude – but I ask because it don't really seem like most Jews believe in God the Father either. Except for the ones with all the hair, the Hassicks – I don't know how to say it –'

'The Hassidim.' He leaned back and laughed. 'You're right. They're like really devout Catholics. Jews like me – we're more like Mario Cuomo.'

'You got it.' Carla snapped a finger at him to indicate he had won a point. 'People who go to college don't really believe in God. People who really know about things don't believe in him. I'm too ignorant not to believe. But I'm not so stupid that I'm going to believe Monsignor O'Boyle when he tells me that my Leo is with God somewhere playing a harp.' She spoke in an annoyed tone but her face was in pain, as if she were about to cry.

Max didn't want her to cry. He said, 'Maybe he's playing a trombone,' as though the subject were absurd.

Carla was surprised. She leaned back on the sofa and her deep brown, almost black eyes looked up at the ceiling. Her face smoothed while she looked. Finally, she said calmly, 'You're right. If he's playing something it would make a lot of noise.'

'But it's all pretty ridiculous,' Max said. He had no desire to be sympathetic. Anyway, it was obvious that pity only made her mad. 'It's just that everyone is scared by the idea that life and death happen without any reason. They think you're born because your mother wanted you so much or because God wanted another great home-run hitter to play for the Yankees. And they think you die because you've been bad or careless – you smoked or you committed adultery or you forgot to put on your seat belt. That way, even though you can never be good enough or careful enough to live forever, at least you can try. But if it's out of our control, if it makes no sense and just happens, then there's no reason to do anything.'

'There's no reason to love,' Carla said to the ceiling.

'People don't so much believe in God as that they choose *not* to believe in nothing.' Max didn't think this was much of a philosophy, but it was the best he could do.

Carla lowered the ancient and lovely form of her face to his level and looked straight at him. Her dark eyes were wide under her thick circular eyebrows. Max watched her pouting and tempting mouth. Being with her in the perfect little living room he felt serene. After a moment of consideration, Carla shook her head no. She said in the relaxed voice of honesty, 'I'm sorry. I can't do it. I believe in him. He may be a fucking bastard – He was a fucking bastard to me –' Max's worst fear came true; her eyes filled with tears and she was crying.

'No.' Max took her hand. He stood up, pulling her hand at the same time. It was cold to the touch. That shocked him. The apartment was hot and she looked hot – in her dark hair and dark eyes and white T-shirt – but her hand was cold and unloved.

His touch stopped her tears. 'What are you doing?'

'Let's get out of here.'

'No!' She pulled to free her hand; it was not only as cold as ice but just as slippery. It slid out. She hid it under her leg. 'I don't go outside! Didn't they tell you?'

'Yes. But you're safe with me. Nothing bad can happen to you with me. Didn't you read about me in the papers? Everyone with me lived. With me you're safe.'

Carla frowned; then she smiled her crooked smile. 'You must think I'm very stupid,' she said in good humor.

'No!' Max was appalled. He slid off the love seat, dropped to his knees and pleaded. 'I'm not lying. You *are* safe with me. I can't explain why. But I'm not lying.'

'You're serious,' she said, more as an observation than a question. 'What are you telling me? There's no God but there's you?'

Max leaned toward her on his knees and extended his hands in a plea. 'Come with me, Carla. I promise you'll be safe.'

Carla beamed at him, as if he had done something delightful. From behind he heard her mother make a noise.

'What are you doing!' the old woman said. He felt her hand on his shoulder, pulling at his sweater. 'Get up. Get off your knees.' She abruptly let go of Max and added softly, 'Carla . . .?'

Carla was laughing. She had opened her mouth – it turned out to open very wide – and was letting go of volleys of laughter, aimed at Max by her bright eyes.

Max took them with a smile. His hands were still out, offered to her. He whispered, 'Come with me?'

Her mother didn't make another move to interfere. She stared in dumb admiration at her merry daughter.

'Sure, I'll go,' Carla said to Max and gave him her hand.

His car was comfortable. It was foreign, a name she didn't recognize or know how to pronounce. Max told her it was pronounced *sob*.

'I don't like that name,' she said and was nervous. The troubles she'd had since the crash whenever she went out had begun. Her hands were moist and her stomach hurt. Each breath stuck in her throat; there seemed to be only a little space left to fill up with air. 'Is this a good car?' she said. Her voice was weak and her ears were stopped up with the noise of her own frightened blood. She could hardly hear herself ask the question.

'It's a very safe car,' he said as he pulled away from the curb. 'Very safe and I'm an excellent driver. Never been in an accident – not while I was behind the wheel anyway. And you know what? It doesn't mean we're going to survive this ride. Because even if I do everything right, even with us strapped in, and with the marvelous technology of the Saab's collapsing cage and its reinforced doors and roof, we could still be crushed to death or hurled to death. We're not safe because of the car or because I drive defensively.'

'What?' she asked. She forgot about trying to absorb air from the small sac of it in her throat. She looked at Max. He smiled at her, at ease and friendly. How old was he? His graying kinky hairs didn't tell her much, because it was the kind of white hair that can come early. His face was lined at the eyes and mouth, but only a little and he had the kind of fair skin that wrinkled easily. He could be as young as thirty or as old as fifty. 'What did you say?' she asked, not really believing she had understood.

'We're not safe. No matter how good this car is, no matter how carefully I drive. I'm not telling you anything you don't know. You know we're not safe – that's why you're scared.'

Carla laughed. 'Everybody else keeps telling me things are safe. You're just saying the opposite to fool me.'

'No. I'm not playing a mind game. It's the truth. It's

not safe. In fact, you're not safe sitting in your apartment. On Mulberry Street you're hardly more than a mile away from one of the biggest faults in the United States. Someday, maybe in a few minutes, there'll be seven plus, maybe even an eight earthquake. This city isn't built for it. You'd be dead. My guess is more than a million people would die right away. And even if you survived you might eventually die. Since this is an island, with all the gas lines and the density – people could be trapped on Manhattan with an inferno around them and no way to escape or to fight it.'

Carla shifted a bit and took a good look at this man, a stranger really, with whom she was now stuck. He looked Jewish to her: very pale skin, a relatively short man with nervous hair who seemed never to have done any physical labor. His hands were smoother than hers; she'd bet they were softer too. But he had good features, a broad smart forehead, beautiful pale blue eyes, a reasonable nose and a wonderful mouth that seemed to curve twice at the ends, subtly down and subtly up so that he could look sad or happy with only a small change in their undulations. 'You told me I was safe with you,' she said, feeling betrayed.

'You are. But not because the car is safe or New York is safe. We're safe because we died already.'

That scared her. Sunlight glared on the cold streets. A beam flashed off a car's fender, blinding her. She was terrified. Maybe she was actually dead; maybe this was purgatory, believing you were alive, but having no feelings except sad ones and hating the people you love. 'I'm not dead!' she yelled.

'No, you're not,' he said. He steered the car crosstown, heading west. He was calm. 'I didn't say that. I said you've died already. You've passed through death. You're alive now. Both of us are. All of the survivors are. Don't you see? Everybody else' – he gestured at the streets, at the people hurrying to their destinations, hunched against the cold, scurrying with the fear of hunted mice – 'they don't know what it is to die in their minds like we did.'

'That's bullshit.' She turned even more in his direction. The seat belt pulled taut against her shoulder. His face looked smooth and very young from this angle. She couldn't see any sign of a beard on those white cheeks. He could be twelve years old. 'I didn't die in my mind. My baby died and I got hurt but I didn't die, I didn't think about dying, I just thought about my –' She stopped.

'You just thought about what? How your baby died?'

He had steered on to the West Side Highway extension heading uptown. 'Where are you going?' Carla demanded. She wasn't scared or nervous. But she thought he was crazy and she wasn't sure if she wanted to be alone with him in a car.

'The Sawmill.'

'The what? You mean out of the city?'

'Yes. The Sawmill is such a great winding road and so pretty. It was built to please the rich.' Irrationally he gestured at the river and the rotting dock structures. 'Well, the middle class anyway. To be a pleasant road for a Sunday drive. The man who designed it –' Max chuckled, 'his name was Moses – he imagined a world full of happy, prosperous self-satisfied people with good-natured servants and shiny cars that never broke down. And it didn't bother him that his own brother died homeless. What an asshole. No, he wasn't an asshole,' he seemed to be arguing with someone else, someone who wasn't in the car. 'He wanted to build his dreams and not just be a good man. A stupid, gullible good man whom everybody cheats and ignores.'

'You talking about yourself?' Carla asked. She had definitely decided he was crazy, but she no longer feared him.

'Yes.' He smiled at her. 'You're smart,' he said and he meant it. He looked sane enough: his pale eyes were friendly; his bush of gray-and-black hair was benign. 'Is it all right if we take a drive and see some trees even if their leaves are dead?'

This was her chance to stop it. He was reasonable and he would let her go back. But she felt comfortable. She had forgotten her small throat and sweaty palms. The car was warm and quiet, her seat ample and soothing. Seeing the miserable, cold, and frightened world through the hard clear glass of the windows felt good. It gave her a kind of strength. He was crazy but he was right – she was safe with him.

Two days later Max returned without phoning ahead and stood in the tiny foyer, his hands folded, to ask if she wanted to see scenic Jersey City. He shuffled his feet like an awkward adolescent asking her out on a date. She said yes, sure that he was kidding about the Jersey City part, but he wasn't, he wanted to see the Newport Center Mall and that's what they did, driving all around it while he made comments on the architecture and the surrounding old buildings, many of them deserted, even burned out. Later, when she returned home her mother made a big joke out of his idea of sight-seeing and probably Manny would have too, if Carla were talking to him, which she wasn't. That was why she tolerated her mother's reappearance from California with the intention of staying through New Year. With her mother there it was easier to ignore Manny.

Carla enjoyed Max's tour. After they went around and through the Newport Mall by car, he pulled into its huge multileveled parking lot and asked if she wanted to eat some lunch. She was hungry. The same sort of gnawing hunger that came on suddenly in the middle of the night, a hunger for comforting foods, a hunger she couldn't satisfy no matter how much she ate and a hunger that so far she had felt only when alone.

She wanted to say yes but she was frightened at the idea of leaving the car. The mall was crowded with Christmas shoppers.

'Remember,' Max said. 'We're ghosts. They can't do anything to us.'

'You're crazy,' she said to him, scared by his idea. She felt comfortable telling him. 'You're really crazy, you know that?'

He smiled with his lips shut; the double curves at his mouth's corners undulated. The sun came across his face through the windshield; his white skin seemed to glow whiter, as if he were made of packed snow.

'I should talk,' she said. 'Okay.' She took a breath and opened the car door. He came around to her side. He put his arm through hers. He was wearing a navy-blue wool jacket, a thin jacket that hugged his upper torso and left the rest of him exposed. 'Aren't you cold?' she asked, shivering inside her goose down.

'Yeah,' he said. 'Maybe I should buy a coat in the mall.' They walked across a covered bridge from the parking lot and entered the mall.

It was beautiful, Carla thought. They had come in on the third floor and she could see down through the open central area to the two lower floors. Everywhere there were Christmas decorations and scenes. Sculptures of reindeer were paused beside plastic pine trees and brilliant poinsettias, all arranged on soft white cloth that looked like snow. There were lights strung along the glass panels at the ceilings and also along the railings of each level so that white, red and green lights blinked everywhere – pretty stars in a small universe.

And the people! Carla had forgotten what crowds of people look like. Haggard mothers shouted after their running children. Harassed fathers stood before store windows filled with goods, their heads bowed, defeated by choices. Giggling teenage girls flounced past, packed together, shoulder-to-shoulder, hair bouncing and trailing them like wedding trains. Solemn boastful teenage boys paraded after the girls; like sullen peacocks, their legs stretched ahead of their torsos with suspicious grace, eyes watching the girls with contempt and mastery.

Max guided Carla among them. She noticed a fat mother with pink beefy arms carrying a newborn. Every other second the mother kissed her baby's bald head softly – a reflex while she studied the mall stores. She wasn't even really in the throes of loving her baby; the constant kissing was routine. Carla didn't hate her, didn't pity her, didn't envy her. She wondered about her life, if she had always been fat, what her husband was like, and if the baby was her first child. She stopped beside them and stared at the newborn's head while the mother paused to look at the shoe store's display window. Carla brought her face within inches of the baby and the mother; neither seemed to notice her. Maybe she *was* a ghost.

Max tugged at her to continue. She felt they were gliding soundlessly to the rhythm of the piped Christmas music, passing unseen by the mob of shoppers: gangs of men, women and children bustling with packages, eyes red and exhausted yet shining with appetite. They weren't gangs, Carla reminded herself. They were families, spinning out and then back to each other, like planets in orbit, loose and yet never free.

'I don't have a family anymore,' Carla said to Max. They were at the crossroads of the mall where it divided in four directions above a large central courtyard. She leaned against a railing that barred her from dropping two floors down to the big open area. Down there a man in a Santa suit in a mock sleigh was being photographed with babies and toddlers. She noticed the long line of children and parents waiting their turn with him. She looked up from that hurtful sight at Max. She felt faint. 'I don't have a family,' she repeated in a weak voice.

'What do you miss?' Max asked. Against the lights and bright decorations he was as pale as a ghost.

'I was going to buy him toys,' she said and sobbed. She tried to stop and then sobbed more. She was embarrassed; she was no longer invisible. She turned away from the startled faces of the mall shoppers and bent out over the banister, shutting her eyes and fighting the pain inside. But the happy music kept on wounding her; and even though she had her lids shut and her eyes were swimming with tears, she could still see the Santa below with awed children on his knee, watched by smiling, satisfied parents, and that hurt so much she wished she could scream herself to death – disintegrate in a single explosion of grief.

'Let's buy them,' Max said. He leaned down and looked at the Santa. Max seemed to be floating in the mall's air, glowing from its clear panels. He looked so different from everyone else, although his clothes were no better and he wasn't bigger or stronger or handsomer. He was at ease, unfazed by her sobs and upset. 'Let's buy him the toys. What did he like? How about a sword? My son used to love swords. He still does but he's too old to admit it.'

She didn't understand him. Or didn't believe she had understood. 'Your son . . .?' she mumbled wiping her wet cheeks.

'How about it? What would your son like for Christmas? Does he play with Legos? No, he's too young. How about the big ones? Or Bristle Blocks? Does he have Bristle Blocks? They're great. They can really use them and they don't get bored by them for years.'

Carla still wasn't sure she understood. 'You want me to buy presents for Bubble?'

'Bubble?' Max said.

'My son, Leonardo.' She understood now; he was crazy. 'You want me to buy presents for him. That's sick.'

'Why?' he asked innocently.

'Because he's dead. It's only going to make me feel bad to pretend he's not.'

'Of course he's – what did you call him?'

Carla lowered her eyes. She felt ashamed. She didn't know of what. 'Bubble,' she mumbled.

'Bubble,' Max said as if he were tasting it. 'Of course Bubble is dead. But your wish to give him presents isn't dead. I like giving presents too. So let's do it.'

'What? Are you serious? You wouldn't do this yourself.' She wasn't angry, but she didn't believe in him suddenly. 'You gonna buy a present for your father?'

'My father,' Max said thoughtfully, again as if he were tasting the word. 'I've never bought anything for my father,' he said wonderingly.

He sagged against the railing, no longer afloat. Carla felt she had hurt him and it was just like hurting a child – he looked crumpled and defenseless. 'I'm sorry,' she said. 'It's not a good idea. That's all I meant.'

But he wasn't hurt. Max's pale blue eyes focused on her, curious and energetic. 'I made him something in school. I carved his name in wood. You know, a nameplate to put on his desk. But I never had a chance to buy him a real present.' He moved close, filling her vision, blocking the pretty stars and talking louder than the happy music. 'Let's do it! Let's buy presents for the dead.'

She wasn't angry anymore or appalled either, but she couldn't accept his idea. She backed against the railing to get some distance from his eager face. 'I can't.'

'Why?'

'What'll we do with them?' she demanded, exasperated and confused.

'Do with them?' Max shook his head of white and black curls. The sparkling Christmas lights in the ceiling shone through his halo of hair.

'Who do we give them to!' Carla almost shouted. His suggestion made goose bumps up and down her back. She was scared of buying things for the dead. Vaguely, she feared it was sacrilegious.

'I don't know,' he said, undeterred. 'We'll figure that out later. Come on,' he took her arm and tugged. 'I know just what my dad would want.'

'You do?'

Max was excited. He pulled her the way a kid would, dragging her down two flights of stairs and hurrying her into a trot until they reached the side of the mall where a large Sears department store took over all the space. He moved with such enthusiasm that they attracted glances even from harried Christmas shoppers. He kept going through section after section until he reached the hardware department.

Max stopped in front of an enormous red metal tool chest, displayed with its top open, its interior drawers out in various levels, each one filled with a tool or a part of a tool that fit precisely in the space allotted. 'He liked to build things,' Max said with a smile of satisfaction.

'Can I help you?' a young salesman asked. He was skinny and his head had a distorted shape, the top extraordinarily wide and flat and then narrowing to an unusually small and narrow chin.

'I want to buy that.'

The chest and tools were so expensive that even the salesman had to be told twice that Max meant to buy both. The salesman's excitement at the effortless sale of an item he obviously thought would never be sold brought a flush to his oddly shaped cheeks. His hands shook while he wrote out the order.

'We lived in an apartment,' Max told Carla while they waited on the clerk. 'So Dad couldn't really have room to work, but he used the maid's room, right off the kitchen, and built chairs – he even built our dining-room table.' His voice, his language, the slouch of his body had become like a boy's. He beamed at her while he talked: 'And he used to fix things for the neighbors for free. Anything he could. Just on the weekends. I'd watch and he'd give me the hammer to hold or have me do the easy stuff. Anytime we had to get something at the hardware store he'd stop in front of one of these' – Max pointed to the display chest – 'they weren't as magnificent as this one – and long for it. He'd look at it silently for minutes and minutes while I pulled at the drawers and then he'd say, "I'd like to have that," and walk away.' Carla saw the tears collect in Max's pale blue eyes. But he was still smiling.

When the salesman took Max's credit card, Max told him that he wanted the tools and chest shipped. The salesman paled. His little chin quivered. He said in a strangled voice that to get the chest there by Christmas it would have to go by UPS and that would cost extra.

'I don't care what it costs,' Max said, his eyes staying wet, but not letting go of their tears. 'It's for my father and I want him to have it on Christmas.'

The salesman paused for what seemed a long time and said nothing. He regarded Max with respect during the silence. When he finally spoke he said softly, 'I wish I was in your family.'

At first Carla had thought Max's idea mad, then dangerous. As she watched him feel this happiness she wanted it too.

'Where are you sending it?' she asked him as he wrote down the address for the salesman.

'Where am I sending it?' Max said loudly and he and the salesman exchanged looks as if Carla were quite foolish. 'I'm sending it to my father. It won't fit under my tree. It won't fit under his either. He's Jewish. He doesn't have a tree.'

The salesman nodded politely. 'Happy Hanukkah,' he said when they were finished.

Max took Carla's arm and said, 'I'd like to buy Bubble a set of Bristle Blocks. Unless that's what you're getting him.'

She saw Bubble reach for a Ninja Turtle figure belonging to another boy in the sandbox and screech when she said he couldn't grab it away. The boy's mother explained her son didn't want to share it because it was a special toy – he had just gotten it for his birthday.

'I want it for birthday,' Bubble said to Carla.

'Okay, I'll get it. I'll get you everything you want. I just do whatever you tell me. I'm your slave,' and she had kissed him and they had had pizza – Ninja Turtle food – and she had never had the chance to buy it. She had promised her beautiful baby a long list of toys for his birthday and she hadn't kept her promise.

Carla could remember the toys Bubble wanted; she could hear his musical voice asking for them. Wanting to buy things for Bubble still lived in her.

'Let's go to a toy store,' she said to Max. 'You can get him the Bristle Blocks. I got plenty on my list.'

After buying the presents they ate madly at the Food Court, a square area in the mall ringed by fast-food stands. They went from one counter to another, eating without any common sense. They each had a hot dog and an egg roll and a slice of pizza and a bucket of fried chicken and two frozen yogurts. While they ate they had Bubble's presents wrapped for a fee; the money went to children with AIDS. They put the presents in the Saab's trunk. Max asked if she minded touring some more of beautiful Jersey. She was glad to stick with him.

He drove through miles and miles of industrial

landscape. She told him about Perlman's group therapy session, reminded of it when they passed a Sheraton. Max made no comment while she recounted all the survivors who had claimed he saved their lives. She tried to prod him by drawing a pitiful picture of Jackie, the cheerleader mother: 'One woman came there just to say thanks to you. She acted like she really needed to see you. She said she and her sons would have died without you.'

But Max wasn't provoked. He said, 'It's so weird the stuff they have to believe.' And he changed the subject, reciting another fact about the warehouses and factories they passed. He seemed to know why every brick in New York and also New Jersey was put there. He was very intelligent, Carla thought, easily the most intelligent person she had ever met, but in a useless and sad way.

'What do you build?' she asked when they were in the tunnel going back to Manhattan. Riding with Max, speeding through the glowing fluorescent coffin buried under the river wasn't scary. She remembered the agony and terror she had felt when coming home from the group therapy session with Manny. She had shut her eyes, put her head between her knees and screamed until they were out. I was so crazy, she thought, comparing that day's hysteria to this calm with Max. Is it Bubble's death or is it Manny that's making me so crazy? Or is it because he's fucking another woman?

No, I was crazy before I knew about her.

'I don't build anything. I design homes,' Max answered after a long pause. She had almost forgotten her question. 'I was going to say houses,' Max said. 'But they're really people's homes. Built for good closet space.'

330

It was only their second meeting yet she knew him well enough to know he meant he didn't think closet space was worth fussing about. 'I've lived in small apartments my whole life,' she said, 'and I'd love to have a big closet.'

'Exactly. That's the way my clients feel. I don't blame them. But you see architecture has nothing to do with comfort or usefulness. Sometimes we pretend it does, but really if it was a choice between people and a beautiful building I'd lose the people. I always thought there was something to be said for the neutron bomb.'

They came out of the tunnel and Carla was surprised by the sun. The sickly white glow of neon had obliterated her memory of it and she was delighted it still existed. She pressed the button, let her window roll down and allowed the warm light and the cold air to wash her face.

'I'm sorry,' Max said. 'That was just a joke. Pretty stupid.'

'You say what you want, Max. It don't bother me. Every time I open my mouth I piss people off. I know what you mean. You love buildings. You love all buildings, even the ugly ones. You can't love all people.'

He laughed. 'That's right. Not even the beautiful people.'

'It's easier to love the beautiful people,' Carla said.

Max laughed very hard at her comment. He cackled for more than a block.

'It's not that funny,' she told him, worried by the energy of his laughter.

'You must make them crazy,' Max said as he controlled himself. 'You're very hard to bullshit.'

He parked his car in a lot and carried the shopping bags of wrapped toys.

'I want to give Bubble's gifts to Monsignor O'Boyle,' she said.

'You could put them under your tree,' Max said.

'No. I got him what he wanted. Bubble didn't mind sharing his –' she couldn't finish that sentence.

'Okay,' Max said. 'Then I'll give the Bristle Blocks also.'

Monsignor O'Boyle wasn't at Saint Patrick's Old Cathedral, they were told by a young priest who answered their knock. Carla explained they wanted to donate the toys to poor children.

'Oh, they picked up for the Foundling Home yesterday,' he said as if they had made a mistake.

'Don't they come again before Christmas?' Carla asked.

'I don't know,' the young priest said.

'Take them,' Carla said with a command and confidence Max hadn't seen in her before. 'If there's a problem tell the Monsignor to call me.'

'What a jerk,' she said about the young priest as they crossed Mulberry Street. Her eyes were bright, Max wanted to gather her wild black hair in his hands and look into them. Instead he walked beside her up the steps of her building and into the vestibule. They were jammed in there like two people squeezed into a phone booth. She pressed the intercom to her apartment. As she turned back to the door, Max's face was right there, up close. He whispered, 'Thanks for coming,' and kissed her on the lips, sweetly. Not for long, but it wasn't chaste either. 'Would you tell your husband that he does some of the finest plastering and painting I've ever seen? He looks to be a good electrician too. And I guess, judging from the window frames, he's a good carpenter also –'

'Who is it!' her mother's electronic voice interrupted.

'Me!' Carla shouted. The buzzing started immediately. She pushed the door open and held it, turning her head back to Max. He was still near her. His pale blue eyes watched her lips; they watched with nervous greed.

He wants me, she realized. It hadn't occurred to her before and it was quite a surprise. So much of a surprise that she didn't know what to think about it.

'Don't talk about my husband,' is what she said.

'I'm sorry.' Max backed away, banging into the front door, opening it enough to let in a cutting ribbon of cold air.

'I'm angry at him. That's why.'

'Oh,' Max said. He was still focused on her mouth. What was he so shy about? Did he think wanting her was a sin? But he wasn't a believer.

Is he scared of me? she wondered and laughed out loud at the thought.

'Don't look so scared,' she said.

'I'm not scared of anything,' he said in that calm tone he had when he said something that was impossible.

'You're scared to kiss me,' she argued gently.

'No, I'm not,' he said in that matter-of-fact voice. 'I just don't want to offend you.'

Carla held the inner door open. Max held the outer open. She looked into his pale blue eyes and then at his white cheeks. He seemed to be such a kind man that he was hardly real at all. Maybe he was actually sent by God. He had done all those good things, saved all those people, he had come to her and soothed her and yet he took no credit.

'Do you believe in God?' she asked. 'I mean for real. You don't think there's anything?'

333

'There are lots of things. I just don't believe any of them are God.'

That's what a true angel would say, she decided. It's just how God would do his works and test her faith. Not that she thought him supernatural. She believed Max was a real person but glowing with goodness like an angel. She liked him. More than that – at that moment she understood she could easily fall in love with him. But she felt if she encouraged him to make love to her that would be a sin and destroy her.

'You're right,' she said testing him. 'I don't want to be kissed. I don't want you to do anything – but – but I want to go with you the next time you go for a drive.'

He was not offended. He smiled with his lips shut. He was as sweet and brave as an angel. 'I'll see you tomorow, Carla,' he said.

18

Max found Debby in her black tights, sweaty and beautiful, seated in a chair near their bed, a wing chair that was usually draped with her clothes, but rarely sat in. He stopped a few feet into the room and readied himself to tell her. He hadn't said hello.

Nor did she. 'I'm going to take a shower,' she said, as if it were a warning.

'I took Carla Fransisca for a drive.'

Debby smiled, a private look of amusement. 'Again?' she said. 'How's she doing?' The edges of her hair were sleek and dark from perspiration. So were the tops of her tights. The fabric seemed to cling even tighter for it, a new skin for her tall lean body. In the black fabric she was a lovely panther.

'I'm in love with her.' He had hurried home, chased by this feeling. Keeping it secret even for the ride uptown had felt corrupting.

Debby sighed. She reached for a towel that Max hadn't noticed before, lying on the floor beside the chair. As she stretched for it she groaned. She hooked it with a few fingers, flipped it up, caught it with her arm and stood. All in a single movement, a graceful talented movement.

She was a living work of art – that was what he had fallen in love with. He had been wrong. It was unfair to her.

'You're in love with her?' Debby asked, more as a wondering repetition than a protest.

'Yes. Nothing's going on. But I'm definitely in love with her and I didn't want to lie about it.' He knew he sounded idiotic. And mean. 'I'm sorry. Not that I'm in love with her, but that I have to hurt you.'

'I don't think I can live with this much longer, Max.' She was upset. Her face showed only a little tightening, but that apparent calm meant the wound was deep and fresh. She walked toward the bathroom door and said loudly as she sought its refuge. 'It's too crazy.' She shut the door hard as if she had made a final decision.

She was right: her response was how the world ought to work. If he didn't love Debby then living with her was crazy.

And Jonah?

Max had come straight to the bedroom on entering his apartment. He hadn't glanced down the hall to check if Jonah was home. Would he be at this hour on a Wednesday? Was today after-school computer? It used to be that Max knew where and what his son was doing at all times.

Going into the living room Max heard the overture of one of his son's favorite video games playing faintly from the hallway leading to his son's room. Should he tell him that he wanted to divorce his mother? He was afraid of that, more afraid than he had felt of anything since the crash. Yet keeping it secret might be impossible. Could he spend time with Jonah and *not* reveal it somehow?

But Max wanted to see Jonah no matter how awkward or risky. Get him to take a walk over to the computer store and see their new games; or maybe to the bookstore to buy him a science fiction novel; or throw a football in Riverside Park, fighting the wind and broken glass.

Max had reached Jonah's door when Kenny, Jonah's closest friend at school, came out and nearly ran him over.

'Hi, Mr Klein,' he said as he went past. There was a black stripe of ink running down his cheek, as if he were a scholarly Apache warrior. 'I need a drink before we fight the Meka Turtle.'

From his room Jonah called out: 'The dreaded Disguised Meka Turtle.'

'Hi, Jonah,' Max said, looking in. Jonah was sitting only a foot or so from the small television in his room, a set used more for video games than watching programs.

'Hi, Dad,' Jonah said fast and melodiously, as if he were a bird chirping. 'Mom's in the shower. She said to tell you he'll be here at four.'

'Who?' Max said, wondering at his child's sudden competence with the world, its errands and relationships.

'Byron,' Jonah said.

'He's coming here?'

'She said you were expecting him.' Jonah made a helpless hands-up-toward-the-sky gesture – a miniature of one of his mother's mannerisms. 'I don't know. Anyway that's the message.'

Jonah was a three-quarter-scale man, freed of Max, and yet always bound to him. Max's heart ached for him. What will he get out of my survival that my father's death robbed me of? he thought. Nothing but what living parents bring – harassment and, soon, disillusionment.

'I forgot about it,' Max said. 'I don't want to see him,' he added, almost calling it out to Jonah.

Jonah studied the frozen image on his television

screen – a video game paused. He shrugged his shoulders and said, 'I don't blame you.'

'I'd rather do something with you,' Max said, painfully aware of how self-conscious he sounded, perhaps even dishonest to Jonah's ears, although Max was telling the truth.

'It's okay,' Jonah said casually. 'I'm busy.'

Kenny returned, brushing past Max in a hurry, carrying two glasses of seltzer, spilling them a little. 'Magic elixir to kill the Turtle,' Kenny said.

Jonah took one of the glasses and sipped it, watching his father. 'Dad . . .?' he asked after a swallow. He gestured at Max, his mouth open wide, almost pleading.

'What?'

'Do you want something else? We're playing here. Do you want to watch?'

'Do you want me to watch?' Max asked, feeling as simple as a child.

'I don't care,' Jonah said.

'Makes me nervous,' Kenny said in a low but audible tone.

'Okay,' Max agreed and left. He returned to the living room and listened to hear if Debby's shower was still running. It was. They would have to discuss living arrangements. Carla didn't want him anyway, so why should he move out unless Debby really couldn't stand him being around? They could maintain the illusion for Jonah, like the joke about the Jewish couple who suffer through sixty-five years of loveless marriage before consulting a divorce lawyer because they wanted to wait until the children were dead.

But if I'm not afraid of death, why should I fear my son's pain?

The intercom buzzed. The doorman told him Byron was coming up; the front-door bell rang a moment later. Byron bustled in with a large portfolio made of handsome black leather, an item so expensive and fine that Max would never have had the nerve to buy it for himself.

'I brought my new design for a shopping mall and a school. They're really good, I think, and you know what? I think they're more like your stuff.' Byron had walked into the living room. He knelt beside the large square coffee table (too awkward for the space, Max had told Debby, but she insisted) and was unzipping the case. 'I don't mean they look like your buildings. I mean they could really get built.'

'Why don't you ask your father to build them?' Max wasn't sarcastic – he believed Byron's father had the necessary resources and vanity.

'He doesn't like my new stuff,' Byron was matter-of-fact. 'Well, he sort of likes the school.' Byron let go of the top of the portfolio, allowing its spine to break open, spreading the contents across the entire surface of the table. He lifted one of his computer printouts from the scattered mess. 'He says he doesn't approve of malls. Here's the school. It's a high school. This is my really cool idea –' Byron spread himself over the drawing to reach a far corner of it.

'But your father could build them, couldn't he?' Max went over to the windows, the new single-pane windows that the co-op had put in. They had not been refitted with anything like the seamlessness of Manny's work. Carla had told Max she was angry at her husband but she was also loyal to him. That was sad for Max and yet in spite of what he should feel about a rival he was struck again by Manny's skill and meticulousness. Manny had done all that work on their apartment by himself, Carla told Max while they were driving on the Newport Mall's elevated parking lot. As she explained that Manny had taught himself those skills to be promoted to handyman, Max noticed the vibrations of the mall's concrete, fairly severe vibrations that were due to shoddy engineering.

Byron explicated his sketches at length, his words blurring together in his excitement. Max seated himself on the windowsill and distanced himself from the boy's blueprints and his speech. He thought about Manny's workmanship in Little Italy and resented Byron, resented this child who was being indulged to blow up his ideas into grandiose and useless monuments to himself, who was being encouraged to learn quickly and carelessly and who might very well one day design a famous building – like the Hancock in Boston, a huge sleek building with windows that fell out by the dozen.

'You're a child,' Max interrupted the boy's lecture.

Byron paused. His arms were spread, his towhead bowed. He lifted it slowly. The hair had been recently cut in a shape that neatly framed his eager face. He looked up at Max, his high cheeks shining. 'I know I'm a child.' He bobbed his chin, irritated, as if daring Max to continue this dangerous line of thought.

'It's ridiculous for you to draw these things without having any idea of the engineering, of the practical problems involved.'

Byron nodded, his lips squashed together in a disgusted frown. He pushed himself off the coffee table, sliding on his belly. The drawing of the mall slid off with him on to the floor. Byron settled on his knees. He

340

held his head in his hands and shook it sorrowfully. 'Not this,' Byron said. 'You're not going to do this.'

'Yes. This. Whatever this is. It's no trick to draw a picture and say here's a high school, here's a mall. Buildings aren't hard to imagine or draw – what's hard is to get someone to build them and then make sure they actually stand, to make them not only look good but also make sense so that people can use them. And will want to use them.' Max had propelled himself off the windowsill. He paced away from Byron and considered leaving the room. He was upset and angry at the child. He was close to saying too much. Yet he turned back to see if he had had an effect.

Byron got to his feet. He was self-possessed. 'I've heard you say that it's people who screw up buildings,' he said in a clear ringing voice. He looked pleased at catching the master in a contradiction.

Max got on his haunches to be level with the boy, speak to him face-to-face. 'The things I say, the things anyone says about their work, are never really true. The troubles I have in my work are too involved with what I can't do and what the world won't let me that I can't speak of them honestly. But I can tell you that it's the practical problems that make architecture a great art form. Buildings have to *work*. A painting doesn't have to support a hundred people dancing. A sculpture doesn't have to have running water and toilets. Look at your idea of a swimming pool –' Max pointed to a drawing that had fallen halfway off the coffee table. 'It's neat to put it on the top floor and cover it with glass windows – only an ordinary floor wouldn't support the weight and it would cost too much to have the extra support and the heating in winter would cost too much

341

and the glass itself would cost too much. Anyone can imagine beautiful things. That isn't talent. Talent is making beautiful things work. You don't know how to make them work. And you're not interested in finding out. You just want to show off. You just want adults to say – isn't he bright? Isn't he talented? And the reason you want that is because your father doesn't know any other way of loving you except by believing that you're talented. He's scared he won't love you if you're ordinary and so you're scared to be ordinary.' Max knew he had said too much. He clenched his hands and swallowed, trying to hold himself in, to stop the flow of hurtful talk.

However, Byron wasn't hurt. He didn't back away. He moved closer to Max while he listened to the lecture. His high cheeks seemed to lift his mouth into a grin. His thin eyebrows rose up and merged with the edges of his haircut. When Max finished, Byron nodded to himself as if he had come to a conclusion. 'You're jealous of me,' he said mildly.

'Jealous of you?' Max rocked back on his heels and tilted too far to the right. He put out a hand to steady himself. The pantomime of being off balance was a good reflection of how he felt. Max assumed Byron meant that Max was jealous Byron had a rich father. 'Jealous of what?' he asked to be sure.

'That I'm so good at it and I'm just a kid.' Byron gestured to his drawings. One of them had slid too far off the coffee table; it began a slow and noisy descent to the floor. They both watched it drop without making a move.

After the paper had settled, Max said softly and gently: 'You're not good. You're precocious. Maybe

342

someday you will be good, but right now you're simply doing something ordinary at an early age.'

'You're jealous,' Byron nodded his head up and down, grinning. 'Yes, you are.'

'Listen to me.' Max took him by his narrow shoulders. The firm grip stilled Byron. His eye were alarmed; they stared into Max's, their usual conviction flickering. 'You're very bright and I'm sure you'll be successful and your father loves you. You don't have to pretend to be grown-up. You don't have to do great grown-up things for your father to love you.'

Byron shrugged Max's hands off. He swaggered away, skidding on to his knees and sliding to the fallen drawings. He picked them up carelessly and shoved them into the portfolio. 'My dad,' he said as if it were of no consequence, 'is a wimp.'

Max assumed he had misheard. 'What did you say?' he asked. He was still on his haunches, an adult cut in half. He stood up; suddenly; he had to be tall.

Byron was done with his sloppy cleaning. He flipped the portfolio together and zipped it up recklessly. The zipper buzzed shut. 'He's a wimp.' Byron faced Max. 'He's even scared of my mom.'

Max slapped the boy. His hand was already back at his side before Max was conscious of the action. He had hit Byron hard. The child's head remained turned to the side where the blow had pushed it. White ghosts of Max's fingers still burned on the clean new skin.

'My God,' Max mumbled.

Byron's face gradually pivoted back toward Max. His eyes were awash with tears and yet they looked fearlessly inward at something ugly. Byron's mouth trembled but made no sound.

Max shivered. He was cold.

The sun came across his jaw, bobbing through the plane's windows. He glanced at Jeff and made a decision – I'm going to sit with that abandoned child so he will not die an orphan. Max saw the look on Jeff's face as he left him. Jeff's eyes were startled and frightened. He mouthed something at Max, a plea . . .

Max understood his partner's last look – *Jeff wanted me to stay with him. He needed me.*

Byron was gone. He heard wailing.

Debby was shouting: 'Max! What's going on?'

She came out of the bedroom with her hair wet, wearing only a towel. Max shook himself, like a dog drying off, to wake up from the memory.

He had forgotten exactly who he was or where he was or what time in earth's history he was living in. His first real thought was that he was living on the Upper West Side and that his apartment needed to be painted. Then he noticed Byron by the front door. From the angle he had of the foyer, Max could only see Byron's legs. He moved until he had a full view. Byron was spread on the floor, leaning his head against the door, clutching his portfolio and sobbing. Debby came beside Max muttering or mumbling something – Max didn't pay attention. He smelled fragrant shampoo.

Max and Debby approached the weeping child together. She talked while they moved, saying things to both Max and Byron. Her eyes looked scared. Max was curious whether the marks from his slap would still be on Byron's face.

Byron lifted his head from the door. He looked at Debby. He paused his sobbing and shouted: 'I wanna go home!' There were no marks, only tears.

'Okay. Max will take you home,' Debby said soothingly.

'He's angry,' Byron said and sobbed again.

'You take him home,' Max said to Debby. Even he was shocked and frightened by the cold fury in his voice. 'I don't want to have anything to do with him.'

Carla was downstairs waiting for him the next day. She smiled at the sight of his black Saab, bleached gray in spots by cold and dirt. Her eyes were lively and her hair was organized somehow – although still looking wild, black and lustrous. She likes me, Max thought and felt as proud as a teenage lover.

'So where are we going?' she said, bustling in, her down coat swishing. She pulled the door shut with a bang and grabbed the seat belt, pulling it across her chest in a hurry. Today, all of her movements had energy.

A dark-skinned man came out of her building, walked up to the curb, rested one foot on a fire hydrant and stared at Max. He was short and broad; his hair was a dulled black, straight and slicked back as if it were a skintight cap. He wore a gray uniform with a name sewn in script over his breast pocket. He didn't have a coat in the freezing air and he didn't shiver or blanch. He was still and ominous.

'Who's that?' Max said although he knew.

Carla had to look; she didn't know he was there. She had been concentrated on fastening the seat belt. She glanced up and frowned a little. She said in a disparaging tone: 'That's Manny.' She finished buckling herself in and said: 'So where to?'

Max returned the stare of her sentinel husband. He wondered: Will I have to fight him to get her?

He drove to the Staten Island ferry.

'Is this safe?' she asked with a sly smile as they were being guided in to park their car in the ferry's wide belly.

'No,' Max said, not smiling. 'It's had accidents. I think there are more boating accidents than with any other kind of vehicle.' He reached the spot where the attendants wanted him to park. He shut off the engine.

'I can't swim,' Carla said. She wasn't smiling anymore but she didn't sound scared.

'I'd like to make this ferry sound especially dangerous, but it isn't. I wanted to show you the dockyard on Staten Island where old ships are hauled to be scrapped for junk. Besides, we'll get a good view of the city on the ride.' Max opened his door.

'I know that. My girlfriend lives on Staten Island,' Carla said and for a moment seemed not to be willing to move.

'Do you want to visit her?'

'No,' Carla laughed. She opened her door. 'She'd ask me a million questions about you later and that would drive me crazy.'

They got out. The other passengers were heading for the enclosed deck. Max took Carla's arm – he could feel her fragile elbow inside the down of her coat – to the open area at the back of the parked cars so they could see Manhattan retreat as the ferry moved into open water.

A gust of wind blew across them. His face felt paralyzed by the cold.

'We're gonna freeze to death,' Carla said but she didn't make a move to go inside.

Max had spent all night alone in a hotel waiting to be

with Carla, expecting that she would make him feel happy. He had spent the night alone in a hotel because when Debby returned from taking Byron home, they had a fight and Max had walked out.

Debby had come in, stood at the closet and told Max right away, 'His mother was very angry. I think you're going to be hearing from them.'

Max didn't answer. He studied his wife to see if the mean truth he had told her had left a mark on her face. She was composed.

'I want you to call somebody,' she said, turning her back on him to hang up the dramatic black cape she wore for a winter coat. She was angry. Everything about her posture and face and tone of voice told him that, but, as had been true since the crash, she was unnaturally holding it in, holding it like a position on the barre. 'It doesn't have to be your psychiatrist,' she said to the closet and then faced Max again. 'Maybe you should call Bill Perlman.'

'Bill? You call him Bill?'

'I told you,' she had to swallow to contain her exasperation. 'I've seen him a few times. He's helpful to talk to. But it doesn't have to be him. It can be your mother. Or maybe a friend. You haven't spoken to Larry or Paul –'

'They're not real friends.'

'Then who is?' Debby insisted.

Jeff. Jeff was the answer. He was the person Max would have talked to.

'You're getting worse,' Debby said.

'I talked to somebody,' Max said.

'Who?' Debby asked. Curiosity wrinkled her high forehead.

'You,' Max said. He reached past her and took his coat from the closet. He held it in front of him and looked at her, asking her to give him a reason not to go.

She tried to hold her calm pose. 'I can't help you,' she said but the words were churned up and suddenly she lost her grip on the barre. She yelled: 'You tell me you're in love with a woman you just met! What am I supposed to say to that!' She seemed relieved for a moment and then sagged into despair. 'I don't know what you want from me,' she added in a low note of resignation.

'I'm going to a hotel,' Max said. 'Just for tonight. I'll call you tomorrow afternoon.'

He had checked into the Carlyle. He had fantasized spending the night there since his youth when he learned that it was JFK's favorite hotel in New York. Later on he read that Kennedy put Jackie in one suite and had his mistress in the adjoining room. That fact didn't make him less curious.

Max asked for and got a room four floors down from the famous suites in the tower. It was a disappointment. Although the elegant room wasn't pompous like the Plaza, it wasn't the good old days either. It had the modern luxury of a video recorder and a CD player. The desk told him a fax machine could be sent up if needed. All that made Max think of business, of what travel had become in the modern world.

He hardly slept, dozing off near dawn and yet waking early. He spent most of the tedious night staring out his window at lights in nearby buildings that stared back at him. All night he waited anxiously to meet Carla.

But he wasn't happy now that he was with Carla.

They leaned against the rail of the ferry and watched

348

the city first grow bigger and wider as they pulled out into the water. Gradually the huge buildings shrank against the widening water and sky, their tops narrowing into needles lost in the clouds, their foundations revealed as resting on only a thin sliver of support. Manhattan was merely a wafer floating on the steel water. The massive works of the city seemed to be a carefully drawn miniature at the bottom of a huge canvas. He felt himself shrink.

'It *is* beautiful,' she said wonderingly, as if she had never seen the skyline before.

Max looked at her face, her young skin even tighter as it clenched against the freezing wind. He didn't have her really. Any more than he had anything. Maybe he was dead after all.

'I had a fight with my wife,' he told her.

'Oh yeah?' Carla smiled. She turned away from the open water. 'I had a fight with Manny,' She shivered and squinted at the wind's force.

'You're too cold,' Max said. They went inside, bought coffees, and sat on a bench. The hot coffees were in thin Styrofoam cups, holding them hurt. Max burned his tongue on the first sip.

'What did you fight with your wife about?' Carla asked. She was hunched over her coffee, bracing the cup between her knees, warming her hands with its steam.

'I told her I'm in love with you.'

Carla sat up straight and turned to look at him full in the face. Her circular eyebrows raised, up there they made an even rounder shape. 'You're crazy.'

'That's what she thinks.'

'Well, she's right. Jesus,' Carla turned away and shook her head.

'It's what I feel. I'm not going to lie about what I feel.'

'There are some things you're supposed to lie about,' Carla said energetically, looking at him again. 'You gotta stop doing that to people.'

'You want me to start lying to you?' Max argued. 'You want me to tell you you're safe when you go out? You want me to tell you Bubble's up there looking down at us, wearing little wings?'

She slapped his arm with the back of her right hand. 'Shut up,' she said casually and shook her head again. 'I'm talking about them.' She smiled slyly. 'The living.' She nodded at the window, at the water and sloppy landscape of Staten Island. 'They can't take it. You have to give the rest of them a break. I'm as crazy as you are – you can't go by me.'

'What did you fight with Manny about?' Max edged closer to her until he felt her coat against him, up and down his side. He noticed her ear – it was little and had the ideal shape of a prototype.

'I told him after my mother left I was going to sleep in Bubble's room. I went in there and started to pack things up. They had kept everything in his room the way it was because they were afraid I would go crazy if they changed anything. And I'm glad they left it so I could do it. I went in yesterday after I saw you and I started packing his little things. I was crying like crazy. But I didn't mind crying and I was getting it done. My mother goes and hides in the kitchen. She was yelling at me from there. I couldn't hear what she was saying. Then Manny comes in and tells me to stop. I told him to leave me alone, to leave me alone for good. He said it was your fault. He said you were a bad influence.' She laughed mirthlessly for a moment. 'A bad influence. You know, like I'm a teenager and he's my pop. "You're running around with the wrong crowd,"' she imitated a deep, rough-voiced man.

Max smiled. He felt sorry for Manny. Manny had had a wife and a son when he put them on that plane and now both were lost to him. 'I *am* a bad influence from his point of view,' Max said.

'He's got no right to talk about who's bad.' She darkened. Her high cheeks and deep-set eyes seemed to become shields; behind them, still visible to Max, she thought something black.

Max was quiet. Staten Island's dock, a dull brown nest, limited their view. He felt better, vindicated in his feelings toward her. He could say the worst to her and she accepted him. The uneasy feeling he had moments ago – that he had been mistaken about Carla – was gone. 'Let's get in the car,' he said.

This time, when Carla strapped herself in she did it slowly and sadly. 'I'm gonna tell you something nobody knows,' she said quietly as they drove off the ferry. Max had studied a map at the Carlyle. He turned right aiming to stay along the water if he could, hoping to find the famous shipyard. He wasn't sure if the street allowed a view. 'Just before the crash,' Carla continued. 'Do you remember? We could see the runway. It looked like we were gonna be okay?' Her voice was tremulous, as if she were weeping in her throat. Her eyes were dry. She said shakily, 'I let go of Bubble.'

Max had never heard a voice in so much pain. He stopped the car immediately, right after a curve. He parked beside a white sea wall, tall enough to block the view of the harbor. He shut off the engine and faced her. Carla was staring ahead, through the windshield. Her hands and arms were out forming a circle, holding something invisible in her lap.

'Do you remember? Or am I crazy? Wasn't it safe? Didn't it look like we were gonna make it?' She stared through the windshield, focused on nothing. Her questions could have been spoken to anyone, to God or her dead child.

Max answered. 'Yes. Everyone thought it was going to be okay. I read in the papers that even the pilot thought we were going to make it.' But I knew, Max thought. I knew otherwise.

'Then didn't the wheels hit the ground? Didn't you think we had landed?' She was urgent, scared he might contradict her.

'Yes.' Max undid his seat belt and shifted to be closer to her. She didn't turn in his direction – he was near to the smooth skin around her lips, to her full pouting mouth. He felt sorry for her and he wanted to make love to her. He agreed softly, 'Everything – for one second – seemed okay.'

'I –' she announced herself loudly and then her lips trembled.

'You . . .?' Max whispered encouragingly to her transfixed profile.

'I had Bubble in my lap. I had crossed my arms over him like a seat belt, I had the fingers crossed – like this –' she locked her hands together in a fist, like a child praying, the skin turning white and the nails red from the pressure. 'And I let go to clap,' she did it now, tears coming to her eyes, although her voice was enraged. 'I clapped.' She released the fingers, put the tips together gently – demure pats, polite applause. 'Then we hit and

I lost him. My hands were open. There was nothing holding on to him.' She whispered in horror, 'I was safe in my belt and he wasn't.' Tears were flooding her eyes but she wasn't sobbing. She stared ahead at her memory.

'I see,' Max said. 'So it was your fault.'

She snapped her head toward him. He had her full attention. The tears stopped. Carla's mouth sagged open, her eyes were wild and scared. She opened her lips in a mute plea.

'It wasn't that the accident killed your baby,' Max said into her horrified look. 'You did it.'

'I wasn't holding him!' she whispered, terrified, as if the words damned her.

'You killed your baby,' Max continued, fascinated by the inexorable, inarguable logic of her guilt.

'His seat belt didn't work – I was supposed to hold him – did they tell you that?'

'Yes, my lawyer told me about your seat belt. He's your lawyer too and he told me about your case.'

'I didn't tell him the truth. I didn't tell him I let go.' Carla's head got erect. Her deep-set eyes stared out at Max, scared. 'Manny wants all this money and I have to talk in court.'

'I understand,' Max said. 'You're a liar also.' She not only had killed her child, she was going to collect for it, compounding neglect with greed.

'I'm very weak,' she said and her body no longer fought against her terror. She dropped her head and shut her eyes. She locked her fingers together, pressed the double fist against her lips and whispered furiously, 'Hail Mary, full of grace. The Lord is with thee. Blessed art thou amongst women. Blessed is the fruit of thy womb, Jesus. Holy Mary, Mother of God, pray for us sinners now and at the hour of our death. Amen.' She repeated the prayer over and over without pause, until the words came so fast and quiet that they were no better than the frightened moans of a child.

'Carla,' Max said. He touched her shoulder and shook it gently to rouse her.

She was oblivious. She keened in the seat, her seat belt swishing along with the whispering words of terror and longing: 'Hail Mary, full of grace. The Lord is with thee. Blessed art thou amongst women. Blessed is the fruit of thy womb, Jesus. Holy Mary, Mother of God, pray for us sinners now and at the hour of our death. Amen.'

He tried again, shaking her shoulder more vigorously. 'Carla. Stop. It's not your fault.'

She didn't react to his touch or his voice. She rocked and prayed, her eyes fixed on her clenched hands, her head bowed as if ready for a blow.

Max's mouth went dry. His tongue felt enormous, stuck, blocking him from speaking. She was lost. He had destroyed her.

What an arrogant meddling fool. He felt contempt and rage at himself. She had no defenses against his fanciful ideas. She wasn't ambivalent about the child she had lost. She loved her baby. Her pathos wasn't diluted by ironies or insights. To feel such a loss was unimaginable to him.

No it wasn't. Losing Jonah would hurt him that much. And no psychobabble on earth or television could convince Max that it hadn't been his fault. The universe had given him a son to protect and any accident was his responsibility.

354

He had done wrong. How could he fix it? What could he do with Carla? How could he explain this to her husband and mother? What did it mean about him that he could so casually harm someone, someone he claimed to love?

Max couldn't speak with his tongue so thick. The heated air of the car was too hot for his nostrils to absorb the oxygen.

Carla's dreadful prayer hurt his ears: 'Hail Mary, full of grace. Blessed art thou amongst women. Blessed is the fruit of thy womb, Jesus.'

Max thought it so natural for her to pray to another mother, to a perfect mother.

'Holy Mary, Mother of God –'

Max opened his door and got out. The cold cleared his eyes of pain. Carla didn't react to his departure.

'– pray for us sinners now and at the hour of our death. Amen.'

Max shut the car door on her.

The hour of our death – the words infected his brain. The hour of our death. Had it come at last? What was Max connected to if he had driven this woman – the only person he had been able to feel comfortable with in all these months – into madness?

Max went to the trunk and opened it. Folded neatly in the corner beside the red plastic box of emergency tools was a plaid blanket. They used to cover Jonah with it when he was little. Max smelled the fabric. He imagined he smelled the sweet dank odor of a child.

The hour of our death. Were they dead anyway? What was the difference?

Max lifted the emergency tool box. The jumper cables inside were so thick the top didn't close completely.

Max felt the weight of the box in his hands, judging whether it was enough. Too light. He looked around and saw – near the base of the sea wall, amidst a broken bottle, a squashed beer can, and a destroyed transistor radio – two partially broken bricks.

He emptied the plastic box of the jumper cables, gloves, tire gauge, the can of pressurized air, black electrical tape and other sundries. He carried the red box over to the bricks and put them in. They fit perfectly and gave it a good weight, in Max's judgement, close enough to what would be needed.

He used the electrical tape to attach the plaid blanket so that it completely wrapped around the plastic box with the bricks inside. He opened the back door on the passenger side and put the blanket and box inside.

Carla's rhythmic prayer continued, '. . . pray for us sinners now and at the hour of our death. Amen. Hail Mary, full of grace . . .'

Max left the back door open and opened Carla's door. He spoke into her small perfectly shaped ear. 'I want you to sit in the back.'

She looked into his eyes, but continued in a whisper, 'Blessed art thou amongst women. Blessed is the fruit of thy womb, Jesus . . .'

'I'm just going to move you to the back seat, that's all.' Max undid her belt and pulled her halfway out of her seat, lifting her by her clenched arms, rigid from her posture.

'No!' she shouted and fought against him, interrupting her prayer at last.

'I'm not getting you out of the car. Just getting you in the back seat.'

He pulled and this time she came out, although still

stuck in her pose, arms locked, hands entwined into a fist she kept at her mouth. Her eyes darted from side to side warily. 'Holy Mary,' she whispered frantically as he guided her to the rear, 'Mother of God, pray for us sinners –'

Max put her in the back, positioning her in the middle where there would be no obstruction from the bucket seats and pulled the lap belt across her, locking it. He took the red box and slid it on to her lap.

She stopped praying at the feel of the weight. She looked down at the box, stupefied.

'That's your baby,' Max said. 'Hold him upright.' He lifted the box so it would stand on its side. It came up to her chin which he imagined would be about right. 'This is Bubble. This is your chance to hold on tight and save him.' Max shut the back and front doors. He raced around to the driver's side, watching her through the window, worried she would balk. She dropped her head to study the blanket. Her black curls covered the top and her face. But she held on to the blanket and box.

Max got into the Saab, put on his seat belt and started the car in a hurry. He pulled out into the street and shouted at her: 'Did you pray in the plane?'

No answer. He saw the road was clear. He pushed on the accelerator, watching the speedometer. At fifty miles an hour that should be enough for a test and yet perhaps not enough to get himself squashed. He glanced in the mirror. Carla's face was white, her eyes wide and pitch-black, staring at him with grave attention.

'Did you pray in the plane?' he shouted.

She shook her head.

'Hold on to him tight! Pray to God to give you the strength to save your baby!'

357

Three blocks ahead the road curved to the right, around a brick warehouse wall. If Max went straight they would smash into it. Nothing was parked alongside to obstruct a direct hit. They were going forty miles an hour. Max pressed the accelerator.

'Pray and hold on!' he shouted and glanced at the rearview mirror.

Carla lowered her eyes. 'Hail Mary –' she whispered. She folded her arms around the box, crossing past each other, each hand gripping the opposite side, holding it tighter than she could possibly have held her child.

Max glanced at the speedometer as the wall loomed – he saw the word PRODUCE written in half-faded red letters – and noted that he had already gone past fifty miles an hour . . .

Too fast for me, he realized. I'll die. Pray for me now at the hour of my death. He shouted, 'Hold on to your baby!' as they hit the brick wall.

AFTERLIFE

19

Carla felt Bubble break away from her. He slipped the entwined grip of her fingers, flung her arms wide and flew out of her lap. Her body tried to follow him, but only the top half could. Her head passed between the front seats. Her cheek gently touched a bloody face that had turned toward her to make a plea. It belonged to Max. Max disappeared. She was yanked to the rear. A hand whacked the back of her head, the way the Sisters at school used to hit her if she talked in line. There was deafening noise, like countless drawers of silverware emptying at once on a tile floor. Yet she kept on thinking through it all, 'He couldn't stay. I couldn't hold him.' Even in the quiet aftermath – all she could hear or feel was something spinning behind her – a corner in her heart opened to a glad feeling of comfort.

'You see –' she heard Max say.

She opened her eyes and screamed. A strange face was staring at her.

'You see . . .?' it mumbled. Max's hand pointed at the smashed windshield: the glass was gone, replaced by bricks; the frame had buckled at the top and sides. The blanket-covered box was where the rearview mirror used to be, stopped from flying out of the car only because of the brick wall. The box looked to be half of its original size.

'You see?' Max mumbled. His face was covered with blood. 'You see?' he repeated. He slumped, his pulpy cheek resting on the bars of a twisted headrest and mumbled, 'Nothing . . .' as he lost consciousness.

Carla pulled at her seat belt. He was badly hurt, maybe dying. She shoved at all the things around her – tiny pieces of glass, a long metal rod, a large brown plastic funnel – and pushed at the crumpled rear door. People were nearby. She called to them as she got her door partly open. Someone took her hand and pulled. She fell out on to the ground. The Saab was several feet in the air, halfway gone into the building. Its exposed rear tires were spinning.

'Help him!' Carla shouted at the man who had gotten her out. A woman ran toward them. She moved in a funny waddle, both hands covering her mouth. Carla yelled at her – and at each person as they appeared – to get them to do something. They just stood and stared. Poor Max was dying, stuck up in the wall, slumped toward the remains of the box, his body squeezed into a tiny space, bright red blood washing down his forehead and nose – and no one made a move. Carla tried to get up to what there was of his window (it seemed to be only a quarter of its original size) to comfort him; but she couldn't get a grip. Finally someone told her an ambulance was on the way.

Fire engines, police cars and two ambulances arrived after what seemed like hours. They urged her to sit in the car or go to the hospital, but she didn't make the same mistake twice; she told them Max was her husband and she wouldn't budge until they got him out.

The paramedics hovered around the wreck, unable to figure out how to reach Max. They were shooed away by the fire department. Two of the firemen, elevated on a platform attached to the engine's ladder, were maneuvered toward the wreck. They carried what appeared to be a gigantic chain saw.

'Stop the bleeding!' Carla yelled at the paramedics.

They didn't respond. Everyone was focused on the two firemen and the machine they planned to use to open what was left of Max's door.

'They have to cut him out of there, ma'am,' said a young cop with dirty red hair and fair skin covered by pimples. He moved to lead her toward his police car.

'Stop the bleeding!' she yelled and got away from the cop. She ran up to the advancing platform that carried the firemen and grabbed hold. She could hang on to it and her feet would still reach the ground. They stopped the engine immediately. It had almost reached the wreck anyway. 'Stop the bleeding,' she yelled at them.

'They can't get up there,' one fireman argued.

'Get outta the way,' the other said.

'Let me try and put something on the wound!' a paramedic called to the firemen. He touched Carla, she let go of the ladder and he clambered up, using part of the platform and part of the broken wall and finally part of the car for his footing. Perched up there he bandaged Max's forehead. Max was unconscious; his head lolled as if he were dead.

Carla got down and watched from below. 'Is he alive?' she called up.

'I think he's gonna be okay,' someone said to her. It was the cop with pimples. What did he know?

Another paramedic came rushing with a plastic pouch of liquid and an IV. He handed the needle and line up to his colleague, who got it into Max and strung the feed around the collapsed roof to the other side. They did it fast and got down so the firemen could use their enormous metal claws. The machine made a hideous tearing sound, as if it were murdering the car.

'Are you Mrs Klein?' the pimpled cop said to her during the agonizing wait as they worked on the car door.

'Yes,' she said, afraid they would take her away if she admitted she wasn't related to Max. The cop asked what had caused the accident; Carla told him the wheels had suddenly begun to skid and Max couldn't control the car. The cop argued with her. He said there weren't any skid marks, that it looked like they must have been going very fast and straight at the wall.

She said, 'My husband may be dying. I have to pray for him.'

She didn't. She thought about praying for Max, but she didn't. She leaned back on a police car and looked up at the sunny blue sky. She watched her breath make small clouds in the pretty air. It was crazy – she felt good.

They carried a limp Max out of the car, swaddled and still, as if he were a newborn. She pushed her way – they halfheartedly tried to stop her – into the ambulance and sat beside him. By then the paramedics had wiped most of the blood off his face. It was puffy all over. His nose was broken. He looked as if he'd been in a heavy-weight fight. She felt pain for him and was amazed at what he had done for her sake. His eyelids were puffy, his cheeks had swollen his head into a square, and his lips had been spread wide. Just before they reached the hospital, he opened his eyes as best he could through the thickening lids.

They focused on her. He didn't seem scared or in pain. The pale blue of his eyes was thoroughly washed out by the sunlight coming through the window. He looked at her expectantly, waiting for her to say something.

'I understand now,' she said and that seemed to be what he wanted to hear. His mouth creased in a pained smile and he passed out again.

She waited until she had to before she called Manny and told him what had happened. First, the doctors checked her and said she was okay. They also said Max had a severe concussion and there was some danger of his brain swelling too much. That was what the doctor actually said. She thought the brain swelling sounded made up, possibly to conceal a more dangerous fact.

She especially thought so when the doctor went on to say that they might have to do surgery on the skull to relieve pressure and they needed permission to go ahead if necessary. That was when she told the doctor that she wasn't Max's wife. He blinked and said in a low but somehow threatening tone, 'How do I get in touch with her?'

Carla promised to get him what he needed if she could make a phone call. The doctor showed her to a waiting room with a pay phone and said he would be back in ten minutes. She called Manny.

'I'm coming for you,' Manny said sternly, as if making a threat. 'Stay there,' he added.

'No,' she said. 'You're going to call that lawyer, the one who's working for us. He's his lawyer too. Tell the lawyer to call his wife and tell her that her husband is okay but they need to talk to her. I'll give you the name of the doctor for her to call.'

'I don't want to,' Manny said darkly.

'Don't want to what?'

'Call Brillstein.'

'Why not!' Carla demanded.

'I don't know,' Manny said.

'You call. Make sure you explain everything to him. Tell him it was just an accident. Tell him Max is alive but he's got a concussion and his wife should call the doctor.'

'Then I'm coming for you,' Manny said.

'Then you come for me. But don't bother if you don't talk to the lawyer first. It's a matter of life and death. And make sure you don't let the lawyer scare the hell out of his wife.'

'Okay,' Manny said.

'Oh. And when you come here, bring some food.'

'Food?' Manny mumbled something in Spanish away from the receiver so she couldn't hear. She knew what all his favorite curses meant. When his voice returned it was louder than ever: 'What for?'

'We're not leaving until I know he's okay. And I'm hungry.'

She stayed in the small waiting room where the doctor had taken her to make the call. It was painted light blue and had a window with a view of a narrow shaftway and large air-conditioning ducts. She sat on a black plastic chair attached by a chain to two others. There was nothing to look at in the room except for the pay phone she had used to phone Manny and a poster explaining how you could be helpful to recovering heart-attack patients. She kept expecting the cops to arrive, angry that she had lied to them. The doctor showed up much later than he had promised he would. He said he had talked to Max's wife and had permission to do the surgery. He said Max was running a fever but that was normal because of the swollen brain. He also said

Mrs Klein had explained everything about Carla and Max.

Carla wondered what Max's wife had explained; she didn't ask.

While she waited, she thought about Max's injured brain. Max was already so smart the idea of his brain swelling sounded all the more painful to her. She knew that was ridiculous; it made her laugh at herself; she felt lighthearted. She knew she ought to be ashamed of her mood. Although she was frightened about Max's health, she was giddy, eager for action.

Brillstein arrived first. 'Here you are,' he said as he entered, his small eyes scanning to make sure no one else was about. 'Quickly. What happened? Just between us.' Brillstein put the flats of his narrow hands together and rubbed gently. The furtive sound of their friction was like a small animal digging a home for itself. He glanced back at the door suspiciously and then at her. 'What did he do? Try to kill himself?'

Carla didn't like him. She couldn't understand how he could be Max's lawyer – it made perfect sense that he was Manny's. 'How did you get here so fast?' she asked. It couldn't have been more than twenty minutes since she had spoken to Manny.

Brillstein's hands stopped. He cocked his head to the right and stared at Carla as if he had just noticed something surprising. After a moment, his mouth sagged open. The worry in his beady eyes went away. They seemed to widen and become curious. 'Luck. I was in Staten Island when your husband beeped me. Incredible luck. I've been lucky lately.' Brillstein backed away. He leaned against the phone, resting one arm on its top. 'I don't know why everything's been breaking my way.

Don't want to think about it, you know? Jinx it. How are you? You look very well for someone who's crashed into a brick wall at fifty miles an hour.'

'I'm okay,' Carla said, now feeling a little uncertain of her dislike for Brillstein.

'Listen. We don't have much time. I bought us some by telling the cops not to bother you now about the accident report. They may call you tomorrow or maybe I can deal with them. But still, Mr Klein could be in trouble. I'm his lawyer. He picked me to represent his interests. You know that. He trusts me. I've got to know – what happened?'

'He didn't try to kill himself. He was proving something to me.'

Brillstein nodded. He gestured with his right hand, a slow wave from her to him, silently asking for more.

'He was showing me I couldn't hold on to Bubble no matter what.'

'Hold on to your son?' Brillstein shook his head with his eyes shut as if he were struggling to wake up; abruptly he opened them and his head was still. 'You mean in the plane crash.' Carla nodded. Brillstein looked astonished. 'Didn't you know that? I told you it wasn't your fault. They should have had a working seat belt in his seat and of course you couldn't have held on, especially in a plane crash –'

For several seconds Carla had been shaking her head no to alert him he was on the wrong track before Brillstein finally noticed and stopped talking. He shut his lips and nodded at her. 'I opened my hands to clap when we started to land,' Carla told her secret calmly. 'When it looked like everything was going to be okay, I started clapping. I wasn't holding on to him tight.' She

could say all that without crying, without rage. She felt
sad, she still felt Bubble's sweaty head bobbing under
her chin, but she was able to keep on talking to the
short nervous lawyer and hold together. 'Also,' she said
after a swallow, 'I always thought he must have been
alive in there. After I got out ... while it burned. I
always thought –'

Brillstein shook his head firmly. 'He would have been
killed instantly.'

At that Carla had to cry. She covered up and let go.
Only the sad fact of her loss was in her heart – no pain.
She felt something soft brush against her cheek. Brillstein was offering tissues. She had just finished using
them when Manny came in. He was carrying a white
bag with Burger King written on it.

'She asked me to bring food,' he explained defensively
to Brillstein instead of saying hello.

'Give it to me,' she said.

'At least she's talking to me,' Manny commented to
Brillstein as he passed him to give Carla the bag.

Carla was annoyed by what Manny had brought. He
knew that she didn't like fast-food crap. Even wrapped
in foil inside the paper bag the hamburger's smell
was nauseating. She took out the french fries and the
Pepsi.

'Here,' she held the bag with the hamburger still
inside to Manny. 'You can throw this out.'

'Throw it out yourself,' Manny said. He leaned back
against the wall underneath the heart-patient poster and
slid down on to his haunches.

'I'll take it,' Brillstein said, obviously nervous that
they were going to get ugly. He grabbed the Burger
King bag. 'I'll check on what's happening and come

back. We have to talk more about the seat belt and everything,' he added in a solemn tone.

'What?' Manny said to the lawyer as he left. Brillstein didn't respond. Manny said it again to Carla after the lawyer had gone. 'What?'

Carla ate a french fry. It was hot and salty – she liked it. 'Thank you,' she said about the food. She took a sip of the Pepsi.

'What the fuck is going on?' He said this hopelessly, sliding down even farther on to his heels. He put his hands in his jacket too. He had made himself into a ball, all round, hiding any part that could be wounded. 'How did you get into this accident? What are you doing to yourself?'

She told him, just as she had told Brillstein, only this time she had no tears, no unhappiness about it. Manny stayed in his crouch while listening, his hands hidden, his head down. He peered out at her from under the hood of his dull black hair. He was like a cornered animal deciding whether to believe the voice coaxing him to come out from his hiding place.

At first Manny said nothing when she was done. He looked away from her and down at the floor. When Manny did talk he was hoarse. 'He crashed the car to prove that to you?'

'I was out of my mind,' she said.

'And now?'

'And now . . .' she ate another french fry. She could feel the grains of salt, there was so much of it. She sipped the sweet soda. 'And now I'm not,' she said at last.

Carla didn't get to see Max. Brillstein told her that the

doctors had decided to let Max's skull be, at least for now. They were optimistic, despite his high fever. He was still in intensive care and couldn't be visited.

'Is his wife here?' Carla asked.

Brillstein said she was, and added that she had asked him to make sure she didn't meet Carla.

'Why's that?' Manny said. 'She thinks it's Carly's fault?'

Brillstein didn't look Manny in the eye. 'No, no, no, no,' he said so fast the nos were hummed. 'She's upset and frightened – she wants to be alone. She doesn't want to see anybody.'

Carla knew from the lawyer's manner that Max's wife must have told him about Max's crazy avowal of love.

She hates me, Carla thought, and understood.

'Let's go home,' she said to Manny. She felt tired all of a sudden. Although her body didn't hurt, she sensed that it would soon.

'One thing,' Brillstein said. He cleared his throat and looked down. He had put the flats of his hands together, the fingertips prayerfully touching his mouth. After a moment of communion he raised his eyes to look at her decisively. He parted his hands. 'Don't talk about – you know, what we discussed – about your worries in terms of the accident. Don't talk about any of that with anyone else. Just for the moment. Talking with your priest is all right. But not with friends. Just for the next few days. I need to think about it.'

'It'll hurt the case,' Manny said in a grave voice. 'We won't talk about it.'

Carla had expected this. She was on her feet, ready to go. She sipped the last of her Pepsi. The back of her neck felt loose and tired. She had to get home and lie down. She wanted to see her mother. She wanted to apologize for yelling yesterday when she was cleaning up Bubble's room.

'I'd better get you home,' Manny said. He took her elbow.

'Wait,' she said and gathered herself. 'I don't want to fight. I don't want to hear any speeches. I don't care about the money. I don't care what happens. I'm telling the truth. To anyone I feel like.'

For a moment Brillstein was eager to answer. His eyes opened as wide as they could. They were still small but they sparkled. He even went so far as to part his lips to talk – but then he squeezed them together, rolled them between his teeth, and made his mouth lipless.

Manny backed a step away from Carla. He shifted to face her completely. He had his arms low and out at his sides, setting the weight of his thick body on to his thighs, like a sumo wrestler ready to absorb a blow. 'Are you crazy, woman?'

'No, Manny.' Carla took a breath and it became a yawn. She was so tired. 'I'm not fighting you about it. I'm not fighting with anybody. But nothing will change my mind.'

'Don't worry,' Brillstein said anxiously to Manny. He leaned forward and touched Manny's left arm gingerly, careful as he tried to soothe the beast. 'I don't think it matters. Let me work with it for a few days.'

'No!' Manny shouted. Brillstein blanched. His hands went up immediately as if Manny were pointing a gun at him. Manny stamped his right foot. It had never occurred to Carla before, but her husband resembled a bull, with his thick body, glowering eyes, and that tight helmet of black hair covering a ramming head. He had no horns –

but otherwise he was a bull. 'No,' he repeated in a deep tone. He sounded very Spanish. 'They killed my son. They were responsible.' He pointed to Carla. 'Not her!'

'Take me home, Manny.' Carla walked slowly to the door. She wondered where Max's wife was waiting. Was there a different waiting room? Or was she allowed into intensive care?

Brillstein tried to soothe Manny with words. 'Of course they're responsible. They're going to pay. Don't worry.'

'They *have* to pay.' Manny's voice sounded at least an octave lower than was normal.

'Take me home,' Carla said again. This time Manny came.

In the parking lot, as they got into his father's car, Manny said, 'Don't worry. I'm going to drive slow.'

'Drive the way you want,' she told him honestly. 'I don't care.' On the way home she fell asleep.

The car's tires hummed on a metal bridge, rumbling underneath her dream. She walked into a white room dressed in a red T-shirt, very bright red and very long. It covered her knees.

Bubble was at her left breast, feeding. He looked up at her thoughtfully while his mouth worked. She felt him pull the sustenance out of her chest, on a string from her heart.

He blinked his eyes.

He was no longer a newborn. Now he stood a few feet away, a toddler. He bent his knees, his chubby legs wrinkling, and laughed hard, showing a mouth of tiny white teeth.

What's so funny? she tried to ask, but no words came out. She was frustrated.

They were outside, on a lawn that rolled down and

away, disappearing into sky, a pale sky, almost white. Bubble came up close, his face as big as the world. She felt his breath on her neck.

'I'm going bed,' he said.

He ran away from her – too quickly – until a man's hand stopped him. Bubble took the hand. It belonged to Max. He smiled back at her.

'I'll get him home safe,' Max said.

Everything was going to be all right, she knew. She tried to tell Max she understood but her mouth still couldn't make sound.

Max led Bubble away. Bubble was pleased to be with him. Hand in hand they walked off the green earth into pale sky.

20

After nine days in the hospital Max's head still ached –
at least dully – all the time. And he felt dizzy if he
walked more than a few steps. He couldn't see that well
either. Everything in his room seemed to have been
covered in cellophane and out his window the world
looked foggy even when the sun shone. They said his
vision would clear up; but he was worried.

When he first regained consciousness, in the dimmed
agony he could feel through the fever, drugs and mental
confusion, he regretted what he had done. Later in the
week, though, when Carla came to see him, he didn't.
She had recovered herself. Her eyes were bright and her
thin body had energy, almost too much energy. Her
darting movements – from the side of his bed to the
tray to get him something – made his head hurt. She
talked nonstop, too, about how she had finished packing
Bubble's room, giving the stuff away to the Church,
how she had visited his grave with her mother and
afterwards they had kissed and made up for all their
crazy arguments of the last six months. 'Poor Mama,'
Carla said. 'I sent her home to be with her new husband.
She's had no time to be with him. I can't believe how
patient she was with me.'

Max enjoyed the lively talk of her awakening – as
long as she kept still.

When others visited their speeches hurt even if they
did keep still, because he had to remember things. It
seemed that to remember used the bruised part of his

brain; listening to Carla's present life required a section that had gone unscathed. The painless present, he called it, and discouraged visits from the past, especially his former office staff, his friends, his mother and sister, Debby's relatives and even Debby herself.

Debby was furious with him, anyway, and probably didn't want to stay much longer than her daily hour-long visits. She made no recriminations the first few days until Max had stabilized. On the fourth day she sent Jonah to the waiting room with his grandfather. She settled by the window – her back erect, her eyes as alert as a cat waiting for prey – and made a speech. Her long face was composed, her profile backlit by the gray winter light. He couldn't see her features distinctly at that distance. The fuzziness acted as a flattering camera lens – she looked as young as when they first met.

'I've had a long talk with Bill Perlman.'

'Another one?' Max said.

Debby ignored him. 'He told me to stop treating you with kid gloves. I've been scared to just say what I –'

'Say what you want,' Max said. It would be a relief to hear her anger. Let the worst happen: it wasn't as terrible as he once thought.

Debby cleared her throat. 'I know you think there's nothing wrong with you since the plane crash. But there is something wrong. Terribly wrong. You don't seem to want to live anymore. At least not with me. And you don't want to do any of the things that we used to do together. You don't want to work, you don't want to make love, you don't want to ... be with me. You don't even want to go to the movies with me. You can't even bear to sit in the dark next to me doing nothing . .' She dropped her head. It was an elegant movement: only her chin and face fell; her long neck remained straight. She was a grief-stricken swan. 'Jonah feels you don't want to be with him.'

Max's nose had been broken in the crash. It was an afterthought for the doctors and a secondary pain for Max. Yet the bridge of his nose throbbed from time to time and it did then. He wondered if the pulsing signified his body was healing. The doctors hadn't done much for his broken nose: a tape, running across from one cheek to the other, held what there was in place.

'Of course something is terribly wrong,' Max said in a moment, once the throbbing stopped.

'Why won't you see your shrink? Or any shrink. You can't tell me you're happy. You used to go to a shrink when you were happy. Why don't you go now when you really need help?'

'I needed help to be happy,' Max said. 'I don't need help to feel sad.'

Debby twisted violently in her chair and banged the hospital's metal radiator cover with her foot – it was a sharp stunning movement for someone usually deliberate and graceful. 'Damn it, Max! What the fuck are you talking about?' she turned toward him as she rose from the chair. He wasn't sure, but she seemed to have tears in her eyes. 'You tried to kill yourself! How the fuck can you say you don't need help.'

Of course she was right to be furious: he had given up his end of the bargain, thrown out the contract of their relationship. Why couldn't she see that she didn't love him, she loved the faker who pretended to care only about her happiness? He had wanted to be her savior, the compensation for the art she had lost. But really he was a transitional object, a teddy husband, a comfort, not a joy. 'I guess – I guess –' he began but he had to stop because of a blinding pain that came across the top of his skull and radiated down to his nose. He actually saw white stars float across the room. He shut his eyes and waited for the pain to pass. He said finally, 'I guess you won't believe me, but I didn't try to kill myself. I have no intention of dying.'

Debby was back in the chair. He hadn't seen her move there. She was folded over, her head draped down below her knees. He envied her ability to make art instantly with her body. An art without compromise. 'You did it for her,' she said in a mumble to the floor.

'It just came to me. I knew what had to be done. I knew it with Byron also. We all lived through death together and I seem to know how they should live. It's the first time in my life,' and he discovered he was crying, 'that I feel talented.'

His nose stung from the tears. He shut his eyes and swallowed tears. He was floating on the bed. He tried to remember sitting in the plane waiting for the crash, but it wasn't there. His head hurt instead.

'How did you help Byron?' he heard Debby ask. 'By hitting him?'

'No,' Max said and didn't elaborate. He knew that to her everything he did was crazy. To her, his real self – which he had finally revealed to her – was frightening and mad. He had dimly felt that was the case all along in their marriage; but he had wanted her love and admiration so much that he was willing to live in hiding. 'Ask Jonah to come in, okay?'

'Why?' she was on her feet, moving soundlessly and gracefully across the room. He guessed she was pacing; her fluid walk had no tension, however.

378

He couldn't face eternity living a lie. He couldn't die a shadow man.

'What are you going to say to him?' Debby insisted, wandering all the way to the open doorway of the bathroom. 'I don't want you scaring him.'

This made Max angry. He knew she was off balance and not to be held accountable; and yet what right did she have to control what he might say to his son? Concussion or no, Max was still shrewd; he didn't show his annoyance. He said softly, 'First you say I don't want to spend time with him and then you don't want me to spend time with him.'

Debby nodded to herself. She turned to the wall and leaned her head against it. 'Damn,' she said quietly.

'You can stay and listen,' Max offered. 'It's not a big deal – I just want to talk to him for a minute.'

'What about my question?' she turned back, put her hands behind her, springing off the wall. She rocked on her toes and then back on her heels until she fell against the wall, only to repeat the process with another shove of her hands. It was a girlish and pretty nervousness. 'Are you going to talk to a therapist? You know, your lawyer says –' she stopped herself, both the talking and the bouncing off the wall.

'What does Brillstein say?' Max prompted. He thought he knew.

'Answer my question first. Will you talk to somebody?'

'Let's get divorced. Then you don't have to concern yourself with whether I'm crazy or not.'

'Why don't you trust me?' Debby said. Her hands went out in spasm, without grace. 'What have I done to you that you don't trust me?'

'I trust you,' Max lied. It was a necessary lie, perhaps even a truthful lie, but it was the kind of untruth he had given up and it hurt – actually hurt: his head throbbed – to resort to it. Yet he had to. He was in danger from her; and probably from others who believed they loved him. She had almost revealed the jeopardy and instead revealed her guilt. Max tried to sound harmless: 'Bring Jonah in for a moment and you'll see.' At least he wouldn't have to tell any lies to his son.

While she was gone he checked the small personal phone book Debby had brought him to see if Brillstein's number was written down. It was. He had to squint to see the numbers clearly.

Jonah came in reluctantly, made even more nervous by an official summons. Earlier he had fidgeted in a chair, averting his eyes from Max's still bruised face. This time Jonah clung to his mother's side, head tilted, looking at some point in between the floor and his father.

'Jonah . . .' Max reached for him with his left hand.

Debby urged him forward. Jonah abruptly rushed to Max and took the offered hand. He bowed his head, staring at the sheets.

As his hand swallowed the small one Max noticed Jonah's nails were dirty. He squeezed the limp fingers and said, 'Did you think I wanted to die?'

Jonah shook his head no and gulped; he didn't speak; to Max that was a yes.

'I don't.' Max raised the enclosed hand and shook it. 'Look at me.'

Jonah's face came up. Max was momentarily silenced by his calm and naive concentration. Jonah's two light brown eyes (the same shade as his mother's) watched and waited for his history to begin.

'I don't just happen to be your father,' Max said. 'I want to be your father.' Jonah's eyes stayed open and focused on Max, although water brimmed at the lower lids. 'That means I don't want to die. You can't lose me because I don't want to be lost.' He let go of the small hand.

Jonah stayed his ground, looking fully at his father's swollen face. The child's tearful eyes dried up; and after a moment, along with their blank and vulnerable attentiveness, there was a glint of armor.

Max's mother was next to come with a grievance. He had known she was angry at him from the brevity of her earlier visits. Moments after Debby and Jonah left (they must have coordinated these attacks) his mother entered and dragged the plastic visitor's chair over to the left side of his bed. She sat down with a firm drop as if she planned to stay for a while. He was glad she had come so close to him; he could see her well from there. 'Max,' she said energetically and patted his hand, 'everyone says I shouldn't bring this up. Your sister especially – that's why I'm here alone. But I think maybe there are a few things a mother knows about her children that even the experts don't.' There it was again – the hint of discussions with psychologists about his condition. Was it Perlman and Mayer, or just one of them, or others he didn't know? He wanted to phone Brillstein urgently. He was sure he could see through the lawyer to whatever was their secret plan.

'Really?' Max answered. 'When I was a teenager it always seemed to me mothers were the easiest people to fool. Freddy, Andy, Barry and me, we could come in stoned out of our minds, tell you we hadn't gotten enough sleep and you'd buy it.'

She squinted at him, annoyed. After a moment she slapped his hand. 'Don't be a wise guy,' she said.

'You were fooled because you wanted to be fooled, Mom. I didn't mean you were gullible.'

'We didn't know about drugs, that's all. It never occurred to us. If you had had extra money I'd have known you were a thief. If you had had bruises I'd have known you were in a gang. If you had thrown up your breakfast, I'd have known you were drinking. I could smell the cigarettes on your clothes. But bloodshot eyes? I thought you'd been up all night listening to rock music.'

Max smiled at her old face. He remembered the shameful secrecy of adolescence, moving his pornography and cigarettes from one drawer to another, rotating them away from her searches. She had found them anyway. 'You're right, Mom. You were no fool.'

'Why did you send that thing to me?'

'What thing?'

'You know –' she winced. She lowered her eyes. They were still young despite the wrinkles around them. They sparkled with humor and curiosity – and pain. 'You know what I'm talking about. Why did you send that box of tools to me?'

He had forgotten about the gift buying. That belonged somewhere in the smashed part of his brain. He thought about it before answering. He remembered the nervous salesman copying the address. He had had to send the gift to his father. Where did his father live but with his mother? 'You didn't look at the card.'

'I looked. That was crazy and it hurt me. But I don't believe you meant it. It was sent to *me*. You were sending me some kind of message.' She tapped his hand again. 'Just tell me what you want to say to me, Max.'

'I wanted to buy Dad a gift. You know I never got to buy him anything.' She turned away from this answer, wounded, ready to walk out. He continued, 'Where could I send it? To his grave?' She looked back at him. Her young eyes wavered in their crinkled settings. 'I bought the toolbox for my living father,' Max went on. 'And where does my father live? With you. His picture – that picture where he's ten years younger than I am – is still on your living-room wall, and there's another beside your bed. You haven't remarried, you haven't forgotten. He's still alive in your house. If I want to give a gift to my father I have to send it to you.'

Her eyes searched him. They went back and forth across his face, in no hurry. She expected him to wait until she had finished her search, just as she used to while interrogating him for confessions of adolescent debauchery. 'You're not crazy,' she mumbled.

'No,' Max said and he gently slapped her hand.

She laughed. Her eyes teared up suddenly. She reached for her purse. She opened it fast, found a tissue, and blew her nose. With that done she looked at him: 'Don't ever do that again. You want to buy something for your father? Do what I do. Make a donation in his name to your favorite charity.'

'That wasn't the idea –'

'I don't care about your ideas!' She got up. 'Don't do that to me again.'

'Why didn't you remarry?' Max shot this past all the sentinels that had always halted the question before it could be given a voice.

It was a shot that stopped her in her tracks. 'Nobody asked,' she said.

383

'Come on, Mom. Did you love him that much? Was he that perfect?'

She smirked. It was a private amused twist of her curvy lips – almost mischievous. 'I had two children, I was almost middle-aged. I wasn't much of a prize.'

Max felt bound by his hospital bed. Its thin sheet was drawn taut across his stomach by the nurse's over-zealous bedmaking. He pushed at it with his belly and pulled at its edges with his hands, but remained trapped. He wanted to get up, in spite of his aching head. His mother came over and pulled them away. 'What are you doing, Max?' she asked. 'You want to get up?'

He was trembling. He was frightened. But of what? 'I'm forty-two years old, Mom!' He got himself turned and slung his legs out of the mechanical bed. It had been raised so high only his toes reached the floor. 'Why don't you tell me the truth! Are we strangers? Do I have to worm it out of you? Do I have to get you drunk?'

She took his arm and supported him as he slid down until both feet rested on the cold floor. 'What do you want to know, Maxy?' she asked, startled into using her childhood name for him.

Standing beside her he looked down at her small skull, sparsely covered by dyed hair. He felt her feeble arm in his. He was astounded at how little and old she was. 'You didn't even try, Mom,' he said, despairing of the interrogation. He pressed on hopelessly. 'Why didn't you try to find another man? You lived without love –'

'I had love, Maxy, I had my children.'

'I mean sex! You lived without sex!' His head seemed to blow up. A bell of pain rang in his ears; a cloud of pain worsened the fog in his eyes. He slipped down into

384

the chair she had moved next to his bed. The back of his dressing gown must have opened. His bare ass slid on the unnatural smoothness of the molded plastic seat. He had to grab hold of its sides with his hands to keep from falling out.

'You shouldn't be up,' his mother said. She didn't sound scandalized. With a child's squeamishness he had expected her to react prudishly to any discussion of sex.

'Answer me,' Max said in a sigh of exhaustion.

'Sex,' she said wonderingly as if she had just discovered its existence. 'It wasn't that important. I didn't miss it that much. I've read books that say I'm wrong. They say it was important to me,' she said without irony, still wondering. 'I missed it sometimes and I –' she met his eyes and caught herself. She didn't blush, but she smiled slyly and smirked with her curvy lip: 'There are ways to have sex by yourself as I'm sure you know, Max.'

'Are you telling me the truth, Mom?' Max felt small and naive looking up at her. He was a middle-aged infant, unable to walk. 'Didn't you live without love for me?'

She considered his question thoughtfully. She frowned a bit, her eyebrows drawing together, but her puffy cheeks stayed smooth and untroubled. 'It had nothing to do with you. Aunt Essie thought I should get married – to almost anybody, even a thief – just to get you a father. But you didn't need a father, Max. "My little man," your father called you. And you were – long before he died – you were a man.'

'No, I wasn't,' Max said. He wanted to weep. He couldn't, his head was too smashed. 'You made a mistake. I needed a man to help me carry my grief. And you've made a mistake with your daughter. She's a widow who's never been married.' There – he had spoken – the terrible secrets were out. He waited for the world to be destroyed.

'I don't think I made a mistake,' she said easily, evidently unaware Max had dropped his nuclear bomb. She reached for his limp right arm. 'Let's get you back into bed.' She urged him up. 'I didn't want to marry the schnooks who were available. Until this thing happened, Max, until that plane tragedy, you were a fine man. Ask my friends, ask yours, and they'll tell you – Max Klein is a mensch. So I don't agree with your opinion of yourself.' She pushed him toward the high hospital bed. Max grabbed for it with the gratitude of a tired swimmer reaching for a life preserver. 'As for your sister,' she said, nudging his legs up on to the noisy sheets, 'she was damaged by what happened. No question. But she was much younger than you; she had less of your father; and she isn't pretty and she doesn't have a good sense of humor. I don't care what anyone says – it's a competition out there for men. You don't have to be a great beauty; you don't have to be a genius. But you have to have something – maybe even a bad quality, a vicious temper – for men to want to marry you. Maybe because there was no man in the house for her to learn how to entertain – maybe you're right.' She rolled Max into the bed; he fell face-forward on to the stiff sheets. His sinuses were hot. He wanted to sleep. The planet was pulverized; listening to her rebuild it was exhausting. 'I didn't want to settle. Most marriages are unhappy, Max. Most women hate the lives they live with their men. I know. They call me with their complaints. Many of them bury their husbands and enjoy life for the first time. Your sister doesn't miss a man. She misses children. I told her – she can have children without a man –'

'You're wrong, Ma,' Max mumbled as his eyes shut. His brain wanted to visit a different part of the galaxy; a place with fewer bomb craters. 'Women and children need a man –' he called back to earth.

'A good man, Max,' his mother said. 'You rest. But if they don't have a good man they're better off alone.'

'No,' he told her as he launched into cool black space.

'We agree to disagree, Maxy,' she said. He fell toward the stars.

Max woke up with a clear head and a nosebleed. He phoned Brillstein, but the lawyer was out; Max left a message. He dozed lightly during the rest of the night replaying yesterday's conversations; by dawn, he was convinced that Debby and Brillstein were up to something.

On his morning rounds the resident told Max he was better, ready to go home tomorrow, although he'd have to take it easy for a while. A psychiatric resident came by half an hour later and said he had to ask some routine questions because of the head trauma. It sounded like a lie. Max pretended his head was aching and asked him to come back later. The psychiatrist left.

Within five minutes Brillstein appeared in an excessively tight brown suit. The lawyer entered with his usual bustle. He scanned the room, obviously empty except for Max, and said, 'You're alone. Good.' Brillstein moved to the foot of the bed. He shifted his weight from one shoe to another restlessly. From his still position on the bed, Brillstein seemed to Max to be a skittish brown bird. 'They want a meeting. About you, Mrs Gordon and Mrs Fransisca.' Brillstein's head had been down while he searched for something in his breast pocket. The jacket was drawn so tight across the chest that his sleeve rode up nearly to the elbow and the right vent billowed like a skirt. 'I just want to get a feel for what kind of numbers we might consider acceptable,' Brillstein said as he produced a small spiral notebook and a ballpoint pen. He looked at Max expectantly, a waiter ready to take his order.

'It's what you're going to get Nan and Carla that's important,' Max said. 'I've got plenty from the partnership insurance –'

'Shh! Shh! Shh!' Brillstein hissed with vehemence. He scolded Max with the ballpoint pen, shaking it at him. 'Don't talk like that. You're not a well man. This whole experience has been horrific for you. We don't know how long it will be before you'll be able to earn a living again even leaving aside the loss of your firm's key man.'

'Key man . . .?' Max pictured a fat man in medieval dress; and around his creased neck, he imagined a dazzling golden key dangling from a chain.

'Key man – Mr Gordon. He brought in the clients and you did the designs. Maybe "key man" is the wrong term from your point of view, but he did bring in the business. Obviously there would be no business to bring in if you weren't doing the designing.'

Max remembered Jeff vividly: *in his chair at his desk, swiveling at Max and then away, talking cheerfully to the phone, 'We can do it – no problem. You'll be as happy as Mr Ben-David,' rolling his eyes at Max as he turned in*

his direction, then smiling at the ugly FIT buildings
across the avenue as he swung away, always coaxing,
always talking, keeping the clients busy with their greed
for more space, more plumbing, more closets, more
things . . .

'It's so simple to you,' Max commented.

Brillstein wrinkled his pale forehead and comically
raised his skinny eyebrows up to the lines. 'Simple . . .?'

'Jeff brought in the business. He died. So I had to
close the business.'

'Mr Klein, I know you're a sensitive and honest man
But those are the facts. No matter what other reasons
there may be, the fact is: the plane crash brought an end
to your business. Under the law you're entitled to be
compensated for such a devastating consequence.'

'I *have* been compensated. I got the insurance
money.'

'That isn't admissible to a jury. As far as they would
know you lost your partner and your business and
that's it.'

'It's all a lie.' Max smiled wanly. His head no longer
hurt. He noticed the absence of pain and then he realized
that his sight, which had been doubled for two days
after the accident and blurry since, was suddenly clear.
He could see distant objects well. He sat up with excitement. He scanned the low buildings near the water and
saw them first as shapes: rectangle, square, triangular
lot; then in height: five stories, four, double-height warehouse; then the details of their condition: bad, bad, bad.
Nothing to look at. If only his room faced Manhattan
he could enjoy its variety of size, and at night, wonder
about the life of its lights.

'It's not lying,' Brillstein said, flitting back and forth

along the foot of Max's bed. 'I don't want you to think that there's anything dishonest about your compensation. That's in your head. I don't know about your head, I'm not a psychologist. In fact – speaking of psychologists – I need you to do some psychological testing to strengthen our case. I need you to take a simple test, it's really just answering a questionnaire. I can have the hospital psychologist do it if you like.'

'Sure,' Max said. He was up to this struggle. He looked at Brillstein and smiled.

'Good, good, good.' Brillstein flipped his notebook shut. He put a finger on his bare forehead; the skin crinkled around it as he frowned. 'Did we discuss a figure? I don't think so. It probably isn't important, but I just need to know when I talk with them. Does a two-million-dollar settlement seem low to you?'

'You're kidding,' Max said.

'Too low?' Brillstein said fast.

'Low!' Max chuckled. 'It's ridiculously high.'

Brillstein relaxed. 'We're talking about your expected after-tax earnings over your prime earning years. The Nutty Nick stores deal alone was a million-dollar loss.'

'We didn't have that job.' Max grunted. 'Aren't they laughing you out of their offices with this stuff? I mean, my share of Nutty Nick wouldn't be a million-dollar net.'

Brillstein had brought his forefinger down to his lips and he nibbled at the nail. 'No?' he mumbled and then flipped his notebook open. 'In his deposition the CEO of Nutty Nick says your and Mr Gordon's fee would have been two million dollars over the course of the years of work he had planned. You were a fifty-fifty partnership, correct?'

'But we didn't have that job. He hadn't seen –'

Brillstein shook his pad. 'In the deposition he says he planned to hire you, but he couldn't because of the accident.' Brillstein smiled so widely he showed teeth. A calm happiness raised his lips. His eyes sparkled. 'It's a strong case,' he said without bluster.

'For Nan it's a strong case,' Max said. 'Jeff's dead. He can't work. But let me ask you something. Unless you prove I'm unable to work, isn't my case weak?'

Brillstein put his notebook away. 'Not necessarily. Just because you're able to work doesn't mean you can earn the same kind of money as you did with Mr Gordon. And it doesn't address the issue of the loss of the Nutty Nick stores contract.'

Max nodded solemnl. Brillstein now paced back and forth in a pattern that took him closer to the door with each pass. Max gestured for him to return to his bedside. Brillstein stopped. He paused and looked curious. Max repeated the gesture. Finally, Brillstein walked to the side of the bed. He held himself stiffly, though, his shoulders back and his head leaning away, as if ready to run. Max said quietly, 'You get a third of the settlements, right?'

Brillstein pursed his lips gravely and nodded vigorously. The expression suggested that he disapproved of this fact.

'You're going to make a big score with Nan's case and Carla's case. Do you need money so badly that you're willing to have me declared insane just to make more money out of me?'

For a moment Brillstein did nothing but blink his eyes. Abruptly he sat down in the plastic chair Max's mother had moved beside his bed. Brillstein rubbed his forehead with his index finger and studied Max. He seemed to come to a conclusion. He exhaled with a rush of words: 'I told you these kinds of cases are almost always settled. And that's true. But sometimes one side or the other decides not to compromise, to go the whole route. Not necessarily because of the merits of the argument. It's for the future, for credibility. If you get a reputation for *always* settling, of being afraid to go to trial, then you can be taken advantage of. I'm up against heavy hitters. Their case stinks. We still don't have the official final judgement of the NTSB but that isn't legally binding anyway. All the data is in and it shows that it was negligent maintenance that caused the engine to come apart and wipe out the hydraulics. So TransCon is going to be on the hook for this. They should settle. They know it. They've already settled seventy-five percent of the suits – got them cheap if you ask me. They did it in a bunch with the two big firms, like a discount sale, using three formulas depending on age. Most anyone got was six hundred thousand. They paid a hundred thousand for the children.' Brillstein shook his head with disgust. 'They may –'

Max was impatient with his tedious logic and cut him off – 'They may go to trial with you to prove a point, since they're safe on the other cases if they lose.'

Brillstein snapped his fingers and then pointed at Max. 'You got it. Also, I'm working on new law here. Well, not new. There's been two rulings so far, but not for airplanes. Have you ever heard of posttraumatic stress syndrome?' Max shook his head no. 'You're suffering from it!' Brillstein said eagerly and with a hint of delight, as though it was clever of Max. 'We can sue them for compensation for the syndrome's effects. It's a gamble for them but they may decide to take it to trial and beat it.'

'But if they lose on that point they're screwed in the future, no?'

Brillstein folded his arms. He smiled without showing teeth. 'They're screwed either way. If they settle on this issue, even if we agree to keep the numbers and the argument confidential, other lawyers will find out and use it again.'

'You know,' Max said. He shifted in the bed, to get on his side and face Brillstein. The sheets and all its plastic undercoverings rustled and swished. He let their surf noise die down before continuing. 'I've never done anything really good or useful in the world.'

Brillstein nodded eagerly, almost encouragingly.

'But at least I've never actually added to what's bad.'

Brillstein's mouth pursed. His eyes were offended. 'Maybe you don't understand,' Brillstein said softly, but with menace. 'If you contradict me on Nutty Nick or Mr Gordon's "key man" status you'll only be hurting Mrs Gordon.'

Max said nothing.

'You'll leave me no choice but to take the line that you're not in your right mind.' Brillstein stood up. His mouth had gotten very tight and severe. He looked too small to achieve the threatening effect he wanted. 'Your wife and I have talked about this. There's a lot of evidence you're unwell.' Brillstein became nervous again. He grinned and said, 'We're both tired and tired talk is no good. Let me know when you want the psychologist to bring you the questionnaire. Get some rest.' Brillstein scurried out in his brown suit, a small, even cute, creature. But the lawyer had meant what he said. And Max knew that sometimes the littlest animals were the most determined and the most vicious.

21

Carla decided to call a cease-fire with Manny. But only after she asked if he was still seeing 'that bitch'.

Manny said no with his head down, ashamed. He mumbled to the floor, 'I ain't seen her since the day in Jersey.'

'I don't believe you,' she said dispassionately.

'It's the truth!' His head came up; his black eyes shone. 'I called her that night and told her I couldn't see her no more.'

'I believe you,' she said and let go of the subject. So they were talking again. Nevertheless, she moved her things into Bubble's old room and slept there. The next morning she bought cans of white paint. Using Manny's brushes and ladder she began to cover the pale blue color of the nursery.

A few days later Manny came home with a dozen roses. They must have cost half his take-home pay for the week. She told him he was crazy. He took off his coat and revealed he was wearing a clean white shirt, a blue tie and his best slacks. She hadn't seen him in a tie since their wedding. For one delighted moment she thought he was going to take her out to dinner and dancing. What he wanted was sex.

She let him – in their old room. The lovemaking didn't bother her although she felt nothing, like always since the accident. But it did bother Manny that she wasn't ecstatic no matter what he tried. He was a skilled lover. Carla assumed he had been taught by experts –

probably his mother's colleagues – but even his fanciest stimulations were of no use. Afterwards he said softly, 'You didn't like it.'

She told him as gently as she could, 'Enjoy yourself. Don't worry about me. I feel fine.'

'I can't.' Manny pushed at his hair with the flat of his palm, agonized. 'If you don't like it, I can't.'

But he *had* enjoyed himself. He had arched to the ceiling and moaned, like always. 'That's your pride,' she said. 'We're married. You don't have to show off with me.'

Manny put his other palm to his hair and pressed with both hands. 'Did you do it with him?' he said in a choked voice.

'No,' she said and was disgusted. 'I'm not you.'

Finally Manny relaxed, stopped asking questions, and began to brag about his triumphs at work. They talked for a while in a friendly way before she went to Bubble's room to sleep. To her room really. She felt no trace of her dead boy in the real world anymore. Bubble did live on in her dreams. There he was always happy and pleased with her.

She visited Max three times. She made sure each time (once with Brillstein; the others with Max) that he would be alone when she came. She worried about his health. They said he was healing okay but she thought something in his brain wasn't working right. When she made jokes he sometimes looked bewildered instead of laughing or smiling; and he didn't say smart things, the kind of things that he used to, that changed the way she thought about the world. On her third visit she found out why. A kid came in a white coat – he was an intern Max told her later, but he looked like a child to her –

and said in a cheerful way, 'How's the vision, Mr Klein? Still seeing double?'

'No.' Max covered his eyes with the fingers of his right hand, as if hiding from the question.

'Good. Let me take a look.' He came up to the bed, snapping on a flashlight in the shape of a pen. Carla thought he was too young to be so presumptuous with Max.

Max persisted in shielding his eyes with his fingers. To coax them down the intern pulled gently on Max's wrist. He shone the penlight into one eye and then the other, each time asking Max to roll his eyes up and then down. 'Good,' the intern said. 'Things blurry, especially in the distance?'

'I can't really see,' Max said in a tone Carla had never heard from him; he sounded afraid.

'You can't see!' the young man was skeptical. 'You can see everything in the room, right? Things are a little cloudy, right?'

'Right,' Max said dully.

'I don't want to put words in your mouth, Mr Klein. You're the patient, you tell me. But you see everything – it's just not sharp, right?'

'Right,' Max said angrily.

'But he can see,' the intern said to Carla.

She understood then why Max wasn't laughing or talking cleverly. She sat by the bed after the kid doctor left and took Max's hand. It was soft and warm. He was quiet for a long time. Finally, he mumbled bitterly, 'It's not seeing.'

When Brillstein came to the apartment that night to ask if he could offer to settle the case for three hundred thousand dollars, she waited through Manny's first excited, then suspicious agreement. At first Manny said, 'Three hundred thousand!' as if it were all the money in the world. Yet only a moment later he said to Brillstein, 'They'd be getting off cheap.' Finally he was satisfied when Brillstein told him that the most any other parent had gotten was one hundred thousand. Carla nodded to indicate it was okay with her and then said, 'Are the doctors telling the truth about Max's eyes?'

While Brillstein assured her that Max's eyes should be fine, Manny sulked. 'He's lucky to have eyes,' Manny commented.

As soon as Brillstein left, Manny sat opposite Carla in one of the metal kitchen chairs and said in a bullying tone, 'I gotta know something. You gonna go on seeing this nut forever?'

'You want me to stop talking to you again?' Carla said.

Manny picked himself and his chair up while still seated and slammed both down. The metal feet and his shoes made a hard and soft clap of thunder. 'You're taking a fuck of a lotta chances with me, woman!'

'When you get your blood money, Manny –' Carla said in a rage, getting to her feet. The white flash of this anger seemed to blind her momentarily. She blinked hard and Manny reappeared. 'You can keep it all to yourself and get the fuck out of my life!' She marched to her room and felt bitterly disappointed.

Manny knocked later, came in without permission, and gave her an espresso. 'I'm sorry,' he said in a mumble.

She took the cup. She had been sitting at the window, looking out at the street, wondering about the tourists and rich New Yorkers passing below. Max had once said that walking through Little Italy made those people feel they were in a *Godfather* movie. She wondered if that was entirely a joke. After a while, she said to Manny, 'Thank you.'

Manny studied her while she sipped the coffee. It was good.

'Do you want a TV in here?' he said eventually.

'No thanks,' she said. She liked the room this way, all white and empty except for the small bed, dresser and rocking chair she had kept from the nursery. A television would spoil it.

'You're my wife,' Manny said quietly.

'Yes, I am,' Carla answered.

Manny nodded and left. She got up early the next morning and made him pancakes. He kissed her with syrupy lips on his way out. He hummed with pleasure and pushed his sweet tongue between her teeth. She eased him out the door.

She cleaned the apartment in an hour. The laundry was done and there was food for dinner. She thought about going to Old Saint Pat's. She could pray for Max's eyes.

I need a job, she thought.

Manny would want her to get pregnant again. She didn't think she could have another child – at least not physically. To raise one, yes; to make one, no. But Manny would never adopt.

Her intercom buzzed. When she asked who it was, she didn't believe the answer: 'Debby Klein. Max Klein's wife. Could I come up and see you?'

Carla was so taken aback she didn't reply, she buzzed her in, wandered to the front door in a daze and opened it.

399

Carla was surprised by Max's wife. She was slight and nervous, not commanding as Carla imagined she would be, and although Debby looked to be around forty years old, she had the uncertain expression of a timid girl.

'I'm sorry,' were Debby's first words as she climbed the last few steps.

'That's okay.'

'If I'm interrupting something –'

'That's okay,' Carla said again.

Debby offered her hand. 'I'm Debby.'

'Hi, I'm Carla.' Carla shook it. 'Come in. How's Max doing?'

Debby passed her and entered the apartment with open interest in the objects. She peered at the furniture and the photographs as they moved into the living room. 'I guess physically he's getting better. I'm worried about what's going on in his head.'

Carla nodded. She gestured for Debby to sit and asked, 'Do you want something? Coffee?'

'No. Thanks. I'm sorry to bother you. I guess this is crazy. I've never done anything like this in my life.' She laughed and it was a surprise. Her laugh was deep and mature and confident. 'When have I ever been in a situation like this? I don't even know what my situation is –' Her amusement shut off, as suddenly and completely as a light going out. 'There are no rules about what's happened to you and Max. I guess that's what I realized last night. What a terrible night.' Debby looked into the distance and there was grief in her eyes, the sort of hopelessness that Carla understood very well. 'It was the worst night of my life. I thought there would never be anything as bad as the night I thought Max had died –' she found Carla's sympathetic eyes and stopped.

She smiled feebly. 'Did Max help you? I talked to Bill Perlman yesterday. He said Max helped you.'

Carla waited to think how she could say it. She felt she owed Debby the truth, if she could figure out what the truth was. She considered and then had an answer that was right. 'He saved my soul,' she told Debby.

Debby's eyes filled with tears. Her lips trembled. 'Well,' she stood up, so agitated that she obviously wanted to hide. 'Well, then, that's that. Thank you. I'm going to go.' She turned away. Carla stood up. She hadn't wanted to make her feel bad and yet she seemed to have hurt her. It was confusing.

Debby moved toward the door. Carla hurried after her. She wanted to say more but she didn't know what else to say; she had an impulse to take care of Debby, she seemed so fragile. Debby was still upset, only barely managing to contain her tears. She pulled at the front door but couldn't get it open. 'I'm sorry,' she mumbled.

'It's okay,' Carla said, unlocking it.

Debby opened the door. Her eyes were awash with tears. 'I think,' she said to Carla and swallowed hard. 'I think maybe you're the only one who can help Max.' And she rushed out, hurrying down the stairs.

It was sometime later that Carla found herself sitting in the kitchen eating from a box of crackers. She had been thinking so hard it was like a trance: What did Debby mean? How could she help Max? Was there anything wrong with him? To her it seemed that he was as great as anyone could be, that he was fearless and kind and smart and loving. Why would anyone want to change that? She didn't know, except that obviously he wasn't being a good husband to Debby. She seemed lost, grief-stricken. Was it Carla's fault, somehow? Had she done this to them? That was an awful thought, a sin she couldn't bear. The crackers were so dry she had to go to the sink and drink two glasses of water. As she put the box away the phone rang.

It was Max, speaking in a whisper. 'Carla. I'm at my apartment.'

'They let you go –'

'Yes,' he hissed in his hurry to tell her. 'Listen. I can't talk long. Can you meet me somewhere? Or do I have to go down to you?'

'Are you supposed to be –?'

'Carla, I don't have much time!' He almost moaned. 'Brillstein and my wife – they're going to put me in a mental institution. I have to get away. Can you meet me somewhere?'

'No!' she said, shocked.

'You can't?'

'No, I mean, they're not going to put you away.'

'I can't talk. Listen, I don't know where . . . Grand Central. Do you know the Oyster Bar Restaurant?'

'No.'

'It's underneath Grand Central. Take the Lex. That's near you, isn't it? Or a cab. I'll pay you back. Go into Grand Central and look for the signs. The Oyster Bar Restaurant. Meet me there at noon. Don't go in. At the entrance. Okay? Please?'

'Sure, Max.'

He hung up. He had sounded crazy. She was sad for a moment and didn't want to move. She was reluctant to go out, blocks away from home, into the underground with beggars and crazies, to the middle of Manhattan filled with people, thousands and thousands, all indifferent, all strange.

It passed quickly. She had wished for something to do. Max needed her. Wasn't that better than a job? If he was really crazy then she owed him her help all the more.

The trip uptown was scary. Everyone in New York seemed demented in one way or another. Many were openly so: in rags, shouting at invisible tormentors, thrusting paper cups and insisting on money as if you owed them charity. Many more were fearful, pretending to be self-absorbed while they peeked from behind newspapers, wearing earphones that disappeared into their clothing or shoulder bags, as if they were switchboard operators wandering sadly to find something they could plug into. The teenagers were scary, especially the black teenagers, whose eyes were so angry and so hopeless that she couldn't believe there was any mercy in their hearts. She avoided meeting their defiant stares.

'Don't look at him,' Manny had once whispered to her because she looked closely at a man on the subway whose pants were gray with filth, who had a cut across his forehead, and whose left shoe top had come off. 'When you're really poor you don't want people to look at you,' he explained later. 'All they got is their pride. You were shaming him. He could kill you for that.'

'Oh, come on, Manny!' She had laughed, nervous at the idea.

'Don't laugh.' Manny had been grave. He pointed to the sky to emphasize the importance of what he was saying. 'I know what I'm talking about. I was one of them in Manila. I didn't care the Americans were so rich so long as they didn't look at me like I was an animal in the zoo.'

She got to Grand Central without incident. The

station seemed to be in another time. The curved interior walls were made of smooth gray stone as thick as a tomb's. The clocks were old-fashioned and so was the lettering embedded in the walls that directed people to the trains or the exits. Carla thought it was too gloomy.

Max probably thinks it looks beautiful, she realized and felt better about this meeting. Grand Central was Max's kind of place. At least he was still partly himself.

She found the Oyster Bar easily. It was also preserved from New York's past. She liked it better. The arched entrance walls were cunningly made with once-white tiles that now had a yellow tint. One half of the restaurant had snaking U-shaped counters to accommodate quick lunches; the other half had tables with red-checked cloths. It reminded her of her hardworking father.

She stood outside in the station's tombs, soothed by the echo of footsteps. She saw Max from a long way off coming toward her. Behind him a cloud of dusty light from the street darkened his face. He walked like an old man.

She hurried to help him.

'Hello, Carla,' he said as she reached him and put her arm through his. He smiled at her anxious grip. 'I'm okay. I'm just getting used to walking distances. I guess I don't trust that my head is better.'

'How are your eyes?'

'They're great!' he said. They paused at the archway leading to the main waiting room. 'Wow,' he said, peering up at the vaulted ceiling. 'Look at how much they've cleaned! It looks so grand doesn't it? A public place designed like a palace. And clocks with faces!' he said, beaming.

'That Oyster Bar looks good. Can we get something to eat?' Carla was hungry, and had been made hungrier by the sight of the lobster tank in the restaurant. But she also wanted Max to sit.

They had a delicious lunch. She loved seafood, but the sweet fat oysters Max ordered for her as a starter were new to her. Max insisted she have a lobster and they shared a thick chocolate cake for dessert. She was so full her stomach ached dully and her eyes felt heavy.

Max ate feverishly and jabbered about how he knew that Debby and Brillstein were going to have him committed. When she challenged this suspicion, he explained the lawyer could get more money that way.

'But your wife wouldn't lock you up just to get more money,' Carla said.

'That's not why. She's got a choice. Either accept I don't love her or decide that I'm crazy.'

'How do you know you don't love her?' Carla said, not as an argument, a wondering question.

'I don't think I ever did love her. I loved the idea of her.'

Carla slid down in her chair a little. The heavy meal was dragging her down. She wanted to yawn. 'I don't know what that means, Max,' she said, again not as an argument.

'I don't even know what love is,' Max said. He yawned without restraint. 'I'm exhausted.'

Carla laughed. 'I could sleep right in this chair.'

'Let's go,' he said. She didn't ask where. She didn't think about where either, although somehow she knew. He hailed a taxi – there were rows of them out on the street – and said, 'The Plaza Hotel, please.' He sagged back, his head against the back seat. His Adam's apple and strong chin made sharp angles. His face had only a trace of puffiness from the crash; a healing cut on his jaw gave his handsome features a romantic wound. 'I reserved a suite this morning,' he said to the car roof. 'Asked them to make sure it was on a high floor. It'll be my last look at New York for God knows how long. I was too tired to figure out where to go. I thought I'd leave the state tomorrow morning. I don't think they can institutionalize me if I move to another state.' He sat up and turned toward her. His eyes were lively, their pale blue as clear as a boy's marbles. He reached for her hands. She gave them to him. His skin was soft and warm. 'I want you to come with me,' he said.

Jonah. If not for Jonah, Max would not have minded the necessity of running away. He was even willing to lose New York City. He knew it too well. He could go to the prettiness of San Francisco; or relish Chicago's earnest skyscrapers. Parody didn't interest him so LA was out of the question. But he was willing to abandon buildings altogether – seek the spareness of the western desert. Or get out of the United States – confront Europe's dead ambitions.

The truth was, he'd rather visit them. He didn't know where to go to live. Perhaps someplace no one wanted to – like Oklahoma. A place where people left to come to New York. There Max could walk on a landscape without challenge. Maybe he could draw again; build himself a house that wasn't fit for a family, that wasn't fit for summering at the beach, that wasn't fit for a person, but that fit only the earth and sky. A useless house, a child's dream. Maybe after that he could believe in the practical world again.

He felt better as soon as he got away from his apartment and was alone outside in the city. He walked carefully, concerned that he was fragile, but nothing hurt. He felt well enough to go as far as Columbus Circle before hailing a cab to Grand Central.

Carla looked beautiful. She had nothing of the pale despair of her grief. The profound black of her thick hair framed her long face. Her chocolate eyes shone out of their deep setting. Her lips were a bold red against the glowing white of her skin. She was a beautiful animal and she didn't know it. She moved with energetic grace but its flow was unconscious. And this healthy Carla had a clarity to her that was also beautiful. There was no guard at attention ready to stop the expression of her true feelings. She asked him whether he was crazy, and nodded at his answer as if that were all the reassurance she needed. She told him about making up with Manny, and yet when she added that she didn't want to sleep in the same room with him anymore she made no attempt to justify her aloofness from her husband, despite his apologies and contrition. She said, I don't like him enough to sleep next to him every night. She was honest in the only way it's possible to be honest – by not knowing there was any other way to be. Max realized that when he was a young man he would have thought her dumb. She was a prize.

'Do you think I ought to work?' she asked while she enjoyed the Oyster Bar's ridiculously sweet and slightly stale chocolate cake.

'When I worked I loved it more than anything,' he told her.

'I don't think I could feel that way about a job,' she said. 'And I don't mean I should get a job for money. I mean I should do something good, you know? Maybe I could volunteer at the Foundling Hospital. I asked Monsignor O'Boyle if he could ask them.'

Max smiled to himself at the thought that no one would pay for her to do good in the world. Of course she was right.

'I wish I could teach,' she said. 'I don't know anything to teach. But I wish I could spend time with kids. Not only sick kids. Healthy kids deserve attention too, right?'

'You want to have another child,' Max said.

'Yeah,' she nodded. 'But I'm a coward. I can't carry a baby and think about losing it all the time. I couldn't take that.'

'You wouldn't lose a baby.'

'No?' She smiled broadly. Her teeth were big and bright. He hadn't noticed them before.

'No.' Max was positive.

'That's good to know,' Carla smiled again. Her mouth opened wide with a laugh and he saw all those teeth again. Why hadn't he noticed them before?

Because she hadn't been smiling or laughing, he realized, and felt dumb. He was so tired from his walk and the big meal that he forgot to ask Carla if she would come with him to the Plaza before heading off to it. When she didn't object to his instruction to the cab-driver he asked her to come with him on his flight from New York. She didn't answer.

The desk clerk smirked when Max told him his bags would be arriving later. Max had forgotten he would need clothes whether he was going to Rome or Oklahoma. Maybe I'm not serious about leaving, he doubted himself.

The view was great. All of Central Park was spread below, the details of its paths, footbridges, hills, buildings, and lake exposed by the fuzzy brown leafless trees. Their room was high enough so that the rectangular borders of tall buildings on all sides could be seen, although the northern end was small. But the height proved the awesome truth that the park was made by man: nature re-created where it had been killed.

This city is what I've loved all my life, Max thought, appalled. A place.

'Lie down, Max,' Carla said. He turned and couldn't find her. She had gone into the bedroom. He was surprised by this forwardness. He walked from the huge sitting room into a narrow bedroom. They must have created this suite from a larger one, Max decided. The bedroom seemed to be for a servant. Carla had drawn the drapes. Only a faint glow of the day's gray light illuminated her. She had drawn the bedspread down but left the blanket and pillows untouched. Her shoes were off, tumbled on to the floor at the foot of the bed. She had lain down on her side, fully dressed, facing the door.

'Come here and get some rest,' she said. Her hand touched the empty place near her.

He yawned. It was hot in the room. He pushed his shoes off and stumbled to her. The pillow was cool; its fabric smooth, but hard. He faced Carla. His hands folded into each other and lay beside her beautiful face. Her eyes were shut. She moved closer. Her hair spilled down over her shoulder and dripped black curls on to his hands. He smelled the sweetly dank fragrance of her hair and he smelled the lunch's shellfish on both their mouths.

'I love –' he began.

'Shh,' she said. She touched his temple. His eyes shut as if she had pressed a button to close them. 'You've helped a lot of people, Max,' she said. 'You deserve to rest.' He felt a soft kiss on his forehead. He smiled and slept.

Carla woke to find Max's hand under her cheek. He was asleep in the deep rest of a baby – eyelids smooth, brow untroubled, jaw slack.

The early sunset of winter had completely darkened the room. Through the open door to the sitting room there was a sickly amber light from the street.

She eased herself off the bed hoping not to wake him. He moaned faintly as she departed; but he stayed asleep. She went into the sitting room. It was a quarter after five. Manny was either home or soon would be. He might be patient about her absence for an hour. Then he would explode. She had to call him soon.

She turned on a lamp. Its switch made a loud noise. She listened for Max. There was no movement. The room – for a place in New York City – was very quiet. Only the occasional faint sound of a car horn or a siren could be heard. Sometimes a dim flow of water from one floor to another in the walls. Otherwise there was only a stillness that left her nothing to hear but the blood rushing in her ears.

She had to make a choice. Delay was no longer possible. Max needed her. He was lost. Although he was the same smart handsome man who had saved her sanity, he was troubled and distracted. But he was not crazy – except maybe about Brillstein and his wife. She could believe the lawyer might want to put Max away, although she had reason to think he was trying to settle the cases; besides she had told Brillstein she was going to tell the truth about what she did in the plane and the lawyer hadn't threatened her. Nevertheless he was capable of putting Max in a funny farm if he could get more money. But she didn't believe for a minute that Max's wife would go along. The woman she met wasn't capable of such a bad thing. Take Manny as an example. He wasn't an especially good man and he loved money so much he could kill for it, still, he wouldn't put Carla away to get more. She couldn't believe Max had married someone more untrustworthy than she had. No. Max wants to run away, she told herself. She understood that much, she understood that Max couldn't abandon his family unless he believed he was forced to and so he had made it up. To her there was nothing crazy about such a delusion – it was desperate common sense, a way of surviving.

She knew how to stop him from running. She knew what he needed. She didn't even like to think about what she understood because it made so little sense to her outside of knowing Max and it was a mortal sin, against everything she had been taught and believed herself.

Well, whatever she decided she had to phone Manny.

Her husband answered on the first ring. 'Hello?' Manny said in the slightly hushed and cautious tone of a child calling into a dark room. When she answered he came to. There was an angry snap to his tone. 'Where are you!'

'I'm with Max.'

'What!'

'Listen to me –'

'You listen to me! You come –'

'Shut up, Manny, or I'm going to hang up on you,' she said in a calm but rapid tone. 'Either I'll come home tomorrow morning and I'll be your wife or I won't and you won't have to see me ever again. But I owe him my time tonight. You can like it or not. If you don't want me to come home tomorrow no matter what, tell me now.'

In the silence that followed her demanding question she heard him breathe through his nose. The inhalations and exhalations were fast and getting quicker as if he were blowing up a balloon. 'You're crazy,' he said abruptly and said no more.

'Manny, I need an answer. Do you want me to bother to come back or not?'

She heard him breathing fast again and then he made a sound that could have been a groan of disgust or a moan of pain. After that the line went dead.

Carla hung up angrily. She tossed the receiver on to the cradle. It made a racket and fell off. She replaced it carefully this time and then tiptoed to the bedroom to check on Max. He had rolled on to his back. His head was turned in her direction, but the eyes were shut. His mouth hung open in a mute plea. His right arm stretched across the bed on to the empty side. The hand reached into the air for help. His position reminded her of something but she couldn't identify it. She returned to the sitting room. The furniture was big and heavy. Even the drapes that hung beside the glittering city views weighed a ton. The carpet was so thick it swallowed the curved feet of the chairs and coffee table. She felt alone. Not lonely. But isolated.

She dropped to her knees. They sank into the thick

rug. She hadn't prayed outside of church since she was a girl. And she prayed for something new. She prayed for Him to explain Himself.

There was no answer or comfort this time. The calm she was used to feeling afterwards – even for only a few seconds – didn't descend. Rising, she was as alone as when she knelt.

'When you don't feel He is with you,' Monsignor O'Boyle had said to her months ago, while she was in the dense fog of her grief, 'then He is *in* you, waiting for you to bring Him forth. He wants you to choose Him.'

She hadn't understood that. It sounded sneaky if true and she didn't believe it anyway. While stuck in despair she knew He was there every minute. During her madness she believed He had killed her baby. After all, she had neglected Him once Bubble was born. For the two years of her baby's life, filled by the happiness of being a mother, she had even forgotten He lived. She believed He had punished her for that sin, and she had hated Him for it. She went to Old Saint Pat's in those days, she now realized, hoping to forgive *Him* – not to be granted forgiveness.

He had been merciful. He had sent Max, with his bravery and his love, to save her from madness.

But to do what?

Now where was He?

What game was He playing with Max?

Max had done His bidding, saving those He wanted saved. Was Max being humbled because his pride wouldn't allow him to acknowledge the Lord? Or was this another part of Max's saintliness – his martyrdom?

No. Max's unhappiness was aimed at her. The Monsignor was right. Christ was hiding *in* her, behind these choices, ready to greet her if she chose correctly. And do what if she chose wrong?

Was she afraid of Him? Yes.

Was that what He wanted? Fear? Was that the purpose of the crash? Did He want her to be afraid?

She thought if Max believed in his family again then he would be all right. Of course Carla would lose him, even as merely a friend she would inevitably lose him once he was truly back with his family. Was that the point? Was that her lesson? That she had to return her angel or He would destroy Max? Just as He had destroyed Bubble because she had loved her baby too much?

She held her head with her hands and pressed as if she could squeeze these ideas out of her skull. It didn't help. She moved to the cool glass of the window and watched the black park. It was infiltrated by the snaking headlights of cars, moving up and down its length and across its middle toward a city that was dark and alien.

She was afraid.

Afraid of sin? Afraid of love? No.

Afraid of God. That was His lesson.

She was thrilled. Doubt left her. The fear was keen, but she wasn't cowed.

All her life she had relied on others to teach her, to explain what was right and wrong. She could fight them or could obey – she had never solved a mystery for herself.

She undressed in front of the window, a slice of cold cutting her thighs, her head warmed by the radiator blowing hot air.

Once she was naked she felt strong. She went to the sleeping Max and lay beside him, curving into the curl of his body.

Still asleep he embraced her. His clothes were cool but his face was hot. His soft hands moved slowly and lightly down her back as if they were creating, not feeling, her shape. She kissed his cheek. The eye she could see opened. The pale blue circle focused on her, her legs tingled in response. His eye was smart and cold and wary. She kissed nearer to his mouth. His lips parted. They were dry. She dabbed them with her own moist lips. Max's hands molded her arched back, skimming her skin, beginning to form her buttocks. The whisper of his touch brought each nerve alive.

'I'm thirsty,' he whispered.

She slid up on to the pillows and brought his head to her neck. She pushed him down. His mouth closed on her nipple. He was so gentle the touch could hardly be felt at first. A hot wet drop – his tongue – circled the nipple until it hardened. Then he sucked steadily and evenly with the patient greed of a baby.

She cupped the back of his head and gradually turned him on to his back, keeping her breast at his mouth. She peered down at him and saw he looked blissful. All of her came awake, her skin stretching into life. She moved his head to the crook of her arm, unbuttoned his shirt and then edged down to open his pants. Max broke off feeding and kissed her underarm, her shoulder, burrowed into her neck, insistent and loving. She reached below and took hold of his yearning penis.

I've fed this big baby, Carla said to God, and now I'm going to take the man into my womb.

22

Max woke alone. He heard the shower running in the bathroom. He yawned and dominated the bed, stretching his arms and legs until he nearly reached all four corners. Outside it was a bright sunny morning and his body had a conviction that he was young again.

They had made love twice, after their nap and then after their late dinner – a romantic meal served in their sitting room. Max drank more than half a bottle of wine and it didn't make him draggy or gloomy. In fact, he felt more vigorous. When they went to bed again he explored Carla's lean supple body thoroughly, wishing to memorize every detail, because she had told him, over coffee, that it would be their last time together.

She had an exciting body, and not only because of her figure; it had energy and tension even when she lay perfectly still. Her physical responses were the same as her emotional responses – direct and passionate.

She had been blunt about why this would be their final time together.

'You have a family, Max. They need you. I have a husband. He needs me.'

Max felt simple. He wondered aloud, 'How do you know?'

'Anyone can tell that a wife and son would miss someone like you, Max,' she said. They were having strawberries and cream for dessert. Max had tasted one of the strawberries, but he left it unfinished because it wasn't sweet enough. Carla ate them as though they were delicious. She cocked her head back and sucked the berry in most of the way before biting off a piece. 'And Jeff's children. They need you.'

'Jeff's boys?' Max didn't know why she thought of them; he didn't think he had even mentioned them to her once.

'I know it isn't fair, Max, but you gotta take care of them too. He was your partner. And you loved him.'

Max hesitated at her saying he loved Jeff. He had been about to dismiss her directive to take care of Jeff's children when she said it. Max heard Jeff's hurt tone answer him at the airport, '*We're not second-rate, Max.*' And what had he added? '*At least you're not, Max.*'

'You loved him, Max,' Carla said again. 'And you miss him.'

This made him feel grief. He thought of his partner's greyhound head, buying cheap tickets and worrying about the security of his wife and sons. He remembered his own pleasure at informing Jeff that they were going to die. He covered his face and wept into his hands.

She left the strawberries, pulled his hands away, and dried his tears with her kisses.

After that, they went to bed again. He had watched her skin meticulously – peering at every pore – desperate to memorize her forever.

When Carla came out of the bathroom wrapped in a towel Max was still stretched out on the bed like Christ crucified. Her long black hair was flat against her head and down her neck, painted on to her shoulders. He had expected the morning would make her less beautiful, but she looked prettier than ever to him in the Plaza towel, rubbing at her drowned hair, and smiling with those big white teeth.

417

'Good morning,' she said as if it were a joke.

'How do you know Manny needs you?' Max said, resuming the previous night's argument. He wasn't ready to give her up.

'You don't know him,' she said. She stopped smiling and moved toward her clothes, draped on an ugly wing chair by the window.

'They might be happier without us,' Max said, rising to his elbows.

'Maybe,' Carla said. She had picked up her red panties. She dropped the towel and quickly put them on, with hasty modesty. 'But we won't.'

Max tried to remember what had already been concealed: her whitest skin, the cheeks of her taut ass; the deep silky black V of her groin; the flat tender skin of her belly. While he made that effort more was lost. She had put her stockings on; her bra; her pale blue blouse.

'I can be happy with you, Carla,' Max argued.

'No, Max,' she said. 'Think about it. You almost went crazy when you tried to run off with me. You want to be free and brave, Max, but you can't be free of your duty to your people. Every time you try to get free of people you just get stuck to another. Like that kid you saved on the plane. Or that blond woman who came to that meeting – on a plane for Chrissake – just 'cause she might meet you.' She had finished dressing. She looked small – a young pretty Catholic girl – a stranger. 'Or me.' She smiled and moved her feet together, coming to attention. 'You ain't never gonna be free of the people who love you. I'll come see you from time to time. But no more of this good stuff.' She nodded at the bed and grinned for a second. 'I got to go home now. I won't be talking to you for a while. And don't call me, okay? I got to make peace with my husband.'

'Wait.' Max scrambled out of bed. The looseness and strength in his body wasn't an illusion. She had healed him somehow.

'No, no,' she pushed at his chest with both hands. They felt little and cool. 'Don't make me cry. I'm happy,' she said and he saw tears begin to well. 'I don't want to cry. Let's say goodbye like it isn't goodbye.'

Max saw she was determined. Nevertheless, he insisted, 'I don't want to.'

'Yes.' She touched his chest with her index finger where she imagined his heart was. 'In there you do. Come on,' she moved off, almost skipping out, 'say goodbye like it means nothing.' She left the room. Her voice called back. 'Bye, Max. See you.'

He didn't answer. He refused to acknowledge her going. The room felt empty. It looked ugly. She had opened the drapes before taking a shower and he could see all of the leafless park, a huge artificial rectangle of dead brown things.

'Please, Max,' she called from the sitting room. 'Be nice.'

'Goodbye, Carla,' he said quickly, but not quickly enough. His voice caught on the last syllable of her name and they could both hear the choked noise of his loss as she shut the door behind her.

Carla walked home, despite the cold gray weather. She wanted to be outside and see all the people and stores and buildings. She went down Fifth Avenue, dignified and wealthy at midtown, seedier below 42nd, and a mess south of 23rd because of repairs on something that had exploded underneath the street. She cried – or rather her eyes teared – for part of the journey. But although her heart was sad, it was also an easy load to carry. She didn't feel she had lost Max; at least not the angel who had saved her. She had lied, of course, about them being able to talk eventually. If what she had done was right, if she had solved His mystery, then Max would be well again and soon forget her. That was not a loss: she had regained herself and what Max had given her she would always have.

When she reached Mulberry she went into Old Saint Pat's and lit a candle for Bubble. She would never go to confession to be absolved for last night's sin – that would have broken the agreement with Him. Instead she knelt and prayed to Him to allow her to conceive another child.

The Monsignor happened by and waited for her by the door. He looked at her curiously and said, 'Hello, Carla. You're looking very fit.'

'Hello, Monsignor. Did you get my message? I wanted to find out if I could volunteer for work at the Foundling Hospital.'

'I already gave them your name and phone number.' He chuckled. 'You're certainly going to be hearing from them.' He followed her down the steps to the street; she watched him negotiate the steps warily. 'Did you hear the news about Pierre Toussaint? He's a candidate for sainthood. The committee's going to exhume his body next month. Cardinal O'Conner himself will preside. He's going to bless the grave and dig the first shovelful. It's very exciting. Toussaint is the first black candidate for sainthood in America.'

'What did he do?' Carla asked.

'It's a very interesting story.' Monsignor O'Boyle lifted his right hand in a lecturing gesture. She noticed his hand trembling faintly. She felt he would die soon. She smiled patiently while he explained that Toussaint was a Haitian slave brought to the United States by the family that owned him. The family lost all its money shortly after emigrating and rather than deserting them, Toussaint had worked as a hairdresser to support them. Years later, when they had recovered their wealth, they gave him his freedom. As a freeman he devoted the rest of his life to caring for the poor and sick.

'They kept him a slave while he was making money for them to live on?'

They had reached the last step. Monsignor O'Boyle was breathing hard through his nose and his white face was even more bloodless. His eyes looked scared. He nodded.

'Are there black children at the hospital?' Carla asked.

Monsignor O'Boyle frowned at her. 'It doesn't have anything to do with race,' he said in a breathless whisper. 'The hospital accepts all children with special problems who need its services.'

'Sure,' Carla said and smiled. She gave him her hand.

His trembling continued while he held it. 'There are plenty of black children there,' he said softly.

She kissed him goodbye on the cheek. She had never done that before; he looked startled. She felt wild and happy, eager to get on with her life. She hurried across the street and up to her apartment. It was just after lunch and she would have plenty of time to prepare a meal for Manny when he got home.

Only he was already home. She discovered him in the living room wearing his handyman's work pants. His shirt was off. His thick powerful chest was almost hairless, the skin dark enough so that anyone might think he had a tan. He had a fifth of rum in his right hand, dangling there as if it were a soda bottle. It seemed to be half gone. She had never seen him drink anything other than beer and never more than two.

Manny looked at her as she stood in the doorway with a mild almost uncomprehending stare.

'Remember me?' she said, trying to be cheerful.

He grunted and took a slug from the bottle. Some of it ran down the side of his mouth.

'You'll make yourself sick,' she said. 'You don't drink.' She went over to the couch and took hold of the bottle. Manny held on and stared at her.

'Bitch,' he said in a mumble.

'Okay,' she said and gently pulled the bottle away. She put it on the coffee table.

Manny spread his arms wide, resting them on the backrest of the couch. 'We're rich,' he said. He slurred the words. 'We're as rich as those fucking tenants I slave for.' Manny tried to laugh, but the sound he made was more like a moan. His head bobbed unsteadily. 'That fucking lawyer called. They made some kind of mistake – I didn't understand. But they offered more than –' Manny tried to get up. He lifted the upper half of himself off the couch but had to fall back. 'We got half a million dollars.' He laughed. 'Five hundred fucking thousand dollars.' He laughed again. Tears were in his eyes, his head weaved and bobbed, and he kept laughing, a sad giggling chortle. 'Unfuckingbelievable. I'm a rich man,' he said and the laughter stopped. He gagged. She sat next to him, put her arms around his strong shoulders and was ready for him to be sick.

Instead the gagging became sobs. 'I'm so fucking rich,' he blubbered through the weeping. 'I'm so fucking smart,' he mumbled and then again, 'I'm so fucking rich. I'm so fucking smart.'

She hugged him and shushed him and kissed him. He didn't cry for long. He smelled sickly sweet. After he had been quiet for a while he said in a croaked voice, 'I love you.'

They were going to be all right. She coaxed him off the couch and guided him toward the bedroom. They passed his discarded shirt in the hallway.

'Stay with me,' he said as he sagged on to what used to be their marriage bed.

'I'm going to be with you from now on, Manny,' she said, sitting beside him.

'I want to have another son,' he said petulantly.

'Me too,' she said and knew that she would.

Max took his time washing and dressing to go home. He felt he was saying farewell to something in that hotel room, something more than just the sex – the unsafe sex – he and Carla had enjoyed. He felt as if he were saying goodbye to himself.

At the door, dressed and ready to go, he was afraid to leave. He tried to think of something that Americans weren't afraid of. When he decided he couldn't he left.

He took a cab to his apartment building. The day was cold and gray. New York's buildings were chameleons to Max; they turned dull with cloudy skies and glittered white with the sun.

The doorman – David – seemed to be surprised to see him. 'Your wife just went out,' he said after recovering from the shock.

Max went up in the elevator wondering about lunch, whether he should wait for Debby and take her out for a fancy meal. Cafe des Artistes was her favorite restaurant. Its campy design gave Max headaches, but to see her smile and feel at ease with him would be well worth it.

Jonah upset that plan. He was upstairs alone. He had felt ill at school and Debby had brought him home. She was out buying Tylenol. 'I've got a hundred and one temperature,' Jonah said. He was very pale, dressed in a long New York Mets shirt, lying in his bed watching a game show on television.

Max shut the set off and sat beside Jonah. He brushed the hair off his boy's forehead. He kissed his smooth brow. The skin radiated heat. They were quiet for a moment.

'Where were you?' Jonah asked fearlessly.

'I stayed in the Plaza Hotel last night. I got a room way up on a high floor and saw all of Central Park at night. It looked great. Spooky and grand.'

'Mom was scared,' Jonah said. 'I overheard her calling everybody. She almost called the police!' Jonah's face flushed at the effort of saying so many sentences.

'I'm here now. I'm not going anyplace. How's your buddy Sam?' Max asked. Carla's instructions about Jeff's children had stuck with him.

Jonah shrugged. 'He's okay, I guess. He's been kind of a pain, actually,' he said softly. He groaned and turned toward his pillow. 'I'm tired,' he mumbled.

Max stroked his head. 'When you're better I'm going to show you and Sam a house his father and I did. The Zuckerman house. It was a pretty good design and Jeff had a nice idea about the patio. Anyway, I'm going to teach the two of you about architecture.'

Jonah rolled away to gain some distance on his father. He propped his pale head on a hand and blinked sleepily. 'I don't wanna learn about architecture,' he said.

'I'm teaching you anyway. I'm your father and I'm your teacher. It's the only thing I know how to teach. You don't have to be good at it. You don't have to like it. You don't have to do it when you grow up. But I have to teach it to you.'

Jonah watched his father for a moment or two. He pursed his lips thoughtfully. 'Okay,' he said at last with a sigh. 'You're the boss.'

'That's right,' Max said. He pulled the bedsheet up to his son's chin. He heard the front door opening.

'I'm back!' Debby called in. She entered Jonah's room. She had no makeup on and she was still in her black cloak. She carried a narrow white bag from the pharmacy. She looked like a sickly child herself, pale and sad-eyed.

'I'm home, honey,' Max said to her. She had come to a halt just inside the door. She stared at him. 'Peace?' he said with a smile.

Debby frowned. She threw the bag at him. 'He needs this.'

Max gave Jonah a dose of Tylenol. Debby fussed around his bed, gathering used tissues, smoothing the sheets, drawing the shades. Jonah protested each action, moaning, 'Just leave me alone. I'm fine.'

Max went to the kitchen and made himself coffee. Debby joined him eventually. She came in and poured herself a cup. She didn't meet his eyes. Her mouth was tight, furious.

'I told Jonah,' Max said, 'that when he's better I want to show him and Sam the Zuckerman house.'

Debby looked at him sharply. Her eyes stared, shifting from rage to wariness. 'Why?'

'I think Sam – I guess I should take Jake too, he's old enough – they should see something their father made. I have to start spending more time with those boys. I have to spend more time with Jonah too. Teach him what I know. It's not much, but that's what fathers do, right?'

'Fathers stay home,' Debby said in a scolding voice. 'Fathers are home to take care of their sons.'

'Not always,' Max said. 'Not all fathers. You can't expect that of every man. Jeff's not going to be home with his children and he was a good father.'

Debby's rigid annoyed face abruptly loosened. Her mouth buckled, her eyes softened. 'What are you saying?' she pleaded, her elegant hands gesturing at him to take her, to dance with her.

He took her hands and reined them in, pulling her toward him. 'Do you want me?'

'Of course,' she said in a whisper.

'I mean *me*! The real me, not just a security blanket.'

'You haven't been much of a security blanket lately.'

'That's right and you don't like that.'

'This is not my fault. Everything that's happened isn't my fault.'

Max looked at her. Her anger was gone. She stared into his eyes as if he had an answer for her, as if he were her best hope.

'You're right,' Max said. 'It isn't your fault.' It was the structure of their world, its rotting design. He had no choice but to accept its danger and fear its risks. He hugged her. She stayed in his arms, huddled in his chest as if he were a strong shelter. He wasn't. He was a partner of her fear.

They made sandwiches and ate them together in almost complete silence. They checked on Jonah. He was sleeping heavily but peacefully. They had more coffee and then chatted in a friendly way – in the way they used to before the crash – about Debby's current crop of students. She had one nine-year-old ballerina she thought very promising. Max proposed they rent a house with Nan and her boys for the summer. Debby agreed, but said with a sly smile, 'You can be their father, but you're not her husband.'

'That's right,' Max said.

David the doorman buzzed them at two-thirty. Debby answered the intercom. She turned from it with a puzzled expression. 'Brillstein's on his way up,' she said.

Max opened the front door and waited for the elevator to deliver his lawyer. He thought about his options: if Nan needed money he could give it to her. Lying wasn't necessary, was it? Well, if it was he would lie. Who was Max Klein to think he could be better than the rest of humanity?

Brillstein hopped out of the elevator in yet another new suit. This one was blue. 'You're here!' he cried at the sight of Max. The blue wasn't a shade Max recognized. It wasn't deep enough for true navy and yet it seemed to want to be that dark. Max didn't care for the color. At least the suit seemed to fit Brillstein better, although it was double-breasted and the short man seemed shorter in the wide cut.

Brillstein carried a bottle of champagne under one arm and a white baker's box balanced on his attaché case. He bustled in. 'I'm here to celebrate. I hope you like champagne. And in here –' Brillstein had put the bottle on their dining-room table. He fumbled at the

427

delicate red-and-white-striped string on the box '– are my favorite indulgence ... chocolate-covered strawberries!'

'Mmmm,' Debby said. And then she looked at Max regretfully.

'What are we celebrating?' Max asked.

'You're not going to believe what happened. We're settled. I can't believe it myself. It's an incredible story. I spoke to Gil Parker this morning –' Brillstein had the box open. 'Take,' he said, offering the contents to Debby. 'He's the outside counsel for TransCon. We *hondeled* and we *hondeled* and we agreed on a figure. One million seven hundred fifty thousand. You have to understand –'

Debby said, 'Wow.' She took a strawberry and said to Max with regret, 'You can't.'

'No, no, that's not what the final figure was.' Brillstein popped a chocolate strawberry in his mouth. He chewed it furiously and spoke through its thick pleasures. 'That's not the whole story.'

'I'm going to get glasses for the champagne,' Debby said. 'Speak up.'

'Sure,' Brillstein said. 'I'll talk loud.' He offered Max a chocolate strawberry. Then he quickly withdrew the box 'Oh, she said you can't.'

Max took it. 'Of course I can. Go on with your story.'

'Well, I had scheduled a lunch today with Jameson, the in-house counsel, the man Parker reports to. He's given Parker the broad range of figures to offer us and left it to Parker to get the best deal he can. By the time Parker and I have agreed to figures, it's time for me to meet Jameson at Gloucester House if you please. Parker doesn't know I'm seeing Jameson for lunch but I figure he's going to talk to him soon because our deal is contingent on Jameson approving the final figures, although it's understood that's just a formality. So, with a four-million-dollar deal almost finished, off I go to Gloucester House.' Brillstein angled himself to one side and then the other; with one turn he buttoned his jacket closed, and with the other he straightened his dashing yellow tie. Evidently he meant to imitate a fashionable man arriving at an elegant eatery.

Debby returned with the glasses. She put them down and looked at the strawberry in Max's hand. 'You're allergic,' she said.

'Not anymore,' Max said. He took a bite. 'I've had them a couple times in the past year.'

'Don't worry if he's allergic. I've got Adrenalin in my bag.'

'Whatever for?' Debby asked.

'We discovered last summer our little girl is deathly allergic to bees. She got bit –' he waved his hand to dismiss the subject. 'You don't want to know. So I've got a hypo with me always, in case her mother forgets to pack it.' Brillstein put a finger to his lips. 'Don't tell her that. She thinks I nag her too much, that I don't trust her to remember important stuff. She's right, by the way. I don't.'

Max ate his strawberry and got to work on opening the champagne. He felt giddy with excitement too – if not about Brillstein's apparent success, at least at the finish of all the maneuvers. Now he wouldn't have to lie.

'Anyway! To be honest,' Brillstein said, taking one of the champagne glasses and waiting for Max to pop the cork and pour, 'I had taken the one point seven million for you and the two hundred for Mrs Fransisca and the two point three for Nan from Parker this morning despite the fact that I thought they were too low. I did it because of you.' Brillstein stared hard at Max and pursed his lips in a childish attitude of challenge.

Max popped the cork. He quickly poured the frothing liquid into the lawyer's glass. It reminded him of the hokey chemical drinks in horror movies – Dr Jekyll's potion.

'I was about to blow your case,' Max said. He filled a glass for Debby and handed it to her.

'No . . .' Debby protested. She had another strawberry between her lips. Chocolate was smeared on them. She looked beautiful.

Brillstein was generous. He waved his glass expansively and explained to Debby, 'Let's just say I didn't want the other side getting their hands on Max the way he was talking. So, one point seven is very good. And I got Nan two point three million, which was okay.'

'And Carla?'

'Even there I thought I'd done great. Two hundred thousand.'

'Two hundred thousand!' Debby choked slightly on the champagne. 'That's nothing. She lost a baby,' Debby insisted in a wounded tone.

Max smiled proudly at his wife and took another strawberry. The champagne was delicious.

'A baby has no earnings you can establish. I was going to argue that the Fransisca baby had a potential career as a child model but they would have shot me down. Really the compensation was for the mother's pain and suffering and because of the negligence of the seat belt. Although she hadn't bought him a ticket and he wasn't entitled to the defective seat –' Brillstein waved at all that with his glass. 'It's craziness. You don't want to know! It doesn't matter! Listen to me!' He put his glass down on the table and spread his hands to show the scene. 'I go to Gloucester House and meet Parker's superior, Jameson. I'm not feeling like such a genius, to tell you the truth, so I don't brag or mention the deal I had just made with Parker. Jameson doesn't either and I figure that's class, that's a real WASP. His people and I have made a deal for over four million dollars that he has final approval of and we don't even mention it. We order. Then he looks at me and says, "I hear your client, Mr Klein, nearly killed himself and that Fransisca woman." I had a piece of bread in my mouth so I nod. Don't want to spit crumbs all over him. He goes on, very haughty, almost angry. "I want to settle your three cases at this lunch. Parker's dragging his feet. I want to get this done." Now I almost choke on the bread because I realize Parker hasn't told him what we've *tentatively*,' Brillstein, grinning, raised a finger in the air, 'tentatively because it still wasn't definite until Parker cleared it with Jameson –'

Max took another strawberry. His throat was dry from the champagne. 'We get it!' he croaked at Brillstein. 'What happened!'

'So I swallow all the bread,' Brillstein's face widened into a grin, 'and I say, "What's your best offer? I'm happy to hear any number and discuss it." So he frowns – he looked incredibly pissed off – and he says, "I won't pay more than four hundred thousand for the baby."' Brillstein giggled.

Max tried to breathe through his nose. The

champagne must have stuffed it. He swallowed the rest of his strawberry and looked around for a tissue.

Brillstein seemed disappointed in the response of his audience. 'Isn't that incredible? That was double what Parker had offered. So you know what I say? And this, I have to admit, was a stroke of genius on my part – I say, "I can't take less than five hundred thousand to settle it at this lunch."'

Debby frowned. 'But you'd already agreed to –'

Brillstein almost jumped in his desire to cut her off. 'Doesn't matter! Once he offered more it was all off the table. He's the one with the real authority to deal.'

'Of course,' Max tried to say, but there was little air to say it. His throat thickened. He sat down.

Brillstein moved to a chair opposite him and tapped him on the knee. 'So Jameson looks furious, just furious, and he says, "Okay. Don't want to quibble. That's done."' Brillstein spread his arms wide. 'And here I made another great move. I took out my notepad and I wrote down Carla's name and put the figure next to it and I had him look at it to see that I've got it right. Now it's as good as a done deal and he can't back out. Then he says, "As to the two architects I won't go above a total package of eight million."' Brillstein clapped his hands together and let his head go back to laugh at the heavens with triumph.

Max struggled to breathe. He sucked from his stomach but nothing could get in through his mouth. His throat had filled in; his nose was sealed. He looked at the box of strawberries and was scared.

When Brillstein brought his head back from his roar of victory, there were tears in his eyes. 'We settled on you getting three point five million and Nan gets four point five.' Brillstein shook his head from side to side. 'He's finding out right now. He's in his huge fucking corner office with his Harvard degree and he's finding out that the Gloucester House lunch cost him four and a half million dollars!' Brillstein collapsed into guttural laughs.

Max's forehead broke out into a sweat. He put his head between his knees. He saw his right hand turn blotchy red. His eyes swelled and ached. There was no way to breathe. He stared at the sanded narrow oak floor, the floors that had carried him from childhood until now, through all the duty and grief and joy of life, and he realized those same sanded boards would soon be his deathbed.

He fell.

The ceiling was flashing yellow. A terrible pain was in his ears.

He heard Brillstein shout – 'Where the fuck is it! It's in my fucking bag!'

Max tried to kick his legs but he couldn't – they were fat columns – dead lumps.

Debby appeared. She was flushed. 'Take it easy, Max,' she said.

'I don't know where to do it!' Brillstein was shouting. 'My wife knows!'

Debby's face covered the flashing ceiling. She pulled at something. 'You're going to be all right, Max,' she said and then he saw her come at his heart with a needle. He tried to scream at her not to kill him but he couldn't make any sound.

She injected him in the upper arm. She cradled the nape of his neck with her hand and tilted his head back. His suffocating mouth opened to her. She covered it

433

with hers. He felt her hot breath enter his throat. The blockage was dissolved. She leaned back and smiled down at him. His nose suddenly cleared. The ceiling settled.

'You're fine, Max,' Debby said. 'Let the Adrenalin work.'

Max rested on the oak floor and breathed easily. I'm alive, he thought. His throat eased and accepted a gulp of air.

I'm alive, he rejoiced. I'm alive. And I'm afraid.

Discover more about our forthcoming books through Penguin's FREE newspaper...

Penguin

Quarterly

It's packed with:

- exciting features

- author interviews

- previews & reviews

- books from your favourite films & TV series

- exclusive competitions & much, much more...

Write off for your free copy today to:
Dept JC
Penguin Books Ltd
FREEPOST
West Drayton
Middlesex
UB7 0BR
NO STAMP REQUIRED

READ MORE IN PENGUIN

In every corner of the world, on every subject under the sun, Penguin represents quality and variety – the very best in publishing today.

For complete information about books available from Penguin – including Puffins, Penguin Classics and Arkana – and how to order them, write to us at the appropriate address below. Please note that for copyright reasons the selection of books varies from country to country.

In the United Kingdom: Please write to *Dept. JC, Penguin Books Ltd, FREEPOST, West Drayton, Middlesex UB7 OBR*

If you have any difficulty in obtaining a title, please send your order with the correct money, plus ten per cent for postage and packaging, to *PO Box No. 11, West Drayton, Middlesex UB7 OBR*

In the United States: Please write to *Penguin USA Inc., 375 Hudson Street, New York, NY 10014*

In Canada: Please write to *Penguin Books Canada Ltd, 10 Alcorn Avenue, Suite 300, Toronto, Ontario M4V 3B2*

In Australia: Please write to *Penguin Books Australia Ltd, 487 Maroondah Highway, Ringwood, Victoria 3134*

In New Zealand: Please write to *Penguin Books (NZ) Ltd,182–190 Wairau Road, Private Bag, Takapuna, Auckland 9*

In India: Please write to *Penguin Books India Pvt Ltd, 706 Eros Apartments, 56 Nehru Place, New Delhi 110 019*

In the Netherlands: Please write to *Penguin Books Netherlands B.V., Keizersgracht 231 NL–1016 DV Amsterdam*

In Germany: Please write to *Penguin Books Deutschland GmbH, Friedrichstrasse 10–12, W–6000 Frankfurt/Main 1*

In Spain: Please write to *Penguin Books S. A., C. San Bernardo 117–6° E–28015 Madrid*

In Italy: Please write to *Penguin Italia s.r.l., Via Felice Casati 20, I–20124 Milano*

In France: Please write to *Penguin France S. A., 17 rue Lejeune, F–31000 Toulouse*

In Japan: Please write to *Penguin Books Japan, Ishikiribashi Building, 2–5–4, Suido, Tokyo 112*

In Greece: Please write to *Penguin Hellas Ltd, Dimocritou 3, GR–106 71 Athens*

In South Africa: Please write to *Longman Penguin Southern Africa (Pty) Ltd, Private Bag X08, Bertsham 2013*

READ MORE IN PENGUIN

A CHOICE OF FICTION

My Son's Story Nadine Gordimer

'*My Son's Story* is a novel of conviction – a passionate novel. But if that passion moves and convinces, it is because we have seen it pass through the checks and balances of a rigorously sceptical, ice-cool intellect' – *Independent*

A Natural Curiosity Margaret Drabble

'This book, like its predecessor [*The Radiant Way*], is a remarkable mixture of rambling but compelling narrative, psychological insight, generous human portrayal, acute observation, humour, horror, beauty and disgust' – *The Times Literary Supplement*

Love in the Time of Cholera Gabriel García Márquez

'A powerful, poetic and comic long-distance love story set on the Caribbean coast ... Unique Márquez magic of the sadness and funniness of humanity' – *The Times*

My Secret History Paul Theroux

'André Parent saunters into the book, aged fifteen ... a creature of naked and unquenchable ego, greedy for sex, money, experience, another life ... read it warily; read it twice, and more; it is darker and deeper than it looks' – *Observer*

Age of Iron J. M. Coetzee

'Coetzee's vision is incisive and yet tremulous, poetic. His intelligence is scabrous, but his prose is aerated and expansive when it needs to be' – James Wood in the *Guardian*